# THE BLUE L*

A new sound threaded into the b......, feminine, and distant, like a woman singing from some far-off place, so quiet that he thought he imagined it at first, but it grew until it mingled with the stream's murmurs. It was the most beautiful music Adam had ever heard and it chilled him beyond measure.

Keeping his gaze low, he slowly turned to face the lobby. The smell of the lake had not diminished. The song continued, and as he brought his eyes up, his body froze and his breath hitched.

Standing near the brook, smiling at him from over her shoulder, the Blue Lady looked coy, playful. Her hair and dress swam around her like living things.

*Do you believe in me now?* Her lips never moved.

Adam blinked hard against the vision.

The Blue Lady turned her head away and continued her slow trek, leaving wet footprints behind her even though her feet never touched the ground. As the distance between them grew, the song faded. When she neared the stone wall, she turned to him, smiled once more, moved to a window and disappeared beyond the glass. As she did, her mad laughter shrieked through the lobby.

"She's real," Adam whispered to himself. "She's real, she's real, oh my God, she's real."

# The Cliffhouse Haunting

**Books by Thorne & Cross**

The Cliffhouse Haunting
The Ghosts of Ravencrest
Mother

**Available as serialized installments**

The Ghosts of Ravencrest
The Witches of Ravencrest

**Books by Alistair Cross**

The Crimson Corset

**Books by Tamara Thorne**

Haunted
Moonfall
Candle Bay
Eternity
Thunder Road
The Sorority
The Forgotten
Bad Things

**Short Stories**

Slippery When Wet

## Praise for The Cliffhouse Haunting...

"Thorne & Cross keep the surprises coming as swiftly as a master magician ...The characters quickly become people we know, but then wish perhaps we didn't ... The laughter of recognition rides like bubbles on the surface of a deep-flowing darkness ...There's something cold in here."
**-Mark Hein, critic and editor at theaterghost.com**

"Thorne & Cross are clever. The plot they create reads effortlessly, and they make us laugh and cringe and widen our eyes, looking away from the text at times to say, "Oh, no you didn't." But they did."
**-Michael Aronovitz, author of Alice Walks and The Witch of the Wood**

# Raves for Ravencrest...

"The Ghosts of Ravencrest: Christmas Spirits is riveting. The characters are wonderful, the subplots are perfect, and the setting is stunning and well-researched. This series is like a roller coaster that goes up and up - the Mannings are literary gold."
**-QL Pearce, bestselling author of Scary Stories for Sleep-Overs**

"In The Ghosts of Ravencrest, Tamara Thorne and Alistair Cross have created a world that is dark, opulent, and smoldering with the promise of scares and seduction. You'll be able to feel the slide of the satin sheets, taste the fizz of champagne, and hear the footsteps on the stairs."
**-Sylvia Shults, paranormal expert and author of Fractured Spirits**

"The Ghosts of Ravencrest by Tamara Thorne and Alistair Cross is a scary, intricate read. The horror is well crafted and the ornate setting descriptions are breath-taking. Most importantly, from page one, readers fall in love with Belinda. We care about what happens to her, and we hope exactly what that is remains deliciously extensive!"
**-Michael Aronovitz, author of Alice Walks**

"Scary and scandalous! The Ghosts of Ravencrest by Tamara Thorne and Alistair Cross will leaving you shivering with excitement and terror as the innocent Belinda breaks free of a minimum-wage hell hole only to move into a sprawling Gothic estate where her body becomes the focal point of a mysterious specter. Out of the pan and into the fire? Only time will tell."
**-William Malmborg, author of Jimmy and Text Message.**

# Praise for Alistair Cross' The Crimson Corset

"Put Bram Stoker in a giant cocktail shaker, add a pinch of Laurell K. Hamilton, a shot of John Carpenter, and a healthy jigger of absinthe, and you'll end up with Alistair Cross's modern Gothic chiller, "The Crimson Corset" - a deliciously terrifying tale that will sink its teeth into you from page one."
- Jay Bonansinga, New York Times Bestselling author of THE WALKING DEAD: INVASION and LUCID

"This drop-deadly tale of seduction and terror will leave you begging to be fanged … "
- Tamara Thorne, international bestselling author of HAUNTED and MOONFALL

"I couldn't put this book down. It's got more hooks than a day boat out of San Pedro Harbor!"
- QL Pearce, bestselling author of SCARY STORIES FOR SLEEP-OVERS

"Alistair Cross' new novel THE CRIMSON CORSET … is taut and elegantly written taking us into the realms where the erotic and the horrific meet. Reminiscent of the work of Sheridan Le Fanu (CARMILLA, UNCLE SILAS) in its hothouse, almost Victorian intensity, it tells a multi-leveled story of misalliance and mixed motives. The language is darkly lyrical, and the tale is compelling. Read it; you'll be glad you did."
- Chelsea Quinn Yarbro, author of the *Saint-Germain Cycle*

# Praise for Tamara Thorne's Novels

"(Haunted) is a wonderful, terrifying book…a worthy successor to The Shining and Ghost Story."
–Nancy Holder, New York Times bestselling author

"…a tapestry of chills and scares that will be remembered long after the lights have gone out."
-Douglas Clegg

"Combines eerie eroticism with page-turning terror."
-Pasadena Weekly

"(Thorne) is one of the best tellers of dark fantasy tall-tales, able to spin a yarn that's both outrageous and surprisingly convincing, peopled with flesh and blood characters you can't help but like and care about ... and she wields her wild sense of humor like a claymore."
-Bill Gagliani, Cemetery Dance

"Tamara Thorne has become one of those must-read horror writers. From her strong characters to her unique use of the supernatural, anything she writes entertains as much as it chills."
-Horror World

"Tamara Thorne is the new wave of horror--her novels are fascinating rides into the heart of terror and mayhem."
-Douglas Clegg

"Tamara Thorne has an uncanny knack for combining the outrageous with the shuddery, making for wonderfully scary romps and fun reading." -Chelsea Quinn Yarbro

The Cliffhouse Haunting
Text copyright ©2016 Tamara Thorne & Alistair Cross
All Rights Reserved
Published by Glass Apple Press
Cover art by Elderlemon Design

First paperback edition April, 2016

No part of this book may be reproduced or transmitted in any form or by any means, graphic, electronic, or mechanical, including photocopying, recording, taping, or by any information storage or retrieval system, without written permission from the authors.

This book is a work of fiction. Names, characters, places and incidents either are products of the authors imaginations or are used fictitiously. Any resemblance to actual persons, living or dead, events, or locales is entirely coincidental. All rights reserved.

ISBN-13: 978-1537265421
ISBN-10: 1537265423

For Robert Thorne and Berlin Malcom.
Thank you for putting up with us.

## Acknowledgements

Special thanks to Q.L. Pearce, Mark Hein, Libba Campbell, Kealan Patrick Burke, Douglas Clegg, Michael Aronovitz, Tracey Weatherly, Wiley Saichek, and John Scognamiglio, for helping us make this book the very best.

More thanks to Doctors June Meyer and Keith Olson for answering our medical questions, Professor Rosemary Channing for her historical insights, Richard Morris, MS, for his expertise on psychological pathologies. Any leaps of logic are the fault of the authors or their cats, and not the experts.

For various and sundry favors and assistance: Chelsea Quinn Yarbro, Pam Stack, Natalie Valenzuela, Michele Dragon, Heather Anderson, Robert Thorne, and our cats, for their fine and unexpected editing techniques.

While the town of Cliffside is purely imaginary, the San Bernardino Mountains, Lake Arrowhead and other mountain areas, including Bloody Gulch, are quite real.

# The Cliffhouse Haunting

by

Tamara Thorne & Alistair Cross

Glass Apple Press

# 1
## *July 2*

Well-marked but never well-traveled, the canyon trail many miles from Cliffside was perfect. Hammerhead had seen only one other hiker so far, but he had been too close to the road to make the kill.

Now he was deep in the woods, his black-gloved hand grasping a makeshift walking stick; the going was steep and while he enjoyed the challenge, he had to be careful because the poison oak was potent and he'd just passed a rattler sunning itself on a rock.

He heard voices and paused. *One male, one female.* It had been a long time since he had taken down two at once. The prospect delighted him, but he was nothing if not cautious; if it wasn't safe, he would wait until another day.

He stepped into the dappled shade of a huge fir, pulled his water bottle from his knapsack and drank. The prey drew closer, and after capping the bottle, he patted the rip claw hammer that hung from a loop on his belt, hidden by his light jacket.

When the voices were no more than fifty feet away, he began walking toward them, timing it so that they would meet near a steep cliff with a panoramic view.

The couple appeared, early twenties, slender and smiling. Hammerhead moved to the side of the trail.

"Hello!" said the young man. "Here for the view?"

He nodded, a smile painted on his face.

"It's worth the hike," the woman said. "It's so clear today."

"It is." As they passed he drew the hammer, whirled, and hit the man in the temple. The hiker crumpled where he stood. Before the girl could scream, he turned, and as graceful as a dancer, spun the weapon around and impaled her temple on the claws. She didn't fall because he held her up by the hammer. He pulled a compact mirror from his pocket, flipped it open and held it up as he lowered her to the ground. Her eyelids drooped, so he held them open with two fingers until she died and her soul was captured in the mirror. He snapped the compact shut, retrieved another, and turned to the young man. Disappointment flooded him. He was dead, his soul already gone. At least he had captured one soul. It felt good; it had been too long.

Hammerhead dragged the bodies to the edge of the rocky cliff. Once there, he lifted one head and brought it down on a sharp rock to obliterate the hammer wound, then dropped the rock over the cliff. He repeated the action with the other on a different rock. Then he pushed the bodies over. The coyotes and hawks would eat well, and in the massive brush and trees below, it was unlikely the remains would be found. There were others down there, after all, who'd been there for years.

***

*I saw what you did.*

The voice, not audible, was clear in his mind and the scent of dark water filled his nose. Hammerhead opened his eyes. "Who's there?"

*I saw what you did.*

There it was again; soft, distinctly feminine, and pleasant, were it not for the accusation itself. He sat up. "What do you want?" His whisper was coarse and brusque in the silence of the night.

*I want to help you.*

Hammerhead flopped back down on the bed, covered his head with a pillow, and closed his eyes tightly. "Go away."

Laughter, light yet somehow terrible, echoed through the room - through his mind - and slowly dissipated, along with the smell of cold water, leaving him alone with the silence.

# 2
## *Cliffhouse Lodge*

**SEPTEMBER**
**SUNDAY**

The great lawn at Cliffhouse Lodge was coated with Labor Day picnickers and revelers. People sat on benches or blankets feasting on fried chicken, barbecued burgers, and ribs. Chief Jackson Ballou rolled down his window to take in the mouthwatering aromas as he drove onto the property, cruising the parking lots by the carousel and miniature golf course before pulling up to Cliffhouse itself.

It stood straight and tall and beautiful, all heavy logs, rugged rock, and glass that reflected the warm afternoon sunlight. Guests dotted the wide veranda that looked out over the dark waters of Blue Lady Lake.

The Labor Day festivities marked the end of the summer tourist season, and by tomorrow afternoon, Cliffside would become a quiet mountain community again, stirring and stretching on mild autumn weekends, remaining sleepy until ski season.

"Chief!"

He glanced up. Teddy and Adam Baxter-Bellamy walked down the broad steps from the veranda toward his cruiser. Jackson waved at the owners of Cliffhouse then pulled the unit to the edge of the roadway, parked and got out. He stretched, sniffing the breeze carrying the delightful fragrances of pine and burgers. "Guys," he called, tipping his hat against the sun.

"Are you trying to scare off our guests, parking out front like that?" Adam asked as Jackson crossed to join them in front of the lodge.

"I'll move it-"

"No, no." Teddy chuckled. "The chief of police can park wherever he pleases."

Jackson glanced at his watch. "It's time for my break. Is it time for yours?"

The guys smiled. "Coffee?" asked Teddy.

"Love some. I'll meet you back here in a minute." He trotted back to the cruiser and pulled around back to the guest parking. By the time he returned, Teddy, Adam, and their daughter Sara were carrying four paper cups of coffee to a white cast iron table with semi-circular benches and a candy-striped umbrella.

Jackson joined them, accepting the tall cup Sara handed him. "It's just the way you like it, Chief. Black and strong."

"And mine's sweet and white." Teddy grinned. "Like Adam."

Sara poked him. "You're awful, Daddy."

Jackson removed the lid and inhaled. "Bliss in a cup."

Teddy gave him a Mona Lisa smile. "Thank you, Jackson."

"So how's life down in the village?" Adam asked. "I sure hope no one's drowned this weekend."

"Not a one," Jackson said. "They've doubled up on lifeguards."

"Good," said Teddy. "I think six drownings in one summer is a little extreme."

"So do I," Jackson said. "I don't even know how many near-misses we had this season. I think next summer we'd better issue swimming licenses or something."

Adam sipped his coffee. "Everyone behaving themselves on land?"

"Surprisingly. The fellas held a traffic stop down the block from La Dee Da's and Boozehound's last night. Filled up our little drunk tank inside of an hour." La Dee Da's and Boozehound's - nee Bloodhound's - were the two bars in Cliffside's seedier area, which was a short block just off Main Street between the Baptist church and the Peppermint Stix Motel. Jackson never failed to find humor in the placement, though he doubted the Baptists were as amused.

"Are we on for our regular run Monday morning, Jackson?" Adam asked.

"Yep."

Teddy shook his head in mock sorrow. "Anyone who willingly runs at seven in the morning has several screws loose."

"I keep trying to get him to join us," Adam said.

"I do the treadmill at nine a.m. like a civilized human being, thank you very much." Teddy sipped his coffee.

"You don't know what you're missing," Jackson told him. "Bracing air, the scent of the forest, beautiful scenery."

"Crazy drivers, packs of coyotes, the occasional bear," Teddy countered.

Sara pointed south toward the band shell across the great lawn. "The orchestra is already setting up."

"Yeah," said Adam. "They're playing this afternoon and then again tonight during the luminaria parade and fireworks. Last night of the summer. Gotta do it right."

In the distance, children shrieked giddily as the carousel's calliope burst into a clanging rendition of *Seventy-Six Trombones*. Jackson couldn't restrain a grin. He wished he could hop a ride.

Sara stood up, the sun making a golden nimbus of her hair as she placed a hand on each of her parents' shoulders. "I need to get back to the desk, but you guys have fun." She looked at Adam. "Dad, you should tell the chief about our latest ghostly encounters."

Adam rolled his eyes, but she was gone before he could respond, her light laughter trailing behind.

Jackson watched Sara trot up the stairs. She'd been a tomboy when she'd left for college, but had returned a beautiful young woman. She still preferred jeans to business attire, but she loved business and intended to run the hotel someday. Her dads were lucky. Most kids wanted to leave home; she couldn't wait to return, claiming the mountains spoiled her for the lowlands.

"Another ghost story?" Jackson tried to sound casual, knowing Adam wouldn't be eager to tell it. Ever since they'd begun renovating the lodge, odd things had been happening, at least according to Teddy - and the occasional guest.

"You're more likely to spot the Blue Lady than a ghost in the lodge." Adam sighed.

Teddy, however, sat forward, his blue eyes coming to life, his cheeks pinking. "They call it Blue Lady Lake for a reason."

"Sure they do." Adam looked bored.

"So," said Jackson. "Let's hear it."

Teddy grinned. "We got a call from one of the guests on the third floor. They said the people in the room next to them were making all kinds of noise - fighting, throwing things, and banging stuff around-"

"It's probably just construction noises," Adam said.

Teddy gave him the stink-eye. "But when we looked to see who was in the room next to them, it was empty. In fact, all the surrounding rooms were empty!"

"Pranksters," Adam said. "There have been ghost stories about this place since the 1880s. People know the rumors. They like to have a little fun. Or, it could be from all the construction."

"Construction in the middle of the night?" asked Teddy. "And none of the rooms had been disturbed."

"It wasn't the middle of the night. It was ten o'clock. And no, they weren't working, but I'm sure things fall over all the time. We *are* tearing walls down, you know."

"You don't sound convinced, Adam," said Jackson.

Adam laughed. "No kidding."

"We have a semi-permanent guest, Miss Maisy Hart, who's an expert on the paranormal," Teddy told Jackson. "She says the remodeling is upsetting the spirits here. I believe her. She's like family."

Adam rolled his eyes. "She's a lovely, if rather tipsy old lady, and she knew Teddy's Great Aunt Theodosia very well. That means she knows the history of the lodge. With that knowledge, it's easy to appear psychic."

Teddy smiled. "You're such a buzz-killer, Adam. She's never claimed to be psychic, but she has studied extensively. And we do have a psychic staying here. Maybe she could give us some answers."

Adam's indulgent smile turned sour. "Ms. Welling is staying here while she does some talks and book signings. She won't be hunting any ghosts at Cliffhouse."

"Did I hear someone say my name?" The three men turned their heads in the direction of the new voice.

The woman approaching them looked like a sugar-frosted flake with her pink streaked platinum hair, raccoon-eyes, and pink plastic earrings that brushed her shoulders. She strutted toward them in jeans so tight Jackson could read her lips. Her cotton candy-colored top had puffy peasant sleeves pulled down to expose her bony shoulders - the left sporting a smiling moon tattoo and the right, a grinning sun. From the unnaturally wide divide between her immobile snow-globe breasts sprouted an especially ugly tattoo. Jackson couldn't tell what that one was, except it was brown. He didn't want to know.

Constance Welling needed no introduction; he recognized her from the posters he'd recently seen plastered all over town. She called herself 'the premiere authoress of the occult.' Jackson's translation: a crystal-packing nutjob.

"Ms. Welling," Adam said quickly. "I merely mentioned to Chief Ballou that you're staying with us, as are many other interesting guests."

"I *thought* my ears were burning!" Constance smiled and her crow's feet glistened in the sun.

Jackson nodded, tipped his hat. "Ms. Welling."

Constance Welling forced Adam and Jackson apart as she wedged herself between them on the bench. "Please," she said to Jackson. "Call me Constance." She winked. "I'm so glad to meet you, Mr. Chief of Police. I've been here over a week and haven't had time to talk to a soul, not even the proprietors of this fine hotel." She ogled Teddy and Adam by turn. Her perfume cloyed in Jackson's sinuses and her bony hip ground into his side as she wriggled in place. It reminded him that he needed to squeeze under the sink tonight and tighten that leaky pipe. "So who are all these other interesting guests?"

Teddy opened his mouth but was cut off by his husband. "All of our guests are interesting and it's up to us as hosts to ensure everyone's privacy, Ms. Welling. Our guests mingle over wine and hors d'oeuvres in the lobby in the evening. You might join them and see for yourself."

"Oh," she said. "Handsome *and* discreet."

The woman's perfume was a headache-inducing blend of scents - rubbing alcohol with a dab of patchouli. Beneath this, Jackson thought he scented liquor, just enough to suggest she'd done a respectable amount of damage to a bottle the night before. His stomach roiled a little.

Just as he was preparing to make his excuses for departure, the dispatcher's voice sounded from his radio. "Chief Ballou?" he heard between two flashes of static.

He pressed himself against Adam to clear enough space to grapple for the radio. "Yup," he said into it.

"We've got a traffic accident out by Elfland"

"On my way. Gotta run, fellas." Jackson stood. "Ms. Welling. A pleasure." He tipped his hat to the hideous woman and trotted toward the black and white SUV.

# 3
## *Walleye*

"Come on, Carrie!" Tommy cried, tugging his sister's hand. "Let's go look in the windows!"

Carrie eyed her little brother - only two years younger but *so* immature - and figured that if she refused to peek in the windows of the little cabin way across the lawn from Cliffhouse, he'd call her a chicken the rest of the day. In truth, the nine-year-old thought it was a pretty wicked-looking place. *Maybe it's haunted.* Or, at least, maybe that's what she'd tell him while he was looking inside. *He'll pee his pants!* She smiled. "Okay."

"Really?"

"Really." Carrie and Tommy stood by the creaky merry-go-round in the playground. They'd gotten bored pushing each other around on the crooked metal wheel. All it did was squeak and groan and go too slow. She turned to look at the carousel. From here, the music was soft, and she could hardly wait until after lunch when their parents would hand them more dollars to ride it. She'd ride it all day if she could. She only wished there were a roller coaster here, too, but Stinky-Pants - aka Tommy - wouldn't go on it anyway and their parents *always* made them do stuff together.

"What?" Tommy squawked.

"What do you mean, what?"

"You rolled your eyes."

"Don't be immature."

He looked confused. "I'm not."

"Are so."

"Am not." He pulled her hand again. "Let's go!"

She gave the carousel one more glance, then cried, "Run!"

And they did, slowing when they were within thirty feet of the cabin. From there they read a little white sign by the door. "No trespassing," Carrie said. "I wonder why."

"They probably store stuff in there they don't want stolen. Boat stuff, maybe."

"That's stupid." Carrie sniffed. "Maybe they store corpses!"

"Huh-uh! *That's* stupid!"

"Dare you to look in a window!"

"Oh, yeah?"

"Yeah. Dare."

"I'm gonna." He didn't move, but licked his lips, which meant he was scared.

"Maybe the bogeyman lives in there!" Carrie suggested.

"There's no such thing!"

"Is so. Remember? You said he lived in your closet last year!"

"Nuh-uh. I said the Evil Monkey lived in Chris Griffin's closet, stupid-head!"

"So go look if you're not chicken." She grinned at him. "Cluck. Cluck-cluck-cluck."

"Knock it off. You just *think* you're funny."

"Hey, Stinky-Pants, you're the one who wanted to come out here."

"Don't call me that!" He crossed his arms and glared at her. "Watch this!"

He sprinted right up to the cabin, staying low, not stopping until he was beside the small square structure. He grinned at her and waved, his thumb stuck in his nose.

"So look inside!" she called.

He crept a couple feet farther and stuck his head up to a window. He stayed there a long time.

"Well?" She was getting antsy.

He motioned her to join him. She thought about it for two seconds, then ran to him. "What did you see?"

"Neat stuff. Look."

"What kind of neat stuff?"

"Look, you'll see!"

"Okay, move over!"

He stepped to the far edge of the window and she peered in. "I don't see anythi- Eeeeeeeeeh!!"

"You immature little brat." She turned on her brother whose hands were still hovering near her ribs. He was grinning like a fool. An immature fool.

"Gotcha!"

"I. Am. Going. To. Kill. You."

"Dad's right. You can dish it out, but you sure can't take it!"

"You. Are. Going. To. Die. NOW!"

Tommy turned and ran the long way around the cabin, Carrie in hot pursuit.

As he rounded the corner, he plowed headfirst into an unmoving mass.

Less than a second later, Carrie crashed into his back.

They squealed as they bounced to the ground.

The object laughed.

Carrie looked up. *It's the Bogeyman!* She scrambled to her feet. Tommy was already on his, running in strange frenzied circles as he screamed incoherent words.

As she swiped at her loony brother, trying to pull him to safety, Carrie heard herself screaming, "It's the Bogeyman! It's the Bogeyman!"

The Bogeyman grabbed Tommy's shoulder and brought him to an abrupt stop.

Carrie panicked. "Don't touch him! Run, Tommy, Run!" She pounded at the Bogeyman with her fist. "Let him go, you … you …"

The Bogeyman just laughed more and grabbed her, too. "Hold on there, little lady," he said. "You've got a wicked left hook. Ever think of taking up boxing?"

Tears streamed down Tommy's face as he gasped to catch his breath.

"Huh?" asked Carrie.

"I know I'm not real pretty to look at, but I'm not a bogeyman, either." The man smiled.

"You're not?" she asked, fear fading.

The man tossed his head back and laughed again. "Wasn't the last time I checked, anyway."

Carrie looked at her brother. She could see relief in his eyes.

"Are … are we in trouble?" Tommy asked.

"Of course not." The man was chuckling. "But what are you doing out here?"

"We were just looking around, Mister," said Tommy. "We didn't mess with anything. I promise!"

Carrie nodded with enthusiasm. "We didn't. We just looked in the window."

"I know."

"You do? How?" she asked. "There wasn't anybody around."

"This eye." He pointed at his face. "It's special. See how it can look off in a different direction while my other one stares right 'atcha? I pretty much can see everything that goes on here at Cliffhouse. That's why I'm the caretaker. Walter Gardner. But you can call me Walleye."

"Mr. Walleye?" Tommy asked.

"Yep, if you like. See how I'm always checking the walls? It's easy."

Tommy nodded. "That's pretty cool. Isn't it, Carrie?"

"Yeah, it is, I guess." Carrie was having a hard time because she couldn't believe how worried she had been about Stinky-Pants. "We should go back to the playground."

"You can come in if you like."

"What?" Alarm bells went off in her head. Maybe he was a kidnapper. Next, he'd offer them candy.

"Really? This is your house?" Tommy's eyes lit up.

"I think I've got some Tootsie Rolls inside."

"Yeah-"

"No, thank you." Carrie was firm, trying to hide a new surge of terror. "Our parents said we can't take stuff from strangers."

"Smart parents," said Walleye. "Guess you better not come in, either."

"Guess not." Tommy was glum. He eyed his sister. "You're no fun."

"You're immature."

"Am not."

"Am so-"

"Kids, why don't I see you back to the playground? I'll tell you a ghost story while we walk. Do you like ghost stories?"

"YES!"

"Tommy, don't yell!" She looked at Walleye. "Yes, we do. Don't mind my *little* brother. He's very immature."

They started across the vast lawn. "Do you know why it's called Blue Lady Lake?" Walter gestured at the rippling water beyond the cliffs.

"No," said Carrie. Tommy shook his head.

"Well, do you know about the Blue Lady?" Walleye paused. "No? Well, that's what we here in Cliffside call our water elemental. The Greeks called it a naiad."

"Huh?" Tommy asked. "What's that?"

Carrie looked impatient.

"Well, it's a spirit - a nature spirit, not a human one - and it lives in water like lakes and streams and ponds. It looks like a woman when it wants to."

"She's the lady of the lake?" Carrie asked. "Like in *The Once and Future King*?"

"Yeah!" Tommy said. "She has King Arthur's sword!"

"Well, yes, kind of like that, but the elemental that lives here is a dark and scary one. She's the Blue Lady."

"Does she have a sword?" Tommy sounded hopeful.

"No."

"A knife?"

"She doesn't need weapons, young man."

"Does she kill people?" Tommy asked.

"Well, she has." Walleye lowered his voice a little. "She lures people into water - like the lake - and drowns them. She's fond of naughty children who don't mind their parents."

They paused, turning to stare at the water. Tiny waves scudded as breezes puffed the sails of small boats, setting them to glide. Canoeists dipped their oars, unaware of what might lurk below.

Tommy swallowed. "How do you know?"

Walleye smiled. "Way back before the Bellamys helped found this town in the 1880s - they run Cliffhouse to this day, you know - there was a group of people who settled up here for a time. They'd first come from Mexico, you know, Spanish soldiers who'd been ordered to plunder Montezuma's gold. Well, some of these soldiers didn't much care for that and instead married senoritas who had arrived years before with their families to settle California. A few married native girls who were rescued from Mission San Juan Capistrano - the monks down there had them working as slave labor." He chuckled. "You know about that?"

"I built a papier-mâché mission in school last year," Tommy said. "It got first place!"

"Congratulations. So you know. Anyway, this little group didn't have a lot of money to set up their own ranch, and they were on the outs with a lot of people because, back then, mixed marriage was a big no-no. So they came here.

"It was spring and they built shelters, planted, and did real well; before the snow flew, they built a nice big log cabin where they could stay warm in the winter. Sort of like an apartment building, but with animal skins for doors between the apartments. The first babies, twins, a boy and a girl, like you two-"

"We're not twins. He's younger than me."

"I see. Well, the first babies were born that February. The parents were a Spanish soldier, Rodrigo, and his beautiful wife, a rancher's daughter, Lupita.

"Everything was fine for several years. They built more log cabins so the growing families all had their own private homes. Fish were plentiful, the native wives were very wise in the ways of nature, and that helped them survive, especially in winter.

"When the twins were three and Rodrigo was gone to trade skins for supplies with a settlement down the hill, Lupita, who was very bored, became infatuated with a handsome French fur trader. She wanted to leave Rodrigo for him, but was afraid he wouldn't want her if he knew she had children. She loved him way too much.

"One night, in a fit of rage, after the kids had been fighting with each other, Lupita took them down to the lake and drowned them, a sacrifice to the water elemental in hopes that she would cause the fur trader to fall in love with her." He paused. "She weighted the children's bodies down with stones to make them sink. No one ever saw them again. But two days later, Lupita reappeared. She was floating in the lake, her face green and bloated as if she'd been there for a very long time. They said it was the Blue Lady that killed her. And that's how the lake got its name."

"The Blue Lady is a real bitch!" Carrie said.

"Carrie! I'm gonna tell! You can't say that word!"

"You're not going to tell."

"Yes, I am."

"If you do, I'll tell them what you put in the vacuum cleaner hose."

The boy turned red. "You wouldn't dare."

"I would."

"You wou-"

"Kids, it's not nice to tattle. Why don't you both keep your mouths shut so I can finish the story?"

"Okay." Carrie's eyes didn't leave her brother's until he looked away. Another victory.

"After that, on quiet nights, the settlers would hear eerie singing near the streams and the lake. Some claimed it was the wind, but most swore it sounded like a mournful female voice raised in song. Those who dared peek out their windows claimed to sometimes see a glowing blue woman with very long hair rise out of the lake and wander the streets, always trying to lure more children out to take into the lake with her."

Tommy's eyes were wide. "Is she still here?"

"Yes, and there's more," Walleye said.

"What?" whispered Carrie.

"Even though that Spanish settlement left within the year - it was no longer a pleasant place to be - the Blue Lady continues to walk along the streams and the lakeside, always searching. When people came here again in the 1870s, she is said to have taken a lot of the early settlers' children, and some adults as well."

"Taken them?" Carrie asked.

They reached the playground and Walleye put his finger to his throat and slid it with a *slash* sound. "Other people have gone missing too, over the years, and have never been seen again." He bent down, staring at them. "She comes at night, so never, ever wander by yourselves after dark. Okay?"

"Okay," they said in unison.

"Now, off you go. You kids have some fun on the swings." He looked thoughtful. "They found a body on that first swing one morning in the 1930s. The playground is haunted, too. I'll tell you about that later, if you want."

Tommy looked worried. "What about Cliffhouse? Is it haunted?"

"Of course."

"Does the Blue Lady go inside Cliffhouse?" Carrie asked. "Like into the pool or the hot springs?"

"Or the bathtubs?" Tommy asked. "Or the sinks?"

"I said that's enough! Now, off you go!"

"Tell us-"

"No more for today." He grinned, then turned and headed for his cabin on the cliff.

# 4
## *Hammerhead Makes a Deal*

*I want to help you ...*

The voice came more and more these past days, riding the smell of the lake, and Hammerhead was growing tired of it. Now she had dared enter his inner sanctum. "Shut up!" He clapped his hands over his ears, a futile gesture because the voice came from within as well as without.

*Give yourself to me...*

"No, no, no! I said, shut up!" He stood in the Hall of Souls before the constellation of small mirrors that hung on the wall. "I'm losing my mind!"

*No, you are not mad.*

"I'm not?"

*Look into the mirror ...*

He raised his eyes and searched the many mirrors, wondering which one she was referring to. Then he saw her in the center mirror, the largest one. *My mirror.*

At first, he saw only a bluish blur. It materialized into the most beautiful woman he'd ever seen. She was slender, elegant. A blue halo of light surrounded her. She drew closer to the mirror, her long blue-white hair moving around her head as if she were underwater. Her gown did the same. Soon, her face filled the looking glass.

*Listen to me.* Her red lips did not move. *You are not mad ...*

He gaped at the phantom. "Who are you?"

*I am the Lady, and I am here to help you.*

"Help me? How?"

Her crimson lips smiled. Her eyes glittered with satisfaction. *We are of the same appetites, the same nature.*

"What do you mean?"

*You enjoy the kill. You need the kill. I share your passion, though my reasons are different.*

"Different how?"

*I am nourished by the body. You are nourished by the soul. Together, we can sustain ourselves more than apart.*

"I don't know what you mean."

*Let me help you. I will see to it that your needs are satisfied and your pleasures are many.*

"But why? Why would you help me?"

*I need you as much as you need me.*

"What do I need you for? I'm doing fine on my own."

*Do you not need more planets to orbit your sun?*

The smaller mirrors seemed to twinkle and the central one bloomed with light, leaving only her eyes and mouth visible. *With me, you will have all you desire and you will never be discovered.*

Hammerhead thought about this.

*You will be caught. It is inevitable.*

He shuddered despite the warmth of his confines. "I'm very careful."

*Time reveals all; do you not yet know that?*

Hammerhead considered her words. It was a worry he sometimes wrestled with. He exhaled and nodded. "What would you have me do?"

The lips broadened, looking more like a red gash than a smile. "I would have you kill."

Hammerhead smiled.

# 5
## *Ballou Family Dinner*

Jackson Ballou pulled up at the little green cabin that his sister Kitty and his father Lee shared in the residential area south of the lake. Stifling a groan, he briefly considered driving off and pleading an emergency call, but he was just superstitious enough to talk himself out of it. On top of that, he was already two hours late due to a fatal hit-and-run near Boozehound's. He'd called Kitty at six p.m. to beg off but she insisted being late was fine. She'd made her "Famous Family Meatloaf" - two of them, in fact - and they would keep.

Boy, would they keep. Like cordwood. Heavy and dry, her meatloaf rarely tasted the same way twice, but it was always boring and a little too sweet. Kitty liked to mix things up. Resigned, he climbed from the cruiser and headed for the cabin.

"Well, there you are!" Kitty opened the door and came out to hug him before he was halfway up the walk. "You're late!"

He returned his sister's hug and, out of old habit, gave her blond ponytail an affectionate tug. "I told you-"

"You did tell me, Jacky. I was just amazed you were *this* late! It's nearly nine."

"Things happen."

"I know, I know, you don't need to give me any excuses - I understand. So anybody get killed?"

"Yes. One fatality, one in the hospital with two broken legs."

"Anybody I know?"

"You told me you had to fire that box boy at the market a while back - Zeke Wilson?"

"Zeke? He's dead?"

"Nope, he's alive, but he killed one person and put another in the hospital." Jackson shook his head in disgust. "Drunk driving. He tried to run but plowed into a telephone pole a block away. Not a scratch on him, of course."

"That's horrible," Kitty said. "Just awful. The day I fired him, he smelled like a gin factory."

Lee Ballou's voice bellowed from inside. "Damn it, Miss Kitty, you're letting all the flies in. Get in here and shut the damn door!"

"Okay, Daddy, we're coming." She took Jackson's hand and led him into the kitchen. "Daddy's such a grumpy bear sometimes."

"Yeah, he's a real cut-up when he's had a sixer or two." That was another reason Jackson didn't want to be here. His dad would probably be on his eighth or ninth beer by now.

"Oh, Jacky, hush now. Dinner's waiting. You need to eat. So does Daddy."

"If he's got any room left for food."

"Hush." She busied herself at the sink. "How's Polly?"

"Fine, as far as I know. Why do you ask?"

"You're sweet on her, aren't you?"

"She's a good buddy of mine. In fact, I'm going by the diner tomorrow for lunch."

Kitty gave him one of those annoying smiles.

"We have good conversations. That's all."

Conway Twitty twanged softly from the radio on the kitchen table. As usual. He was Kitty's favorite singer and she called him an "old dreamboat." He was her first crush and, evidently, her last. He'd died, what, twenty or thirty years ago? *Old dead dreamboat.*

"Jackson, boy, get in here and get yourself a cold one. Get me one, too."

"Don't roll your eyes," Kitty whispered. She went to the fridge and drew two Buds out. He took one and shook his head when she tried to push the other on him. "Jackson," she whispered, "You know he hates to drink alone."

"Is that why he's been doing it for thirty years?"

"Why do you have to be so obstinate? You act like a little boy sticking his tongue out at his father."

"I'm a big boy and I don't drink. He's why."

"Oh, nonsense. You can't blame him for you not liking to drink."

"Yes, I can. And I do."

"Jacky … Why do you have to be so difficult?"

From the living room: "Jackson? Where's that beer?"

"Look Kitty, you're my sister and I love you. I can never thank you enough for living with the old man, but I will not be pressured into drinking with him. You remember how bad it could be."

"He doesn't drink like that anymore."

"Ah, he's cured, huh?"

"He's not a drunk anymore. You were just really late and-"

"So it's my fault he's drunk? I won't accept that. Maybe I'd just better leave before things get worse. You and I are never going to see eye to eye on this one." He turned to leave.

Kitty grabbed his arm. "Okay, okay, let's go in and be nice. It's just dinner, then you can leave."

"Okay. Just don't push me about the drinking." He thought he saw tears in her eyes. "Look, Kitty, you've done a great job with him. He really is better than he was, but he and I will never be pals. You're just going to have to accept it."

"He's your family."

"You're my family, Kitty."

"So is he."

"I believe in choosing my family, not letting blood decide it."

"Damn it, where's that beer?" Lee Ballou hollered.

"Fine, fine." She pushed the Bud into his hand. "Take him this. I'll have dinner on the table in ten minutes."

He took the beer and entered the living room. At one end, there was a large fireplace. Catty-cornered from that was a big-screen TV and across from it was a threadbare La-Z-Boy in which Lee Ballou sat, one hand wrapped around an empty bottle, the other around the remote control. He was watching a ball game, the announcer babbling behind the song stylings of Conway Twitty in the kitchen. He didn't seem to mind.

"Hand me that beer," Lee said, showing a wide toothy grin.

"Here ya go, Dad." Jackson took the empty and gave him the fresh bottle.

There was a paper grocery bag on the floor next to him and it was half full of empties. Jackson averted his eyes and, for Kitty's sake, kept the empty and sat down on the sofa facing the fireplace. He held the bottle as if it were full and looked at the TV instead of his inebriated father.

"Cheers." The old man twisted off the cap and raised the bottle to him.

"Cheers." Jackson tried to look engaged.

"You think you're pulling the wool over my eyes, sonny-boy? I know you're not drinking. What's the matter with you? Got a little too much pussy in your makeup?"

"Mom didn't drink either."

"There ya go then. Pussy. I'm glad Miss Kitty's got some balls. Takes after her daddy. And here she is now!"

Kitty bustled into the dining room area at the far end of the living room and set a platter down in the middle of the table. Jackson rose and went to help her get the last of the dishes while Lee belched happily and got to his feet. Jackson watched him from the corner of his eye. To give the man credit, he didn't come close to falling down, but his walk was creative, to say the least.

"Sit down, you two," Kitty commanded. "You boys can get started passing the food in a sec. Jacky, you want to say grace?"

"I'll pass."

Lee chortled. "Good boy."

That almost made Jackson want to pray. Almost.

Kitty sighed. "I'll do it." She folded her arms and bowed her head. After a moment of silence, she spoke. "Lord, we thank you for this food, and we hope you're enjoying some, too. Amen."

Lee pulled the platter closer and eyed the shoebox-sized brown meatloaf topped with greasy slightly burned ketchup and surrounded by a nice looking assortment of roasted baby potatoes and broccoli. "Broccoli? Miss Kitty, I told you, I don't like that shit."

"You eat it up, Daddy. It's good for your prostate. You know what Doc Siechert said."

"Yeah, well, okay, but only because Nurse Cornhull has her eye on me. Cute little thing, Nurse Cornhull."

Jackson and Kitty traded looks. There was nothing cute about Tessa Cornhull.

"I'm thinking of asking her out," Lee added, taking a long swig of Bud.

"Daddy, she's a lesbian, isn't she?"

Simultaneously, Jackson said, "She's dating Siechert."

Lee looked confused, then whooped. "Guess I hit a nerve there, huh kids?"

Kitty started to open her mouth but Jackson silenced her with a look. "Dad, why don't you carve?" When it came to Kitty's meatloaves, "carved" was the proper expression.

Lee already had the big butcher knife in his hand. "Who wants the end?"

"Not me." Jackson said.

"I do, Daddy. I like it crunchy."

In a few minutes, everyone had their meat and vegetables. Jackson eyed the meatloaf with trepidation. There were little pale green things in it. And what looked like pineapple niblets.

"Well, go on then, Jacky. Taste it. Tell me what you think!" Kitty was proud of her kitchen prowess.

He cut a piece of potato and broccoli and put it in his mouth. "Mmmm. Good."

"Taste the meatloaf, Jackson."

"Pass the ketchup first, Kitty."

"You kids, you rib each other just like you did when you was little."

"Were, Daddy."

Jackson gave Kitty a warning look. It had never been smart to correct their father when he was drinking. Sure, she always got away with more than he had, but … bad idea. He popped a bite of meatloaf in his mouth and chewed.

"Um, what are your secret ingredients this time, sis?"

"Can you guess?"

"Something green."

"Daddy's favorite nut!"

Lee grinned. "Miss Kitty, that's where my pistachios went?"

"Sure did, Daddy. I hope you approve!"

"I do, indeed. This is going to make some fine sandwiches."

Kitty beamed. "I'll bring another bag of nuts home from the market. We put them on sale this week."

Jackson forced down another piece. "Is there pineapple in this?"

"That's my secret ingredient, Jacky. Good for you."

*Not so good for me.* "It's interesting, Kitty."

"Oh, Jacky-"

"Speaking of secrets," Lee boomed, startling them both, "my pal Larry called me. He says there was quite a ruckus by Boozehound's earlier. Said you were there."

"He doesn't want to talk about it, Daddy," Kitty interrupted. "Somebody died. It's not dinner conversation. Let it go."

"I'm his daddy. He's going to tell me. Who got put down, Jacky-Boy?"

Jackson recognized the temper in his father's voice and shifted in his seat. His stomach knotted around the meatloaf. "Sorry, Dad. Kitty's right. Not something I care to discuss."

"Oh, come on," Lee slurred. "I can take it. Give me the gory details."

"No, Daddy!" Kitty's voice rose a notch.

Jackson's temper was near the boiling point.

"Oh, bullshit!" Lee roared. "Bullshit! You'll tell me and you'll tell me now!"

"Okay. Hit and run." Jackson forced himself to speak softly. "A drunk driver, probably one of your pals, killed an innocent woman, splattered her all over the road, blood everywhere, and her 10-year-old daughter got to watch it all. She was a lucky girl, though, Dad. She's still alive, but her spine is broken. Likely, she'll never walk again." Jackson's fists curled with rage as he rose and left the table.

Lee gawked at him but said nothing.

"Kitty." Jackson turned to his sister. "I need to make my rounds. I'm sorry I have to leave you."

"Let me wrap up some meatloaf for you, Jacky. I can give you slices off the second one."

"No, that's okay."

Lee slapped a hand on the table. "Pussy!"

Jackson glanced at him. "Yeah, Kitty, get me some meatloaf."

He followed her into the kitchen where she opened the fridge. "No, Kitty. I don't want any. I just want to make sure you're okay. Are you?" he asked softly. "Do you want to stay at my place tonight?"

She turned and looked up at him, her blue eyes shining with restrained tears. "I'm fine," she said. "He never threatens me anymore. Jackson, he's getting old. Why can't we be a real family?"

"Kitty, you and I, we're real family and always will be. You sure you want to stay here?"

"He'll be dead to the world in twenty minutes, trust me. I just need to get some food into him. I'm fine."

Jackson wrapped his baby sister in his arms and held her long and tight. "You take good care of yourself, Kitty." He moved to the door and turned the knob. "Good care."

"Don't you worry about me, Jacky."

But he did worry.

# 6
## *Sara and the Poltergeist*

Sara Baxter-Bellamy left her apartment and went downstairs to Cliffhouse's large kitchen to forage for food. Her own refrigerator was empty except for several bottles of green tea and some out-of-code yogurt.

She opened the large stainless steel refrigerator and found sliced ham, Swiss cheese, lettuce, and mayonnaise, and took them to the counter. Retrieving a loaf of rye, she started piling the ham and cheese between two slices.

After twisting the bread package closed, she crossed the room for a knife. As she returned, something caught her attention. She gasped as the loaf of rye slide from the middle of the counter, out into the air - at least a foot - then fall to the floor.

She dropped her knife. "What the …?" She looked at the bread on the floor and waited for it to move again. It didn't. The sight was so unexpected that she burst into laughter. Maybe it was one of her dad's tricks.

Bending, she picked it up, and looked for a telltale thread. There was nothing. Her smile faltered. She looked around the room, but she was alone. *Weird.*

She finished making her sandwich, then poured herself a glass of milk, and sat at a small table they used for making grocery lists. She watched the counter while she ate. Nothing happened. She wasn't sure if she was relieved or disappointed.

# 7
## *Booteous Maxima*

Labor Day weekend was in full, boisterous swing and Hammerhead cringed as another volley of fireworks exploded over the lake. He had chosen to walk far from downtown proper with the whore, near the Presbyterian church and the park, to avoid crowds, noise, and even the sight of the fireworks. It was so distracting. He hated the noise, the proximity to people, the whore's cheap perfume. But his new companion, the Blue Lady, didn't mind.

The whore, who introduced herself as Booteous Maxima, smiled. "What's the matter, lamb? Jumpy tonight?"

He didn't answer, but remained civil as she pushed her hand through the crook of his elbow and sidled closer. In her platform heels, she was taller than he by several inches, making her companionable move ludicrous.

Another explosion boomed over the lake; he saw gold and silver glitter above the trees as his body jolted with the shock.

"Oh, lamby, you *do* hate noise, don't you?" She squeezed his arm. "I bet you were scared by fireworks when you were just a little boy. I'll bet you were the cutest little boy ..." She bent and brushed her red lips against his cheek, a presumptuous move that made him cringe inside.

Her perfume was so strong now that he could barely hide his disgust despite the soothing, sensual mental blandishments of the Blue Lady, who watched and waited. "I'm fine," he said to the whore, trying to sound pleasant.

*Just a little while, now ...*

The whore gave him a painted red smile. "Want to have some fun, lamby?"

"What do you suggest?"

He controlled his revulsion at the touch of her, the smell of her, at the very thought of this pestilent woman thinking he wanted carnal relations with her. He had seen her just three days ago at the doctors' office laughing and joking with the receptionist about her need for antibiotics to control the venereal disease she'd been spreading like poison throughout the town.

"Well, what turns you on, lamby?"

He paused. "You tell me."

"We could go behind the church and find out." She withdrew her arm from his elbow and took his hand.

He suppressed a shudder at her damp touch, then glanced around; there was no one in sight. The population of Cliffside was gathered at the lake, staring up at the sky like sheep as fireworks bloomed. "All right."

She led him up the driveway, along the building, then turned behind it, guiding him to the brick trash enclosure. She steered him inside, pausing to kick at a pile of old blankets by the single Dumpster. Then she pushed him against the back wall farthest from the half-empty bin. Clearly, she'd done this before. His repulsion grew and a new smell, the dark-water smell of the lake, drowned out the cheap musk the hooker wore.

*It's almost time ...*

He reached in his pocket for the mirror as she worked his belt buckle.

"Damn," the whore whispered. "It's like the fucker is glued shut! But don't worry, lamby, Mama's fingers are nimble. There we go."

She unzipped his trousers and before he could stop her, shoved a hand into his shorts and grabbed him. "Somebody needs his pillow fluffed," she murmured. He sensed her readying to lower herself before him and he brought the compact mirror out, snapping it open. He felt the Blue Lady's excitement growing.

The whore already had his genitals exposed and was moving her lips toward them. In horror, he watched her kiss the tip of his penis.

He felt violated, diseased, and grabbed her hair, yanking her head back hard.

"Wha-? What the hell are you doing?" She stared up at him with clownish eyes.

*No. Do nothing.* The Blue Lady's voice filled his head. *Let me.*

With his fist still tight in her hair, he used all his self-control to keep from drawing the hammer from his belt loop.

*No. You have only to continue touching her. Watch.* The scent of water surrounded him.

The whore coughed once, twice, and then the only thing keeping her upright was his hand in her hair. She coughed harder, eyes glazing. He lowered her to the ground and knelt beside her.

*No. Continue to touch her,* the Blue Lady ordered. *Touch her shoulder. It is time.*

He heard the phantom sound of rushing water as the whore looked at him with eyes that swam and wandered.

*Now. Take her soul.*

He brought the mirror up, moving it to catch her gaze.

She coughed, turned her head, and gasped for breath. Water bubbled out of her mouth and she began jerking beneath him.

He steadied the mirror in front of her, forcing her own reflection to become the sole image of her dying moment.

She gagged, hacked, coughed up more water, but her eyes were wide and fixed on the small looking glass.

Her skin began to change. At first she looked blue, her lips purpling with the lack of oxygen. Then, as her movements weakened, the blue tint of her skin went grey; he could see it despite her heavy makeup.

The whore stopped moving.

Her eyes, wide and fixed, glazed over.

Within him, he felt the Lady buzzing with contentment.

He snapped the compact shut, his own prize captured. "Never touch me," he whispered. "You're a whore." He crouched to get a better look at her.

As he watched, a drop of water slid from her left eye and slid down onto the greasy, stained blacktop. He wondered what she'd been thinking at the moment of her death, and what it was like to watch yourself die.

He bent down, picked the carcass up, and hefted it into the Dumpster. He looked at the pile of dirty blankets on the ground, and then threw them in, covering the corpse.

The Lady was content, silent. Her watery scent faded. He exhaled and she left him, his mind, and his body.

He watched a moment as damp footprints parted from his own. As he disappeared into the night's shadows, he knew they'd both sleep well.

# 8
## *Jackson Relaxing*

Jackson sat in the golden glow of his porch light decompressing after the uncomfortable dinner with his sister and father. On his iPod, Springsteen sang of hard times and young love as Jackson put his chip knife to a small block of linden wood. Whittling soothed him.

He'd started this block a few nights ago with no idea what it would reveal as he stripped away layer after layer of wood. Now he saw an owl appearing beneath the blade. Sometimes he found a whale or a bear inside the wood, or various birds, even the occasional squirrel. Once, there was a beaver with a big flat tail.

Kitty was fine, but Lee Ballou was a drunk. He always had been, and probably always would be. While he had doted on Kitty - Miss Kitty, as he called her - he'd been hard on Jackson, who never was any good at sucking up to the old man. Lee, tall and slim, good-looking to this day, was a charmer when he wanted to be. He charmed everyone but his son.

Until Kitty moved up to Cliffside a few years ago, Jackson hadn't seen the old man in a decade, and he liked it that way. But after Kitty came up, it wasn't long before she invited their father to move in with her. *God, I wish she hadn't done that.* He found the edge of a wing in the wood and worked his way around it. Things could be worse; Kitty wanted the three of them to be a family and kept trying to bring them together over dinner, but at least she only pushed for monthly visits.

Tonight's torture had been typical. Kitty cooked and made peace while Lee Ballou swilled Budweisers and called Jackson a pussy for refusing to join him. He had way too many bad childhood memories about his father's drunken actions for that. Jackson might down a beer with his friends if the situation called for it, but never with his father.

He reached for his iced tea and finished it off, then rose and stretched. Yawning, he gathered his things, went indoors and shut off the porch light. He had to be up early to run with Adam before going to work. *Time to sleep.*

# 9
## *Sunday Night Ghosts*

At 10:30 on Sunday night, the vast lobby of Cliffhouse Lodge was nearly deserted, despite the holiday. Tonight, it was warm and those still celebrating were out on the lawns, down by the lake, or in town taking in the local production of *Oklahoma!* Within Cliffhouse's public area, the only sounds were those of the lodge's famous natural creek, which bubbled and babbled down the lobby and the soft music coming from the grand piano. Peace reigned in Cliffhouse Lodge this evening.

Across the great lawn, even the miniature golf course was still open. The carousel's calliope drifted in on the breeze and guests sat in Adirondack chairs on the wide terrace, nursing drinks and making small talk, enjoying the night air. Tomorrow was Labor Day, and everyone knew this was the final official night of summer, so they stayed out late, trying to absorb every last drop of the fleeting season.

Tonight, Jordan Cartwright had come in to tickle the ivories of the gleaming grand piano, something he did only on Friday and Saturday nights. He played the blues with exquisite finesse. Sara loved the blues. She and her dads were relaxing nearby, chatting and sharing a bottle of wine after a long day. Paul Butters, owner and manager of the on-site restaurant, La Chatte Rouge, had joined them after his last dinner guests departed to wait for his crew to finish cleaning up before locking the bistro for the night. He nursed a bottle of Cliffhouse's own Blue Springs Sparkling Water.

"So, Sara," said Teddy. "You're not just joshing us?"

"I'm not making it up, Daddy. The bread slid right off the counter and didn't fall until it was a good foot out. Then, *bam*, it just dropped."

Adam sat forward in the deep leather chair and lifted his wine glass from the massive coffee table that had been hewn from a giant redwood, back in the days before that was considered a bad thing to do. "This happened when?"

"About an hour ago. I thought you guys were pulling a trick on me, but there were no wires."

"There has to be a rational explanation," Adam said, settling back and sipping his Chantrieri Merlot. "This is delightful. We need to feature it at this month's wine tasting."

"Good idea. Valentyn Vineyards wines are excellent."

"I'll place an order tomorrow," Adam said.

"Good," Teddy said. "Now I want to hear more from Sara. What else happened?"

"Nothing."

Teddy rubbed his chin. "The poltergeist. It must be. But what's it doing in the kitchen all of a sudden? It's never performed off the second floor before." He looked hopeful. "I've always suspected we have more than one."

"Poltergeist?" Paul Butters asked. "Really? You have one here?"

"That's up for debate," Adam said. "I think there's a simple scientific explanation. Likely it's related to fault lines or underground streams."

"Whatever it is, it's spooky," Butters said. "You ought to play it up and get some of those ghost hunters up here. That might amp up your bottom line."

"No." Three Bellamys spoke as one.

"Think of the business you're passing up. There are plenty of old ghost stories attached to this place, aren't there? Between those and your poltergeists, you're in like Flynn. You could be on all those television ghost shows. Do the whole circuit." Paul's eyes lit with excitement. "We'd all make lots more money. I could expand La Chatte Rouge, you could renovate rooms faster-"

"Paul," Adam said. "I respect your entrepreneurial instincts. I admire them. But we will not invite that sort of thing. Most of those shows are hoaxed and we want nothing to do with fraud. And I don't care to have a bunch of would-be ghost hunters traipsing all over the lodge annoying our legitimate guests." He shook his head. "We refuse ghost-hunting privileges here every month. It's nothing new. Cliffhouse is supposed to be a haven, not a circus."

"I'm afraid that I must agree with my husband." Teddy poured two more fingers of wine. "I adore ghost stories, but our guests come first. 'Guests before ghosts.' That's our motto here."

"That's right," said Sara. "We're going to keep our poltergeist to ourselves, right everybody?" She looked straight at Paul.

"I would never betray a trust. You know that."

"Hello. Excuse us?" A tall fortyish man approached, his hair graying at the temples. His wife, slim and elegant even in shorts and a T-shirt, and his kids - a fidgety boy and girl - stood behind him. "May I ask you folks a question?"

"Mr. Collins." Sara stood up. "How nice to see you. Mrs. Collins. Kids. What can I do for you?"

"We were wondering about tomorrow. What time will the festivities end? We're trying to figure out when we should head down the mountain."

"Well, things will end around five o'clock, but people get anxious to get off the hill without getting in traffic. Some have quite a way to travel to get home."

The kids groaned and Mr. Collins threw them a stern glance, then turned to Sara. "Thank you. Might I ask what activities you recommend tomorrow?"

"The 11 a.m. paddlewheel tour is going to feature live folk music and free popcorn. That's always fun."

"We already went on that boat," the little girl said. "It was boring."

The mother put a hand on her shoulder. "Hush."

"Is there gonna be a Civil War show?" the boy asked.

"No, but later this month we have our Civil War Days Festival."

"Can we come back, Dad? Can we?"

Mr. Collins looked pained. "I'll check my calendar, Tommy, I promise."

The girl looked disgusted.

Teddy smiled at her. "There's a doll museum over on the other side of the lake, just off Main on Spruce. It's pretty great."

"Ugh. I hate dolls."

"Carrie!" said Mrs. Collins. "Mind your manners."

"Well, I do."

Teddy chuckled. "Excuse me, folks." He rose and headed for the piano.

"I'm sorry," Mrs. Collins said to Sara. "They're tired."

"Too many rides on the carousel," added Mr. Collins.

"You should get a roller coaster," Carrie said. The piano music stopped as she spoke and her words boomed through the lobby. Over in a corner, just outside the entrance to Omar Siam's Tavern, Maisy Hart looked up from her martini in surprise, then rose and wandered into the bar, no doubt for a fresh one. With three olives. Old Aunt Maisy was a creature of habit.

"All right, children," Mrs. Collins said. "It's time for bed. George, we'll see you in a little while?"

"Yes, I'll be up," her husband replied.

The mother herded her chicks - the boy whispering, "Can we? Can we, Mom? Can we?" and the girl stomping her feet as her mother pushed her along with a subtle shoulder pinch. They disappeared into the hall near the elevator.

As the piano music stopped, Sara looked at Mr. Collins. "Won't you come with me to the desk? I can give you a print out of all the activities in town tomorrow." She led him to the reception desk, worked her magic, and then returned, smiling. "He's decided to join the hotel BBQ tomorrow. I told him it's $20 a head, kids eat free, and they can play in the playground and, well, you know ..."

"And maybe they'll be worn out by the time they drive down the mountain," Adam finished.

Sara grinned. "Am I good or what?"

"What?" said Teddy.

She punched him affectionately then poured an inch of merlot into her glass. "Mr. Collins took the Civil War Festival brochure and booked a room. It's his son's birthday weekend."

"Glutton for punishment," Adam said.

"Indeed," agreed his husband, who had returned, the pianist in tow. Jordan Cartwright, standing behind an empty chair, sipped from a blue bottle of sparkling water, smiled, but said nothing.

"Speaking of ghosts, I guess he's been reading up on ours because he requested the Theodosia Suite, but I'm not inclined to share." Sara smiled. "I gave him the McGill Suite instead."

Teddy laughed. "Maybe Mary McGill will haunt them."

"The Theodosia Suite is where your aunt lived, isn't it, Teddy?" Jordan Cartwright asked.

"That's right. She lived and died in that room." Teddy paused. "It's a full-sized two bedroom apartment, and it was the most expensive suite in the hotel, until Sara talked us out of it."

"In return, I'm the one who gets to deal with night time emergencies," Sara said. "And it's worth it. It's haunted by Theodosia and her cat, Omar."

"That's the room that's been written up on a lot of ghost sites," Paul said.

"Really?" Jordan sipped his water.

Teddy smiled. "It has been, but we deny it. I think Aunt Theodosia prefers her privacy."

"And your unofficial response?" Jordan asked.

"I-"

"It's nonsense," Adam interrupted Teddy. "Jordan, have a seat. Your playing was enchanting, as always."

Jordan smiled, showing dimples. Cliffhouse's part-time piano player was in his mid-thirties, but he looked ten years younger, with boyish features and short sandy hair. "I need to get home, but I'll be back early tomorrow to tune her." He nodded toward the piano. "She needs it."

"Well, we appreciate it." Adam stood. "I'll walk you out."

Adam set his wine glass on the table then the two men crossed the lobby and disappeared into the hall, heading for the parking lot.

"Now that Adam's out of earshot, tell me more about the ghosts," Paul said. "I've never heard the story, only read it on the Internet."

Teddy rolled his eyes. "The Internet ... The true story is that Great Aunt Theodosia and Great Uncle Aaron took me in after my parents died. Aaron died a couple of years later, so Aunt Theodosia and I were pretty close. She'd always been quite a character, but after Aaron passed, she got downright wacky." He paused. "Theodosia performed rituals to keep the ghosts of the hookers and various murder victims at bay."

"Hookers?" Butters asked. "You admit you had hookers here? I saw that on the Internet, but ..."

Teddy grinned. "Cliffhouse served as a hotel, casino, saloon, and even a house of ill repute back in the 1880s, when it was brand new. That was pretty common in those times, in these places. And during Prohibition, things sort of repeated themselves. We had rum-running gangsters, lots of bathtub gin, big parties and party girls - things that were tough to come by in that era." He cleared his throat. "But back to my great aunt. She walked every hall at night, ringing a small bell and calling for the ghosts to be peaceful or leave. She made me do it with her when I was a kid. It was spooky. By then, the entire lodge was empty except for us. She only rented the cabins out for many years."

He glanced at the rear door, and then continued. "Omar was the only other person - creature - living with us then. He was a big, beautiful Siamese cat, her pride and joy. He lived to be twenty-three." Teddy looked a little misty. "I loved that cat. I always tried to talk him into sleeping with me, but he would sleep with no one but Auntie." Teddy glanced at the bar. "The tavern is named after him.

"Anyway, when Auntie - and Omar - were getting on, Adam and I met and fell in love and Theodosia let us move into one of the cabins. In return, we did the chores, kept up the property as best we could - she was very private and didn't like workmen around. She hired Rosa, our head housekeeper, to help her out, but she didn't stay nights.

"One night, poor old Omar Siam died peacefully, sleeping with Auntie. She was overcome with grief and we held a proper funeral. If you go to the little garden with the juniper - where the marigolds are in bloom - you'll see a big stone with a bronze cat sculpture on top and a little plaque. He's buried there. Great cat.

"My great aunt passed two nights later." Teddy poured himself the last drops of merlot. "We buried her ashes in Omar's grave. It was very touching.

"I saw Omar twice after he died. The first time was the night Auntie passed. It was about two in the morning and I woke up from a nightmare hearing meows. It sounded like Omar, but he was in the ground. I got up and was sure something was wrong - I didn't know why, but the feeling overwhelmed me. I pulled on my shoes and robe, grabbed the key and walked up to Cliffhouse. I heard another meow. It sounded just like Omar. I was a little frightened.

"I let myself in and there, in the middle of the lobby, sat a Siamese cat, staring at me. Omar. As soon as he had my attention, he turned and trotted to the stairs. I followed. I was baffled.

"I lost sight of him a couple of times, but he always reappeared and when I rounded the last corner, there he was, sitting in front of the double doors of Aunt Theodosia's apartment. It was Omar Siam. I even saw the little scar on his forehead.

"I knocked on the door and called out to my aunt. There was no answer. I let myself in and knew that she was gone. She, like her beloved Omar, had died in her sleep."

"I'm sorry," Paul said.

Teddy shook his head. "She was very, very old. I think she only lived as long as she did because of Omar. Once he left, she was free to go as well. I didn't see him again that night."

"When did you?" Paul asked.

"A couple of weeks later, the day we added Auntie's ashes to the grave. We'd put Omar a good four feet down because that's what she wanted.

"We were pretty weepy, but also happy for her - she was free of that old arthritic body. Free to go wherever she wished and we knew she and Omar were together again. When we finished replacing the earth, we planted a small juniper over the grave.

"And there was Omar, no more than ten feet away, watching us. He faded away before our eyes." Teddy wiped a tear.

"A beautiful story," Paul said. "May I ask a question?"

"Of course."

"You said Omar faded away before *our* eyes. Who else saw him?"

"Adam. But he insists it was a hallucination, a trick of sun and shadow. Promise me you'll never mention this to him."

"I promise. Did he ever admit to seeing him?"

"Yes, but it was long ago."

"Sara, were you there?"

"Yes, but I was just a kid and I wasn't looking where they were. I wish I had been."

"Has Omar been seen since then?"

"There have been sightings, yes. I've seen a shadowy cat in the halls on occasion. So has Sara. And guests often ask if we have a hotel cat. Guests in the Theodosia Suite used to report feeling something hop on the bed at night and hearing purring, but there's never anything there."

Sara nodded. "I've heard him purr and meow since I moved in a few months ago. I've felt him on the bed, too. It's nice."

"And your aunt," pressed Paul. "Has anyone seen her?"

"Sometimes we smell her perfume. She liked White Shoulders." Teddy smiled. "Of course we can't be sure it's not a coincidence, but we think it's her. She wouldn't leave without Omar."

"Excuse me?"

Sara smelled gin and olives and said, "Aunt Maisy?" before she even turned around.

"Yes, dear. Might I trouble you for some bath salts? I've run out again and I want to have a nice warm soak before I go to bed."

"Of course. I'll have them sent right up."

"Thank you, dear."

The old lady, dressed in finery circa 1965, started to turn.

"Aunt Maisy?"

"Yes, dear?"

"We were just talking about Theodosia. You knew her your whole life, right?"

The older woman's smile took years off her face. "She practically brought me up."

"Can you tell us about that?" Sara asked.

"There's not much to tell. I was born out of wedlock to a maid who worked here. Theodosia didn't fire her, like most people would have. Instead, she helped take care of me. She was my second mother. I loved her." She looked around. "She's here, you know. She loves you, Sara, and you, Teddy. And Adam. She's glad you live in her apartment, Sara. She likes your company."

"Thank you."

"She protects you from some of the others." Maisy Hart smiled again. "I must have my bath now." She turned and tiptoed away as quietly as she had appeared.

"Excuse me, I'll be right back." Sara crossed to a house phone, gave instructions, and returned to her seat just as Adam showed up, guest "authoress" Constance Leigh Welling hanging on his arm. Her assistant, a handsome young man named Luke Donovan hovered behind them sipping from a bottle of Blue Springs. He and Sara caught each other's eyes. His were blue; a flattering contrast to his glossy dark hair, which was pulled back in a low ponytail. She wanted to undo the band and see it hang free around his face. She felt herself blush and was glad of the low lighting.

"Oh hello there, Mr. Bellamy," Constance said. She didn't take her eyes off Adam as he returned to his seat by Teddy. She leaned against a chair back, looked him up and down, then bent forward, showing too much cleavage.

"Good evening, Ms. Welling," said Teddy.

Sara looked at Adam. He appeared irritated and it occurred to her that Welling didn't realize the men were a couple.

"Have you all met my assistant, Luke Donovan?" Welling hooked a thumb toward Luke.

*Oh my, yes, I've met Luke.* Over the last week, Sara and Luke had managed to chat every time he came down on errands for his boss. A toothbrush, dental floss, lots of clean towels. She'd told him he could call down for them but he said he'd rather come himself and that made her happy. They were on the verge of serious small talk. Now he looked at her and smiled. She smiled back. They locked eyes again and butterflies stirred in her belly.

In Constance's company, Luke was more reserved, almost shy. Although witty and well-spoken when he and Sara talked at the desk, he barely mumbled greetings in front of his boss. Sara could tell the woman was hard to work for and on top of that, she eyed him with an interest that obviously wasn't professional. Now, Constance was licking her lower lip and staring at Adam. Teddy was watching.

"Would you like me to top off your drink, sweetie?" Teddy asked Adam with exaggerated affection.

Constance's gaze flickered between the two men.

Sara could see realization dawning as Welling's mouth became a firm line. She straightened a little and then snapped her fingers twice in the air. "Luke?"

Luke Donovan stepped closer. "Yes?"

"Go get me a drink, will you?"

"Do you want something from the bar?" he asked.

"This soldier's dead, but I was about to fetch a new bottle," Teddy said nodding toward the merlot. He rose. "Do you like wine, Ms. Welling?"

"I'd love a glass of whatever you're having," she said, turning her snake eyes on Paul Butters as Teddy departed for the cellar. She looked straight at the restaurateur and licked her lips again. "But just one glass," she said. "Constance must get her beauty sleep for her talk at the Crystal Cavern tomorrow." Without turning, she added, "Luke, why don't you run along? We'll see you in the morning."

"Okay," Luke said. "Do you want me to run your bath for you before I go to bed?"

Constance laughed. "What?" *Tsk.* "That's ridiculous. We aren't even in the same room."

"You said that's why we had to have connecting rooms-" He turned his head slightly toward Sara and gave her a wink.

"Go to bed, Luke," she ordered, her voice harsh and nasal. She huffed. "Forgive him. He's new and has no understanding of propriety. He's very young, you know. But he's learning, aren't you, Luke?"

Luke looked incredulous.

"Do as you're told," she said. "Chop chop." Snapping her fingers, she dismissed him, then looked at Paul Butters as if he were a side of beef. "I'm an authoress," she told him. "But you already know that."

Sara hadn't been able to stand her from the moment she'd checked in. The woman seemed to think she was in her twenties, but she was fifty if she was a day and if she hadn't been so condescending, Sara might have been embarrassed for her. The perfume she wore cloyed around her like a second assistant and her dangling earrings jingled like wind chimes. In fact, Sara was pretty sure that's what they were supposed to be. Welling was trying to be flamboyant but all she managed was tinsel cheapness.

"I hope you all can come by the Cavern tomorrow. I'll be signing my books. They're bestsellers, you know. International." As she spoke, she perched on the edge of a chair arm across from Paul Butters. Sara stared in amused horror as Welling first crossed one leg over the other, showing off her underwear - or lack thereof - to Paul, then switched legs, like a pathetic knobby-kneed Sharon Stone with varicose veins and no tan. Paul had the courtesy to blush and look away. It didn't faze her. She recrossed. "The next installment in my *Crystal Method Series* is called *The Kiss of the Wild Crystal.*"

Paul nodded unenthusiastically while Adam wore a rictus smile. Constance didn't notice.

"Next weekend, the store will also have my new kids' book. It's called *My Crystal and Me,* and it's just delightful! There are fun games and pictures of crystals to color." She paused to pinch her face into what was probably meant to be a display of intellectualism, but she just looked constipated, and that made Sara smile. "It's very important that children know that rose quartz is pink, and that amethyst is purple, you know."

Teddy returned with another bottle of Chantrieri Merlot.

"Daddy! I'm glad you're back! You were gone so long that I thought you got lost!"

He gave Sara a quizzical look. "I doubt I was more than three minutes."

"It seemed *much* longer, didn't it, Dad?" She looked at Adam.

"Indeed."

"'Dad' and 'Daddy?'" Constance said as Teddy uncorked and poured. "You adopted a baby?"

"My sperm, and Adam's sister's egg and womb. Sara is very much *our* daughter." Teddy's eyes sharpened, but not his voice.

"Sara," Constance asked. "Does your mother live here, too?"

"She died."

Constance plowed on with no hint of a soul. "So you *were* adopted, then!"

"No," Adam said in a chill voice. "My sister agreed to be a surrogate for us."

"That's just so-" Constance paused. "That's just so ... nice."

"I read in the Cliffside Weekly that you're a ghost hunter," Paul said, changing topics. His heart was in the right place, but not his words.

"Oh, yes, I most certainly am!" Constance lit up like the sign outside Boozehound's - flashy, pink, and not very bright. "I've resolved many hauntings and sent multitudes of spirits into the light." She pulled a pack of Virginia Slims out of her bag, and corked one in the corner of her mouth.

"There's no smoking in Cliffhouse," Sara said. "You'll have to take that out to our designated smoking area. Do you need directions?"

Constance rolled her eyes and tucked the cigarette between her breasts. "*Anyway,* all the famous ghost hunters on TV have consulted with me. You've seen me on some of the shows." She paused, but no one took the bait. "The super-professional ones who don't go on TV consult with me, too. You know - the *real* scientists."

In the silence, Teddy proffered a glass of wine to Constance, who took it, recrossed her legs, and sipped. "Mmm. I like red wine."

"It's a merlot from a specialty vineyard on the central coast," Adam said, looking disgusted.

"And it's red!" She polished off her glass in one swallow and set it on the coffee table, evidently giving up on Paul. "Constance needs her beauty sleep. I hope to see you all at my workshop and signing."

"Have a good night, Ms. Welling," Sara said as the woman clicked away on gold stiletto sandals.

Paul Butters stood. "I'd better lock up the bistro. Thanks for the wine and the ..." he glanced back, saw Constance dawdling nearby, fishing the cigarette out of her cleavage, "the interesting company." He headed briskly for the hall that led to the restaurant.

"So." Teddy's cheeks had pinked now that he'd indulged in a second glass of wine. "Rosa Morales told me something intriguing today."

"What?" Adam refilled his glass.

"Evidently the two newest rooms on the third floor have a little problem. They share a very talkative ghost. It's scaring the tar out of Jenna and Maggie."

\*\*\*

Constance rounded the corner, took a quick look to be sure she wasn't being watched, and hunkered down behind a potted fern.

"What does this ghost allegedly say?" asked Adam.

"The girls' names," said Teddy. "It whispers in their ears while they're working. Jenna and Maggie won't go into the two rooms by themselves."

Adam sighed.

Teddy continued. "Rosa says it scared Jenna so badly she's considering putting in her notice."

"I'll talk to her. We don't want to lose either one. They're both good housekeepers." Adam sounded tired. "Or maybe Sara should talk to her. She likes Sara."

Teddy's voice now. "Yes, good thinking. Rosa hasn't heard the voice, but she believes the girls." A pause. "Can you imagine hearing a disembodied voice say your name right in your ear?"

Adam shushed his husband. "No. I can't, but I think I've seen it in a few horror movies."

"I'll speak with Jenna tomorrow," Sara said. "And I can imagine it, too, after what I saw with the bread. I think things are getting a little more active around here."

"I agree," said Teddy.

*More active?* Constance leaned closer.

"We have to nip this in the bud," Adam said.

"How?"

"We can clean the rooms ourselves until the maids get over this nonsense."

"We only finished renovating those rooms in August," Sara said. "And the season is over. We have at least until first snow before we really need them again. That won't happen before Thanksgiving."

"Sara's right," Adam said. "We have a dozen new rooms up there and those two can stay empty for now. Let's assure the maids they don't have to clean them until the situation is resolved."

"Good idea," Teddy said. "Do we have anyone in either one tonight, Sara?"

"Yes. Room 337 is occupied through next weekend. Newlyweds, the Kirbys. George and Maryanne."

Constance made a mental note. *Room 337.* She would find a way to check it out. It had become clear to her the Bellamys wouldn't support her plan to write about the paranormal activity in Cliffhouse that she hadn't even broached the subject. But it was a great idea. It would be her first full-length book. *The Lost Spirits of Cliffhouse.* It even sounded like a number one bestseller. She smiled, imagining herself on television, being interviewed by the biggest names in the business. *My name is Constance Welling and I'm a famous authoress. I am young, desirable, and talented.*

After her mantra, she listened for a few more minutes but the conversation turned to business and other boring things. Constance rose and slipped toward the elevators. It was early for her, but she intended to have that bath. And Luke. Not necessarily in that order.

# 10
## *Jackson at the Crime Scene*

**MONDAY**
**Labor Day**

Cliffside Presbyterian Church sat at the east end of Main, across from the lake between a small park and a ski shop. Jackson rubbed sleep from his eyes as he pulled up. Reverend Bob Poole, nearly dancing with anxiety, beckoned him forward. Jackson was anxious himself; murders were not common in Cliffside. He followed the minister up the long driveway and parked his cruiser at an angle to restrict access.

"The Dumpster," Poole sputtered as Jackson climbed out. "She's in the Dumpster. She's dead."

"You're sure?"

"Well, I didn't climb in and check."

Jackson reached for the radio. "Dispatch, would you send Gene Holmes to this location, pronto?"

"10-4. Anything else?"

*Meat wagon,* he thought, but decided to wait. "Not now."

Poole hung back as Jackson entered the brick corral. The body was hidden under filthy old blankets, but the face stared up at him with glazed eyes. He could smell perfume and the faintest whiff of decay.

"You found her?" he asked Poole.

"Y-yes. I saw the blankets and thought there might be a homeless person sleeping under them. It happens, you know. I-I called out but there was no answer, so I reached in and pulled back a corner and …"

"There she was," Jackson finished.

Poole nodded.

"When was the last time you or anyone working at the church was here, Bob?"

"Yesterday. Sunday services. In the morning."

"No evening services?"

Pool looked a little embarrassed. "Normally, we have them, but last night was the celebration; we had a potluck by the lake."

"So as far as you know, none of your people came around again?" He stared at the face of the corpse, recognizing her. Booteous Maxima, aka Norma Bailey, the thirty-something star of the Crimson Corset Burlesque Theater. He wondered where her partner, Copious Maximus - Brad Bailey - was right now. The two were long-married and seemed genuinely happy, so he had a sinking feeling he was going to be delivering some bad news to Brad, rather than arresting him. *Catch-22*.

Jackson returned to the unit to request an ambulance then turned as he heard the unmistakable sound of the medical examiner's big black Hummer coming up the drive. Holmes tucked the ridiculous hunk of machinery in next to Jackson's unit.

"Jackson? This better be good. I gave up golf for this."

"What's the matter? You subpar on the windmill hole?"

"Fuck you," Holmes said amiably. "So what's going on?"

"Dead body. Booteous Maxima."

"No shit?"

"Know her?"

"Who doesn't?"

"Yeah. Reverend Poole found her."

Both men looked toward the reverend, who stood a good twenty feet from the bin, his back to it, as if willing it all to go away.

"Poor guy," observed Holmes. "He must have done something to really piss off God."

"Ready to take a look, Doc?"

"Ready as I'll ever be."

# 11
## *About the Playground*

"You get back here this instant!" cried Abby Collins.

Carrie and Tommy bolted down the hall toward the elevators. The family had been heading downstairs for breakfast but Carrie didn't want to get stuck sitting there eating when there was still so much to do before they left this afternoon.

"You kids can play outside but not until you eat something." Their father didn't sound nearly as angry as their mom.

"We'll hit the breakfast bar," Carrie lied over her shoulder. She and Tommy wanted to do some *real* exploring, including walking the nature trail, paying a final visit to the playground ... and getting Walleye to tell them another ghost story.

"Wait up!" called Tommy.

"Hurry! We don't have all day!" Carrie slowed a little and her brother quickly caught up. Seeing the sign for the stairs, Carrie yelled, "Come on! This will be faster."

They bounded down the steps, their footfalls echoing off the walls. Reaching the first floor, they burst into a hallway by the pool, and then ran through the lobby and out the front doors. Outside, Carrie darted past the playground, her hand closed hard on her brother's, dragging him along.

"Wait!" cried Tommy. "Where're we going?"

"To see Walleye. I want to hear another ghost story!"

"Wait," he said. "Let's walk."

Carrie slowed a little. "Are you chicken?" she asked.

"No! Why?"

"Because I can tell you don't want to hear another ghost story. Or maybe you're afraid of Walleye because he might really be the bogeyman."

"I'm not afraid!"

"Are so."

"Am not!" Tommy broke into a run, leaving Carrie behind.

She caught up and grabbed his shirt collar, bringing him to an abrupt stop. "Look!" She pointed. "There he is."

Walleye was raking a little garden several yards away.

"Walleye! Walleye!" Carrie cried as she and Tommy ran toward him.

The man looked up and the wrinkles on his face deepened as he smiled. "What are you kids up to now?"

"We want to hear another ghost story," said Carrie. "You promised!"

Tommy was doubled over, trying to catch his breath.

"Well, *I* do, anyway!" she said. "Tommy's scared!"

"Am not!" he said through ragged breaths.

"Am too! You're so immature."

Walleye's smile faltered. "I have some work to do now."

"But you promised!" cried Carrie. "You promised and today is our last day! You *have* to tell us another ghost story!"

"I'll tell you what," he said, glancing around then leaning on his rake. "Why don't you kids go have some fun at the playground and in a few minutes I'll be over to tell you one more story."

"All right!" said Carrie. "Is it going to be a scary one? A *real* scary one?"

"Well," he said, drawing the word out. "Since it's your last day, I guess I better tell you a big one, huh?"

"Yes!"

"All right," he said. "Go play, but remember, the playground is haunted, especially that first swing on the left."

\*\*\*

Walleye Gardner leaned on his rake and watched the kids. It was the nature of children to love a ghost story and he loved telling them. He raked a stray candy wrapper out of the little garden memorial to Theodosia and Omar Siam, and then stood looking at the grave. It was a beautiful spot, the juniper having grown to shade the brass cat atop the monument. He paused to read the plaque on the pedestal, as he always did. He loved what it said: "To those who inhabit Cliffhouse, be Wary the Night, be Kind to the Cat and His Mistress, or suffer Fates hitherto Unknown to You."

*That's some weird shit, but the old lady was okay.* As he raked between the bright marigolds and leafy coleus bordering the garden, he wondered how long the flowers would last. While the days would remain warm for some time yet, it would soon get nippy after sundown this high in the mountains, and despite the unseasonably warm Labor Day weekend temperatures, first frost wasn't far away. *No more lawn mowing until late spring, hallelujah!*

## 12
### *The Girl on the Swing*

"It's this swing," Carrie insisted, tugging on a chain.

"Huh-uh," Tommy told her. "He said the one on the left. That's the right!"

"No, he didn't."

"Yes, he did!"

"You're so immature!"

"Huh-uhhh!" Sometimes Tommy really wanted to bop Carrie, but she was at least half a foot taller than he was, and hit harder. He contented himself with sticking out his tongue. Carrie advanced on him.

"Kids!" Walleye Walter surprised them. "Better stop fighting before the Blue Lady hears you!"

"Mr. Walleye!" cried Tommy with great relief. "Which swing is haunted?" He pointed. "The left one, right?"

"That's right, son. That's as left as it can get." He glanced around, saw a few kids nearby. "Let's keep it down, okay? Can't have the whole world listening to us. It's our secret, right?"

Tommy nodded and Carrie made a quick face at him, then turned to Walleye. "Right. Tell us," she demanded.

He hunkered down. "You kids ever hear of the Bodice Ripper?"

"Those books my mom reads with those naked people all huggy and kissy on them?" Carrie asked.

"Barfaroni!" Tommy added. He had taken one of those books to first grade show-and-tell last May and Miss Firebush wouldn't let him show *or* tell.

"No, no. Nothing like that." Walleye laughed.

"That's what Daddy calls those books," Carrie informed him. "Bodice rippers."

"They look stupid," said Tommy. "Those guys are all sweaty like they need a bath. Some of them wear plaid skirts."

"This Bodice Ripper is not the same thing. This one was a murderer. A serial killer. You kids know what that is?"

"A cereal killer?" Tommy was intrigued. "I wish he'd come and kill the Shredded Wheat Mom makes us eat."

"Not *that* kind of cereal, stupid-head." Carrie rolled her eyes. "With an S. Hannibal the Cannibal is a serial killer."

Walleye smiled and nodded his head. "Except this killer was real. And he did a lot of killing right here in Cliffside during his heyday. It was at a time they called the Roaring Twenties."

"Why?" asked Carrie and Tommy in unison.

"Well, I suppose he liked to kill people."

"No, why was it called the Roaring Twenties?"

"Because it happened during the 1920s, when World War One was over and everyone was celebrating. It was a pretty happy time. People had lots of money."

"Tell us about the Bodice Ripper!" Carrie ordered.

"Well," Walleye began, after looking around. "In 1928, during Prohibition - that's when alcohol was illegal - there were still plenty of people who liked to drink, so there were lots of places that served alcohol on the sly. Illegally. Cliffhouse was one of them."

Tommy yawned and watched Carrie. He could tell she wanted to wind her hand in a *hurry-it-along* way like she did to him when he took too long getting to the good stuff.

"The hotel had a speakeasy." Walleye paused. "A speakeasy was a place that served alcohol. They had music and dancing, too. Anyway, on Labor Day weekend, just like it is now, there was a young woman sitting on that very swing early one morning." He pointed. "This woman was about to find out why they called him the Bodice Ripper."

"Did he rip them open?" asked Carrie.

"How'd he rip them?" asked Tommy.

Mr. Walleye gave them a spooky smile. "With a knife," he said. "A great big knife. He started at their throats, and cut all the way down." He dragged his finger slowly from his neck to his belly.

Carrie made a sick noise and Tommy tried not to think about it too much.

"So this young lady on the swing, her name was Mary McGill, and she was only nineteen years old, just a few years older than you, Carrie." He winked at her and Tommy felt a shiver down his spine.

"Mary McGill was beautiful and by all outward appearances, she had it all. A good family, plenty of youth and beauty, and a promising career in theater. She was acting at The Lucky Tiger, which was a theater in the lodge. They had musicals and vaudeville plays and Mary was a big hit."

Carrie wound her hand. "Get to the ghost stuff!"

"Yeah," said Tommy. "Get to the ghosts!"

"All right," said Mr. Walleye, his eyes twinkling, "straight to the good stuff. The Bodice Ripper had already killed nine ladies since 1925. One night, Mary performed as usual, and then went down to the speakeasy for a drink before going to bed. That was the last time anyone saw her alive except for the people who reported seeing her walk out onto the terrace with a tall man.

"The next morning, a guest out for an early walk saw a woman sitting on a swing in the playground. She was so still he thought maybe something was wrong. When he called to her and she didn't answer, the guest approached - and found out why she hadn't answered. She was all bloody down the front and he saw she'd been cut wide open, clear from stem to stern."

"Eww!" said Carrie.

Tommy swallowed hard.

"Only that wasn't the worst of it," said Walleye. "Turns out, the killer had twined her intestines around her waist then wrapped one arm with them all the way up the chain, then across over her head, and down the other arm so she wouldn't fall off. I guess he thought that was pretty funny. Of course, there was no question who'd done it. This was right up the old Bodice Ripper's alley."

Carrie's eyes widened "And she haunts the playground?"

"Yep," said Mr. Walleye. "And the second floor of the hotel, especially the room she was staying in. The McGill Suite."

"That's our room!" Carrie cried.

"It is," chimed her brother.

"Is it, now? Well, she's nice. Don't worry too much," Walleye said. "Some have reported seeing her in the lobby, too, but mostly, I think she stays close to her room." He eyed the swing set. "And the playground of course."

"Did they ever catch him?" Carrie's voice was a croak.

Walleye shook his head. "Nope. They never did. A couple weeks later, he killed another lady and left her in the lobby. She walks near the fireplace some nights."

Carrie looked as terrified as Tommy felt.

They heard someone clear his throat and all three of them turned to see a man - the dark-haired hotel owner - leaning against a nearby tree. He didn't look mad exactly, but it was clear he'd been listening.

Mr. Walleye gave the other man a smile and hunkered a little closer to the children. "Time to wrap this up but before you go, I gotta swear you to secrecy." He lowered his voice. "Do you promise not to repeat this story to anyone? Ever? It's top secret."

Carrie and Tommy exchanged looks. "We promise," said Carrie.

"Both of you?" asked Walleye, looking at Tommy.

"I promise, too," Tommy said, knowing he would tell Bobby Taylor as soon as he got home.

Walleye smiled and straightened. "All right then," he said. "You kids run along and have a nice day."

# 13
## *Monday Morning Autopsy*

Jackson would have been a lot happier if Doctors Gene Holmes and Roger Siechert had a refrigerated holding room at their clinic. Instead, he stood in Casper Hill's workroom at the Cliffside Mortuary and watched, along with Casper, as Holmes finished up his autopsy. It was bad enough being in the room while Gene was scooping innards out of the corpse's body as if he were simply dishing up runny lasagna, but watching it here, in a mortuary, somehow made it even worse. He wished he was still out running with Adam.

The workroom was barely twenty by twenty, but Booteous Maxima wasn't the only deceased occupant. There were two others - a retiree named Bruce Culpepper who had landed face first in his crème brulee at the ripe old age of 103 and Glenda Simms, who, according to her Bible-thumping family, slipped into Jesus' arms yesterday - but not before falling out of her bed and breaking a hip, two ribs, and her neck - at the Cliffside Retirement Home. They were both under sheets, and as patients of Doctors Siechert and Holmes, they were certified to die without autopsy, and were simply awaiting Casper's handy trocar and the cosmetic talents of his wife, Beverly, before seeing their families and friends for their final sendoffs.

Casper was as Milquetoast as his name, and while his work was piling up, he waited for Holmes to finish before getting down to business. Being Casper, he wouldn't rush him. Politeness was a great asset in morticiandom.

"How much longer?" Jackson wasn't so polite.

"Almost done, Chief. Casper, do you want me to replace the guts?"

"I can manage," Casper said. "But thanks for the offer."

"Welcome. Chief, Ms. Bailey appears to have lost her life sometime yesterday afternoon. She drowned."

"How could she drown?"

"I don't know." Holmes nodded at the lungs, grayish-pink sweetbreads on a scale nearby. "They're saturated with water. Five liters if there's a drop. If anything other than water had filled her lungs that full - mucus or tumors, for example - she wouldn't have been walking around. No, sir. We have to wait for the bloods to come back to see if anything else was going on."

"When will they be back?"

"Slower than usual because of the holiday. Skeleton crew, you know."

"No bones about it." Casper sounded amused. He'd used the line before.

"Get them to me as fast as you can, Gene," Jackson said.

"Will do." Holmes looked at the mortician. "I guess you don't want me to sew her up, either, Casper?" He gestured at the gaping body-long incision.

"Nope, I like to do it just so." Casper's smile was solemn despite a slight twinkle in his eye. "Beverly says I'm too fussy, but my customers have never complained."

"Gene," Jackson asked, "how could she drown on dry land? She hadn't been in water when we found her. Her hair was done and her make-up was relatively intact. It doesn't make sense."

"It doesn't." Holmes picked up a magnifying glass and examined the dead woman's face. "Water could have been forced in through the nose. There are no marks on her face indicating use of force, though if she was unconscious it might have been possible. She died by drowning. This wasn't done post-mortem." He stood straight and half-smiled. "I'll do what I can to help, Chief, but I'd say you have a real mystery on your hands."

There was a rap on the door. Speak of the Devil. Beverly Hill didn't wait for an invitation but entered, her rabbity nose wrinkling in disgust as she saw Dr. Holmes replacing Norma's heart in its natural-born holder. Her eyes brushed over Jackson and came to land on her husband, Casper. "We're supposed to be arriving at the Lake Club for lunch with the Wellbornes in thirty minutes and you haven't even showered yet!"

"I showered this morning, dear, and I haven't even gotten my hands in anything yet today."

"You know you smell like death just from being in this room. You need to go shower now." Beverly's finger, as skinny as the rest of her bird-boned body, pointed at Casper. "Go," she said, then wagged the finger at Holmes and Jackson. "You gentlemen will excuse him." It was not a question.

"Of course," Holmes said. "You go on Casper and don't worry. We'll turn off the lights and lock up on our way out."

"Thank you." He gave them each a nod, then rushed from the room.

"And we promise not to shoplift or look in your drawers, Beverly."

With an unamused harrumph, Beverly turned on her heel,

slamming the door behind her.

"You know, Gene, she's going to take that mad out on Casper."

"Hmmm. I probably shouldn't have said that. Poor Casper. What the hell was he thinking when he proposed?"

# 14
## *Constance Wants a Bath*

"Lukey?"

Luke Donovan cringed as his new employer, Constance Welling, knocked playfully on the door separating their adjoining rooms. *I didn't sign up for this.* "I'm getting dressed, Ms. Welling."

"I told you to call me Constance. Can you do that? Can you call me Constance?"

"I'm getting dressed. Constance."

The day he'd answered her Craigslist ad looking for an assistant to accompany her to a mountain retreat while she wrote a book and did personal appearances, he had no expectations of getting such a wonderful job; after all, he was just another English major trying to make a living without resorting to teaching. But she had called him back a day after his interview and hired him. He'd been amazed at his luck.

The doorknob jiggled. "Do you need any help in there?" Constance pitched her nasal voice high and sing-songy.

He shuddered at the sound of it. "No. What do you need? I haven't even had breakfast yet."

"I need you to come run my bath, Luke. Then we'll go to breakfast."

*You can't fill your own bathtub? You can't even let me have a single meal by myself?* That's what he wanted to yell through the door, but there was no point. She wanted in his pants, that was all there was to it, and he wanted to stay in the mountains while he thought about career paths, so he held his tongue and ignored her advances. *She must think I'm incredibly naive.* With an ego like Constance Welling's, he figured that's all she could think; it would never occur to her that he didn't want her body. She was old enough to be his mother.

"Lukey, Constance needs her bathy-wathy. You don't have to dress yet."

"Yes, I do." He groaned to himself as he brushed his dark hair into a ponytail at the base of his neck. What he really wanted to do was go downstairs and see if Sara Bellamy was on duty yet.

\*\*\*

Luke Donovan was so innocent that Constance wanted to slap him before she fucked him. Impatient, she lit a cigarette and blew smoke out the open window. Stupid smoking laws. Stupid Luke ... but what a hunk. That long, lean body, the perfect chin, and the dark silky hair he refused to let loose for her. Yet. He had six-pack abs that she'd managed to spy by following him to the indoor pool near the gym. When he pushed up out of the water and saw her waiting with a towel, he'd nearly turned purple with embarrassment. Oh, was he going to be a fun pupil. She would teach him every facet of pleasing a woman. He'll be so grateful.

There was a knock on her door. "Who is it?"

"Luke."

Taking another drag, she set the cigarette on the windowsill and answered the door. Exhaling a cloud of smoke in his face, she smiled at him as he coughed. "Poor baby, I'm sorry about that."

"It's illegal to smoke in hotels in California."

"Fuck the rules." She pulled him into her room. "Why did you come to the front door? You're supposed to use the adjoining door."

"I'm more comfortable using the front door."

She led him to the bathroom. "You're such a silly boy, Mr. Lukey. There's no reason to even lock that door. You're working for me and we must have instant access to one another."

He stiffened, but not in the way she wanted. "You want me to turn on the bathtub again? I showed you how."

"You work for me. You're my personal assistant; you do it."

She spotted rebellion in his eyes as he started the bath. It made her happy; he kept his emotions hidden, but now they were stirring and she knew she would have all of him very, very soon. He stood up and started to leave the room. "You need to stay and turn it off, you know."

"I don't think-"

"Do you like my robe? It's real satin, from gay Paree!"

He nodded absently.

"Constance will be right back. I need to get something." She went to the bedroom and spritzed cologne in her hair. "Not too hot!" she called, untying her robe.

Just as Luke turned off the faucets, she returned. Stepping around him, she carefully engineered a slip and fell against him, squealing. He grabbed her just in time. She looked up. "Thank you. You saved me!"

His nose twitched as he gently pushed away. "It wouldn't be good to break your hip." He backed toward the door.

"My hip?" Constance's lady parts dried up instantly. "Just how old do you think I am?"

"Sorry." There was a subtle lack of respect in his voice.

"You know," she said. "If you want to be a writer, you'll need to learn some better people skills." She looked at him pointedly. "It' all about who you know. You may leave now."

"Yes, ma'am." He was gone in a heartbeat.

Fuming, she settled into the warm water, watching it lap at her body and engulf her in a comfortable embrace. Luke was a challenge she would soon conquer. She took a deep breath, closed her eyes and thought of the conversation she'd overheard the Bellamys having last night. Now she knew there were ghosts on the third floor and if she could just get the Bellamys to open up to her - or at least open up the rooms - she could turn out the bestseller she was born to write, instead of just another book on shit-diddling crystals.

But how to get them to open up? She hadn't even been able to get the maids to talk yet. The websites offered nothing of value about Cliffhouse, just a repeat of the same old stories. What she needed was to expose a new scandal. She just had to get someone to talk. And she needed to get into those rooms.

First, she would use her profession to the fullest extent, introducing herself to the newlyweds to get invited into their room. Surely they'd love to meet a famous writer and share their story with her. She'd take her cell phone along to take pictures. Damned thing was almost useless for anything else up here anyway.

Secondly, she'd get to the fat one - Teddy - one way or another. It would mean getting around his hateful husband, of course, but she'd find a way to do it. Idly, she wondered how faithful they were to each other. Perhaps Luke, eye candy that he was, might help persuade the fat one to talk a little. She knew that soon Luke would do anything for her.

Thirdly, she would make friends with the young maids. What were their names? Jenny and Mary ... something like that anyway. Whatever. Maybe she'd call for some extra towels and get one of them up here to spill some dirt. She laughed. "Maids spilling dirt," she said to the room. "Thank God for my sense of humor."

Beyond that, there was just one more thing to think about: Paul Butters. He, she was certain, wasn't gay. Of course, she hadn't guessed the owners were gay either, but generally speaking, Constance had an amazing sense about these things.

And even if he was gay, there was that piano player. And the fitness director. What was his name? It didn't matter. She intended to meet him in her bikini so he'd really appreciate her.

She let her thoughts drift to the fitness stud while her hand explored more familiar places. The shiny piercing that had brought her so much pleasure was still upholding its value. As she stroked it and gently tugged, she considered getting a second one.

Lost in pleasure, she squealed as the hot faucet shot on, dousing her toes with scalding water. "Son of a bitch!" she screamed as she bolted up and fumbled with the handle. It spun around uselessly. "Luke! Get in here!"

She was out of the tub, bent over twisting the faucet to no avail. "Luke!" Soon, the tub was full enough she needed to open the drain. "Luke! I said get in here!"

She smacked the handle then gave up, wrapped a towel around herself and stomped out of the bathroom. Luke was not in the room. Little bitch! She pounded on the adjoining door but there was no response. Finally, she dialed the front desk.

"Guest Services. How may we help you?" said a friendly voice.

"Well, you could start by getting someone up here immediately. Something's wrong with the plumbing. The hot water faucet has turned itself on and no matter which way I spin it, it will not shut off. I was bathing and could have been seriously burned!"

"Oh, I'm sor-"

"I am in room number 202. You people get someone up here immediately!" She slammed the phone down.

While she waited she went into the bathroom and stared at the running water. The whole room was beginning to fog. She tried shutting it off again. It didn't respond.

Soon, someone knocked on the door.

Constance, still in her towel, threw it open and glared into the face of a short middle-aged Hispanic woman in a blue and white uniform. She wore a nameplate that read, Rosa.

"I don't need a Christing maid! I need a plumber!"

"Well, I'm all you got, lady."

Constance made an exaggerated come in gesture. "In there!" she pointed at the bathroom.

The maid went in, bent, turned the faucet and the rush of hot water came to an immediate stop.

"What the shitting hell?"

"Maybe you don't know how to work this kind of faucet. You want me to show you?"

Constance huffed. "I certainly do not need any lessons from you. Now get out."

The maid's eyes landed on the windowsill. "No smoking, lady."

"Get out!"

As she ushered the woman to the door, Luke appeared.

"I wouldn't go in there if I were you," said the maid as she hurried past him, crossing herself.

Constance grabbed Luke's shirt and pulled him into the room. "Where the hell were you?"

"Getting breakfast." He smoothed his shirt.

"You work for me, Luke Donovan. I'll decide when we eat breakfast."

The younger man's eyes glittered with defiance. Somehow, this only made him more attractive.

# 15
## *Teddy and Adam Stroll*

"It's glorious today." Teddy stepped off the veranda, leaving shadows for sunlight. He breathed deeply. "Absolutely glorious!"

"You should have gone with Jackson and me on our run this morning. It was even more glorious." Adam patted Teddy's belly. "If you don't start exercising more, you're going have to break out your size 40s."

Teddy looked down. "You're right, of course. I'd better start walking more."

"And eating less."

Teddy rolled his eyes. "You're such a nag."

"It's my job." Adam took Teddy's hand and squeezed it. "Love you."

"Love you, too. Shall we stroll?"

They started off, going south, paralleling the cliffs above the lake until they were just past the far edge of the playground. They turned east. It was only 10:30 a.m. but people were already arriving, choosing picnic benches, spreading blankets on the lawn, and staking out the brick barbecues that dotted it. This side of the playground was the primary picnic area, with the big cement band shell at the farthest point south. Some music fans were even setting up near it to get the best seats when the afternoon concert began.

The playground was full of kids. Adam stopped opposite the old metal merry-go-round. Walter Gardner was busy oiling the creaks out of it. "So, Ted, I caught Walleye telling a couple of kids ghost stories again."

"Good for him."

"He was giving them quite a scare."

"Hmm. Interesting. He's a good storyteller and he's got that spooky look the kids love. I can't wait to try one of Paul's gourmet burgers. I'm glad he decided to man the grill so we don't have to." Teddy sighed. "I think I'll have a bleu cheese burger first. Mmm."

"First?"

"Yep. After I digest that, I'm going back for a plate of his ribs. Talk about perfection. What are you going to have?"

"I have no idea. Teddy, you need to stop thinking about food so much."

"Oh, stop it, Adam. In half an hour this whole place is going to start smelling like carnivore heaven." He inhaled. "It already does." He peered at the huge stone barbeque at the rear of the playground where Paul Butters and several assistants had been cooking ribs for at least an hour already. "So what are you having?"

Adam laughed. "You're incorrigible."

"That's why you love me."

"I know. You're a very bad influence. I think maybe I'll have his hickory onion burger. It's delightful." He paused. "There are the children Walter was talking to."

"I remember them from last night. I think that girl is a real handful. Something in the eyes."

"She looks like Scout from To Kill a Mockingbird," Adam said. "She's nearing that age when children start getting hormones and turn into little monsters. Two more years, tops, and she'll be hell on wheels."

Teddy chuckled. "Just like Sara. Oh, was she a handful. Remember when she decided to dye her hair black and started wearing mourning clothes?"

"Oh, dear lord. A ten-year-old Goth. It was something right out of South Park. I never knew kids could get so weird so young."

"She's always been an overachiever. At least she was over it by high school." Teddy nodded toward the Collins kids, who were both attempting to sit in the same swing even though the one next to it was empty. "The boy's going to lose this battle."

"He's small, but he has moxie."

"What the hell is moxie, anyway, Adam? Oh, she's almost unseated him."

"Moxie will win out. Care to make a small wager?"

"Breakfast in bed?"

Adam nodded. "You're on."

The kids were a tangle of arms and legs. Suddenly, the boy yelped and fell into the sand and the girl shrieked, "You lose, Stinky-Pants!"

The boy was motionless as the girl got ready to launch herself on the swing.

"Keep watching," Adam said. "He's not done yet. I'm winning this bet."

"Sure, Adam, sure you are."

The boy had to hurl himself sideways to get out of the path of his sister's feet as she swung past him. She did it once, twice, and on the third pass, he lunged, grabbed her ankles and yanked. She flew off, furious. "I'm telling on you!" she shrieked as she rose, dusting sand off her arms and legs.

"You are not!"

"Am so!"

"Are not!"

"Am so!" The girl plunged a fist into the sand and hurled a stream of grit at the boy's eyes.

"You're right," said Teddy. "She's going to be hell on wheels. Do you see their parents anywhere?" Their noise had become truly irritating.

Adam scanned. "No."

"Probably enjoying a little peace and quiet. Can't blame them. Do you think we should go break that up?"

Adam sighed. "I suppose. But look! Walter is headed their way."

They watched as Walleye worked his magic. The man never failed to astonish Teddy. He had such a way with children. "Too bad Walter never had kids of his own."

"I know. He's amazing."

Walter was crouched in front of them and they were silent, nodding at his words. "I wonder what his secret is."

Adam rubbed his chin. "Honestly, I think he might be scaring them shitless and at this point, I don't care. It's working. Let's walk."

A moment of strolling brought them to Omar's monument in the little garden. "I miss your aunt," Adam said. "And that big old cat of hers."

"Me, too."

Adam began walking again. "We need to figure out our order for the winetasting."

"Definitely the Chantrieri Merlot." Teddy smiled, thinking another bottle might be an appropriate nightcap this evening. It was so smooth, so perfect.

"What would you think of featuring all Valentyn Vineyards wines? We might get a discount doing that."

"I think it's a fine idea. Valentyn's produces exceptional wines. Chantrieri is simply amazing. I wonder how they do it. On our next vacation, we have to stop there. I want to meet the owner and shake his hand."

Adam laughed. "And drink his wine."

"Let's go in the spring. We can visit the winery and stay in that wonderful little B&B in Crimson Cove."

"Yes, absolutely. I love that little town," Teddy said. "Adam, do you think we might make some bottles of Blue Springs available for sale during the tasting?"

"Hmm. Maybe a few; we need a better bottling system first. It's a good idea, though. Let's use Blue Springs for palate cleansing."

Teddy nodded. "Perfect."

As they passed the massive stone barbecue where Paul Butters was working his magic, Teddy inhaled deeply and almost tripped because he had closed his eyes in bliss. His stomach growled, but it was too early; Paul's chest of burgers had yet to be cracked. Adam tugged his arm.

Behind the barbecue and to the south more picnic benches dotted the lawn. The area also held a couple of tennis courts and badminton and volleyball nets festooned the greens in between. There was another gaming area behind the lodge's parking lot where croquet, horseshoes, and similar summer games were available. Farther out, to the south and east were the miniature golf course and carousel. They continued walking.

# 16
## *In Room 337*

"At least we don't have to clean 339," Maggie O'Connor whispered to Jenna Holstrum. They stood outside 337, the room the newlyweds were staying in through next weekend.

"I don't want to go in there," Jenna whispered. "If I hear that voice again, I'm quitting."

"It'll be okay." Maggie was as scared as Jenna, but she couldn't afford to quit and she didn't want Jenna to, either. "Come on, it's okay." She rapped on the door and called, "Housekeeping."

"If you think nothing's going to happen, why don't you go in alone?" Jenna asked, her fingers tapping nervously on the cart handle.

"It'll be fine. The newlyweds tip well and together we can be done in ten minutes, tops."

"I don't want to go in there."

Neither did Maggie. She'd had no trouble with the room until a few days ago.

While the newly renovated room wasn't a suite, it was large and luxurious with a kitchenette, and a nice loveseat tucked into a small living and dining area across the room from the bed. This room, like 339, came with a fireplace, Jacuzzi and French doors that opened onto a balcony overlooking Blue Lady Lake. The rooms were instant hits with honeymooners.

Last week, while Maggie was hanging fresh towels in this room, a voice said her name, right in her ear, so close she could feel the cold breath. She had almost fainted in fear. The following day, she'd wanted to foist the room off on the part-time maids, but they were busy on the second floor, so she got Jenna to go with her without explaining. Nothing happened, at least not in 337, and the cleaning was done so quickly with both of them working that they decided to do the rest of the third floor together. Everything was fine until they entered 339. While they were putting fresh sheets on, Maggie heard the voice say her name again. Simultaneously, Jenna yelped. They'd both heard their names. Their own names. They rapidly finished the bed, then were out in a shot. Maggie told her the same thing had happened in 337, and immediately wished she hadn't.

Three days ago, she was stuck with the third floor once more and asked Jenna to team up again. Jenna had been reluctant, but money talks and in the end, Jenna helped her, happy to share in the generous tip. A twenty apiece, who could complain? And nothing happened; it was easy to get Jenna to team with her again the next day.

But the day after, as Jenna scrubbed 337's toilet, she heard her name again. The next day, she absolutely refused to work the third floor, so Maggie went to her boss, Rosa Morales, and told her about the voice, warning her Jenna was ready to bolt. Rosa nodded and told her she'd do the third floor with her.

While they worked, Maggie tried to get Rosa to talk about the experiences she was rumored to have had in her twenty years as Theodosia Bellamy's housekeeper and maid for the cabins. Rosa wouldn't say much though; she never did - except to encourage speed so she could get back to her other duties. When they finished the floor Maggie was almost sorry nothing had happened because she wanted to hear the voice. She even asked her boss point blank if she believed there were ghosts in Cliffhouse. Rosa had folded her arms and looked her in the eye, then said, "What do you think?"

And that was all, damn it.

"Did you hear me, Maggie? I don't want to go in there."

Maggie used the passkey. The door snicked open. "Jenna, please. You can have the whole tip. All of it." She pushed the door open and silently thanked God the newlyweds had left the drapes open, allowing warm, friendly sunshine to stream in.

Jenna followed Maggie inside, looking around cautiously as she made her way to the dresser to check the tip. "Forty dollars," she said. "I guess I'll do it, but let's be quick."

"We will be."

Jenna crossed to the bed. "I'll make this and vacuum, you do the bathroom."

"Deal." Maggie was glad just to have company. She started by sanitizing the toilet. As she scrubbed, she looked over her shoulder trying to discredit the feeling she wasn't alone. *It's just a case of the creepy-crawlies.*

She heard Jenna vacuuming in the other room and after finishing the toilet, Maggie did the bathtub, running hot water over the cleanser. The rising steam felt good on her face as it wafted around her, fogging the mirror.

She moved to the sink, hosing it down with some bleach-based spray. The hum of the vacuum from the other room was a soothing sound, almost tranquil.

As she polished, movement in the mirror caught her eye. She looked up and saw her own face staring back at her through a heavy glaze of condensation on the glass. Something was different, though. At first she thought the mist distorted her reflection, but as the glass cleared, she realized she wasn't looking at her own face.

She was brunette with dark green eyes.

The eyes in the mirror were solid black and the hair billowed around the delicate face - sometimes silver, sometimes pale blue - like an animated halo, as if the specter were underwater.

Maggie gasped and stepped back.

The face floated closer.

"Oh, my God ..."

Pale skin, slightly blue. Crimson lips, full and pouting, like a movie star's. The mouth curved into a smile and the face somehow became even more beautiful.

*Maggie ...*

The word was delivered in a feathery singsong.

The woman swam upward, displaying a lithe, willowy figure. She disappeared for an instant as if the mirror were a window in a water tank - then glided downward, moving with long arm-strokes and scissoring legs. She drifted one way then the other, stretching and arching her body as she chanted Maggie's name.

Maggie was enraptured.

The woman neared until only her face was visible. *Maggie ... Maggie, come to me, help me ...* The black eyes went wide. Her arms flailed and her body jerked and heaved, not with the grace of moments before, but with panic. She pounded at the glass.

Maggie was afraid to touch the mirror.

*Maggie ...*

Maggie could hear the thud of the woman's fists on the glass.

The face began to change, the structure of bone beneath the skin rising to the surface; what was once a beautiful woman was now a monster.

"No!" In a panicked frenzy, Maggie drove her fist into the mirror. The glass splintered, webbing around the point of impact. Pain shot through her hand.

"What are you doing?"

Maggie turned.

Jenna stood in the doorway. "What's going on?"

Maggie looked back at the mirror and lowered her bloody fist.

A few loose shards of glass clattered into the sink.

The phantom was gone.

"There was someone in the mirror." Her knees were rubbery and weak. "She tried to make me think she was drowning, but she was going to hurt me."

"What are you talking about?"

***

Rosa Morales was at her desk in her office behind the kitchen making out the following week's schedules when Jenna's call came over her two-way radio. "Rosa? Can you come up to 337 on the double?"

"Why - never mind. I'm coming." Rosa stuck her pencil in the notebook, then bustled from the room. She crossed herself as she headed for the service elevator, praying it wasn't a ghost report but something simple like dropping a bottle of bleach into the Jacuzzi.

The elevator arrived and a moment later she stepped onto the third floor and saw the housekeeping cart in the hall. She entered and found Jenna and Maggie sitting on the bed, Jenna's arm around the other maid. Then she saw the blood dripping on the carpet.

Without a word, she entered the steamy bathroom and grabbed a hand towel. The mirror was shattered, and the tub faucet ran full blast, but she kept moving, going back to the girls and putting the towel under Maggie's bleeding hand, before removing the sodden wash cloth. Oh, don't they ever think?

"Wrap it tight," she ordered as she took the bloody towel to the bathroom, careful not to let it drip. After dropping it in the sink, she turned off the faucet. The second crazy faucet today. Despite the heat, gooseflesh rose on her neck as she turned to look at the mirror.

In the bright light, shards of glass glittered crystal and crimson where Maggie's fist had made impact, and the web of cracks extending from it covered several feet. Looking at the ruined mirror, she crossed herself and muttered a prayer under her breath, grabbed another towel, and then went out to her girls.

"Come sit at the table, Maggie," she ordered. "Jenna, get working on those blood stains!"

As soon as Maggie sat, she unwrapped the hand. The bleeding wasn't so bad now, but there were lots of cuts. "You might need some stitches," she said, gently unfolding Maggie's fingers. The girl whimpered a little, but it was obvious nothing was broken. Rosa examined the hand. "Do you want to go to the doctor?"

"I think a few Band-Aids are all I need." Maggie spoke without looking up at Rosa.

"I think probably you're right. We'll clean and bandage your hand downstairs, then you take the rest of the day off to rest or maybe enjoy the picnic? Jenna and I will finish up."

"Th-Thank you."

Rosa gently wrapped Maggie's hand in a fresh towel. "Maggie? Look at me."

Slowly, Maggie raised her eyes. She looked like a child under those dark bangs.

"What happened?" Rosa asked.

The little color in Maggie's cheeks drained away. "I saw a woman. A horrible woman. A ghost, I think."

"In the mirror? What did she look like?"

"I don't - I don't know. She looked blue. She wanted me to help her."

Rosa's breath caught on a wave of dizziness. Santa Muerte. She tried to hide her reaction. "Maggie, where are you from?"

"San Diego."

"How long have you been here in Cliffside?"

"About a year. Since you hired me. Why?"

"I just wondered. Sometimes locals play mean tricks on newcomers. You know, tell stories." She paused. "Has anyone told you stories about this place? About Cliffside or Blue Lady Lake or this lodge?"

Maggie hesitated and Rosa became aware that Jenna was listening intently. That one was ready to leave. Maggie probably was, too. She couldn't let that happen; they were the only two maids who were truly efficient and trustworthy. "I don't think so," Maggie said at last. "I mean, I've heard about the lady of the lake and all-"

"The Blue Lady."

"Yeah." She paused. "You don't mean I saw the Blue Lady, do you?"

Rosa smiled gently. "No, no. It's just nonsense. Fantasy. You know that, right?"

"It sounded pretty silly," Maggie admitted.

"Jenna," Rosa called. "Do you agree?"

"For sure. What scared me isn't some stupid lake monster. It's that voice I heard saying my name. The same one Maggie heard. That scares the sh- stuffing out of me."

"But you didn't hear it today, right?"

"No," said Jenna.

Maggie said, "But I did. I heard my name over and over."

"What?"

"It was almost like she was singing it. 'Maggie, Maggie, Maggie' - she wanted to hurt me."

"And you heard nothing, Jenna?"

"No. I was running the vacuum."

"Maggie, you had the bathroom door shut while you were cleaning?"

"Yes."

"You had bleach in there and lots of steam. Maybe too much bleach from the smell of it. I think you maybe got a little faint and imagined the singing. Don't you?"

"Maybe ..."

"I didn't imagine the voice in 339," Jenna said.

"I didn't say you did," Rosa replied. "I'll tell you what, both of you."

"What?" Maggie asked.

"Neither of you have to clean this room again. Or 339. Those are the only rooms that scare you, right?"

Jenna joined them at the table. "Right."

"Right." Maggie echoed.

Crisis averted. Rosa hid her relief. "You two go downstairs to my office. I'll be right behind you."

The maids left the room. Rosa, refusing to acknowledge her own fear, gathered the cleaning supplies and dirty towels, put them in the cart, then reentered the room to make sure all the faucets were off. She would send Hank, the maintenance man, to clean up the glass and let Sara Bellamy know they needed to move 337's guests to another room if Noble Mason couldn't come to replace the mirror today. People shouldn't stay in this room anyway.

She glanced around. Everything appeared to be in order and Jenna had obliterated all traces of blood on the carpet. As Rosa approached the door, the Jacuzzi roared to life.

"Mother Mary!" She turned and raced to the hot tub and flipped the switches. The power went off but the water continued to roil and bubble. "In the name of Mary, stop!" She crossed herself and prayed.

Instead, the dark cold smell of lakewater overwhelmed the chlorinated Jacuzzi water and shrieking laughter whirled around her on a cold wind.

*Rosa ...*

She ran, slamming the door behind her.

# 17
## *Broken Window*

The fragrance of barbecue filled the air as Teddy and Adam passed the carousel and squinted in the bright sunlight. Simultaneously, they pulled their sunglasses from their pockets and slipped them on.

Teddy grinned. "My lord, this place smells heavenly. This is where I want to go when I die, you know."

"I know." Adam saw that Teddy was about to turn back, undoubtedly toward Paul Butters' grill, and stopped him with a touch to his arm. "Let's finish making the rounds, then we'll have lunch. Sound good?"

Teddy looked like one of those cartoon characters who was about to lift off on the curls of aroma and float toward the food, but he nodded. "I hope he doesn't run out of ribs."

"Don't worry. That won't happen."

They walked behind Cliffhouse, dipping down through the parking lot. It was solidly packed with cars now that it was past noon. At the rear of the lot, Adam spotted Loyd McRoid's beat up old Chevy pickup, its pale blue paint barely recognizable under the rust, dust, and mud. "Lookie there." He pointed.

Teddy looked. "Loyd the Roid, as I live and breathe. I wonder if he's paying for a ticket to the barbecue."

Adam snorted. "Dream on. But he'll find a way to get something for free, mark my words."

"Marked. We'd better keep an eye on him."

"He does annoy the guests," Adam agreed as they approached the pickup. The windows were down, revealing a rump-sprung bench seat with upholstery the color of old dirt. A 1989 Thomas Guide for San Bernardino and Riverside Counties lay on the passenger side under an eclectic sprinkling of burger wrappers and donut boxes. A partially emptied bottle of 7-Up, the green plastic as faded as the label, lay in easy-reaching distance and it looked bloated, ready to explode.

"Hey guys!" McRoid's head popped up from the bed of the truck, his raw-boned face sunburned and smiling. A faint whiff of Thunderbird accompanied him. Slowly, he climbed out of the bed, with groans appropriate for a guy who claimed disability for a perpetually bad back. Maybe his back really was bad, since McRoid made most of his money selling scrap metal, refrigerators, stoves, and such, and usually conned the people paying him to haul away their junk into loading it for him, too.

"Hello Loyd," Adam said, measuring his words.

"Nice weather we're having, isn't it?" Loyd sidled up next to them - too close - looked around and gave a long, low whistle. "Looks like you got the works here this year fellas."

"We do," said Adam. "Did you bring your own picnic?"

The Roid slapped his pocket. "Got it right here."

Adam almost asked what he meant, but Teddy nudged him and said, "We have clowns for the kiddies, a mime to annoy the adults, folksingers, an acrobatics show, and of course, the concert in the band shell later."

"All I need is the sunshine and I'm happy," said Loyd.

"Well," said Adam, "luckily for you, that's free." He took Teddy's elbow and slowly steered away from McRoid. "Enjoy your day, Loyd."

They were almost clear of the parking lot when Noble Mason's truck pulled up. "Here for the picnic?" Adam asked.

"Wish I was, but I'm working today. Pat and his family are around here somewhere. Gave him the day off," Noble said.

"We just saw them," Teddy said. "They're picnicking by the carousel."

"That's nice. I'll leave them to it."

Teddy laughed. "We won't tell them we saw you."

"Thanks," Noble said, and all three laughed.

Noble Mason only had one employee, his brother-in-law, Pat Matthews, a man who quickly got on everyone's nerves. Everyone but Noble's little sister, Taffilynn. He evidently just got on Taffilynn as often as possible. They were as fertile as a pair of teenage rabbits in June.

"So what are you doing out here, Noble?" Adam asked.

"Sara called, says a bathroom mirror in one of the rooms broke."

"Oh, okay." Adam looked at Teddy. "Do you recall if we have any spares in storage?"

Teddy shrugged. "I've no idea."

"Not to worry, fellas. I've got the right one with me, if necessary."

"Truly, you are the king of repairmen, Noble." Teddy said.

Adam pulled a ticket out of his pocket. "Before you go, take this over to the hotel barbecue and get yourself some ribs. Thanks for coming on a holiday."

"You're a gentleman," Noble said. "I'll do that."

"The parking lot may be full. Just go park in the red."

"Thanks, Ted."

They waited for Noble to pull away then began walking again, heading for the far side of Cliffhouse. Here, the ground was natural, clad in pine needles and acorns from trees punctuating the ground. Straight ahead, about twenty yards away, was the Forest Kelly, which ran all the way to the cliffs fronting the lake. He and Teddy had had the help of several troops of scouts when they decided to refurbish and reopen the Forest Kelly Nature Trail, which wandered past the springhouse and through the trees. The trail was just a half mile loop, but it was pretty, had lots of benches and plenty of engraved placards pointing out native plants and animals. They were proud of it, and as they left the parking lot they saw a Boy Scout troop starting to pack up their camping gear. They got to camp near the forest in exchange for trail maintenance. It was a good deal for all. Two of the boys were tossing a ball back and forth near the springhouse.

The sound of broken glass rang out as the ball went through a window. The Scouts cringed. "Boys will be boys," Teddy said, approaching the springhouse. The two Scouts were already examining the damage.

"Have an accident, guys?" Teddy asked.

The boys turned, looking sheepish.

"Don't worry about it," Teddy said as Adam pulled his two-way radio out of his pocket to let Sara know Noble had another job.

"Go on back to your troop," Teddy told the kids. "No one need know."

They ran to the campsite.

Adam unlocked the big padlock that secured the door and they entered. Teddy picked up the ball. "I love it in here," he told Adam.

They could hear the spring bubbling in the stone well - the wooden cover was half-off yet again. They looked around; the old-fashioned bottling equipment and stacked cases of Blue Springs Sparkling Water bottles were untouched. Adam figured gasses from the spring probably pushed the light cover off, which explained why the old metal one had been chained down. He watched Teddy slide the cover back in place.

The springhouse had a good cement floor they'd put in when they revamped it all last spring, but otherwise it looked as it had perhaps a century ago. The shadows were shot with sunlight. A hanging lantern, a table, a set of shelves, and a chair were the only furnishings. The clean scent of fresh water filled the room. It was lovely.

"We'd probably need to enlarge the springhouse if we want to bring in modern bottling equipment," Adam said.

"It would be a shame to do that. It's exactly like it was when I was little - and when Aunt Theodosia was a child. Who knows? It probably hasn't changed since the 1880s."

They walked outside and Adam left the padlock undone for Noble.

Teddy tossed the softball to the scouts, then they walked toward Cliffhouse, passing the original built-in hot springs spa. The hulking little building was low slung and mainly underground. Eventually, they planned to renovate and reopen it.

They walked another twenty feet to the outdoor hot springs. Recently renovated, the rocky, natural bottom had been smoothed by cement; equally smooth natural stones and boulders had been brought in to provide seating. Young pines, barely six feet tall, acted as a surround, making the entire warm spring pool an idyllic retreat. Only two guests lazed in it now.

Adam and Teddy nodded greetings and kept walking. Their cabin, as well as the five guest cabins, stood to their right, on the cliffs among the thinning pines of the forest overlooking the lake.

They passed them, and headed for the dock. As they neared, they smiled at each other when they spotted their favorite odd couple on the bench closest to the dock steps: Maisy Hart, retired scream queen, and Jon Daniels, Cliffhouse's bartender.

Aunt Maisy was a fan of all things watery, except for drinks. She preferred those straight up. Around seventy now, Theodosia Bellamy's old friend was easy to spot, as was Daniels. She loved sunhats, the more broad of brim and colorful the better. Today's was purple, its inevitable long scarf a brilliant flutter of cherry red. Jon Daniels was identifiable by his straight-backed posture and long narrow head. They made quite the pair.

"Folks," Teddy said, as they looked around.

"Good afternoon," Aunt Maisy said. "It's a lovely day, isn't it?" She held up a paper cup of something that looked like lemonade but was surely far more potent.

"It is lovely," Adam said. He nodded at Jon then he and Teddy walked down the dozen stairs to the wharf below.

Three benches lined the rear of the narrow wharf, snug against the cliff, wildflowers still blooming between them. At the south end of the dock was an enclosed boathouse to keep their little fleet of half a dozen motorboats, rowboats, canoes, and kayaks safe from winter weather. Two motorboats and a kayak were tied to the short docks; the rest were out on the water.

"I wonder where Bill Wasserman is," Teddy said.

"In here," came a voice from the boathouse. Bill appeared a moment later, brown, grizzled, and shirtless. His khaki shorts, at least, were neat and clean. It was hard keeping their employee attired. Unless it was freezing out, he shed clothes like ducks shed water.

Roger Siechert, M.D., came out of the boathouse and squinted against the sun. "Teddy, Adam, nice to see you."

At least Siechert was fully clothed. "Doctor," said Teddy. "What are you doing here?"

"We're playing a little poker," Siechert said. "Care to join us?"

Teddy chuckled. "Looks like strip poker." He glanced at Wasserman.

"I think we'll pass," said Adam.

"Excuse me then." Siechert disappeared into the boathouse.

"When is the next boat due back?" Adam asked.

Bill consulted a non-existent wristwatch. "Maybe twenty minutes."

"Well, put your shirt back on in fifteen, or if you hear anyone else come down to the wharf, will you?"

Bill nodded his shiny head. "'Course I will. Always do."

Butter wouldn't melt in his mouth, but he was a good and honest employee, so Adam pretended to believe him. "Thanks."

"How's business?" Teddy asked.

"Steady, Teddy." Bill squinted across the lake, where dark water reflected clouds and blue sky and sailboats scudded on rippling waves. "They've been going in and out all morning. Great weather. Hot. So, what can I do for you?"

"Nothing," Adam said. "Just checking in. You're making them wear life vests, right?"

"Always do. If anybody else decides to drown before the end of summer, it won't be on our hands."

They started back up the steps. "Bill Wasserman and Doc Siechert?" Teddy asked.

Adam chuckled. "Takes all kinds."

# 18
## *The Hall of Souls*

He stood back and admired his work.

The large circular mirror took center stage on the wall in the long narrow closet that was the Hall of Souls. This was his mirror and he hoped the Blue Lady would respect that in the future. The other mirrors, small satellites, spread out like a freeze frame of planets orbiting the sun. These souls belonged to him.

Beneath the central mirror was a glass shelf holding a flickering white candle. Otherwise, his shrine was bare. He'd begun his collection several years ago. There were eight now - one for each of the victims taken since he'd decided to collect their souls. The mirrors were not representations of his crimes, if in fact, it could be said that any crimes had been committed. They were the casings in which the life forces of the men and women he'd conquered were confined - they were his flock; he was their shepherd.

Sometimes, from the corner of his eye, he thought he saw movement within the mirrors. He imagined the faces of his acolytes staring at him, watching him visit his private altar. He wondered if they were surprised when they looked upon the face of their God. Perhaps, he thought, they expected the peace-filled bright light of the stories survivors of near-death experiences told. Or perhaps, some of them even expected that almighty white-bearded Santa Claus, surrounded by a golden celestial glow as He welcomed them home with open arms from His throne, too fat with joy and too drunk on love to get up and meet them halfway.

He closed his eyes, remembering his first capture, though it was, by no means, his first kill. He had wielded his hammer with practiced skill. She was a lone hiker, far from civilization, young and stupid and sure she was immortal. It was a beautiful spring day near Joshua Tree National Monument when he spotted her. He trailed her for miles before taking her. His swing had been too hard, sending the flat end deep into her skull; when he pulled it out, grayish-pink brains came with it, spattering his sand-colored pants.

But it was worth it; he captured her soul in a mirror, the one that hung just to the left of his own, and there it remained ever since.

As far as he knew, the body was still buried behind a huge outcropping of boulders not far from a stand of Joshua trees. The girl had achieved immortality after all.

He looked to the newest mirror, where the Cliffside whore now dwelt. While it was certainly a safe kill, it had not been so satisfying.

Perhaps allowing the Lady to take the physical body lessened his experience. Perhaps he needed to kill alone for the soul to be fully his.

Time would tell.

His reflection wore a contented smile. It was the simple things that made him happy. Simple things like the roses that lazily climbed the trellises of his home and bloomed with great white vibrancy in his gardens. Simple things like quieting his mind in the Hall of Souls. This was, after all, the sole place where all those small simplicities he cherished combined to create the only environment in which he truly felt the buzz of life.

Here, in the Hall of Souls, he was free from the material world and its demands. Here was his romance - here was the absence of need and duty. Here, he was God.

# 19
## *Chad Armstrong*

Cliffhouse's fitness director, Chad Armstrong, was halfway into the first of his two turkey sandwiches - six ounces, skinless and boneless on multi-grain bread, with fresh lettuce, tomato, no mustard, and of course, no mayonnaise - when the urge struck him. Setting the unfinished sandwich down, he walked into his bathroom and seated himself on his beautiful new porcelain throne.

He loved his job and had built the lodge's little gym and spa into a facility that was now in daily use not only by guests, but by the townsfolk as well. When he began, two years ago, he was basically the lifeguard for the indoor pool and in charge of keeping the place clean. The gym room had had only one treadmill, an Exercycle, and a few free weights; but now there were multiples rooms, lots of equipment and classes, from weight training to spinning to Pilates and yoga. He'd done well and now he'd earned the biggest bonus of all: the BB Boys, Teddy and Adam, had given him a newly renovated suite on the third floor, rent-free, with maid service. *Life is good.*

He sat, enjoying himself, content. Until he heard the voice.

*Chad ...*

He straightened. The word seemed to come from all directions, yet from nowhere at all somehow. "Who's there?"

The silence was thick. Then the voice came again.

*Chad ...*

The odor of dank water rose around him. Beneath the bulking armor of chest muscles, his heart hammered against his ribs.

*Chad ...*

Something cool, like an invisible finger, moved up his thigh. Then, shrill feminine laughter ricocheted off the tile walls. Chad Armstrong shot to his feet, yanking up his pants as he fled from the room.

# 20
## *Moving the Kirbys*

"It was an easy fix," said Noble Mason.

"I'm glad to hear it." Sara smiled at Cliffside's handyman from behind the registration desk. "And I almost forgot. Would you have time to fix a broken window at the springhouse?"

"Not a problem."

"Thanks."

Noble smiled and headed for the rear exit. As he left, the Kirbys entered the lobby from outdoors, arm in arm, looking every bit the newlyweds they were. Sara motioned them over to the desk.

"I'm sorry to ask this, but one of the maids accidentally broke the bathroom mirror in your room ..."

Pixie-faced Mrs. Kirby stopped smiling as her mouth formed a little 'O' of concern. "Is she okay?"

"She's fine, but we'd like to move you to the room next door, room 339, for safety's sake. It's the same floor plan as 337."

"That's not a problem." Mr. Kirby was a handsome man with striking blue eyes.

"I'll send Jerry up with a cart to help you move."

'Thanks," said Mr. Kirby.

Mrs. Kirby nodded and smiled.

"Okay, hang on." Sara programmed a new key card and handed it to them.

The Kirbys smiled, engaged arms again, and disappeared.

Sara watched them go, wondering what it was like to be in such a close relationship. Her love life - on the rare occasions it existed at all - had thus far never been satisfying. Then she thought of Luke Donovan. *Who knows?* Smiling, she picked up the phone and dialed Rosa. "The Kirbys are back and are going up to move their things to 339."

Rosa cleared her throat. "No one has been in yet to vacuum again in case there are still shards of glass."

"It's okay. Jerry's meeting them." Sara paused. "Rosa," she said, "what *did* happen to Maggie in 337?"

"I'll come down," Rosa said and hung up. A moment later, the head housekeeper appeared, looking anxious. Rosa never looked anxious.

"So," said Sara. "What's happened?"

Rosa crossed herself and whispered a Hail Mary, then gazed steadily at Sara. "I think you know there are things that happen here that can't easily be explained."

Sara nodded.

"People hear voices. They see things. And it's been getting worse."

Sara thought of the flying loaf of bread. "Yes."

Rosa smoothed her uniform then met Sara's eyes again. "Maggie saw something in the mirror. A phantom woman."

"I don't understand."

"She says the woman was floating in water, and then drowning."

"Drowning? In the mirror?"

"Yes." Rosa whispered something to herself in Spanish. "The woman in the mirror was banging on the glass, trying to get out. Maggie panicked and hit it, trying to help her. That's how it broke."

Sara looked at Rosa a moment. "Do you believe her?" It was a needless question. She could see the conviction in Rosa's eyes.

"I do," she said. "She's back."

"Who's back?"

"Santa Muerte."

Sara shook her head. "Who is Santa Muerte?"

"You call her the Blue Lady. Your great-great aunt told me about her. She saw her when she was young, many years ago."

"Okay ..." She'd have to ask her dads about that story; she'd never heard it. "You're saying Maggie saw the Blue Lady, as in, Blue Lady Lake?"

Rosa nodded. "She is the spirit of death. The Blue Lady is Santa Muerte.

"Well," Sara said, "I hope Maggie's hand is okay."

"Listen to me, Sara. I saw her walking a few weeks ago, late at night. Someone drowned in the lake the next afternoon."

"Did you see her in a mirror like Maggie?"

"No. She was walking by the lake."

Sara could see the other woman believed what she was saying, and a chill tiptoed up her back. "But Maggie is okay?"

Rosa nodded. "She's fine."

The silence was awkward now. "Well," said Sara, "would you mind checking on the Kirbys in a little while?"

"I will." Rosa looked at Sara for a long moment then turned and headed toward the elevators.

## 21
## *In the Lobby*

"Let's check in with Sara," Adam said as they walked through the big glass and wood lobby doors.

"Okay, I want to find out how that bathroom mirror broke," Teddy said. "But then we need to get ourselves out to Paul's barbecue."

"Things break," Adam told him. "As long as no one was hurt …"

The huge lobby was quiet; almost everyone was outside enjoying the entertainment, the barbecue, or the lake on this perfect, summery day. Within, the creek babbled its way down the center of the lobby, bordered on either side by low log railings, and disappearing under the marble floor so guests could pass over it. Hewn-timber posts, lacquered and polished, studded the tall room and skylights dotted the ceiling, letting the sun in. Potted ferns bookended the groups of dark leather chairs and sofas throughout the vast room and the fireplace on the east wall commanded attention in its huge rocky surround.

Twenty feet away was their prized Steinway & Sons grand piano, one hundred and one years old and in perfect condition. Only the three Bellamys and Jordan Cartwright, the town librarian and official pianist, were allowed to play it. Jordan was as protective and possessive of it as they were; perhaps more so. Adam smiled. Jordan would be coming to play again late this afternoon.

"Looks like Sara's on break with her new friend," Teddy said. Bellhop Jerry Belvedere, elegant if a bit nerdy in his navy bellman uniform, manned Reception, humming along with the Beethoven concerto playing behind him. Louis, the plump, red-cheeked concierge, sat at his desk in a cubby to the side of the registration counter, his chubby hands absently conducting along with the music.

Over near the open corridor that edged the lobby, Sara stood talking with the handsome young man who worked for Constance Welling. They had their heads together as if telling secrets. Sara's laugh pealed across the room.

"Those two have been making eyes at one another," Adam observed.

"It's nice to see," Teddy said as they approached the front desk.

"How's business?" Adam asked Jerry, in library tones.

Jerry, tall and slender, dark and earnest with a gold-edged blue cap and brocaded epaulets on his skinny but squared shoulders, nodded. "It's very quiet right now. Oh, hello Ms. Welling. How are you this morning?"

Adam turned to see Constance Welling coming toward them. The woman had put him off from the first moment she'd waltzed in with her crystal-this and psychic-that. Her much-touted books were nothing but cheap booklets, but her narcissism knew no bounds. He cringed every time she referred to herself as an 'authoress,' and suspected she knew how to throw a tantrum. He hoped the young man talking with Sara was well paid to put up with it.

Adam tried to hold his tongue because Teddy was fascinated by her and would become all the more interested if he protested, maybe even giving her permission to prowl the premises in search of ghosts. That would be disastrous.

"Hello, the Bellamys," she said as if this were the most clever line on earth.

"Hello, Ms. Welling." Teddy dimpled up at the woman who was dressed in skin tight lime green pants, complete with camel toe, and a loud flowered peasant blouse with long sleeves hanging off her bony shoulders and laced up low in the front to show off her bulging breasts. Today, the sleeves were pushed down to a record low, showing off several more tattoos that hadn't been visible when she'd barged in on their coffee klatch with Jackson.

"Ms. Welling, I hope you're enjoying your stay at Cliffhouse." Adam could barely look at her. She'd obviously killed an Avon Lady and stolen all her makeup.

She smiled, smug as a snake, then shook her head, making her gold bangle earrings jangle like bells. "We had an incident this morning."

"And what was that?" Teddy asked. "Anything we can help you with?"

"Your bathtub nearly burned me to death!"

"Pardon?" Adam said.

"I couldn't turn the hot water off. It just turned and turned." She huffed. "I barely got out in time." She clicked her tongue and *tsked*. "I called your desk and they sent a maid up! A *maid!*"

"That would be the most expedient person to send, Ms. Welling," Adam told her calmly. "After all, we don't have a plumber on staff." He glanced at Teddy, who looked slightly shell-shocked by her vindictive tone.

"Well, at these prices, you should have a plumber on staff! You're lucky I wasn't burned." She *tsked* again.

"Was our maid able to help you?" Adam was starting to enjoy himself.

"She turned it off, if that's what you mean. And she was very rude about it!"

"Rude?" Teddy asked.

"Yes." *Tsk.* "She actually offered to teach me how to operate the faucet, as if I were a complete imbecile!"

Adam quelled an incipient smile. "I'm sure she was only trying to be helpful. Faucets can be tricky if they're unfamiliar."

Constance's eyes narrowed. "I know how to operate a faucet!" *Tsk, huff.*

Adam watched her assistant walk toward them. He was nearly on tiptoe when he laid a soothing hand on her arm. "We need to leave, Miss Welling, if we're going to be at the Crystal Cavern on time for your talk."

She let out a breath. "Where the fu- heck have you been, Luke? I've been looking all over for you!"

"We were chatting, Ms. Welling," Sara said as she joined them.. "It's all my fault."

Constance glared at her, at Luke, then back at Sara. "He is on the clock, young lady! I'll thank you to keep your hands to yourself!"

Teddy started to chuckle and put his hand over his mouth.

Constance Welling glared at him.

"I just told myself the funniest joke about a carrot and turnip. Do you want to hear it?" Teddy asked.

Adam grinned despite himself. "I think Ms. Welling needs to leave now, isn't that right?"

Welling looked angry and flummoxed as she searched for something to say. "That's right. We can't keep my fans waiting." She eyed Adam. "I expect you to get a plumber here this afternoon to make sure everything is working properly, or you'll have to move me to a new room." She huffed again. "And if you do that, you must move Mr. Donovan, too, so that we have a connecting door. I'm paying good money, you know."

"We'll have our handyman check it out while you're at your engagement."

"Not a handyman. A *real* plumber. Remember, the customer is always right!"

"So be it," said Teddy. "Don't you worry about a thing. I hope you have a wonderful talk and book signing. I only wish I could be there." That last part, he gushed and that made Adam happy because it was totally false.

She bought it completely. "Why don't you come by, at least for a little while?"

"I'm afraid it's impossible today, but you'll be giving more talks before you leave us, won't you, Ms. Welling?"

She actually batted her eyelashes at him. "Yes, I have several more talks!"

"I'll do my best to make it to one," Teddy said.

Constance looked satisfied as only a person of her perceived virtue could. "Come along, Luke. Here, carry my bag to the car. There's a good boy."

The three Bellamys watched them until they got out the lobby doors, then Teddy shook his finger at Sara. "Keep your hands to yourself, young lady." He broke out laughing.

Adam shook his head, staring at the doors. "So *that's* what happened to Baby Jane."

# 22
## *At Polly's Diner*

Polly's Diner was the best thing Jackson Ballou had laid eyes on all day. He hadn't eaten before the autopsy - he never ate before dealing with carnage - and now, refreshed by a quick shower and change of uniform to get rid of the lingering formaldehyde perfume, his stomach was growling and grousing.

Polly's looked like a diner should. Taking up the corner of Main and Pine, the cafe was in a long narrow building dating back at least sixty years. Next door was Trudy's Antiques and across the way was Golden Bear Water Sports. Between them, Pine dead-ended into Cliffside Beach's parking lot. It was a great location.

When Polly Owen bought the place about a dozen years back, it had been a run-down rat's nest, an eyesore that had stood empty for years. That was before Golden Bear built on the other side of the driveway to the beach and Trudy's Antiques had been struggling in its less-than-stellar location. Then Polly came and changed things with her business sense, common sense, and intuition about what people wanted. The area thrived now.

Jackson peered through the glass as he pushed the stainless door handle. It was a little on the late side for lunch and most everyone in town was out at the lodge, so there weren't many customers. There was only one man at the counter near the window sipping coffee and a couple Jackson didn't recognize sitting in one of the booths that lined the other wall.

At the cash register was Polly herself - tall, slender, chestnut hair pulled back into a bun. Though she owned and ran the place, she always wore the uniform, a neat dark-purple shirt with matching pants, a black apron, and a colorful neck scarf tied under her collar. She passed a large bag across the counter to Prudence Pender Pope, lady-friend and right hand woman to Francis Trudy, then turned and beamed at Jackson.

"Chief Ballou, what brings you here today?"

"You do." He felt himself blush. Prudence dimpled up at him, her soft powdered face and gray hair reminding him of someone's grandmother.

"You're the best cook in town," he added hastily.

"Hey, you better be talking to me!" called Dale Ham, Polly's short order cook.

Jackson put up his hands. "That's it. I'm here to see if Dale will grill me one of those cheddar and grilled onion burgers before I fade away."

"That's better," Dale grunted from the kitchen. He was a retired army cook, grizzled and seamed, and he knew exactly what he was doing.

Prudence looked in her bag. "Did you put in the extra mayo? Frannie loves his mayo."

"I did," Polly assured her.

"You're a saint."

"Hey," called Dale. "What about me?"

"You're the right hand of God, Dale."

"That's better."

Polly handed Prudence a couple bottles of soda pop. She put them in her big shoulder bag and took the brown sack of sandwiches from the counter, then turned and smiled at Jackson. "You need to make an honest woman out of Polly, young man."

Jackson laughed. "She's the most honest woman I know."

Prudence eyed him, and nodded. "See? You can have it all if you'd just get off your duff and kiss her."

"She'd slap me for sure, Pru." Jackson chuckled. "Wouldn't you, Polly?"

Her look was fathomless. "Probably. You'd have to try it to find out."

They watched Prudence bustle out the door, then Jackson took his usual stool.

"Anything to drink?"

"How about a Cherry Coke?"

"You got it, mister."

Polly clinked ice into a tall glass then pushed it against the dispenser. She turned and handed it to him. He took a swallow then glanced at the other customers; the one near the window was just leaving, and only the couple in the rear lingered. "Where are your waitresses?"

"Nancy and Vickie are probably out at Cliffhouse. I gave them the afternoon off. We're closing up at three today, or as soon as the last lunch stragglers get their fill." She arched her eyebrow.

"That would be me."

"Right."

"You knew I was coming?"

"You told me you were coming yesterday, remember?"

"I don't remember," he confessed.

She chuckled, moving a little closer. "You say it every day."

"I guess I do."

She bent and lowered her voice. "How'd it go this morning, at, you know …" She cocked her head in the general direction of the Cliffside Funeral Home.

"Guessing it's homicide."

"Guessing? She was found in a trash bin. Tell me something I don't know."

There was no one off the force that Jackson would tell before a public statement, except Polly. As much as she loved hearing things, she never told a soul. He'd tested her early on with an outrageous but harmless tale about a deceased donkey. Polly was the only one who passed that test, ever. On top of that, she was better than anyone else at helping him brainstorm. "I think it'll be hard to prove murder. Doc doesn't know anything for sure, yet," he said after glancing around. "She probably drowned."

Polly's eyebrows shot up. "You're kidding me."

"Swear to God."

"Maybe somebody drowned her in the lake then left her in the bin?"

Jackson shook his head. "She hadn't been in water. Her hair was in perfect condition, just like her makeup. Doc will have everything analyzed, but … It's a weird one."

"Order up," Dale called.

Polly took the order from the pass-through window and placed it in front of Jackson. The burger was on a big fluffy Kaiser bun with lots of cornmeal sticking to the top. The beef was juicy, the tomato red, the cheddar golden, and the grilled onion shreds thick and fragrant. Perfect.

"Cleaning out the grill," Dale called to Polly. "I want to get some of those ribs Butters makes. I'm trying to figure out his recipe for the sauce."

"Sounds good." Polly went to the door and flipped the Open sign to Closed as the tourist couple left. Then she grabbed a dishpan and quickly bussed the place, taking it all to the kitchen. Dale grunted insincere thanks.

Jackson heard her sweet talk him. She could sweet talk a mountain lion if she wanted.

She returned a moment later and hunkered down a little. "So why do you think she drowned?"

"God, this burger is good!" He waited a moment to see if Dale would reply. He didn't. *Good.* "Her lungs are full of water.

Completely saturated. We won't be telling anyone about that - I shouldn't be telling you, Polly-"

"You know you can."

"I do." He took another bite. "God, this is good."

"He can't hear you right now."

"Humor me. Anyway, we will say - and this is true - she drowned. That's it. I'll release the statement in the morning."

"So, any theories, Jacky?"

"You're being disrespectful now." He gave her a big shit-eater of a grin.

"Oh, you love it. You know you do."

"Well, Pollyanna ... From you, it's okay. I guess."

"That's not my name."

"But you always find a silver lining."

"Can't argue with a man when he's right. So-"

Jackson's radio came to staticky life. "Bronco 1, you read?"

"10-4."

"We have a call from Surfside Salon. Vandalism. They're hoping you can come by right away."

He glanced at his watch. "Tell them fifteen minutes."

"Will do."

He popped the last bite of burger in his mouth and chased it with Cherry Coke. "Perfect."

"Thanks," Dale called.

He stood and paid, and waited for his change. "Are you going over to Cliffhouse, Polly?"

"As soon as the last dish is put away. I don't want to miss the concert. It starts at four."

"What a coincidence. Theoretically, I'm off the clock at four. Theoretically." He paused, a little squiggle of something in his solar plexus. "Maybe I'll see you there?"

"I'll watch for you," she replied. "Theoretically."

# 23
## *The Crystal Cavern*

Obviously, Jim Stone hadn't advertised her appearance properly.

When Constance walked in at 2:10 p.m. - she always made a point of being ten minutes late in order to build suspense - only four people occupied the five rows of folding chairs set up in the event area of the Crystal Cavern, a pretty little occult store in the middle of the businesses on Main. It was a typical shop, dark and creaky, full of books, bells, and candles, not to mention assortments of gazing balls, talking boards, and magic wands. She suppressed a snort. *Such tomfoolery, those wands. Who could ever believe in that nonsense? Go to hell, Harry Potter, you four-eyed geek!*

Stone, the Cavern's owner and manager, had greeted her with moist hands when she and Luke, who carried a large box of extra copies of her books, arrived. Jim was a good host, gracious enough to find moist towelettes for her when she asked. Of course, she had pre-requested towelettes since she always wiped her hands after touching fans.

Jim, a man who obviously trimmed his own gray-brown beard, was an average guy in an inappropriate polo shirt and khakis. He was the sort who could probably go unnoticed in almost any situation - except a formal party. There, he would look as out of place as a tattoo on a Mormon's ass. He looked at Luke. "You can put the box of extra books behind the checkstand, and if we need any at the signing, I'll come get them."

"*If* we need them?" Constance said, but the men didn't hear.

Jim returned, Luke in tow. "A few folks are already here, so let's get you settled before any more arrive." With that, but without offering her any refreshments, he ushered her into the room where she would give her talk - "Making the Occult Crystal Clear with Constance Welling" - and sign books.

She looked at the four people and, furious, hissed at Jim Stone, "You didn't even put this in the newspaper, did you?"

"I didn't forget. There was a short piece in the Cliffside Weekly Chronicle this morning."

"Show me."

The four fans heard her and stared. It was humiliating. "I mean, I'd like to have a copy for my scrapbook," she amended, smiling brightly.

"I'll get you one." Jim Stone escorted her to the little podium and accompanying table, where he handed her a pen that said "The

Crystal Cavern" to sign with. "It's a gift," he told her. "You can keep it."

She stared at him. "Might I have a cold bottle of water?"

"Of course."

"Perrier, please."

"We don't have that, but I have something even better. Our own Blue Springs Sparkling Water. It's bottled right here in Cliffside. I went out and got some especially for you, Ms. Welling."

She sighed. "I guess that will have to do, but I'd prefer Perrier."

"I'll remember that for next weekend's talk." He ran to fetch the water and was back before she had her notes out. "Here you are."

"Thank you." She took a tissue from her pocket and wiped the bottle top. "Luke," she said icily, "Where is my straw?"

She had instructed Luke to hover behind her during events, legs apart, hands behind his back. It was a pose she liked her assistants to take because it prevented trouble should one of her fans become aggressive. He had already assumed the position, but now he went to her bag and rummaged for a straw.

"You will never speak to that little slut again, do you hear me?" She hissed the words in his ear.

He didn't react at all.

The audience of four watched with impatient expectation.

Constance raised a hand and snapped her fingers twice at Luke. "Andale! andale!" she said, then plastered a smile on her face and turned to the fans. In the front row two Goth girls, probably in their early twenties, gazed in awe. Then Constance realized their eyes were on Luke. He brought her a straw, and she cleared her throat and squared the pages of her notes, clacking them down hard on the podium. When she had the audience's attention, she sipped.

Finally, she brought her hands together, as if in prayer. Next she glanced at Luke. He had resumed his bodyguard position. *At least he did something right.* "I'd like to start by inviting you all to take some cleansing breaths with me." She closed her eyes, drawing air deep into her lungs, then exhaling slowly.

After a few breaths, she opened her eyes and smiled. "I hope you'll overlook my eccentricities. It's just that I like to be centered for these things and I think you all will benefit as well." She squared her notes again. "Shall we begin?"

The two wide-eyed Goths in the front row nodded their heads with enthusiasm. The other two attendees, a man and a woman who sat several rows back and a few chairs apart from each other, exchanged glances.

"First, let me tell you some things about myself that you may not know. I'm Constance Leigh Welling, authoress, paranormal expert, and medium. I am the bestselling author of *The Crystal Method Series*, published by Faerie Dust Press, as well as several other standalone works on the subject of the healing properties of gemstones." She paused a moment, letting her accomplishments settle in.

"As a paranormal expert, I have spent the majority of my life on a very particular quest. My mission is to obtain the answers to life's most difficult questions through the most reliable source available: Mother Earth." She sipped her water.

"As for my mediumship, those of you who follow my career on Twitter, Facebook, and other avenues of media will surely already know about Eliza, my confidant and spirit guide who has been with me since the age of twelve, after I had a near-death experience in a boating accident." Another sip. "Apparently, Eliza wanted to come back to Earth with me because she's been with me since the moment I woke up in the hospital. So," she said, raising a hand to the invisible air beside her, "I'd like you to meet Eliza, my spirit guide." Constance chuckled.

The audience blinked.

Apparently, they had no sense of humor.

"Just a little joke," said Constance. "For those of you in the know, Eliza is *within* me, not beside me." This was going to be a dud, she could tell. Still, she sighed and carried on. She was a professional and this was her job. "And now let's talk about crystals."

The girls in the front row lit up, nodding their heads.

The man in the back yawned. The woman a few chairs away was texting.

Constance cleared her throat. "Let's turn off all our electronic devices and concentrate on the subject at hand, shall we?"

The woman rolled her eyes and departed.

# 24
## *Surfside Vandalism*

Surfside Hair Salon was on a narrow street about three blocks from Polly's Diner. It was small and pricey, just like many of the other businesses in town. Jackson always got his trims there, since Troy and Derek gave discounts to the locals, and were good at what they did. Also, the only competition was Ye Olde Barber Shoppe, run by a man in his nineties called Chuck. Jackson was afraid he might lose an ear to Chuck's shaky razor.

Tourist traffic was picking up as people began heading home from the three-day weekend, but Jackson made it to the salon without encountering a single fender bender. He pretended not to notice an entitled-looking Volvo run a red light because he wanted to get to the four o'clock concert to see Polly.

He parked in front of Surfside Salon, hopefully blocking most of the display window from view. The window, normally pristine, had a ten-foot bright red penis on it, balls at one end and a dripping fireman's helmet at the other. *Vandalism, indeed.* It even had veins. *Damn kids.* At least the salon was closed today.

Despite himself, he was amused, but he kept his face stern as he grabbed the camera and got out. Half a dozen shots later, he walked up the driveway to the tiny parking lot behind the shop. Troy's red Corvette and Derek's Jeep were both there.

He knocked on the back door then let himself in.

"Chief? That you?"

"It's me."

Troy Doheny came out of the office, dressed in shorts and a Hawaiian shirt loaded with pineapples.

"You saw it?" Derek Sand asked as he appeared from the lavatory. He wore shorts and a Hawaiian shirt coated with hula girls. He flipped carefully styled blond surfer-boy hair out of his eyes.

"Couldn't miss it."

The three of them walked to the front of the salon. Like its owners, it had a Hawaiian motif, the upper walls sporting surfboards, leis, pineapples, and pina colada art. It should have looked tacky, but somehow, Derek's eye for decor had turned it into exclusive-looking kitsch.

"Any other damage?"

"Not that we could find. And it doesn't look like anyone tried to break in," Troy said.

Derek nodded. "It's just this big ... wang."

They unlocked the door and went out to the sidewalk to examine the graffiti. There was a little overspray on one side of the window. "Do you have any pissed-off customers?" Jackson asked.

"Not that we know of."

Jackson kept asking questions and they kept answering, but no clues surfaced.

"Chief," Derek said. "We already called Mason's - this has to be gone by morning - and he'll probably be here any minute. It's okay if he cleans it up, now, right?"

"No. You guys have to leave it intact for at least a week. Evidence."

"What?" they cried in unison.

Jackson laughed. "Sorry. Of course, get rid of it. I doubt we'll find the perpetrator anyway. Probably some idiot kids."

"You scared me, Chief," Troy said. "If my wife saw this, she'd run away screaming!"

"And mine would say, "You don't satisfy me anymore, Derek."

Noble Mason's service truck pulled to the curb and Mason got out, grunting. "Busy day today." He threw a cursory glance at the window then shook hands with all three. "Busy day."

"Anything like this, Noble?" Derek asked.

"Nope. Mostly broken glass and some funny plumbing." He nodded toward the window. "This has to be the work of the same guy who's been trashing stuff all over town."

"What?" Jackson asked. "I haven't had any graffiti reports for two weeks."

"We've been getting quite a few calls at the shop about graffiti. It's been minor, on walls, fences, like that. At least I have plenty of work for Pat these days. Good thing, too - they're expecting another baby." He rolled his eyes. "He's already got more than enough. I must have the most fertile sister in the state." He paused, chuckling, then turned and carefully studied the graffiti. "I must say, gentlemen, this penis is quite a work of art."

# 25
## *Life of an Authoress*

Constance's talk went well. Two more people had come in halfway through and listened politely, and the two girls in the front row proved to be worthy fans; they both owned every single one of her books. She had signed one book for the man who'd yawned, but the other two people left without even coming forward to thank her for the talk. *Oh well*. Such was the under-appreciated life of a writer.

Jim Stone walked in as the two girls stood before the table, enraptured, while she told them about the healing wavelengths of crystals. "Sorry to interrupt, Ms. Welling, but I need Lacey and Belle to go back to work now. We've got a nice little crowd out there."

"They *work* for you?"

"Of course. You didn't know?"

"No. I didn't."

"Oh, Miss Welling, we'd have been here even if we'd had to travel, like, thirty miles, to see you," said the blonde.

The brunette nodded.

They hefted their little stacks of autographed books and left the room.

"Ms. Welling," Jim Stone said, placing about twenty of her books on the table. "Would you mind signing some stock?"

"Certainly. But do you think this is *all* you'll sell before I come back next weekend?"

"Well," he said, "if I sell more, I'll make sure to tell the customers they can come back next Saturday to have them signed. You're giving your workshop on writing, correct?"

"Yes. But I do think you'd better advertise a lot more."

"We'll do all we can."

"You have flyers, of course."

"I'll make some more up."

"No need." Constance snapped her fingers. "Luke, go to the car and get a master of our flyer." She looked at Stone. "You can use mine - it's much more professional looking than anything you could run up. Just scan it in and add the time, date, and location and take it to the printer's. It's simple. And they ought to work much better than the flyer you made for this appearance, don't you think?" Constance picked up her water bottle and sucked on the straw until it rattled with air.

Stone cleared his throat. "Thank you. I'll have the girls take care of it."

"What-"

"Ms. Welling," he continued, "next Saturday will be better, I'm sure. The town is full of aspiring writers who will be eager to attend your workshop. Will you need anything? Besides Perrier, that is?" His smile looked rather false.

"A better audience. And never mind the Perrier. I'll have more of this." She brandished the bottle of Blue Springs.

"Very well. I'm glad you liked it."

"I mean, I would like more of this right now. Do you think you can you manage that?"

"I'll get you a bottle to go."

"Get me several, please."

"I'm sorry, I only have one more. They're rather expensive, so I only bought you two. You can purchase them at Cliffhouse. I believe you're staying there?"

*The impertinence!* "Of course I'm staying there. Where else would I stay?"

"A lot of our authors stay at the Doc Holiday Inn. It's more affordable and-"

"Constance Welling does not stay in a *three*-star hotel!"

"I meant no offense."

"I'm sure you didn't. Most writers are not as successful as I am." She favored him with an understanding smile.

Luke returned and handed Stone a white flyer.

"Thanks," Stone said. I'll see you next Saturday promptly at two."

Constance tried not to roll her eyes. "Very well. Get our things, Luke." She snapped her fingers at Luke to follow, turned on her heel and walked out the door. Little bells, like angels, tinkled as she left.

# 26
## *Constance, Interrupted*

That little bitch Luke pled a headache and vanished as soon as they got back to Cliffhouse. She waited until he left her room, then peered into the hallway to see if he was really returning to his. He did, and after she heard locks snapping into place, she closed her door, but kept very quiet to see if he was really going to lie down or if he planned on sneaking downstairs to talk to that hotel skank again.

No man turned down Constance Leigh Welling, not ever, and Luke would not become the first. Clearly, he was a latent homosexual. There was no other explanation. His interest in the Bellamy girl was surely based on fashion and other gay stuff, not on sexual desire.

Within ten minutes, no sounds came from his room, and after half an hour of silence, she decided she could stop worrying and go for a swim. She changed and left the room.

The gold-fringed bikini tickled her fanny as she swayed her hips, practicing her moves in the elevator. The skimpy metallic cloth under the nearly transparent golden wisp of a cover-up took twenty years off her figure. Not that she needed it.

Constance got off on the main floor, and although she knew the pool entrance was straight down the hallway edging the main lobby, she exited the elevator, assumed a bewildered expression, and wandered into the lobby, hoping there might be some single *heterosexual* men who might appreciate her swimwear. She ignored the "POOL" sign and its gigantic red arrow and headed for the reception desk.

The lobby was nearly empty. The Bellamy slut worked the desk, where a woman was checking in. A few children ran through the room, their parents calling after them. Then she saw the piano man.

She supposed he was handsome, in a bland kind of way - short-cropped sandy hair, good bone structure, a slender frame. She couldn't see his eyes because he had them closed as his hands moved across the keyboard. He was nothing special, but nothing to sneeze at either.

The version of *Rhiannon* he played echoed through the room, enchanting, almost a duet with the babbling of the little creek, and she found herself walking toward him. As she neared, his hands caught her gaze. They were slender, graceful, long-fingered. Constance bet the man knew how to play a woman's body just as well as a piano.

"Excuse me." She leaned into him over the piano.

He didn't stop playing. In fact, the man didn't even open his eyes. She cleared her throat noisily.

He looked up, his fingers never stalling. "Yes, ma'am?"

She nearly recoiled at the use of the word *ma'am.* Instead, she pushed her breasts out a little, giving him an eyeful of something that she was sure would change his perspective.

His eyes didn't leave her face. They were blue, surrounded by lashes darker than his hair, making him more handsome than she'd thought.

"I hate to interrupt you." She tried to sound breathy. "But I'm looking for the pool and I seem to be lost."

The man smiled and she saw dimples. Rung by rung, he was moving up the stud ladder. "Go back to the hall, pass Registration, and follow the signs."

"Oh, I don't know *how* I missed it."

"Nor do I, ma'am."

Constance suppressed another jolt of anger. *Ma'am? Do I look like a shitting ma'am?* But those dimples ... they made it easy to give him another chance.

He closed his eyes again.

Constance cleared her throat. "Do you take requests?"

"Some nights, yes."

She wriggled a little closer to him. "Do you know any Metallica?"

"No, ma'am."

She wasn't sure if she wanted to slap him or kiss him. "Pity. Well then, I'll be sure to stop by and have you play *Piano Man* for me. You know, the old Billy Joel tune?"

"I know it. I don't sing." His fingers danced as *Rhiannon* neared its end.

"Don't be shy, now," Constance said, wagging a finger at him. "I'm sure your voice is just as fine as those fingers."

"I guess we'll never know."

"Oh, all right, then. I'm Constance by the way. Constance Welling."

He gave her a tight smile.

She wondered if he was going to offer his name. She waited. Apparently not. "And what is your name?"

"Jordan Cartwright, ma'am."

Clearly, this Jordan man was another homosexual. She wondered what it was about the place that turned so many men gay. *The water?* Surely not. The water was fabulous.

"I'll be on my way." She put an extra swing in her step as she walked off. After just a couple of yards, she looked over her shoulder, deciding to throw the man a final bone. "I'll see you later tonight, then?"

He was silent, too involved in his art to notice the *real* art that stood just in front of him.

*He's gay.* She stalked toward the main hall, her cheeks flaring with humiliation.

\*\*\*

The man in blue Speedos at the pool definitely wasn't gay. He was too manly to be gay. He must have been six-two, a good two hundred pounds, all solid muscle, nearly bursting out of the smoothest, tannest skin she'd ever seen. She looked him over, from the short spiked blond hair to the broad expanse of heavy shoulders and bulging pectorals, down to the V of his abdomen where it disappeared into the luckiest swimsuit on the planet. And his legs … Constance felt a welcome moistening of her lady parts.

It was clear the man waxed and she wondered if he gave as much attention to the areas she couldn't see. She closed her eyes, exhaled, and imagined she was taking care of those hard-to-reach places for him. She needed to find a way to get close to this man … needed a reason to approach him. She ransacked her imagination, trying to find a viable excuse to approach the muscle god at the other end of the pool.

She walked his way, slowly removing the gossamer wrap from around her hips, and putting some real pop into her step. The closer she got, the hotter he looked, but just as she came near enough to appreciate his chiseled jaw, he dove in and began swimming away.

*Jesus Christ! I've never had to work this hard in all my life!* She rolled her eyes, sighed, and turned around.

He was headed to the shallow end. Constance began an indiscreet walking race with him. She beat him by a couple of seconds, crouched down at the edge of the pool, and hoped like mad he'd come up for air once he reached her. He did.

He emerged from the water like Adonis, droplets streaming down his sculpted, hairless body. He startled a little when he opened his eyes and stared into her crotch.

"Hello, there," she said. "I'm sorry to interrupt you, but I couldn't help noticing how beautifully you swim."

The man wiped water from his face. She watched his bicep flex with the motion. "Thanks." His voice was smooth, deep ... pure sex.

A plan hatched, involving man candy for herself, and for her sexually confused assistant. If the likes of this muscle god didn't get Luke's blood flowing, nothing would.

"I wondered if you give lessons. I'm afraid I'm not a very good swimmer and I think it's time I learned some ... moves."

He blew out a breath and Constance caught the scent of something wet and male.

"I'm Constance Welling," she said, holding her hand out to him. "Authoress."

His large wet hand encased hers. "Chad Armstrong. Nice to meet you." A familiar glint of interest shone in his eye. Finally, one that wasn't gay. "I'm the personal fitness director here at Cliffhouse." His pec flexed right on cue.

*Oh yeah. Luke is going to love this guy. And I am, too.*

"I'm not a professional swimmer but I can give you some tips."

Constance smiled. "I would really appreciate it. In return, I'll take you to dinner at La Chatte Rouge."

Chad Armstrong smiled. He had the nicest set of teeth she'd seen in a while: white, straight, strong. She couldn't wait to find out what he could do with his mouth. Slowly, she slipped into the water, as near the hunky bodybuilder as she could get without rubbing herself right on him. Once in, she feigned slight terror, letting herself sink a little before flailing her arms.

His hands shot to her waist and brought her up just as she neared his crotch.

"The water's so *cold!*"

Chad's brows furrowed. "It's ninety-three degrees," he said. "The pool is partially fed by the hot springs and it's quite warm."

"Well *I'm* cold. I have hypoglycemia."

"And how does that affect your body temperature?"

"When my blood sugars get low, I get cold." She was losing patience with this guy.

"You shouldn't be swimming if you haven't eaten. Hasn't your doctor explained that to you?"

Constance rolled her eyes. "Yes," she said. "He has. And I've eaten. It takes a few minutes to get my blood sugars up, that's all."

"Then you should get out and wait."

"I feel so faint." Constance let herself slip under the water and flailed her arms, feigning panic.

Chad's reflexes were as quick and healthy as she imagined they would be. Within seconds, the bulging muscles of his arms were wrapped tight around her, pulling her up.

The moment they broke the surface, Constance threw her arms around his neck, squeezing him hard. "Oh!" She slithered around within the confines of his firm embrace, enjoying the feel of the hard smooth peaks and valleys of his manly physique. He was enough to inspire even a romance novelist - not that Constance would be switching genres any time soon. The crystal business was lucrative. And Chad had her lubricated.

"Oh, no!" In her faux panic, she threw herself against him, thrashing and wailing. She slyly pushed one breast out of her bikini top, and rubbed it against his chest as he tried to calm her down.

A shrill whistle echoed through the pool room and the slaps of oncoming feet broke her concentration.

"Are you okay, ma'am?" The lifeguard stood at the edge of the pool, eyes wide, whistle dropping from his lips as he spoke.

"I've got her," said Chad. "She just panicked a little, but she's okay now. Aren't you, ma'am?"

*Ma'am?* Furious, Constance slipped her breast back into her bra. "I'm fine!"

"Ms. Welling is a guest here and she's interested in swimming lessons," said Chad. "Steve's our official lifeguard and he gives lessons."

Steve the Lifeguard might have been a hunk were it not for the eyes, which sat a little too close together. Not as bad as Nicholas Cage's, but bad. *He's got rat-face. I'm not taking lessons from him!*

"I'm fine," she said again, holding onto Chad's mountain-like shoulder. "The water is just too cold for me. I don't think I'll need lessons."

The men looked at each other and shrugged. Then, to her shock, Rat-Face reached down and Chad handed her up to him as if she were a load of laundry. "Let's get you out of here," said the lifeguard as he led her away.

"Please." She looked at Chad. "Won't you escort me?"

Chad shrugged and pushed out of the pool. She took in his entire glistening body and nearly went weak in the knees as she grabbed his arm. It was a shame he hadn't gotten a look at her bared breast, but win some, lose some. In fact, other than him calling her 'Ma'am,' everything was going according to plan.

## 27
## *Chaos in the Lobby*

Jackson Ballou, off-duty but still in uniform, pulled into the Cliffhouse lot around four-thirty. As he exited his cruiser, he could hear the concert in progress in the band shell. The band - about forty pieces, mostly horns - was doing a decent job belting out Joplin's *Maple Leaf Rag*. *What am I doing here?* He locked the SUV. *You told Polly you'd come. Yeah, but it's not like it's a date or anything ... is it?*

The question made his stomach flip. He started off through the crowded lot, taking his time, checking out the other vehicles. He came to Loyd the Roid's eyesore of a Chevy pickup and automatically looked into the bed. There was a flat spare tire, a length of chain, some rusty bolt cutters and a hammer, what appeared to be a squirrel's tail, and a stack of old Playboys in a milk crate - but Loyd was nowhere to be seen. That was never good.

He kept going, heading past the hotel barbeque pit, the busy playground and picnic tables, toward the white band shell. People had filled the concrete benches and many more fanned out across the lawn.

He nodded at Walter Gardner, who was hammering a nail into a redwood trash enclosure, then at Father Malone of St. Mary's, and Harold Beaver, pastor of the Baptist brigade. They were caught up in deep conversation, thank heaven, and didn't try to engage him. After that, he said hello to Merlin Skinner, proprietor of The Wizard of Ink, whose blond ponytail blew in the breeze. Merlin looked annoyed at having to acknowledge him. *Kind of a snob, that one.*

The Joplin rag ended and the band struck up *Seventy-Six Trombones* with more enthusiasm than skill. He cringed a little and scanned for Polly. And scanned some more. He finally spotted her, smack in the middle of the benches, hemmed in on both sides by wide women in polyester. He took this as a sign, and headed for Cliffhouse, trotting up the broad wooden steps of the veranda. A few people relaxed in Adirondack chairs and lounges, but despite the warmth and the still-shining sun, Labor Day was ebbing. In a few hours, Cliffhouse would be comparatively empty, at least until the next festival - and since Cliffside made its money as a tourist town, there was a festival nearly every weekend. Even the weekend after Labor Day, though it was for the locals. The End of Summer Beach Party was the town's private way of saying goodbye to the season and it was always a hoot, raunchier and louder than any tourist event. His officers would be pulling overtime, but despite an occasional drunken tiff, the party likely would still be pretty tame because that's just how things rolled in Cliffside. And he didn't want it any other way. As a detective in the lowlands, he'd seen more than his share of ugliness and violence; that's why he had taken this job.

By day, the lobby was lit only by skylights, and it was shadowed now that the sun was thinking about setting. Only a few people sat in the chairs, some with luggage, some with drinks. The little brook babbled and Jordan played the piano, going the way of Elton John rather than The Beatles for now. It was nice. Jackson saw that Sara Bellamy was manning the registration desk, so he ambled over.

"Hey, Sara."

"Chief. Are you here on business?"

"Not a bit." He paused. "Any idea when the concert will end?"

"I give it another twenty or thirty minutes. How do you feel about coffee?"

"I feel good about coffee. How about you?"

"Just a minute."

She walked over to the concierge and spoke with him. Louis got up and moved to the registration desk. Then Sara disappeared for a moment and came back with a couple of paper cups and handed him one.

They walked over to the first clutch of leather chairs and sat. "If I had one of these in my office," he said, "I'd never leave."

"No kidding. I love these chairs. Especially after hours and hours on my feet."

"Did your dads stick you with front desk all day?"

"Eh, I volunteered. They just love to stroll around and shake hands with everybody. They've made at least four rounds of the grounds today."

"Rounds of the grounds. I like that."

She grinned. "So do they." Her face turned serious. "Anything new on the killing?"

"No, nothing yet." He wished he had something. "So," he said, sitting forward. "Anything interesting happen around here lately?"

"Nothing criminal, unless you count flying bread."

"What?"

"I watched a loaf of bread slide across the counter last night, sort of float in the air for a second, then drop."

"Right …"

"I'm not kidding."

"And I'm the Queen of the May."

"Chief, I swear. On my honor."

He studied her. "You're really serious, aren't you?" He'd never known Sara to be much of a joker and now he could see it on her face - she meant it.

"I am."

"What did you do?"

"Well, I picked it up and made a sandwich."

"I like a woman who's hard to ruffle." He looked up and saw a young man who looked vaguely familiar wearing only Speedos and escorting a bony woman in a fringed gold bikini up the corridor from the pool. The woman was practically hanging on him. "Who's that?"

"Chad Armstrong, our fitness director. The woman." Sara waited for them to reappear from behind a portion of solid wall. "The woman. Yes, of course. It's one of our guests. Constance Welling."

"I remember her all too well."

Sara's smile was almost invisible. "She's an authoress, you know."

"Yes. She made it abundantly clear within sixty seconds of introducing herself." He watched as Constance tapped the young man's arm and made him stop walking while she adjusted her gold sandal. She didn't notice them, but Chad looked up and waved. He didn't look happy.

"He really attracts older women," Sara said. "And younger ones, too."

"He must have an active dating life."

They watched the pair continue toward the elevators just as a huge ruckus arose at the front doors. About a thousand children poured in followed by two adults. "Kids, stay together!" called the weary-looking mother.

Instead, the kids started running toward the center of the lobby, no doubt intent on inflicting themselves on the peaceful creek bubbling through the room.

"Be reverent!" the woman called in a husky voice.

The kids were not reverent, and as one boy careened past his chair, Jackson simply reached out and grabbed his T-shirt. "I'd mind my mother if I were you, son."

The kid, face covered with chocolate and snot, took one look at Jackson and began screaming. "Mom! Help! I got arrested!"

Taffilynn Matthews tromped up to her spawn and, with a practiced pinch, relieved Jackson of his prisoner. "You're not arrested, Anakin Lehi, but you should be! No running. You promised.

You know who's watching, don't you?" She looked toward the skylight, but the boy's cringe was unworthy.

"Princess Josephrania!" yelled Pat Matthews, as a girl with brown braids flying behind her nearly tripped Jerry Belvedere, who was pushing an empty luggage cart through the lobby. The girl managed to twirl and jump onto the moving cart, reaching up to swing on the top rail - but the cart tilted and she jumped off, nearly taking the bellhop down with it. Jerry's face was an unreadable mask as he righted the cart and pretended not to be angry. Pat Matthews called out in a less-than-commanding tone, "Stand in position."

She did.

"Great, Princess. That's just great!"

And then she took off in the direction of the piano.

"Great. Just great," Pat said without enthusiasm.

Sara was on her feet, attempting to corral the feral children; Jackson supposed he ought to help her, but he was really enjoying the show.

Two girls, older twins who wore identical dresses and reminded him of nothing more than *The Shining* twins in puberty, walked up to him. "Are you a cop?" asked one, her face bland except for a pimple that pulsated on the verge of eruption.

"I'm Police Chief Ballou."

"Do people tease you about your name?" asked the other one, differing only from her sister because her pimple had two heads, both quivering.

"Um …" *What the hell is she talking about?* "No." For lack of anything better to say, he asked, "What's your name?"

"You don't have to tell him!" Anakin Lehi screeched. "Not unless he arrests you."

"Humph," said the double-header twin. She extended her hand to Jackson. "I'm Truthanne Matthews. Pleased to make your acquaintance, Mr. Ballou."

Jackson shook her hand solemnly, then wiped the stickiness off on the side of his pants. "Pleased to meet you, Truthanne."

"This is my sister, Shrudilee," continued the sticky-fingered one. "She's my *little* sister."

Happily, this one didn't try to shake hands. She glared at her sister instead. "By three minutes. You just never stop, do you?"

"Oh, grow a weasel!"

"Truthanne Delightra Matthews!" her mother cried. "You will go outside and wait by the van right this minute, and when we get home, you are going to hold a bar of Ivory in your mouth for fifteen minutes! Indeed! Where did you learn such language? You know who's watching you!"

Truthanne's eyes rolled toward the ceiling. She was not impressed. "I learned it from Ensign and he learned from Brigham and Hiram. And they learned it from Daddy!"

Jackson was having trouble not smiling.

"Hiram, Brigham, Ensign, come over here right this minute."

Three boys looked up from their assault on a group of chairs. "Ah, mom, we're building a fort."

"Now!" Noble Mason's little sister was a force to be reckoned with, but evidently only her husband, Pat, realized it. He was nearly cowering at the sound of her voice. And with good reason. "Patrick? Take these boys out to the van. They are not going to get any treats today." She paused. "And take Truthanne with you as well."

Taffilynn watched the father and kids traipse toward the parking lot door then turned to Jackson and Sara, her voice as sweet as her name. "I'm so sorry for the trouble they caused. You know how children can be."

"I do now," said Jackson.

"Don't worry about it," Sara said. She'd plastered a big fake smile on her face that wouldn't fool anyone if they looked twice. "I hope you all enjoyed your day here at Cliffh-"

The bang of the grand piano lid stopped all other sounds and movement in the lobby, save for the oblivious creek. Its harp vibrated and echoed under the closed lid.

Jackson found himself sprinting across the lobby as if there'd been a real explosion, and came up short by Jordan, frozen fingers still on the keys. His face was white with a pair of little red spots starting to grow on his cheeks.

And the powerful voice of Taffilynn Matthews thundered, "Ralphene Celestia Matthews! What have you done?"

A girl of ten ducked under the piano and two more, not much younger, giggled and ran toward the back door.

"Jordan?" Jackson asked. "Everything okay here?"

Jordan nodded.

"Are you Ralphene?" Jackson bent and eyed the sticky-looking girl under the piano. Pink cotton candy streaked through her hair, making him think of the platinum and Pepto disaster on Constance Welling's head. She nodded.

"Go to your mother. Now."

"Do I have to?"

"Yes."

Taffilynn arrived and marched the girl toward the back entrance.

"Two others went that way, too," Jackson said.

"Yep. I saw them." Taffilynn turned and yelled across the lobby. "The rest of you kids follow me. There will be no Kool-Aid tonight. Or for the rest of this week for anyone except Shrudilee, Jenteel, and Twyla Dawn. They were reverent children and they will get double Kool-Aid."

Sara arrived at the piano and put one hand on Jordan's shoulder. "I'm so sorry."

"It's not your fault." Jordan stood up, reset the piano lid on the prop, and returned to the bench. "The show must go on."

"Can I get you anything?" Sara asked.

"No. Wait, yes. If you don't mind, I'd love a bottle of sparkling water."

"Certainly. On the rocks, with a twist of lemon or lime?"

"Just a cold bottle would be fine." He gave her a grateful smile. "Thanks, Sara."

She trotted away, leaving Jackson with Jordan. "I'm glad I don't have kids."

Jordan nodded. "They can be difficult, that's for sure."

"Big families baffle me," Jackson said. "I wouldn't have the patience for even one or two kids. A dozen like that, well, I'd probably either run away or shoot them." He chuckled.

"I understand completely." Jordan smiled and put his hands on the keys. "Do you have any requests, Chief?"

"Classic rock. Something mellow."

"*Strawberry Fields Forever*?"

"Perfect.

# 28
## *Constance on the Prowl*

The toe of Constance Welling's gold stiletto kept rapping into Luke Donovan's shin as they sat on stools at a tall table in La Chatte Rouge's bar, waiting for Chad Armstrong to appear. Luke was doing a good job of ignoring her ... so far. The little bitch hadn't so much as apologized for speaking to the hotel harlot, but there was no doubt he would before she let him off the hook. She had plans for the night and she wasn't going to let Luke act like a baby and ruin them.

Constance had hit bottom on her second Sex on the Beach and held the glass up as a barmaid passed by. "Another please," she called.

Luke had barely touched his mojito and evidently thought the mint leaves were supposed to be eaten. He was toying with one, holding it and mindlessly putting the tip between his lips.

"I'd like you to do that to me, sometime, Lukey," she said, laying a hand on his knee.

Startled, he dropped the leaf. "Excuse me?"

"I'd like to be that mint leaf." She giggled. "I'm a little drunk. You have to take care of me tonight."

"Yes, ma'am." He moved his leg away from her just as she began to edge her hand up his thigh.

"Stop calling me 'ma'am.' That's an order."

"Yes, Ms. Welling."

"You have to call me Constance. You work for me." She licked her lips and blew him a kiss, her lady parts tingling. Sex on the Beach was an aptly named drink. "Say it."

"Say what?"

"Don't be coy with me. Say my name."

"Constance Welling."

Her good mood started to fade. "You little bitch."

"You are drunk, Ms. Welling. I may be your employee, but that does not give you the right to call me names. Why don't we just go in to eat now? You need to eat."

"I'm sawwy," she said in a little girl voice as she looked up at him from beneath fluttering lashes. "I got you a gweat big supwize. We have to wait for it to awwive. It will make you all better."

He stared at her without answering. Her irritation returned, but was forgotten as Chad Armstrong entered the bistro. Constance waved. "Over here, Chad! I've saved you a seat!" She poked Luke. "Surprise!"

"What?" Luke looked incredulous.

"Well, what are you waiting for? Get Chad a stool."

"I think he can pull up his own stool, don't you?"

"Don't be a little bitch. Do it."

Luke stood and brought over a stool from an empty table and started to fit it between his and Constance's.

"No, you idiot," she hissed. "Put it on my other side. Don't you know anything?"

He rolled his eyes, an action he would pay for later, but he obeyed and the fitness director, dapper in a stretchy dark blue T-shirt that showed off his muscles, tucked in next to her.

Now she had a stud on either side. Constance smiled and tingled.

"Thank you," she told the waitress who brought her a fresh Sex on the Beach. "He'll have a fresh mojito with extra mint leaves, and what would you like Chad? Tonight is on me."

"Sparkling water," he told the waitress.

"Blue Springs?"

"Yes, Pammy," he said to the barmaid. "Absolutely. Thank you."

Constance stopped the barmaid. "I'm sure you'd like some Absolut in that water, wouldn't you, Chad?"

"No, ma'am, I don't drink alcohol."

"Why ever not?" Disappointed, she let the bar girl go.

"Personal choice," he told her. "My body is my temple."

*Oh, groan. One of those.* "Won't you excuse me, just one moment?" She slipped off her stool and casually walked toward the barmaid.

"Miss, uh, Pammy?"

The girl turned to look at her. "Yes?"

"Do me a favor, hon, and slip a couple fingers of Absolut or Grey Goose into the sparkling water."

"You want me to spike Chad's drink?"

"Well, I wouldn't put it that way." Constance dug in her pocket and pulled out a twenty-dollar bill. "This is for you, honey. You know what to do." With that she returned to the table.

Not three minutes later, Pammy appeared with a tray of drinks. A mojito for Luke and a bottle of sparkling water accompanied by a shot of vodka for Chad. She served, then Constance snatched the shot away and said, "This was for me, I believe." *Stupid slutty barmaid.*

She downed the vodka. One way or another, she was going to get lucky tonight, and if it took bringing another man into the mix to get Luke in the mood, so be it. Besides, there were few things Constance loved more than being the meat in the middle of a man-sandwich. It was a win-win for everyone. Constance was always amazed by her own innovative ideas. Now it was time to put the plan into action. "Oh, it's so hot in here, don't you think?" She unbuttoned the filmy shirt she wore over a Spandex tank top. "Help me off with this, Chad, honey, won't you?"

"Uh, sure." He let her shuck the shirt then handed it back to her. She passed it off to Luke.

"What do you want me to do with this?" he asked, obviously mouthy from the second mojito.

Ice in her voice, she said, "Hold it." As she turned her attention to her other guest, another party entered the bistro. She squinted. The Bellamys, all three, plus that old lady who hung out in Omar's. *What luck!*

She waited until they were inside, and then spoke to Luke. "Go get us a table right next to them. You can do that, can't you? Secure it, and then have them call us for dinner. And if you as much as look at that little tramp, I'll have your balls on a platter."

# 29
## *La Chatte Rouge*

La Chatte Rouge was appropriately dark, cool, and quiet this Monday night. Soft jazz filtered through the sound system, blending with the murmur of guests.

"It's so nice of you all to take an old lady out to dinner," Maisy Hart said to Adam, Teddy, and Sara. The four of them were seated at a table by a window that looked out at the forest beyond. Maisy could just make out the stone springhouse. The forest behind it looked dark and spooky. "I love this place."

"The bistro?" Teddy asked.

"Yes, I love all of it. The lodge, the property, those woods. I love what you've done with this place. Theodosia, bless her heart, would be so proud of you all."

Another party arrived; a pair of tall young men, and - *oh hell* - that annoying woman who called herself an authoress. She wore a tight hot pink tank top that showed off her breasts. Feathery pink earrings brushed her shoulders. Even back in her go-go dancing days at the Whisky, Maisy wouldn't have been seen on the street dressed like that. To make matters worse, the hussy stared straight at her as the hostess seated her party at the table next to theirs, not four feet from them. Maisy looked away. There were plenty of prime tables near other windows, so why? *She asked to be seated here, that's why. The nerve.*

"Pardon me. I'm Eduardo and I'll be your server tonight." The handsome young man handed them their menus then listed off the house wines. They ordered a red and an appetizer plate. The whole time, Maisy could feel the obnoxious woman staring at their table. *Maybe it's your imagination.* But she didn't dare look.

*Maybe I should say I'm getting a chill here by the window and ask to move.* But she knew she was probably just overreacting. Sometimes certain fans at horror and sci-fi cons gave her the same creepy-crawly feeling. Could the woman be a fan? It seemed unlikely - and that was more disturbing.

The other table received their menus and the woman loudly announced to the server that she would be paying the entire check.

At that, Adam, seated by the window, looked past Maisy and saw who was talking. A look of pain swept across his face. "Miss Maisy, would you like to move to another table?"

"That would be rather obvious, wouldn't it?" She leaned over and whispered, "What does that creature want, have you any idea?"

"She's nosy and I think she wants to write about the lodge's ghosts. Do you want to move?"

"I'd rather not give her the satisfaction. She's a writer of some sort?"

"So she claims. She's booked two rooms for at least another month," Teddy said softly.

"That doesn't give her the right to intrude on our other guests," Adam said.

"Keep your voice down!"

"I am."

Maisy put her hand on Adam's. "It's okay. I've survived worse."

"You're the very voice of reason," Adam told her.

She smiled. "As I was saying, I do love it here."

They paused while the server poured wine and took their orders.

"To Cliffhouse," Teddy said, raising his glass.

"To Cliffhouse," they echoed.

"You mentioned the Scream Queen Festival in Los Angeles next month," Teddy said. "Are you a guest?"

She laughed. "Yes. They're running *Creature of the Indigo Swamp* and *The Scream of the Shrew Monster.* Neither film is my best, but I did do some fine screaming in both of them, if I do say so myself." She paused. "I'm hoping you'll give Jon the weekend off so he can escort me. I need an arm to lean on these days."

"Naturally," Adam said.

There was a *clunk* at the next table. Maisy spared a quick glance and saw the authoress snatching her fork from the floor. She'd somehow managed to drop it barely two feet from their table.

"Clumsy me," cackled Constance Welling.

Everyone ignored her.

Eduardo the waiter brought an appetizer plate and they all forgot about talking.

\*\*\*

Constance's hungers were many. Her stomach growled despite the infusion of a third Sex on the Beach. The scent of male musk surrounded her, igniting her lady parts with ideas. She continually brushed her hand against the solid muscle of Chad Armstrong's thigh. He had to have noticed, but he was doing nothing to stop her. *Progress.*

Her other hand lightly stroked Luke's thigh. She knew the little bitch loathed scenes and wouldn't react in public, so she moved her hand a little higher. His leg muscle stiffened and he pulled away, but he couldn't escape her touch completely. She stopped her advance, but kept her hand in place.

"Why don't you have some bread?" Luke passed her the basket. You need to eat."

"Yes, Ms. Welling," echoed Chad. "You must watch your blood sugar."

"I'm watching my figure." She gave Luke's knee a hard squeeze, using her nails. He jumped a little but said nothing. He'd pay for his words later.

"You have a very trim body," Chad said. "It's rare to see someone so fit in middle age."

Fury, the kind that could kill, threatened to overcome Constance. *Who's he calling middle aged?*

Eduardo appeared. "Would anyone like another drink?"

"I'll have another sparkling water," Chad said.

Before Constance could speak, Luke said, "Why don't we all switch to sparkling water?" He nodded at his barely-touched mojito. "I'm done with this. Please take it away."

*Prude.* "We'd like a bottle of red wine," she told Eduardo.

"Very good, madam. Would you like to see our list? We have some excellent-"

"Just bring something sassy. Something with a bouquet."

"What sort of bou-"

"Just bring it!"

"Very well. And are we ready to order?"

"It's about time you asked," Constance said. "I'll have the chicken Caesar salad with low-fat Italian dressing. And the red wine, of course. Don't forget that. And Chad? Luke? Order anything you want. My treat."

The waiter turned to Luke. "For you, Monsieur?"

"The lobster tail-"

Constance cleared her throat. "He'll have the same salad and a side of steamed broccoli."

The waiter looked at Luke, eyebrows raised. In turn, Luke glared at Constance. "She's paying, so she's ordering," he said, much too loudly.

"And for you, Monsieur?"

Chad glanced at her, eyebrows raised.

"You have whatever you want, Chad. Remember, it's on me."

"Great! I'll have the tenderloin, rare. Vegetables on the side. No potato."

Eduardo nodded. "Will that be all?"

"Yes," Constance said, then paused. "No. These boys also need a dozen raw oysters."

"None for me," Chad said. "They're unclean. They're not good for my body."

"So half a dozen?" Eduardo looked at Luke.

"No, I don't want them either."

"Luke, you'll have them and you'll like them. Chad doesn't look like he needs them." She smiled at the fitness god.

"Very well. I'll bring a half dozen oysters to the table." The waiter left and Constance put her hand back on Luke's knee. He sighed audibly.

"Chad," she said.

"Yes?"

"Luke and I would like you to join us later tonight."

Chad blinked. "Join you?"

"Yes."

He blinked again. "You mean ... in your room?"

She laughed. "What else would I mean, silly boy?"

Luke stared at Constance, mouth hanging slightly open. She pinched his leg, letting her fake fingernails dig in even harder.

"I guess I can stop by for a few minutes," Chad said.

Her heart pounded and her nether regions moistened. Tonight, Constance would be in beefcake heaven. She downed the rest of her cocktail in one long swallow, demonstrating her oral prowess.

*\*\*\**

Sara had feared the evening was going to be a rocky one when drunken Constance Welling planted herself, Luke, and Chad Armstrong adjacent to their table. For a while, it was. Welling was trying to eavesdrop, Dad was looking incensed, and Daddy, well, he was making nice, playing down the woman's rudeness. Maisy Hart, her honorary aunt, did the same, though it was obvious she was uncomfortable - or perhaps, amused. She couldn't tell which.

Sara vehemently wished Constance Welling would cancel her reservations and go home. Poor Luke looked so uncomfortable that she really wanted to plant her foot halfway up the woman's ass.

But about the time their food arrived, Constance became less nosy. The drunken old bitch had her hands on Luke's and Chad's legs and was trying to feel them up. They both looked supremely uncomfortable.

"So, Maisy," said Teddy. "What do you think?"

"About what?"

"About the maids' experience on the third floor. Have you heard any other stories like that?"

"Of course. Forgive an old lady's wandering mind." She winked at Sara, who smiled back. "Your great aunt told me about something like that happening when she was a young girl."

"Really?"

"Yes, as I recall, some people - guests, maids, I'm not sure - experienced something similar. It was at the time the Bodice Ripper was active, I think. I'm sorry I can't tell you more." She paused. "I'll see if I can't remember some details."

Teddy smiled. "I remember when I was little, Aunt Theodosia used to sit at her desk and write for hours. I wonder if she was keeping journals." He shook his head. "I never saw any. Did you, Adam?"

"No, not that I recall."

"If she did, perhaps she put them away, or burned them," Maisy said.

"I'd love to find them," said Sara.

# 30
## *First Date*

"Despite the name, this place grills the best tenderloin in town," Polly told Jackson as she swabbed up juices with the last bite of beef.

Jackson wondered how such a slender woman could put away such a big dinner. He'd left half his loaded potato on his plate, too full to finish it. "What's the matter with the name? Spunky's Steak-Out. I like it."

"You would. It just makes me giggle."

"Why?"

"You know why."

"I can think of a couple reasons." He sat back, wishing he could undo the top button of his pants.

"Oh, stop it." She eyed his plate.

"You want to finish that?"

"No, no. I was just thinking that you probably would rather skip dessert."

"No, it's okay, if you want to split something." *Please say no.*

"No. I'm having a great time," Polly said.

"So am I." But his mind kept wandering back to the morning autopsy. Lungs full of water. The body dry and found in a garbage bin. It didn't make sense. The husband, Brad Bailey, had been out of state for more than a month taking care of his mother, who'd broken a leg. His alibi was air tight and he was due back next week, when the cast came off. Telling him about his wife's death had been torturous. Bailey was devastated.

"Surprised, Jackson?"

"What?"

"Are you surprised you're having a good time?"

"Oh. No. Are you?" He wasn't surprised, but he was nervous. Polly was his best friend, his confidant, but they were in unfamiliar territory. With one bad marriage and a couple of horrible relationships in his past, he had run shy of romance for years. He had very bad taste in women, and while he knew Polly was nothing like the others, he was a little afraid none of his romances had worked out because there was something wrong with him. He didn't want whatever that was to ruin their friendship. But looking at her now, he really wanted to kiss her.

"How about we go back to my place and have a nightcap?"

"Good idea."

# 31
## *Sex Sandwich*

Back in the hotel room, Constance slipped into the bathroom to freshen up, leaving Luke Donovan and Chad Armstrong sitting in awkward silence on the sofa. She'd tried to lure them straight to the bed, but neither took the bait. *They'll both be hot when they see what I'm wearing!*

She'd taken her bra off so her breasts could sway freely under a black lacy top that didn't quite cover the bottoms of them. Tiny matching panties drew attention to her midsection. Black nylons gave her legs a smooth, touchable appearance, and the black stiletto knee-high boots added height. As a final touch she sprayed some vanilla musk into the air then moved through the mist to be sure every inch of her body was covered by the scent.

The ensemble was perfect, showing off all her tattoos and flattering her figure. Her breasts were plump melons, perky thanks to Dr. Roth. She frowned however, when she turned to look at her ass. That was the next thing she'd need to have plumped up.

She applied red lipstick and dusted her lids with violet-blue shadow. Finally, she rubbed rouge into her nipples, then her cheeks and lined her eyes in an extra thick layer of kohl. She blew her reflection a kiss. "I am still young, I am eternally beautiful, and any man is lucky to have me." She repeated the mantra three times, as she did at least once per day.

She stepped into the living room.

Both men looked up. They were speechless, as she expected. "Hello boys," she said in her best Marilyn Monroe imitation. "Do you like my outfit?"

Luke's jaw dropped.

Chad's face reddened.

Constance turned around, bending forward to give them a full view of her behind. She waggled it a little. Then, turning back around, she slid the straps of her top down, lowering it until both her luscious breasts were exposed. She tweaked her nipples and giggled.

Luke gasped.

"Take out your ponytail," Constance ordered.

"No."

"Luke, you shit-diddling little bitch, do as I say." She turned to Chad. "And why don't you stand up and take your shirt off, Mr. Hunky-Man?"

Chad stood, but he made no move to undress. "I'm sorry," he said. "I clearly misunderstood your intentions. I thought we were having coffee." His gaze flitted to Luke.

Luke held up a hand. "I wasn't in on this, either." He turned his gaze on Constance. "This is inappropriate and I won't tolerate it." He stood.

"How dare you speak to me like that, you little shit!"

Chad gave her a long disbelieving look before turning to Luke. "Why don't you come with me, Luke. You don't need to tolerate this."

Luke nodded. As they stepped toward the door, Constance's voice shrilled through the room: "You are *my* employee, Luke Donovan, you shitting ingrate!" No amount of booze could quell her humiliation. "You get back here this minute, both of you little shitters!" She jabbed a finger at the floor.

As the door clicked shut behind them Constance collapsed, ready to begin one of her anxiety attacks. But Luke didn't return, so she rose to her knees, and screamed at the door. "You shits!"

She threw a pillow at the door and decided to go down to Omar's Tavern and see what kind of man-candy she could score. "I'm still young, I'm eternally beautiful, and any man would be lucky to have me." She recited the mantra as she tucked her breasts back into her top.

# 32
## *Hammerhead*

The urge was coming upon him again. The need. He sat cross-legged in the Hall of Souls, the tips of his thumbs and third fingers touching as he calmed his desires.

*There is time for all things. Time is infinite. I am infinite. I will wait.*

When the Lady had come to him this evening - touching, caressing, demanding - he allowed her entrance into his body, even though he wanted to refuse because he preferred being alone.

Now the Lady whispered in his ear from inside his mind. She was his constant companion tonight, urging him, filling him with her need, mating it with his own. She was aware of all the people, all the annoyances, all the drama of the narcissists and clowns who surrounded them. How he hated the constant babble of his fellow man! How the Lady hated all men! She valued them only as food, as energy upon which to feed, and he understood that clearly; he felt much the same way.

*Just a few days,* she whispered. *Just a few days more, and we shall have what we most desire.*

He took a slow deep breath. "Just a few days."

# 33
## *Omar's Tavern*

Constance added her last painkiller to the mix in her stomach and sang *The Pina Colada Song* as she headed for Omar Siam's. Dressed in her favorite neon pink angora sweater and matching capris that showed just a sexy hint of butt cleavage, she arrived at the entrance and paused to pet the "Open" sign, which featured a painted image of a fat Siamese cat. "Nice kitty," she said, too loudly, then entered and sat on a barstool.

The bartender appeared, and she saw in the mirrors behind him that while he was probably pushing forty, he lacked a bald spot. *Nice.* He was cute - in a dour, horse-faced sort of way.

"What's your name?" she asked.

"Jon Daniels, madam," he said as he wiped the bar. He was tall, thin, and fit looking. Of course, that could have been the black jacket. Underneath it, for all she knew, he might be bony. His little red bowtie was a nice touch, too.

"So, tell me, Mr. Daniels, how long have you been the bartender here at Cliffhouse?"

"I've always been the bartender," he said. "I came over from The Sommelier's Cellar when Cliffhouse opened."

"I've never heard of it. Kamikaze, please?"

"You'd have to be a wine connoisseur to be familiar with it, I'm afraid."

"I'm fine with wines." She winked at him.

"I'm sure you are, madam." He left to make her drink.

A new voice sounded from a table behind Constance: "Speaking of wine, I'd love another glass of chianti."

Constance turned. It was the old biddy who had been to dinner with the Bellamys. She was obviously up past her bedtime; she had to be seventy-five. Her hair was too dark and her black cocktail dress and jacket were inappropriate for someone her age. She swayed in her seat, just a little.

"Of course, Miss Hart." Jon Daniels set Constance's kamikaze down in front of her, and took a chianti bottle to the old woman and refilled her glass.

"Maybe she'd like some fava beans with it instead of peanuts," Constance muttered as she downed half her drink.

The old lady raised the glass to her lips and Jon the bartender waited, as if to make sure she was satisfied with its taste. Constance noticed the glint of four rings on her hands, rings that were heavy with diamonds. *Ostentatious old bitch.*

After taking a sip, the biddy set the glass down. Jon Daniels topped it off. The woman reached into the top of her dress and pulled a bill out. As he snagged it, Constance saw it was a fifty.

When Jon returned, Constance raised her eyebrows at him. "Who is that woman?"

"That's Miss Hart. She's a treasured guest at our lodge."

"You two are close?" She touched the tip of her tongue to the lime wedge in her drink.

Daniels paused, his brows knitting together. "Come again?"

"You seemed to be quite ... chummy, if you know what I mean."

A subtle smile flirted with the corners of his mouth. "I'm afraid I don't follow you, madam. All our guests are our good friends."

"Well," said Constance, straightening in her seat, "she flashes red to me."

"I don't understand."

She leaned forward as if she were about to disclose a great secret. "A lot of people don't know this, but I'm gifted."

"Gifted, madam?"

"Yes. As a girl, I had a close brush with death and I returned with a new friend."

Daniels appeared to be waiting for a punch line.

"Her name is Eliza. She's my spirit guide. She's here right now."

"Here? With you, madam?"

She swigged the last of her drink and tapped it on the counter to indicate she was ready for another. Jon Daniels read her cue. "Are we charging this to your room, madam?"

"Uh huh. Constance Welling's room. I'm a famous authoress." She licked her lime slice. "Eliza first spoke to me when I was recovering from the accident. At first, I was frightened. I didn't know what she was and thought I was going crazy."

He brought her a new drink.

"She advises me." She took a long pull. "It's difficult sometimes, you know?"

"I wouldn't know, madam."

"Call me Constance. Not very many people do understand. It's quite rare, you know. Plus, being a famous authoress on top of it, well, it can be very pressing to say the least."

"I'm sure, madam."

"Call me Constance. Anyway, what I was saying about that Harpy woman-"

"Miss Hart, madam."

"You can call me Constance. Anyway, sometimes … I see auras. I think Eliza shows them to me. And when a person flashes red, I know they're bad news." She drank, her glass dangerously close to being empty again. Do you know what color your aura is?"

"I'm sure I don't, madam." His smile looked almost like a smirk now. He was handsome when he smirked. She was certain he was flirting with her, and that, she thought, took quite a lot of nerve after his touchy-feely exchange with the rich old bag at the table.

"Well, I know what color it is," she said. "Your aura is deep purple. Do you know what that means?" She finished her drink.

"Another kamikaze, madam?"

"Yes. And please, call me Constance." She stifled a burp as the man mixed her drink. When he returned it to her, she continued. "Purple means you're very sensual, very passionate. Probably an artist of some kind. You're carnal, and you have an insatiable appetite for all things."

He nodded calmly and began wiping the bar.

"Want to know what color my aura is? It's usually a nice healthy pink, meaning I have very profound healing abilities. It actually makes sense, considering the profession I ended up in. But anyway, tonight, my aura is purple. Like yours." She tried to give him meaningful eye contact, but he evaded her, busying himself with minor duties. He was shy.

A voice startled Constance. "I'm going up for my bath, Jonny." It was Miss Hart, and up close, she was especially hideous. "Thank you for the chianti. It was lovely. An excellent choice." She tossed another fifty on the bar and appraised Constance. "And you," she said. "You shouldn't try so hard, dear. It makes you look … well, cheap. Plus, I doubt you can afford Mr. Daniels." She smiled as if she'd just given Constance a compliment. Then she winked at Daniels and left the bar.

"Well, that was quite rude, don't you think, Jonny? I mean, I never! What a horrible, horrible woman."

"It's Mr. Daniels, madam." He gave her a studied look. "Finish up your drink. The bar will be closing in just a few minutes."

"But it's nowhere near two a.m."

"True, madam, and if you'd like to continue drinking until then, I might suggest Boozehound's in town. Though I dare say you've had enough and ought to go back to your room."

"How dare you talk to me like that? I'll report your rudeness to those nice gay men."

"If you're so inclined. Have a pleasant evening, madam."

***

"There she goes, off to take her nightly bubble bath," Teddy said with fondness as they watched Maisy Hart walking regally but carefully out of Omar's and up the hall toward the elevators.

"She does love her bubbles," Sara said, smiling after her. "I think she's very happy here."

Teddy and Adam nodded. "She says our water is special."

"She dines with us nearly every night," Paul Butters said. "A lovely woman." He blushed slightly. "She gave me an autographed DVD of *Screams of the Sorority Sisters* for my birthday." He shook his head. "I'd only mentioned that film once, months before, and she remembered."

"Excuse me!" Maisy's voice echoed down the hall with the sound of the elevator.

All four turned that direction. A young couple appeared, moving fast, faces white, hair flying. They were buttoning their clothes as they headed for the front desk.

"Mr. and Mrs. Kirby?" Sara called.

They halted, stiff as boards, and then turned. They looked like they'd seen a ghost. Maybe several. "Oh shit," Teddy said softly. It wasn't just the ghosts he was worried about, but the fact that Constance Welling had just staggered out of the bar and was headed straight for them.

They all stood as the newlyweds approached. Mrs. Kirby pushed her hair off her face. "We're leaving."

"Why?" Adam asked. "Is something wrong?"

The couple looked at each other then back at Adam. "No. We just have to leave," said Mr. Kirby. He put his arm around his bride.

"Please, what happened!" Sara said. "Is there something wrong with the room?"

Mrs. Kirby laughed and the laugh spiraled out of control. "You want to know if something's wrong with the room?" she sputtered. "You don't know?" She hung onto her husband.

"We need to take this out of the lobby," Teddy said as Constance teetered up and leaned against the back of a chair for support.

"P'raps I can help you," she slurred. "I'm Constance Leigh Welling and I'm-"

"So drunk you can't stand upright," finished Adam. "Please, Ms. Welling, go to bed. This is none of your concern." He looked at the couple. "Let's go into my office and talk."

"No," said Mr. Kirby. "There's nothing to talk about. We just want you to send our bags over to the Doc Holiday Inn as soon as possible."

"We can send someone up to get them now." Teddy began.

"I'll go," Constance muttered, staring down at her own tits.

"No. We're leaving. Just send the luggage over."

With that, the couple turned and hurried toward the exit. Constance attempted to follow them, but tripped on her stilettos and fell onto a couch. Teddy sighed. "Jerry's off now, so I'll see she gets to her room."

"You're a saint," Adam told him as he watched his husband wrangle the drunken woman, who just kept babbling. He cringed as Constance Welling made a sound that announced the imminent departure of the contents of her stomach. Teddy, uncharacteristically gruff, pulled her off an area rug and onto tile then held onto one arm from as far away as he could, his face twisted in disgust as she regurgitated all of the evening's sins. She probably broke the Guinness world record for projectile vomiting.

Paul Butters looked green and headed for La Chatte Rouge, but Adam just smiled.

# 34
## *In Room 339*

"What do you think happened in here?" Sara followed Adam into 339, the room the Kirby's had fled moments before.

"No idea."

She stood still, taking in everything. The newlyweds had obviously been in bed watching TV. The set, tuned to a Jennifer Aniston rom-com, was still babbling happily to itself while Jen tried to figure out which hunk she adored most. The Kirby's robes were on the floor near the Jacuzzi, which was off, and there were a couple of empty Coke Zero cans, two sparkling water bottles, a half-eaten bag of potato chips, and a pack of Pecan Sandies on the table.

Adam opened the closet, pulled out the suitcases, then placed them on the bed and began filling them. Sara began putting smaller items from the dresser in an overnight case, working quietly, trying to feel the room, to soak up the atmosphere. Something felt wrong.

"Christ on a cracker!" Teddy Bellamy cried as he arrived.

Sara jumped. "Geez, Daddy, you scared the hell out of me!"

"Yeah, well, let me tell you, I got the worst job tonight. I practically gave myself a hernia trying to put that woman on her bed without getting any of her sick on me. Adam, you don't have to worry. I'm not a fan of Constance Welling anymore."

Adam laughed. "I'm glad you saw the light. We'd better send her assistant in there to take care of her."

"I knocked on his door. He's not there."

"I saw him with Chad a little while ago. They were swimming. Probably trying to get all of Ms. Welling's fingerprints off themselves." Sara paused. "Should we send a doctor up there?"

"Oh, maybe," said Teddy. "But I wouldn't bother. I checked with Jon. She's just drunk. Maybe we should have a maid leave some aspirin on her pillow."

Adam laughed. "Let's ask Rosa to check on her in the morning."

"I should have let her fall in her own sick, but I didn't want to have to touch that mess." Teddy shook his head, and then looked around. "So have you figured out what happened in here yet?"

"Not a clue so far," Sara told him. "We're getting their things together so I can drive the luggage over to Doc Holiday's."

"Why are you going?"

"Because I have the best chance of getting one of them to talk."

"Can't argue with that," Teddy said. "It feels peculiar in here. Did you notice?"

Adam grunted.

"I feel it," Sara said. "It's almost like the room is holding its breath."

"Sara, are you trying to scare me out of here?" Teddy chuckled and headed for the bathroom. "I'll get their toiletries. What the-"

Sara and Adam peered inside. The bathroom was damp. Everything in it was damp, the neatly folded towels, the floor, the walls, the tub and shower, too. But not wet. They hadn't bathed yet - there were no used towels. Beads of moisture clung to the toiletries, fogged the mirror, and coated the hair dryer attached to the wall. The toilet paper roll was damp but not sodden. A single set of wet footprints led from the bathroom to the room door; Sara hadn't noticed them before, but they were easy to see now.

"What happened in here?" Teddy asked.

"I've never seen anything like it," Adam said. "It's as if the room has been painted with steam."

"Well," Sara said, scooping up the rest of the toiletries. "I'm going to dry these off. No need to remind them of whatever happened in here."

The sensation she had felt in the main room was stronger in the bath and she was glad to leave it. She and Teddy dried the toiletries on the hotel robes by the Jacuzzi, but the air kept feeling heavier and heavier. She began to hear a high buzzing and glanced at Teddy. They locked eyes.

"You hear that?" he asked.

She nodded. Now she felt static electricity and looked at her arms, saw the fine hairs rising with goosebumps.

From the closet, Adam said, "We need to have the central air checked. There are blotches of cold all around me and the a/c isn't even on."

"Gather their luggage. We're leaving this room *now*," Teddy announced.

"Yes," said Sara, feeling cold air on the back of her neck.

"What?" Adam asked. "It's just the central air."

"Now!" Teddy's voice rarely held such authority. When it did, everyone listened.

Within thirty seconds they bustled out of the room, not bothering to speak, because the sense of urgency was too strong. They had to get out.

Teddy was last out, shooing the others ahead of him. He paused only long enough to make sure the door had locked, then the three of them carried the Kirbys' luggage downstairs and out to the hotel van.

# 35
## *Breakfast at Polly's Diner*

**WEDNESDAY**

Jackson Ballou faked a leg cramp and looked up at Adam Baxter-Bellamy as he massaged his calf. "I could use some bacon and eggs."

Adam, breathing easy and maintaining a stationary jog, grinned at him. "Your leg inevitably cramps in front of Polly's Diner."

"Must be something in the air."

"The smell of bacon." Adam looked at his watch and his stationary jog came to a stop. "Dale's egg white and spinach frittata is to die for."

Jackson grinned. "I'm going for bacon and eggs, hash browns, and pancakes."

"You're as bad as Teddy," Adam said. "Well, almost. At least you run a certain percentage of it off."

Jackson patted his abdomen. "Pure muscle."

"Showoff." Adam smiled.

"Thanks! Adam, how can you smell bacon and resist it?"

"It does smell good, but nothing tastes better than being thin feels."

They entered and Jackson led Adam to a table across from the cash register where Polly usually stationed herself. He didn't see her, but the diner was busy. She'd be around.

"Jackson," Adam said. "Let's take that table in the back where it's not so noisy and we don't have people's rear-ends in our faces while they're paying."

Jackson sighed. "All right. We'll do it your way this time, but you do understand that, as police chief, it's my duty to stay in the middle of things."

"You just want to be near Polly." Adam slid into the rear booth, taking the side facing the wall. "I'll let you keep an eye on the whole place. How's that?"

"Thanks." Jackson nodded at Nancy as she arrived with his black coffee and a green tea for Adam. "Careful, it's hot. Do you two want your usuals?"

"Absolutely," Jackson said.

"Coming right up." She bustled away, her purple pants looking ready to split, but in a nice way.

"Interesting crowd this morning." Jackson sipped his coffee from the thick white cup.

"Enlighten me."

"Well, Mr. Trudy and Pru from the antique store are finishing up what looks like a mountain of pancakes between them. They look happy. And Merlin Skinner just came in and is heading our way." He nodded a greeting to the sensitive-looking tattoo artist who took the booth next to theirs. Merlin barely nodded back. He was so famous for his inky artistry that customers came up from all over the state to get needled by him.

Nancy soon returned with refills and their breakfasts.

"Is Polly around this morning?"

"She sure is, Chief. She's in back with the produce delivery guy." Nancy shook her head. "I wouldn't want to be him right now. He tried to give her old tomatoes. I'll tell her you're here." She hustled off.

The front door opened. "Noble Mason," Jackson said, biting into a crisp strip of bacon.

"Good." Adam turned and waved at the handyman. "I need to talk to him."

Returning the wave, Noble approached. "Adam. Chief. How are you this morning?"

"Fine," Adam said. "I wanted to ask you about the bathroom you checked out for us yesterday up at Cliffhouse. Join us?"

"I'm waiting for my brother-in-law." Noble checked his watch. "He's running late. As usual." He sighed and sat down. "I'll tell you, business is a little too good these days."

"Too good?" Adam asked, digging into his frittata.

"Awful lot of small stuff lately. Graffiti, mostly."

"Surfside Hair?" Jackson asked. "We haven't had any more calls since then. Our only other call about graffiti was from the mortuary last month."

"Oh, yeah," Noble said. "That vandal was really tacky, putting skull and crossbones across those nice wooden entry doors of Casper's. Took a lot of work to put those doors right."

"Yeah." Jackson sipped coffee. "You've had other calls?"

"Sure have, all summer. Smaller stuff, like I told you. I've been paying Pat a lot of overtime lately." He shook his head. "So tell me, Adam, what happened on the third floor? Seems weird, having problems in rooms right next to each other."

"Same people. We moved them from the one with the broken glass to the one you checked out yesterday. They aren't at fault, though."

"What happened?"

"The mirror in 337 was an accident, but I wanted to talk to you about the bathroom in 339. Teddy and I meant to be there when you came by, but you know how that goes."

"Indeed. I'm sure Sara told you I couldn't find a damn thing wrong in there. The vents worked, the plumbing was fine. No leaks. She said the room was damp?"

"It was," Adam said. "Damnedest thing. The guests - newlyweds - came downstairs Monday night, scared out of their minds. They wouldn't talk. They couldn't leave fast enough. They wouldn't even wait for their luggage - we delivered it over to the Doc Holiday. Teddy would tell you they acted like they'd seen a ghost."

"What would you tell me?"

"I don't know what they saw, but they didn't like it," Adam said. "We - Teddy, me, and Sara - we all went up immediately. Everything seemed normal except for the bath."

"Was the bathroom door closed before you went in?" Noble asked.

"No, it was open."

"That's strange," Noble said.

"Quite." Adam glanced at Jackson. "There was something more to it. The couple had dropped everything and raced out of the room. I doubt they'd even been in the bathroom; they hadn't used the shower. I think they were watching TV. They hadn't used any towels but every single one of them was damp. The rugs, too. The toilet paper looked like it had sat in a sauna for an hour. Everything in that room was moist."

"Weird," said Noble. "Unless they were doing something freaky in there with a humidifier - after all, they're newlyweds. I surely can't figure it out."

"A humidifier?" Adam laughed. "I doubt that, but I guess we should consider it."

"They were scared?" Jackson asked.

Adam hesitated before answering. "Terrified."

"No idea why?"

"None. I just don't get it. I will say, though, that the room felt funny. Teddy and Sara were nervous as cats." He paused. "Honestly, I felt nervous too, and I don't know why."

"Aha," Noble said. "Maybe I should check the wiring. Feeling 'funny' wouldn't explain the damp, but sometimes you can get a funny buzz from electricity. Plays with your brain or something."

"There's something wrong with the central air in that room, too. It was creating cold spots even though it was off. Adam looked relieved. "Can you come out today?"

"Probably not. How about Friday? We're swamped."

"Please."

Noble nodded. "Of course, it might not be the wiring making you feel hinky. Maybe the Blue Lady is up to her old tricks. Somebody down at the market heard a couple of people say they saw her walking near the lake the night Booteous - excuse me, Norma Bailey - was killed."

"What?" Jackson asked. "As in the ghost of Blue Lady Lake?"

"What else?" Noble slurped coffee, a little smile trying to crook up one side of his mouth. "They say that when the Blue Lady walks, death walks with her."

"That's just what Teddy's aunt used to say."

Jackson sighed. Fairy tales wouldn't help him solve the murder of Norma Bailey. He watched as Francis Trudy and Prudence Pender Pope went out the door. For a couple well past retirement age, they moved quickly, bounces in their steps. *Must be love.*

Noble looked at his watch. "I'd fire Pat if he wasn't married to my little sister. Damn guy makes me wait too much."

"Speak of the devil," Jackson said as Pat Matthews walked in.

"I'll say. See you later, good talking with you." With a sigh, Noble joined Pat at the counter.

"Twelve children?" Jackson asked Adam, who had craned his head to look.

"Can you imagine?"

"No." Jackson pushed his plate back and grunted. "I'm stuffed."

Adam studied him. "What do you make of Cliffhouse's newest mystery?"

"'Once you eliminate the impossible, whatever remains, no matter how improbable, must be the truth.'"

"Spoken like a true detective. The question is, *what* remains in this case?"

"Good question. I-"

Polly Owen appeared at their table. "Nancy told me you were here, Chief. Was everything satisfactory?"

"It was great," Adam said.

"You two look as thick as thieves."

Jackson grinned. "We're telling ghost stories."

"Yeah, right." She turned to Jackson, "Are we still on for Friday night?"

"That's what I wanted to ask you."

"We're on, Chief."

"Good. I'll pick you up at seven."

"It's a date."

Polly laid a hand on his shoulder and gave it a quick squeeze before she left.

"Glad to see you're finally appreciating that woman," Adam said.

"I've always appreciated her."

"You're dating."

"Nah. We do things together."

"If you say so." Adam smiled.

"Excuse me. Chief Ballou?"

Jackson looked up and saw Francis Trudy bustling up the aisle toward him.

"What can I do for you, Frannie?"

The neat little white-haired man was out of breath, his cheeks pink, blue eyes focused on Jackson's. "I'm sorry to interrupt you, but would you mind coming next door?"

Jackson stood and put a ten down on the table. "What's up?"

"A vandal struck. Pru went out to the alley to throw out today's junk mail - my, there was a lot of it. The point is, she nearly fainted when she saw what someone has spray-painted across our back door."

"Let's go. I'll see you later," Jackson said. He followed Mr. Trudy out of the diner.

Trudy led him through the antique shop, past Prudence, who sat behind the cash register fanning herself, her face flushed. A moment later they exited the back door and stood in the alley. "Look. Look at this obscenity."

Francis Trudy reddened as he gestured at the six-foot-long red penis that ran across the door and wall. "It's obscene. I hate to think of Pru seeing that!"

"I recognize the style," Jackson told him. "I'm going to run over to the station. I'll be back soon. Don't touch anything."

"Chief Ballou, you couldn't pay me to touch that!"

# 36
## *The Boys at Chad's*

Chad Armstrong came out of his bedroom. "I smell coffee."

"Freshly made," Luke Donovan said. He sat at the kitchen table, his hair mussed with sleep.

"You didn't have to make coffee."

"Well, you didn't have to let me crash here, either." Luke stood, took two mugs from Chad's kitchen cabinet and poured.

"Not a problem." Chad took his coffee and sat down at the table. He yawned and stretched. "Have you made any decisions about work?"

Luke joined him. "I'm resigning."

"Good. Constance Welling is impossible." Chad had a hard time imagining how anyone could work for that woman. "How long have you worked for her?"

"Only three weeks. I hate the idea of breaking a commitment, but I can't do it any longer. I should have quit last night."

"She was too drunk - it would have been pointless," Chad said. "You'd just have to do it again."

"I suppose I should probably give her some kind of notice …"

"Don't be so honorable - she doesn't deserve notice. She's lucky if you don't press sexual harassment charges." Chad slurped coffee. "You do have a case, you know."

Luke shrugged. "I don't want the hassle."

"So what's your plan?"

"I don't want to go back to the city - at least not right away."

"What about the living situation? Do you have a place there?"

"I gave up my apartment when Constance hired me. I was at the end of my lease and it was a dive, anyway. It was so bad, I was starting to name the rats."

Chad laughed.

"I wouldn't mind staying here and finishing my Master's online if I could find new work and somewhere to stay."

"What are you studying?"

"English lit. It doesn't do me a whole lot of good in the real world, but I want to be a writer. That's part of the reason I wanted to work for Constance. I thought I might learn some useful things, even though her personality sucks."

Chad smiled. "Well, I'm sure you've learned some things *not* to do, anyway."

Luke nodded. "Indeed, I have."

"What do you like to write?"

"Historical fiction. That's what I like to read, too."

"Nice. I'm into sci-fi myself." He paused. "So you really like it up here, huh?"

"I love it."

"You and Sara got a little thing going on? Is that why?"

"There's nothing going on yet, but I'd be lying if I said I wasn't hopeful." He gave Chad an embarrassed smile.

"Sara's a great girl. I can tell she likes you."

"You think?"

"I really do."

"Does she have a boyfriend?"

Chad shrugged. "Not that I know of."

Luke smiled. "Well, regardless of whether or not that goes anywhere, I'm ready for something new. It's just time to start over, you know?"

Chad looked at him, an idea forming. "You work out, right?"

"I jog, lift weights, the usual. I hit the gym about four times a week."

Chad nodded. "One of my instructors left to go back to school. I need to hire a new one. Would you be interested?"

Luke's eyes brightened. "That's really nice of you to offer, but I'm no pro."

Chad leaned in and clasped his hands together. "You already know how to work out. I can teach you anything else you need to know."

"I-"

"The pay is decent to start, there's insurance, and you'd get raises. You'd have plenty of time to write. And, you can have the sleeper sofa here as long as you like."

"Don't you have to clear this with the owners of the place?"

"Don't worry about that. I do my own hiring, so consider it done. If you want it, that is."

Luke gave him a wide smile. "I'd be an idiot to say no."

"Great." Chad finished his coffee and stood. "I'm going to hit the shower. You're welcome to get yourself something to eat if you're hungry." He grabbed a blue bottle of sparkling water from the fridge.

"I'm fine," Luke said. "And Chad?"

"Yeah?"

"Thank you. For everything. I mean it."

Chad shrugged. "Not a problem, man." He headed to the bathroom and turned the shower on, glad that Luke would be staying.

He'd be a great addition to the Cliffhouse staff and although Chad hated admitting it, it would be nice having someone around, especially since he'd been spooked by the phantom voice. He wondered if he should have told Luke about that. *He'd only think I was crazy. And it probably didn't even happen, anyway.*

He took a swig of Blue Springs then set the bottle on the counter, stripped, and stepped into the shower. The water was hot and he relished the feel of the spray as it warmed and massaged his muscles. The steam thickened, and he leaned out of the shower to hit the switch to the overhead fan, then slid the glass door closed and lathered his face, the scruff along his jaw letting him know he could use a shave after his shower.

As he scrubbed, he felt something cool move across his abdomen. He rinsed his face, looked down, but saw nothing at first. Then he noticed the steam. It was even thicker now, unnaturally dense and oddly cool as it moved back and forth just inches from him.

"What the hell?"

He put a hand in it. It felt heavy, more solid than it should have. And it was cold. He stared, frozen in place as it changed from white to icy blue. It seemed to be lit from within.

Then he saw the face forming; eyes, nose, the horizontal slash of mouth.

He gasped and stepped back.

The foggy steam roiled into what looked like shoulders, and from there, two breasts, full and ripe. Then lush hips and legs.

"Oh, my God."

The woman smiled as chill wisps of fog formed into arms. She extended her hand and traced one cold finger along the edge of Chad's jaw.

"What the hell's going on?" Chad's whisper was hoarse. He blinked, rubbed his eyes. *It's real, it's really real.* "Who are you?" He stepped back and the phantom swayed, bobbing with the gentle currents of air.

The ghostly woman still smiled, but there was no joy in it; it was empty, lunatic. The grin widened, showing too much madness - and too many teeth - to be pretty anymore. She moved closer, wrapping cold arms around him. Frozen by terror, Chad felt the cold wispy fingers slide down his back and prod at the cleft of his buttocks.

"Stop!" He swiped at her.

Her form shattered and a shrill screech rent the air. The head jerked around and the face was inches away.

Chad threw himself back, crashed against the tile wall, slipping, nearly toppling over before gaining his feet.

The phantom's eyes widened with black hatred. Its lips drew back into a sneer, then widened as she screamed again. The shriek went on and the face began dripping like streams of hot wax until all Chad could see was a screaming skull.

The phantom shot into the shower doors. The glass exploded outward, shards splintering again as they hit the wall, mirror, sink, and floor. The Blue Springs bottle toppled and shattered as the scream faded.

Luke was banging on the door. "Are you okay?"

Chad grabbed both towels from the rod. He wrapped one around his waist and tossed the other over the shattered glass and stepped out of the shower. He threw the door open and stared at Luke, who was as white as the bathroom tile. "I heard screaming-" He looked at the shower door with wide eyes. "What happened?"

"You heard?"

"Yes! What the hell was it?" Luke stepped into the bathroom.

"There was a woman ... well, not really a woman, but a - I don't know what." Chad was having a hard time catching his breath.

Luke moved toward the shower and peered inside, then looked around the small room, and finally at Chad. "A woman? In here?"

"Yes," said Chad. "She ran out of the room." He pointed to the door. The woman was gone, but he saw something else. "Oh, my God!" He stepped out of the bathroom.

Luke was at his side. "What is it?"

"Look." Chad pointed to the floor. On the carpet, a trail of wet footprints led from the bathroom, across the living room to the balcony slider.

Luke's eyes were saucers. "What the hell?"

Chad moved to the glass door, slid it open and saw that the footprints continued. They seemed to walk right off the edge of the balcony. He opened the door, stepped to the railing and gazed down. *Where did she go?*

Luke was beside him, his knuckles bleached white as he gripped the railing and gazed down.

Chad turned to his new roommate. "I guess there's something I need to tell you."

# 37
## *More Broken Glass*

"I slipped and fell and the shower door just shattered," Chad said. He took a long pull on a bottle of water. "It was intense."

"I'll bet." Sara Bellamy looked the fitness director up and down. He wore shorts and a clean white T-shirt. "You're okay?"

He nodded. "Not a scratch, I'm fine."

"Good. I'm going to send someone to clean up the glass. Do you want to supervise or maybe hang at the gym or something?"

"Yeah, I'll go down and do some paperwork I've been putting off." He paused, looking anxious. "When will the shower be fixed?"

"Probably not before Friday. Do you mind showering in the gym?"

"Would it be a problem to put me in a guest room?"

"Not at all. Let's see." She consulted the computer. "You live in 310, right?"

"Yes."

"I can put you in 314 ..." She paused, thinking about all the plumbing problems on the third floor. "Can I ask you a question, Chad?"

"Sure."

"Did you see anything before this happened?"

"Like what?"

Now she was sure he was frightened. "A lot of mist. You know, maybe you tripped because the bathroom fogged up badly?"

His eyes widened. "Yeah, I mean, how did you know?"

"It's happened before. Noble Mason is going to look into it as soon as he can. Anyway, how about I put you on the second floor instead. 212? King bed, fold-out sofa, mini-fridge and microwave. That should be okay for a couple days, right?"

Chad smiled, his relief evident. "It would be super. Thanks."

She handed him the key. "Can I ask you something else?"

"Sure."

"Constance Welling was down here looking for Luke. Do you know if he's okay?"

"He's fine. He's giving notice. He's staying with me for now. By the way, remember, I was looking to hire a new gym instructor?"

"Of course."

"I hired Luke. He has the qualifications, he loves it here, and I think he'll be excellent with our clients."

Sara barely kept her jaw from dropping, then had an even harder time not hugging Chad. "I think that's wonderful!"

He cocked an eyebrow, and then grinned back. "Glad you approve."

"Oh, yes, I approve. So will my dads." Sara regarded Chad. "Now I want to ask you something really weird."

"What?"

"Footprints."

"What?" His eyes widened.

"Wet footprints. Did you see any? I know it sounds crazy, but there were footprints in one of the other rooms with the fog problem."

"Yes, we saw them. Small, like a woman's."

Sara nodded. "Don't say anything to anyone other than myself or my dads. I want to talk to someone who knows more about these things than I do."

"Not Constance…"

"No, not Constance. Maisy Hart. The older woman who was at dinner with me and my dads last night."

"I know her." Chad nodded. "She's a nice lady."

"I'll tell her what happened. She might have some insights."

# 38
## *Ghost Stories*

"This smells as good as it looks," Jackson said as Teddy set a platter of fragrant glazed Cornish game hens on the table. Adam arrived next, carrying bowls of roasted broccoli and whipped sweet potatoes.

"My dads are fine cooks!" Sara said, passing Jackson the potatoes.

"Indeed." Jackson hadn't expected to be sitting down to dinner in Teddy and Adam's cabin this evening, but he was enjoying himself. "I don't know why I was invited," Jackson said, "but I'm glad I'm here."

Teddy took his seat as Adam opened a bottle of white wine and poured.

"This looks great." Jackson sipped his water and tasted the wine. "Nice."

"Chablis suited to poultry," Adam said. "It's another offering from Chantrieri Winery. Very smooth. We're featuring it at the wine tasting this weekend. I especially enjoy the citrus notes."

Jackson nodded. "So I have to ask: Why am I here tonight?"

"It was my idea," said Sara. "I hope you don't mind, but we want to pick your brain a little about what's going on at Cliffhouse."

"Uh, sure," Jackson said. "I heard a little about it this morning."

Adam nodded. "I was going to tell you more about it at breakfast, but it didn't work out." He looked at his game hen, picked up a knife and started carving.

"You're all being very mysterious," Jackson said.

"Sorry." Teddy nibbled a wing. "Perfect, Adam. Superb."

Jackson did the same. "Delicious. Don't keep me in suspense. What's going on at the lodge?"

"Weirdness," Sara said. "A lot of weirdness. We had another incident today."

"Somebody enlighten me, for Christ's sake."

"He's fun to tease," Teddy said to Adam. "Isn't he?"

"He is."

"Stop that." Sara laughed.

Adam set down his fork. "This morning at breakfast, you heard about the odd things that happened in the bathrooms on the third floor."

"Yes."

"You haven't heard all the details." Adam studied his plate.

"And it happened again today, in another room," Sara said. "This morning, our fitness director, Chad, broke the glass doors on his shower. He said he slipped and fell, but there was more to it than that. He was really frightened. He saw the heavy fog and wet footprints on the carpet, like the ones the maids saw in 337."

"Footprints?"

"Yep. They started in the bathroom and disappeared off his balcony. I've seen them before. We all have. And I think Chad saw something more, but I don't know. He was terrified and asked to switch rooms while repairs are made. And I have a feeling he's not going to want to move back up to the third floor."

"We're doing renovations on that floor and the rooms with problems haven't been open very long," Teddy explained. "That may be why things are happening up there. The renovations are stirring things up. I've been doing some reading."

Sara nodded. "Real research, he means. Not watching ghost shows on TV." She glanced at Adam. "This afternoon, I talked with Maggie, the maid who was injured when 337's mirror broke. She told me she saw a ghostly woman in the mirror who said her name multiple times."

"Maggie and Jenna both heard their names in those two rooms on several different occasions before all this happened," Teddy said.

"It's easy to imagine images forming in steam or fog," Jackson said.

"Exactly," said Adam. "And water pipes sometimes hum. That might be all it is."

"I spoke with Maggie's supervisor after that," Sara said. "Rosa calls the phantom *Santa Muerte*, the feminine equivalent of the Grim Reaper. That jibes with the Blue Lady stories."

"Noble Mason said that when the Blue Lady walks, death is imminent." Jackson said. "I have to admit that when he mentioned people had witnessed her the night Norma Bailey was murdered, it caught my attention. Wish it was a real clue." He looked at Sara. "But you want my opinion on what's going on at Cliffhouse?"

"Yes, a cop's opinion." She smiled.

"Well, have you checked out all the physical possibilities? Plumbing problems, things like that?"

Adam speared a broccoli floret. "Noble's checked 337 and found nothing wrong, but he's coming back Friday to recheck the third floor. He said something funny in the wiring could cause people to feel odd things."

Jackson nodded. "Could someone be messing with you or your employees? Do you have any enemies who might play destructive jokes?"

Teddy and Adam looked at each other, then at Sara, and all three shook their heads. "None we can think of," Adam said.

"I'd check with the maids about recently dumped boyfriends, things like that, and see if there's anything else your fitness guy wants to tell you." He paused. "I can take some prints, but I doubt we'll get anything useful. If it happens again, call me before cleaning up."

"Thanks," Adam said. "We'll do that. Any other ideas?"

"Not offhand. It's an interesting problem. I'd like to see those rooms on the third floor. Just have a little look around."

"Of course," Teddy said. "Do you have time for a quick tour after dinner?"

"I do." He sipped his water. "You know, all the time I've lived here, I've never thought of the Blue Lady stories as anything but campfire tales." He chuckled. "If grown people are claiming to have seen her, it makes me wonder if UFOs will be landing here soon."

Teddy grinned. "Let's hope not. UFOs are too much, even for me."

"I like our poltergeist," Sara said, "but that's enough for me."

"Poltergeist?" Jackson asked.

"The one who moved my bread."

"Things like that happen from time to time," Teddy said.

Jackson was surprised Adam didn't look annoyed. "I've seen a few things I haven't been able to explain over the years," he said. "But not many."

"Like what?" Sara asked.

"When I was twenty-two, living in my first apartment, some funny things happened now and then."

"Such as?" Teddy asked.

"Well, similar to your poltergeist. I guess I had one, too. Sometimes things moved by themselves. It never occurred to me that it was out of the ordinary. I thought maybe there was a gravitational glitch, to be honest."

Adam laughed. "Really?"

Jackson raised his hand. "Swear to God. My point is, usually there's a plausible explanation for things. But not always."

# 39
## *Constance in the Closet*

Today was a shit-fest from start to finish. Constance Welling stubbed her cigarette out on the windowsill. She'd had high hopes the newlyweds' story of being driven from Cliffhouse by an evil haunting would provide the linchpin in her book about the lodge. She had driven herself around the lake to the Doc Holiday Inn to talk to them, but the shit-diddling manager wouldn't let her go up to their room, let alone tell her the number. Instead, he phoned them and proceeded to fall all over himself apologizing for interrupting their precious honeymoon. No wonder they said no, when he approached them like a shitty little snake in the grass afraid of his own shadow.

And when she'd arrived back at Cliffhouse, she'd found a letter from Luke under her door. The little bitch had tendered his resignation, not even giving two weeks' notice. And he obviously had waited until she left to do it.

She hadn't seen him since he'd taken off with that muscle-bound lunkhead, Chad Armstrong. They were probably gay for each other; that would explain a lot about the way they had treated her. *Tough luck, Skanky Sara. He doesn't want you, either!*

Constance stomped across the room and tried the adjoining door. *If he thinks I'm going to pay for his room, he's very much mistaken.* "God damn it." The door was locked. She got out a credit card and jimmied it.

The room was empty, his clothes gone, even his toothbrush, which she'd intended to dip in the toilet. In fact, the only thing left in the bathroom was the bottle of aftershave she'd given him. *Ungrateful bastard!* She checked everywhere and found only a pile of her books and flyers.

She took all of it and slammed back into her own room. She thought about burning the flyers in the wastebasket, but the smoke would attract the idiots who ran the place.

Taking a deep breath, she centered herself. *I am Constance Leigh Welling and I always get what I want. Nothing will stop me from getting my story and writing this book and becoming even more famous! I am Constance Leigh Welling and I will prevail.*

After repeating the mantra three times, she pulled a satchel out of the back of her closet and extracted a small electronic device she'd procured online for "research." It had cost a small fortune, but it would pay for itself when it allowed her to enter room 337 and take photos. *And now is as good a time as any.*

She crammed the device, disguised to look like a marking pen, into one pocket and her phone into the other. Then she left her room, headed for the elevator, and when it arrived, punched in the third floor. It was a quick trip.

Stepping out of the car, she looked around. The floor was silent; she was confident she'd have no problems. She followed the hallway, counting down the room numbers as she passed - 343, 341, 339, and finally, 337. She was still alone.

She reached into her pocket and withdrew the tool. She uncapped it; there was a small circular piece where the felt should have been. She reached under the door handle, feeling for the tiny opening in the lock box, then plugged the circular part of the marker into the hole. The lock unlatched, easy as an ugly girl.

She slipped the device out and stepped into the room, letting the door click closed behind her then turned on the light.

The room was vacant and immaculate, smelling of clean sheets and chlorine from the Jacuzzi. *I can't believe I'm paying so much for my room and it doesn't even have a hot tub! Maybe I'll come back and take a dip later. And pee in it!*

Eyes closed, she took a long, deep, cleansing breath, the kind she taught at her metaphysical workshops. *I am Constance Leigh Welling. I am a famous authoress. I always get my story.* Centered now, she opened her eyes. The room felt empty. She explored, pausing to lift the bedspread up and spit on a pillow, then entered the bathroom, finding absolutely nothing out of the ordinary. She kicked the toilet, then took another deep breath. *I am Constance Leigh Welling. I am a famous psychic and channeler.*

"Hello? Is anyone here? Do you know my name? Can you say it?"

Silence answered.

"Damn it, my name is Constance. What's your name? Silent Sam? Talk to me."

There was nothing and it was beginning to piss her off. She wished she wasn't out of happy pills. "I don't have all night. Show yourself!"

As she left the bathroom, she heard the entry door click, sending her about a foot into the air. As the handle depressed, she slid a closet door open and stepped inside, closing it just as several people entered the room. *Now what the hell am I supposed to do?* She would be found out the moment the guests started unpacking. *People shouldn't be allowed to check in after six p.m.!*

"The maid must have forgotten to turn off the light."

"I don't blame her."

"Me, neither."

The voices belonged to the Husbands Bellamy and their daughter. They began talking about a broken mirror in the bathroom - and an apparition. *What broken mirror? What apparition? What are they talking about?*

"The maid saw the Blue Lady in here," said Sara.

*Blue Lady? Sweet!* Constance's creative juices began to flow.

Footsteps passed by, and then she heard a new voice, masculine, say, "Looks like a normal bathroom to me."

*Ballou! They brought the Chief of Police up here! Was there a murder?* She closed her eyes, barely able to contain her excitement. That would guarantee her a bestseller. *Oh, delight! But what if they find me? He'll try to arrest me. Damn you for the little shit-bird you are, Luke Donovan. How DARE you desert me? You should be here to take the rap. Maybe I'll say you made me do it.*

The voices moved toward the hot tub. Constance controlled her breathing, straining to hear every word.

It began getting damp in the closet, a little chilly. She ignored it, listening to Slutty Sara talk about the phantom the maid had seen. She called it a water elemental, the Blue Lady, Santa Muerte. Constance memorized the words that would put her on the New York Times Bestseller List for at least a year.

She caught the scent of the lake suddenly; she could almost taste it. It was nonsense, but she thought she felt fog moving over her skin. The fat Bellamy started spouting off about folktales concerning water spirits, and it sounded like a load of crap, but she could hear the others, evidently all in fine moods, egging him on for every footnote he could dredge up. *Hurry the fuck up and get out of here!*

Constance was getting a little freaked out in the darkness; she felt thick mist clogging her lungs. *What the hell?* She listened and heard them talking about moving the couple - the Kirbys - to 339 because of the broken mirror. So that was the room they'd fled, not this one. *Well, shit.*

*Constance ...* The voice was a feminine whisper in her ear.

She nearly screamed.

*Constance ...*

It moved into her other ear on a chill breeze.

Something touched the back of her neck, then she felt cold moisture trickle down her spine. *Oh bloody shit! What's going on? Leave me alone!*

The human voices drew closer, talking about visiting 339.

Something slithered around her shoulders. *Go away! Go! I've gotta get out of here, damn you!*

*Constance ...*

The voice was so close it seemed as if it were inside her head. Invisible cold fingers tried to pry open her mouth.

She heard the room door open. *Go, go, go, go, go!*

*Constance ...*

The door closed. She didn't wait, but slammed out of the closet. Behind her, in the blackness, she saw a woman's face, angry and terrible, for just an instant.

*Constance ...*

The lights were off and she stumbled and fell. The rug felt damp under her hands as she crawled.

*Constance ...*

The voice was following her in a cloud of dank lake fog. When she reached the tiled entry, she stood and grabbed the door handle. Edging it open, she waited one horrible second, cold fingers caressing her neck, for the others to disappear into 339.

Then she fled without looking back.

# 40
## *Hammerhead in the Dark*

The urge was upon him but the Lady was not. At his very core, he felt the need to take a soul. If it were morning he would be out now, hunting for a stray hiker or a tourist with a flat tire. But hunting at night, in town, was foolish.

While her presence irritated him, he missed her at this moment, because of her ability to let him kill without worry. It would feel so good to take a life, to look into eyes as the soul poured out of them and into one of his mirrors. He burned with desire.

From the darkness of his porch, he stared into the night. Pines hid much of the sky, but he saw the brilliant moon and a swath of the Milky Way overhead. *I look forward to your next visit.* He sent the thought out, but no one answered.

As he was about to turn and go into the house, he clearly heard her voice on the wind. *Soon. Very soon.*

# 41
## *In the Theodosia Suite*

Sara sat at Theodosia's antique desk in the living room of her apartment. Tall windows gave her a view of the Kelly Forest to the north and the lake to the west.

She had loved this suite since she was a little girl visiting her aunt. Much of the furniture had been Theodosia's, from the desk and four-poster bed to the cherrywood dining table and chairs, and the Tiffany lights that hung from the ceilings. Her dads had moved all the Tiffany table lamps to their own cabin before they began renting the suite to guests, but now Sara intended to bring some back. She had already returned the blue shell Tiffany to its rightful place on the desk. It was her favorite, and Theodosia's, too.

Gone were her aunt's antique Oriental rugs, auctioned to help pay for the lodge's restoration. They'd replaced them with new Orientals that were just as beautiful.

Beyond the windows, moonlight rippled on the lake and cast just enough light to let her see the stone springhouse nestled against the pines. She suppressed a shiver; it reminded her of the evil witch's house from an old fairy tale her aunt used to tell her.

She walked into the kitchen for a bottle of water from the spooky springhouse. She drank deeply. The taste was pure and certainly not evil.

Since her dads reopened the well, the demand for Blue Springs had steadily risen; now they were even selling small quantities to gourmet shops in town. It wasn't the first time the well had been a commercial venture. On the wall in the lobby there was a print of the Naiad Springs label from the 1920s featuring a Maxfield Parrish-style girl in a bathing suit on a swing.

Sara returned to the desk, wondering why the spring had been sealed all these years. *Maybe the water table was low or something. Maybe the girl on the swing took on new meaning when the Bodice Ripper struck.* That gave her a little shiver. She doubted her dads knew, but thought Aunt Maisy might. *Maybe I'll invite her up for tea and a chat.*

The old-fashioned desk phone rang. "Hello?"

"Sara?"

"Yes, who's this?"

"Luke Donovan."

"Luke! I'm so glad to hear from you. Congratulations on your new job. When are you starting?"

"Tomorrow. Chad's going to train me. I just wanted to thank you and your dads for approving of me."

Sara felt a little squiggle in her belly. "We're very glad to have you here."

"I have a question."

"Go ahead."

"Does working for you preclude my asking you out sometime?"

"We're pretty informal up here," she told him.

"Does that mean …"

"Yes. You can ask me out." She smiled to herself.

"Then I'm going to ask you if you'd like to go with me to the End of Summer Party this weekend."

"Sure, if you don't mind picnicking with my dads. It's a tradition."

"That would be great. I'd love to."

"Pizza's here." She heard Chad's voice in the background.

"You'd better go," Sara said. "See you tomorrow!" Hanging up, she decided a shower would be nice.

The huge bathroom held a separate shower and a big whirlpool tub in addition to double sinks. The whirlpool had replaced an equally oversized clawfoot tub; the fixtures and mirrors were new, but the tile dated back to the Twenties. The floors and walls were done in shell pink with narrow blue tiles accenting them. It was retro to her eye and she loved it, partly because it reminded her of Aunt Theodosia.

The room felt a little damp so she turned on a fan. There was a light mist on the mirrors and walls, almost as if she'd already showered. *Odd.* She pulled a couple of the big fluffy bath towels off the shelf.

They were damp. Folded and damp. Like in the newlyweds' room, but not as damp, just misted. The tiniest thrill of fear shot through her. It was likely nothing; after all, the door had been closed all day. She left the bathroom to call for fresh towels. As she waited for Housekeeping to pick up, she thought she heard a faint meow near the bed and caught the faintest whiff of *White Shoulders.*

"Aunt Theodosia?" she asked. "Are you here?"

She heard another meow, louder, and smiled.

# 42
## *Pat Matthews*

Pat Matthews, brother-in-law to Noble Mason, husband to Taffilynn, father to a full count of disciples, always needed money. That was the way it was when you had a fecund wife and a Xanax habit.

Xanax had played a minor role in his life when he had enough kids for a bowling league, but as he and Taffilynn humped their way toward an entire baseball team - *be fruitful and multiply* - he required more and more benzos to offset the sleepless nights spent worrying about money.

Now he had enough kids to supply Jesus with a new set of apostles, and was working on number thirteen. At the rate they were going, in another five years, he'd have a hockey team. *Maybe sooner. Twins run in both our families.*

He popped another few milligrams.

Noble was a generous employer, no doubt because Taffilynn was his little sister, and he refrained from hiring another employee because he knew Pat needed the overtime. Noble picked up the slack instead, always kind, always tired. Pat felt bad for him sometimes. Still, when business was slow, there was nothing Pat's brother-in-law could do for him.

Pat swallowed another Xanax as he shook the can of Fire Engine Red spray enamel. He wished the little bbs weren't so noisy, and looked around. Main Street was deserted at ten on a weeknight and nobody was near the library. It was safe.

Guilt about making work sometimes ate at him, but he had mouths to feed, and taking care of your family was the only thing that really mattered. Taffilynn insisted on working from home. She counseled new mothers on breastfeeding; she was an expert there. But he still hated that she needed to contribute to the family income, even though her Internet consultations brought in less than fifty dollars a month.

Pat, feeling a tad more relaxed now, wished she could do it simply as charity work, because needing more income meant he wasn't doing his job as well as a husband should. *Except for getting her pregnant. I'm a pro, there.* The thought made his mind jump to Dr. Siechert. He needed to see him for more Xanax soon. Once, the doctor had told him that if he ever wanted a vasectomy - the ultimate stress relief, Siechert counseled - he would be happy to provide it on the sly. Pat prayed about it, but couldn't get an answer. He always came away knowing the Lord wouldn't be happy; if God didn't want him to be fruitful, he wouldn't have given him lively sperm and a fertile wife. He pushed the sinful thought from his mind.

Instead, he would continue creating extra jobs for himself. He gave the can another shake and uncapped it and began spraying a tall red penis on the glass double doors of the library. It only took a moment. He added some hairs to the testicles before shading in some veins, defining the helmet, then adding the exit point and an explosion of semen above. He carefully kept the paint to the glass doors because the library facade was brick and would be very expensive to clean. If the town had to pay that much, they might try harder to catch him.

He stepped back into the shadows and surveyed his work. *Perfect.* Though smaller than the penises he'd left on other public places, this was the first time he'd dared to emblazon a front entrance on Main Street, and the first on a publicly-owned building. It was a risk, but one he wanted to take because he was angry with Jordan Cartwright for glaring at his kids when they closed his precious piano lid on Labor Day. No one had the right to look angry at his children except their parents and Jesus. At least the man hadn't chastised them; if he had, he would have found a red penis on his house!

Pat put the spray can in his pocket and began walking to his van, keeping to the shadows, still thinking about Cartwright. He'd parked blocks away.

When the kids had gotten a little out of hand and made Cartwright glare - as if a piano were more important than a child! - he had also been very unhappy with Sara Bellamy, who was abrupt with them for running in her precious lobby. He'd considered marking Cliffhouse for that, but they had been guests there that day, so he cut her a little slack. He really wanted to paint a penis on Chief Ballou's black and white for his disciplinary behavior, but that was too risky so God would have to see to that.

Pat saw vehicle lights approaching and ducked into the shadowed entryway to Trudy's Antiques. It was one of the police cruisers patrolling the town. *They might see the library doors.* The paint would be fresh, still tacky, and he wasn't far enough away yet to be safe. He prayed they wouldn't notice the graffiti.

He allowed himself one more Xanax - *I wish there was a Pez dispenser for these!* - he quickly walked the remaining blocks to the Presbyterian church where he retrieved his van and drove home to his family. *A good night's work. Thank you, Lord.*

# 43
## *Jackson Visits the Library*

**THURSDAY**

The graffiti artist had struck again, this time defacing the Cliffside Library. Jackson put down the almost-useless lab report on Norma Bailey; the only interesting item was that the water in her lungs came from the lake.

He pulled into the slot next to Jordan Cartwright's white Honda in the otherwise empty lot, then checked his watch. The library wouldn't open for a few more minutes.

Jackson saw the damage from several yards away; it covered the front doors. Immediately, he could see why Jordan had sounded upset on the phone. There was no mistaking the illustration: it was another giant phallus, erect, red, and in the throes of ejaculation, complete with a hairy set of low-hangers. As he neared, he saw Cartwright on the other side of the glass, covering the image from the inside with newspapers.

Jackson took several pictures of the damage from the outside. All in all, the grotesquery had been painted with pride - not necessarily by someone who had taken much time to do it, but rather, Jackson figured, by a person who had developed substantial skill at his craft. *Given the recent amount of tags, this guy ought to be a pro by now.*

He tapped on the glass and Cartwright let him in.

"Welcome, Chief," Jordan said. "I'm sorry to bother you so early." His eyes fluttered between Jackson and the floor.

"Morning. Looks like you had a night visitor."

The librarian's cheeks pinked. "Uh, yes. I'm trying to get it covered up till we can, uh, get it taken care of. It doesn't come off with water."

"Have you called Noble Mason?"

"Not yet. I wasn't sure what the protocol was on something like this." His eyes flickered toward the obscenity. "The library opens in five minutes."

"I'll give him a call when I leave. Meantime, let's get the outside covered. Can't have the kids seeing this."

The two men stepped outside and began taping up paper. Within two minutes the door was covered.

Jackson stood back. "Well, it isn't too pretty, but it is an improvement."

Jordan nodded. "At least we can open the doors."

"All right. Let's go inside. I need to ask you a few questions, then I'll be out of your hair."

"Okay. My help called in sick today, so I'm here alone. We usually get an influx of people in the morning."

A warning bell went off in Jackson's head. "Who's your help?"

"Herman Mudgett."

"Sick, is he?"

"Yes, he sounded pretty bad on the phone." Jordan flipped the "Closed" sign to "Open." On cue, a car pulled into the lot.

Jackson filed Herman Mudgett's name away in his mind. There seemed to be two kinds of criminals - those who were ashamed of their crimes and didn't like facing what they'd done, and those who showed up at a crime scene the next day to see the shock on everyone's faces. In his experience, most perps fell into the latter category, and Jackson wanted to see who would appear at the library this morning. He wasn't discounting Herman Mudgett; it was possible he'd done it and was now too ashamed to come into work, but he doubted that was the case. He didn't fit the profile. Mudgett was heavy-set, over thirty, and slow in movement and wit. This graffiti artist probably fell into a more common category - kids with more opportunity than imagination.

"Pardon me, but I need to station myself at the desk," said Jordan.

Cartwright wore a suit, but otherwise, he looked very much the same person he was when he played piano at the lodge. Jackson followed him to his post, took out his notepad and leaned against the counter. "Nothing else was out of place when you got here?"

"Nothing," said Cartwright. "Everything was normal, except the door."

It had been the same in every other case; still, he had to document it. As Jackson wrote on his pad, the front doors opened.

"Hello, Mrs. Mudgett," said Cartwright.

Herman Mudgett's mother scowled. A well-dressed little army tank of an old lady, she seemed to roll toward the front desk. The only thing Jackson knew about her was that up until her fifties, she'd had a habit of closing down bars and getting handsy with other women's husbands. Some time in her sixties, she'd found Jesus; now, at seventy-something, she was in charge of the Baptist's baking club. "I'm here for those herbal remedy books I phoned you about." Her voice was a rasping croak. Apparently, she'd polished off one too many cigarettes before the Lord had intercepted her soul.

"I hope Herman is feeling better." Jordan reached under the desk and produced a short stack of books.

"He has a head cold, poor baby." Mrs. Mudgett eyed the stack. Her down-turned mouth crawled as if she tasted something unpleasant. "Humph. I'll look around some before I go. You have any others on the subject?"

Cartwright pointed. "Last aisle."

Her head followed his finger and she trundled away.

"I hear they spray-painted the hair salon. Do you think it's the same vandal?"

Jackson nodded. "I'm certain. Same style of ... artwork."

The librarian flushed again.

The front doors opened and two children entered, followed by their *shushing* mother. They gawked at the papered-over doors. The boy reached out a hand to touch the tape, but his mother grabbed his wrist and led him and his sister deeper into the building. Before the door had a chance to close, Beverly Hill arrived. The mortician's wife was a woman Jackson had never cared for.

As if she owned the place, Mrs. Hill approached, a book in hand. "It seems you've had some trouble with vandalism."

Jackson wondered how she knew it was vandalism, then chalked it up to common sense. Beverly Hill was a hawk. The Cliffside grapevine seemed to have a direct line to her, and surely the previous graffiti incidents hadn't escaped her vigilant watch.

Jordan nodded. "It's being taken care of."

She turned to Jackson. "You haven't even been able to catch the hooligan who marked *our* doors yet." She glanced at the door. "Kids can be such bastards," she announced for all to hear. She was thin, nearing fifty, with constipated features, expensive jewelry, and hair landscaped into a perfectly puffed dark brown halo.

"How can I help you, Mrs. Hill?" Jordan spoke softly, as if hoping Beverly would follow suit.

"Well," she said, just below a bellow, "I checked this book out a couple days ago and once I got it home I discovered it was missing some pages." She plunked the hardcover down: *Dr. Richard Akin's Tea Remedies for Indigestion*. On her wrist, she wore a gold Rolex Oyster, which had to be a knock-off, unless Casper had more money than good sense.

Jordan picked the book up and thumbed through it.

"I'd like to return it," she said, digging into her purse - a gym bag-sized monstrosity of what was certainly the finest leather. She found her library card and set it on the counter. "I want a refund."

He blinked at her. "A refund?"

From the corner of his eye, Jackson saw Mrs. Mudgett's head swivel.

"Yes," said Beverly. "A credit toward my account." She tapped her library card.

"Do you want to ... pick something else?" Jordan Cartwright seemed to be having trouble understanding.

Jackson, too. *Who in their right mind demands a refund on a library book? What does that even mean?*

"Yes," said Beverly. "I want another copy of this book and I'll take no responsibility for the damage to this one."

Cartwright looked at it. "I'm afraid this is our only copy, but I can put in a request and see if another library has it." He looked at her apologetically. "It will take a few days."

Mrs. Mudgett trundled up and stopped at Beverly's side. The two women, one the wealthiest in all of Cliffside, the other wanting to be, exchanged unpleasant glances. "I guess that will have to do," said Beverly sidling away from Mrs. Mudgett as if she hadn't bathed.

Cartwright took her card and ran it through the computer. As he did, Mrs. Mudgett gawked around Beverly. Cartwright cleared his throat. "May I help you, Mrs. Mudgett?"

The old lady pursed her lips. "I can't read some of the titles you chose for me."

Her voice reminded Jackson of a piece of gravel stuck in a garbage disposal.

"The writing's too small. Would you read them off to me?"

"It will be just a moment." Jordan's voice was calm and friendly, and Jackson admired the man's patience.

"Maybe you could help me, Chief," said Mrs. Mudgett.

Before Jackson could reply, Jordan spoke up. "Chief Ballou is here on business, Mrs. Mudgett. I'm afraid you'll have to wait a moment." He looked at Beverly Hill. "There are some missing pages?" he asked. "Is there anything else?"

"A few pencil markings. Very distracting and disrespectful. Makes it difficult to read. I got a headache trying and ended up having to lie down."

"I'm sorry to hear that." Cartwright typed something into the computer.

"It was very inconvenient for me." Beverly eyed Mrs. Mudgett, who had stepped forward, her eyes on the damaged book.

"You're returning it, you say?" Mrs. Mudgett took a corner of the book, pulling it toward her. At the same time, Beverly Hill slapped a hand on it. Herman's mother was not deterred, and managed to get a grip on the bottom corner. Beverly, just as determined, held onto it at the top.

Jordan looked up from his computer.

Jackson watched, waiting for one of the women to let go. Neither did. They faced each other, the book the only distance between them. Both pairs of eyes glinted with challenge.

"Mrs. Hill?" Cartwright's voice held the cautious uncertainty reserved for men standing on the ledges of tall buildings. "You intended to return the book, didn't you?"

Beverly faced the librarian. "Since I have to wait for another copy, I've changed my mind." She yanked the book from Mudgett's hands with a snap of her wrist, her alleged Rolex flashing. "I'll return this one when my other copy arrives."

Mrs. Mudgett wasn't a graceful loser. She huffed, spun on her heel, and steamrolled back into the stacks.

Beverly unzipped her purse and stuffed the book into it, looking around as if she were afraid of being accosted by another book thief. "Very well," she said. "I'll not be responsible for any late charges should the other copy take its time arriving." With that, the mortician's wife stalked out of the library.

"I'm sorry about that," said Cartwright.

Jackson held up a hand. "No problem."

"Let me go help Mrs. Mudgett, then I'll be right with you." The librarian stepped around the desk and disappeared. Within moments, he returned with the woman and several books. He got her checked out, ushering her along with a constant, if strained, smile.

"Give Herman my best," said Jordan. "I hope he'll be able to work tomorrow."

Mrs. Mudgett gave him a smile or a scowl - Jackson couldn't tell which - and trudged out of the door.

"Do you have any suspects yet?" Jordan asked.

Jackson shrugged. "Not really, but I would guess it's high school kids."

"What happens when you catch them?"

"Usually, if it's a kid having a good time, we just instill a little fear in him. At this point, though, it's destructive enough that I think charges will be pressed. In that case, the perpetrator will be arrested and fined."

"I'm sure it's just some kids who should be in here reading instead of out there creating mischief. It's sad, really."

Jackson glanced up as the doors opened and saw the town tattoo artist entering. "Interesting clientele."

Cartwright replied so quietly Jackson had to lean in to hear him: "Merlin comes in early because he doesn't open his shop until noon. He checks out a lot of classical music CDs and art books. I wish he wouldn't doodle in them, though. It's in pencil and masterful, but he likes to draw nudes of both genders. I've asked him not to; children may be exposed."

"Doodling's a hard habit to break," Jackson said, wondering if the Wizard of Ink was doodling on more than books.

"Here comes your father," Jordan said.

Jackson's stomach did a little flip as Lee Ballou walked in, stopped cold, and stared at his son.

"Well, Jacky-Boy, don't you look nice today! Didn't expect to see you here. You chief of the Library Police, too?" He chuckled.

"Hello, Dad."

His father tipped an invisible hat at Cartwright and ambled by. At least he didn't smell of anything stronger than Old Spice. Jackson whispered, "He's a regular?"

"Yes. He spends most mornings reading newspapers."

There was a rustle of whispered giggles as a pair of girls in their early twenties entered, carrying stacks of booklets and pink papers. Their makeup was vampiric and both wore short black skirts and too-tight shirts. They approached the desk.

"May I help you?" asked Jordan.

"I'm Lacey and this is Belle and we're from the Crystal Cavern? Our boss wanted to give you some books by Constance Welling? We have too many and he thought you might like some?" Lacey pushed the stack of books toward Jordan. "They're autographed and everything?"

Jordan perused the stack of a dozen small books, took three titles, and pushed the rest back across the desk. "'I'll take these."

"That's all?" said Lacey. "Also? Can we put this flyer up in your window about the writer's workshop she's giving tomorrow afternoon? And here are some more to leave on your desk?"

"You may leave them."

"Thank you!" squeaked the girls, clattering out of the library on ridiculously high heels.

Jordan shook his head and dropped the entire stack of flyers into the trash. He opened one book and scanned through a few pages, set it down and pushed them all to the side. "Everyone thinks they can write these days."

The library door burst open in a silence-shattering tangle of voices, chief among them, a shrill cry of children's names:

"Ralphene! Lehi! Twyla Dawn! Be reverent!" Taffilynn Matthews grappled for several of her offspring, missed, and accepted her lot with a look of resignation as they scattered to the winds.

"Well," Jackson said. "I think I've got everything I need. You'll let me know if you think of anything else?"

Jordan jumped as a child squawked. "I will. Thanks, Chief. Again, I'm sorry to have troubled you."

"Not a problem." Jackson smiled, happy to be leaving. The sounds of *shushing* from various points of the building could be heard over the squealing, giggling, and hollering of Pat and Taffilynn Matthews' very irreverent children.

# 44
## *Dr. Feelgood*

It was an atrocious morning. Constance had barely slept - and what little sleep she did get was plagued by nightmares about the ghostly face in the closet. The smell ... the eyes ... that voice. She had almost convinced herself she'd imagined it all. Sara Bellamy had been talking about the Blue Lady, as in Blue Lady Lake. *Did they really believe that nonsense?* She'd never encountered anything that wasn't faked in her entire career.

Whatever the hell it all was, between that and Luke's desertion, she'd had two horrible nights in a row. *Little bitch, it's all your fault. You'll never make it as a writer now, Luke, I'll see to that! I'll sue you for dereliction of duty too!* She was sure she had a case. Her assistants were never reliable. *What is it with all these shit-diddling employees? The world's gone to hell.*

This morning was even worse than Thursday. She woke with a pounding neck ache from sleeping wrong on the dreadful hotel pillow and knew it was time to seek out the local doctor for Percocet and Ambien.

To that end, she'd stopped at the registration desk and asked Slutty Sara to make her an appointment. There was an opening with a Dr. Siechert in just half an hour. Pleased, she told the slut she was no longer paying for Luke's room and was humiliated that Sara already knew he'd quit. The girl looked like she'd swallowed a canary. *You'll pay for that!*

Now, she sat on the edge of an exam table waiting for the doctor. Five minutes had already passed and he was still keeping her waiting. His nurse, however, a mannish woman with the longest fingers she had ever seen, wouldn't leave her side. The woman - Tessa Cornhull according to her nameplate - was annoying Constance with unending questions.

"The pain started this morning, you say?"

Constance blew out a noisy lungful of air. "Yes. I woke up with it. I have a writing workshop to teach, and I'm not looking forward to it in this condition. I'm a novelist."

"A novelist? What do you write? I have always wanted to be a writer," prattled the nurse. "I'd like to write detective fiction. I have the heroine of the stories all fleshed out in my imagination. I think I want to do a series. I started-"

"Constance Welling does *not* write fiction. It's a waste of the intellect."

"Oh? I thought novels *were* fiction."

"Not always." *Impertinent woman! How dare she question me?*

"What do you write? Have I read any of your books? Where do you get your ideas?"

Constance rolled her eyes. "I write about the healing properties of crystals and gemstones. My latest book-"

"Crystals and gemstones? That's interesting. I was thinking of naming my detective heroine Crystal-"

"I also teach writing workshops. As I said, I have an event coming up that-"

"Oh, when is it? I'd love to attend. I always thought if I wasn't a nurse I'd be either a writer or a teacher. And look at you. You get to do both!"

*A person's ability to string a sentence together does* not *make her a writer.*

Behind Cornhull's noise, Constance heard someone whistling *The Happy Wanderer.* Then the door opened. A handsome auburn-haired man wearing a white coat and a stethoscope entered the room with a broad smile and sparkling green eyes. He held her chart in one hand and one of those wonderful blue bottles of water in the other. "Ms. Welling?"

She wet her lips and smiled. "Miss Welling. I'm not married."

He gave her an odd look, then peered at her chart. "A stiff neck?"

"Yes. I woke up with it and, as I was telling the nurse, I have a writer's workshop to teach and I need some relief. I'm a authoress, you see, and-"

"Well," said Siechert, sitting down on a stool beside her, "we can't have that, can we?"

Constance shook her head with a little too much enthusiasm, then brought her hand up to her neck and rubbed to be sure he understood the severity of her pain. "No, we can't. I'm a busy woman."

The doctor gently turned her head one way, then the other. His hands were strong, warm. She imagined what else he could do with them and found herself wishing she'd made the appointment for a pelvic. Something about Dr. Siechert gave Constance the impression he'd really appreciate her lower body jewelry.

"Tell me when it starts to hurt." He turned her head further to one side.

Constance gave a small chirp when the ache flared.

He righted her head and smiled. "That wasn't so bad, now was it?"

She beamed at him. "You were *very* gentle."

The nurse, who'd been watching the doctor's every move with keen and calculating eyes, cleared her throat noisily. Constance assumed the woman must be jealous. The envy of other women was a burden Constance had learned to accept many years ago, so she shrugged it off with the grace of a swan shaking a droplet of water from the tip of its wing.

"I'm going to send you home with a printout of some neck stretches which should help."

Constance blinked at the man. "But I need something more immediate," she said. "I have an event tomorrow. I can't depend on exercises!"

"What pain medications have you taken in the past?"

Relief settled over Constance's solar plexus like a contented kitten with a bowl of warm milk. "Percocet has given me the best pain relief in the past." She gave him a pointed look. "I also have a hard time sleeping."

He produced a pad. "I'll give you a prescription for Percocet and Temazepam."

"Couldn't I have one for Xanax, or maybe Ambien?"

"Temazepam is specific for sleeping problems. I think it will be a better combination with the Percocet."

She sighed.

As he wrote, Constance had a feeling that were it not for his pesky nurse, he might have asked her out. *Oh well. Can't win them all. I'm Constance Welling. I'm beautiful, interesting, and any man would be lucky to have me.*

She took the prescription from the doctor.

"Nurse Cornhull," said the doctor. "Please get Miss Welling the printout for the neck exercises."

The nurse scowled and opened a drawer.

Constance smiled. "If you're not busy tomorrow, I'd love to see you at my workshop. Perhaps we could have coffee afterward?"

He said nothing.

The nurse rattled the printouts before thrusting them into Constance's hand. "I'd be there, Ms. Welling," she said. "But by tomorrow afternoon, I'm on an Alaskan luxury cruise for almost three weeks."

"You *want* to go to Alaska?" She didn't wait for a response. "Doctor, what about you? Might you drop in on my workshop?"

"I'd love to," said Dr. Siechert. "But I have a golf date over at the course in Lake Arrowhead."

She looked at him and knew that if it weren't for that overbearing nurse, Dr. Siechert would be singing a different tune.

The nurse cleared her throat again and crossed her arms. "I'll see you in the waiting room momentarily."

*You shitting bitch. You know competition when you see it.* "Thank you." Constance stepped into the back office area, letting the door swing shut behind her. On a counter was a cell phone. She glanced around then turned it on. It belonged to Dr. Siechert. So far, she'd found almost no cell service in the damn mountains, but it wouldn't hurt to have his number, just in case. Quickly, she snagged a pen off the counter, found his number, and wrote it on her hand.

# 45
## *Siechert Gets the Finger*

After giving that vixen Theo Pelinore - Cliffside's new real estate agent - the pelvic to end all pelvics, Dr. Roger Siechert was left with a hard-on that would have made his thirteen-year-old self-envious. The woman, a healthy specimen with marvelously dense natural breasts and excellent blood pressure - absolutely wriggled on the speculum … then asked for a bigger size. He would have given her something much bigger indeed, had Nurse Tessa not been shooting him the stink-eye the entire time.

The Pelinore woman was gone now, the soft floral scent of her perfume the only proof she'd been in the office. *Well, that and my ruthless erection.*

"Will you miss me while I'm on vacation?" Tessa Cornhull tried to bat her eyelashes, but it looked like a nervous tic. "I'll be gone almost three whole weeks. Will you be faithful?"

"Of course," he said, thinking about Ms. Pelinore's snatch.

"Do you think she's prettier than me?"

Siechert sat, legs crossed, hiding his trouser dragon. He looked at his nurse, from her new George Clooney haircut to her white rubber-soled nurse clogs. There was only one way to answer her. "Of course not, Tessa. Why would you even ask such a thing?"

"Well," she said, leaning against the wall, "she's tall, dark, and exotic. She could be a model."

"I'm not a photographer. Would you pass me my Blue Springs?"

Cornhull handed him the bottle. "You still find me attractive, don't you?" She stepped closer.

He sipped. "Of course I do, Tessa." The truth was, he never had. The nurse's appeal lay entirely in a singular sexual practice she performed.

"Then prove it." She took the chart from him.

"Damn it, Tessa. We're working."

A smile crawled across her mouth and she raised her index finger, waving it back and forth, taunting him.

Her long slender finger, gentle when he wanted it to be, and rough at just the right times, wagged in the air, nearly causing an explosion in his pants.

"Do you need me to take your temperature?" she asked.

Siechert blew out a breath. "Get over here, Nurse, and check me for fever." As he stood and began undoing his pants, Cornhull wedged a chair under the doorknob.

She undid her blouse and pulled out a floppy breast, which she began to stroke.

Siechert focused not on her breast but on the finger she was using to tweak a brown nipple. *It looks like a piece of pepperoni on a flapjack.* He shuddered.

"I will, but you know what you have to do first." She grinned through a mouth full of crooked teeth. She undid her pants, dropped her panties, hefted herself on the exam table and spread her legs. The odd, unpleasant smell of lakewater filled the room and Siechert glanced down at her pudenda, concerned, but everything looked fine.

Trying to show no hint of displeasure, Siechert positioned himself between her thighs, and thrust into the canyon of her womanhood. *It's like throwing a hot dog down a hallway!* He suppressed a chuckle and continued thrusting. The watery smell grew stronger.

Soon, her hands were on him, her fingertips teasing the tops of his shoulders, then trailing down his back, playing his spine like an instrument. He felt himself harden even more when she reached his lower back, teasing the top of his butt crack. *Ah, it won't be long now.*

Then, with no warning at all, she stabbed into his anus. He yelped, slamming his buttocks together, his thrusts coming to a halt.

"What?" she asked. "What's wrong?!"

"Jesus Christ, Tessa!"

"What? What is it?"

The pain subsided a little. "I don't know. I guess I just wasn't ready."

"Ready for what?"

"The invasion of the Chocolate Wanderer."

Cornhull looked confused. "But I didn't." She held up both hands and wiggled her fingers.

Just then, the pain inside his rectum sharpened. Siechert spun around, fruitlessly trying to get a look at his own ass, like a mastiff chasing its tail. "What the hell?" Something was in him, he could feel it. He crammed a hand between his buttocks, found his anus, and palpated it. Nothing was out of the ordinary, but the throb of chill pain with each beat of his pulse assured him he hadn't imagined it. That and the overwhelming cramping that urged him to vacate his bowels immediately.

"Roger! What it is?" Cornhull was on her feet, trying to get a look at his behind. "Did you get bitten?"

"Bitten! By what?"

"I don't know, a bug or something?"

"Goddamn it, Tessa, it wasn't a bug. Unless it flew up my ass! What did you do to my ass?"

She looked at him, dazed. "Nothing. Not yet. I was going to, but..."

Siechert grabbed a hand mirror from a drawer, squatted over it, and continued inspecting himself. It looked normal. As he probed, the sensation of fullness in his bowels eased. Then he felt something cold snaking through his insides. "It feels like I've got a goddamned icicle up my ass!"

Cornhull, wide-eyed and useless, stood there like a mannequin, hand over her mouth.

Siechert groaned, almost doubled over, when - just as suddenly as it had begun - the sensation ceased.

Hand on his abdomen, pants around his ankles, mirror on the floor between his feet, he blinked at the useless nurse. "Oh, Tessa, honey. I think I need to use the bathroom." He yanked his pants up and fled the room.

In the staff lavatory, Siechert sat down on the porcelain throne and waited. Nothing happened except an occasional cold flutter inside him. It was higher now; closer to his stomach. After several moments, he stood, flushed, and washed his hands. He stared at his reflection. He wondered if he was losing his mind.

*No, Roger. Your mind is not lost. I will return it when I am done.*

He didn't hear the voice exactly - not with his ears, anyway. The icy feeling inside exploded now, blossoming like fireworks, and shooting down his legs and up into his arms. It was not entirely unpleasant.

# 46
## *The Wizard of Ink*

"I'm ready for you," Merlin Skinner told the woman in the waiting room.

She raised her chin. "It's about time." The woman stood, her gaze crawling up and down his body, settling finally onto the exposed skin of his chest, where the laces of his black poet shirt were loose.

Her clothes were too tight, her hair too big, her makeup too heavy. She seemed to think she belonged in a 1980s hair band music video, stretched out on a black Jaguar, gyrating to the cacophony of too many guitars. She never would have made the cut, though, even if she wasn't about thirty-five years late for auditions.

She held out her hand. Her perfume was a nauseating blend of roses and patchouli. "I'm Constance Welling."

He shook her hand. "Merlin Skinner." Only one of her fingers was free of gaudy rings set with colorful baubles that she probably thought were expensive gemstones.

"Oh, my. Your hands are so smooth. You must give wonderful massages."

He let go of her hand. "I don't give massages."

"You should consider it. With hands like those, you could make a fortune."

Silently, he led her into the ink room.

"As I told you on the phone," her voice was the sound of a fork being dragged across a plate, "I want a new tattoo." Constance slithered into the work chair. Because the clients enjoyed watching the process from various angles, there were several mirrors on each wall, and she eyed her reflection as she stretched out, jutting her chest forward. She seemed quite pleased with her appearance.

Merlin took great care to keep his distaste concealed. "Have you decided what you want?"

"I have." That voice could curdle milk. "I am, as you know, an authoress, so I've decided to get a quill pen to represent my devotion to my craft." She raised her chin and *tsked*.

Merlin, wishing no further pontification on the profundity of the writer's mind, said, "There are several different styles that are popular." He grabbed his black portfolio from the counter, flipped it open, and handed it to Constance.

"We can do any of those," said Merlin, "or a variation."

Constance turned a page. "There don't seem to be many to choose from."

She turned a few more pages. "I want this one." She stabbed a finger at an ornate image. "It befits my station in life." She closed the book and gave herself another sideways glance in the mirrors and pushed her chest out again.

"And what area is it going on?"

Constance jutted her chin. "My left buttock."

Merlin cleared his throat. "Okay," he said. "I'll need to adjust the chair then we'll begin the sanitizing-"

"I don't need a run-down of your processes," said Constance. "I've had this done many times." The *tsk-click* sounds she made with her tongue were starting to irritate Merlin. "Do you also do piercings?"

He averted his eyes as she peeled off her pants. "No," he said. "I don't." He flattened the chair and Constance oozed back onto it, sliding around on her stomach before reaching back and pulling the bottom of her red lace panties into the cleft of her buttocks. She wiggled her rear end coquettishly. It was an unfortunate move.

He began the sanitization process without a wince. Merlin Skinner was nothing if not a professional.

# 47
## *Whispers*

Luke Donovan spent the morning with Chad Armstrong, becoming familiar with the gym and its equipment. He felt good about his new job and could tell Chad was pleased he was a quick study. After the lesson Chad suggested a workout in the empty gym; they completed a twenty-minute cardio warm-up, then headed for the free weights. That's when Chad realized he'd left his weight-lifting gloves upstairs, and asked Luke to go get them.

Now Luke stood just inside their temporary room on the second floor fighting off an uneasy feeling that someone had been in here. *Constance? No, she doesn't know I'm staying with Chad.* It wasn't the maids, either. They'd been there; the beds had been straightened, the floor vacuumed - but something felt wrong.

And the bathroom was foggy, as if someone had just taken a hot shower. The strangest part, though, was that the bathtub, toilet, and sink were all brimming with water, their surfaces as still and smooth as glass.

Then came the whispers.

*Luke ...*

The voice set his teeth on edge and thrust his heart so high he could feel his pulse in the back of his throat. He spun, his mouth so dry he could barely swallow.

*Luke ...*

It came from the other direction this time and he turned, every muscle in his body tense and charged.

*Luke ...*

He followed the whispers out of the bathroom to the bar sink between the microwave and mini-fridge. It brimmed too, yet not one drop of the glassy water had spilled.

*Luke ...*

He spun to the right.

*Luke ...*

Now it came from the left.

*Luke ...*

This time it came from behind. His grip on his key card tightened.

*Luke! Luke! Luke!*

The whispers overlapped, crawling toward him from all directions, like a mob of starved cockroaches at lights out. He clapped his hands over his ears, his only defense against the maddening voices. Squeezing his eyes shut, he tasted terror, sharp and sour, on the back of his tongue.

*Luke! Luke! LUKE!*

The whispers - hundreds if not thousands of them - rose and fell. With fresh horror, he realized they assailed him from without and within.

He screamed, jolting away from the sounds which now, somehow, touched him. He felt their cold caresses at the base of his neck, the side of his face, the back of his hands, crawling up between his legs, each of them syncing perfectly with the sound of his name.

*Luke! Luke! Luke! LUKE! LUKE!*

He bolted from the room.

The door slammed shut behind him. He pressed his back against it, standing ramrod straight and panting. Relief flooded him; the whispers hadn't followed him. His skin began to tingle. A cold, clammy rash of gooseflesh covered him and he could smell his own sweat. It wasn't performance sweat. It was terror sweat; he knew the difference.

His vision swam and he felt lightheaded. He saw two women down the hall approaching the Theodosia Suite. He stepped out of the doorway.

Sara Bellamy and an elderly woman stared at him. "Luke? Are you okay?" Sara approached him.

"I, uh." He couldn't find the words.

The older woman stepped forward. "You've had a scare, young man. Would you like some tea?"

"I'd love some, but first, would you mind checking out my room with me, Sara?"

"Sure," said Sara. "We both will. Let me introduce you to my honorary aunt, Maisy Hart. She knows a lot about this place."

Luke faced the door, the key card in his hand. The poor young man was terrified.

"Let me." Maisy gently took the card from him and slid it into the lock. The light blinked green and the young man still didn't move, so Maisy placed her hand on his. "It's okay," she said. "I've seen some very scary things in my day and I'm still ticking. Don't be afraid."

He opened the door and she slipped in front of him, taking the lead as they entered.

Once inside, Luke came to an abrupt stop. "No," he said. "No way."

Maisy followed his gaze to the bar sink.

"It was full of water when I left." Luke looked from Maisy to Sara. "I didn't fill it. Please, come with me." He led them to the bathroom doorway and flipped on the light, but Maisy couldn't see past him.

"No!" he almost shouted. He turned to face them, his eyes wide. "I swear, a few minutes ago, the toilet, the tub, the sinks ... they were all full!"

Sara looked at him. "You're sure?"

He nodded. "Yes! And now ... now look at it." He stepped aside and Sara and Maisy stared into the bathroom. Nothing was wrong. "I must be losing my mind."

Maisy looked up at Luke. "How long were you gone before this happened?"

He blinked. "I don't know. Maybe an hour?"

Sara pointed to the toilet paper, which was folded neatly at its ends. "It looks like the maids have been here recently."

Luke nodded. "Yeah, they came while I was gone. I know they were here, but I'm also sure they didn't do ... that thing to the sinks and bathtub." Maisy saw him suppress a tremble. "They couldn't have. They were too full, you know?"

"I know," Maisy said.

Sara stepped away from the bathroom. "Did anything else happen?"

Luke opened his mouth, paused, and then spoke. "Yes," he said. "There was something else."

In the years since she'd stopped making movies, Maisy had immersed herself in the study of the occult, and she'd seen enough to know that the truth wasn't always explainable. "Do you want to talk about it?"

Luke looked bewildered. "I heard my name over and over. They were whispers, thousands of them, and they touched me."

"They touched you?" asked Maisy. This was unusual.

Luke nodded. "Yeah. I felt them. All over me like bugs. Or maybe fingers. Have you ever even heard of such a thing? Am I going crazy?"

Maisy shook her head. "No. You are not crazy. In my years with Theodosia, I heard many stories about this place, and I've heard more since. It's one of the reasons I love it here." She looked around the room. "I've never heard of anything exactly like this, but I'm not surprised." She turned to Sara. "You told me others have reported voices, correct?"

"Yes. A feminine voice that speaks their name." Suddenly, she froze.

Maisy saw Sara's gaze flicker to the bathroom door. "Oh, my God."

Maisy turned, and at first saw nothing, then spied wet footprints forming. One after another, they walked on, continuing until they disappeared through the balcony glass. Maisy Hart had never seen anything like it, though she remembered hearing a similar story from Theodosia. "Let's go have some tea," she said, trying to keep a quaver out of her voice. "I want to tell you a tale."

## 48
## *The Hunger*

The hunger was fierce and brutal. Once it began, it was too savage and constant to be likened to a beast, no matter how wild and ferocious.

It had always been there and always would be, thoughtless and inanimate; and yet, when it sliced into your soul, it became the only thing that held meaning. Then it became a living thing, a force to contend with.

Hammerhead battled that hunger now.

It twisted into him, taunting and teasing. That was the worst part - the teasing. Teasing, teasing, the way a poker teases hot coals. Serving its purpose. Bringing fire to life. The hunger.

Cold beads of sweat dotted his hairline. The tips of his fingers trembled and his stomach roiled. But these things weren't real. None of them. They were phantom symptoms of a much deeper need that had gone too long unsatisfied. A need he intended to quench as soon as he could. The Lady, however, was nowhere to be found.

*Where are you, you fucking bitch? Where are you now? I'm ready. I'm hungry. It's time. Where are you?*

It wasn't time though, and he knew it. It wasn't even the weekend yet. And he might even have to wait longer than that. It all depended on the Lady. *You stinking cunt! Where are you?*

A stranger passed by and gave him a smile. It was heartfelt and genuine. Despite the twisting of the knife blade beneath his skin, it was vital he appear calm, like a mote of pollen on a breeze.

He smiled back.

# 49
## *The Lady and the Doctor*

Roger Siechert arrived at the stately gated community of Bavarian Pines and waited impatiently for Larry, the gate attendant - *slight case of scoliosis* - to deal with the two Volvos and the BMW ahead of his black Jaguar XK Touring Coupe. Larry finally waved him through and he wove the Jag along the curving streets of his forest-scaped community until he pulled up to his Bavarian Dream home.

One of the reasons he'd bought the spacious sanctuary was the builder's name for it: "Bavarian Dream." He parked in the driveway and got out, stretching and popping his long bones and joints with pleasure. He had a little arthritis now and usually he felt it every time he drove home - *maybe it's time to trade the Jag for a BMW* - but this evening, he felt young and utterly acheless. He wondered if it had anything to do with that strange chill he'd experienced earlier. *Nonsense.*

His residence was two rambling stories of beautifully hewn logs and gleaming glass, on half an acre. It had cost him a mint but the privacy it afforded was well worth it. Happy to be home, he sighed as he unlocked the massive entry doors and let himself in.

An instant later, a rash of cuckoos began singing. He had Black Forest clocks in almost every room; one of his pleasures was winding them once a day or once a week, depending on the model.

"Good evening, my fine feathered friends," he said as he locked the door behind him. "I trust you've had a pleasant day."

*Roger ...*

"Who's here?" he called, alert. He waited. *Must have imagined it.*

He went up to his bedroom, stripped, considered a shower, but decided to wait until bedtime. He dressed in a pair of gray sweatpants and an Angels T-shirt. Humming *Happy Wanderer,* he hung up his suit, then tossed his shirt in the hamper. The ping of his cell phone made him jump. There was virtually no service in the mountains, but Bavarian Pines had its own private cell tower that worked reasonably well when the gods were smiling. He picked the phone up and saw the text: *Is Constance Welling. r u bussy this eveneing?*

*How did she get my number?* He considered ignoring it; Ms. Welling - *possible early stages of cirrhosis, based on the subtle jaundice of her sclerae and skin* - wasn't his stein of beer. Apparently she wasn't much of a writer, either, if her text was any indication.

Then again, Tessa Cornhull wasn't attractive, yet she'd brought him hours of pleasure.

*No,* he typed. *Just relaxing at home.* He sent the text and stared at his phone a moment. It took its time sending but finally found a signal. *The gods are smiling.* He slipped the phone in his pocket.

Daylight was beginning to fade as he padded barefoot to the kitchen. After pausing to fill his favorite German stein with icy lager he kept on tap, he went foraging in his massive fridge. He found salad and omelet makings and went to work. A few minutes later, he sat down and picked at his dinner. He only finished the omelet; the salad - and the beer - made him feel chilly inside.

***

Constance couldn't believe Roger Siechert had received her text, let alone answered it. She'd had nothing but rejection since she'd arrived in this Christing town, and her self-esteem was ruined, but the painkillers - along with a few shots of tequila - had restored her confidence. She'd found a bench outside Cliffhouse where there was nothing but lawn below and sky above, and sent the text. She was gazing at the early moon - it seemed to be weaving - when the doctor replied. With effort, she focused on the words. He was relaxing at home. That was an invitation if she'd ever seen one.

She looked out at the lights and activity across the lake where the End of Summer partiers were beginning their revelry. She heard music, voices, laughter. Thanks to the pills and booze, they were soothing.

Maybe she'd have a little party of her own. She texted the doctor back.

***

Roger Siechert scraped his dishes and set them in the sink, then brewed a pot of tea, hoping it would warm him up. He hadn't felt quite right since the icy invasion of his sphincter. Not wanting to argue, he hadn't pressed Tessa about it, but he had no doubt she had hurt him on purpose. She always got pissed off when patients flirted with him and that had happened twice today. *And that's my fault?* His phone pinged.

*I wsa hoppingf we coud get 2gether maybee later 2nite? I hav teqilla.*

He texted her back: *You seem to be feeling much better.*

A new text came: *The pils u give me hepped a lot and I feel bettr.*

*Of course she mixes painkillers with booze.* The slight jaundice made that a given.

His thoughts returned to Tessa. She'd hurt him because she was a jealous bitch who hated it when he examined beautiful women. *And ugly ones.* So she rammed him like a sailor on shore leave, fast and hard.

*Roger ...*

The voice was back. He whirled, saw no one. "Hello?"

*How dare she hurt you!*

The voice sounded friendly. She sounded like she cared, unlike Tessa. *Who does Tessa think she is, to cause me pain?* he thought. *She works for me!*

He poured a cup of tea and sat down at the kitchen table, warming his hands, then went back to the fridge for a bottle of Blue Springs. Seating himself, he downed the sparkling water in three long gulps then, refreshed, put his hands around the warm teacup again.

*She uses you ...*

It was true. Today wasn't the first time Tessa had been rough on his sphincter. Just six months ago, after he performed an especially thorough - and necessary considering the dense tissue - breast exam on Norma Bailey, Tessa had actually cut him with her nail. Little Roger gave a twitch.

*Norma Bailey - Booteous Maxima. She's dead.* The thought surprised him and he remembered his partner, Gene Holmes, telling him about the autopsy, the lungs saturated with water. Little Roger went back to sleep.

*Roger ...*

The voice was in his ear, the breath chill. "Who are you?" he whispered. "Where are you?"

*I am here. I am the Lady. You are mine. We will be together.*

The air seemed colder and he could have sworn he smelled lakewater on a phantom breeze.

"I'm imagining things," he told himself. He chuckled. "Maybe I'm going insane."

An image of Tessa Cornhull flashed across his mind; she was smiling at him, waving her finger - *the Chocolate Wanderer* - but her grin wasn't playful. Her eyes were black, and as her lips curved upwards, blood dribbled from their corners and down her chin. He shuddered.

*She could ruin you. She knows too much.*

"What the hell is wrong with me?" He had never before heard voices in his life.

*She could expose you.*

His eyes shot open and he sat up, worried. "She wouldn't," he whispered.

*Not as long as you let her use you ...*

Cool beads of sweat prickled at his hairline.

*She will not let you go. You know this.* The voice filtered through his mind like cool water.

Was the voice right? He wondered what Tessa really wanted.

*Don't be foolish,* the Lady whispered. *You are her prisoner.*

Siechert swallowed. Was Tessa really that vindictive?

*Try to leave her and you will see. Why do you think she watches you so closely?* On a deep level, he knew the voice spoke the truth. He also knew the voice wasn't his own: It was something else, something feminine and dark, sensual, full of power. Something from the lake.

*She saw how you enjoyed that woman's body today.*

That was true.

*She was watching. She was watching. She was watching.*

He rose and paced the floor, the voice taunting him, seeming to be many voices now.

*She knows. She's going to tell. She knows ...*

Siechert slammed his hands over his ears. "Stop it! Shut up!"

*She knows all your secrets ... She knows ...*

The voice came from inside his head this time. Panic took him. All that money he'd spent on medical school ... his parents, who had prepared him since he was a child. *How could I have been so stupid to have an affair with a nurse? She'll ruin me! She'll tell people about the Chocolate Wanderer and how I like to use anal beads when I'm on my treadmill.* He'd never work in Cliffside, or anywhere else, again.

*You'll be humiliated. You'll be ruined.*

*Fuck!* He paced, paced, paced. *What the fuck am I going to do? Shhh ...*

The voice soothed him and he stood still, his breathing heavy.

*You must stop her.*

Images flashed before his eyes; images that showed him what to do. They eased his mind and slowed his pulse. His breathing returned to normal and the black pit of spinning panic in his gut dissolved.

*You know exactly what to do.*

Yes. He did. His cell pinged with another message, but he ignored it as he walked to the landline, took it off its cradle, and dialed Tessa Cornhull's number.

She picked up on the first ring.

\*\*\*

Tessa's phone jangled out the chorus of Exile's *Kiss You All Over*.

*It's Roger.* "Hello, Doctor."

"Tessa." He sounded out of breath. "How are you?"

"I'm fine, Doctor."

"You know how much I like it when you call me that."

"I do." *In* and *out of the office. Especially out of it.*

"Would you like some company tonight?"

Her heart tripped then resumed its course. "It sounds like someone needs a checkup."

"Yes." He sounded breathy. "God, yes."

"I'll be waiting." She listened to his ragged breathing. She thought he might be pleasuring himself. She'd never heard him quite so excited, and it made her tingle. "Doctor?" she said in a feathery tone.

"Yes, Nurse?"

She took an audible breath to keep him in suspense. "The Chocolate Wanderer will be ready."

The sound that came from the other end was an outright growl. The doctor disconnected and Tessa stared at her phone a moment. He'd come over after hours before, many times, but his mood tonight was unusual. Ordinarily, he was impassive, almost chilly. This new side of him was refreshing and she intended to reward it.

She set her paperback down on the end table. It was a mystery novel and even though she wasn't finished with it yet, she was certain she already knew the killer's identity. That was one of her talents: Tessa Cornhull always knew *whodunit*, and one day, she intended to rob Agatha Christie of her title as *The Queen of Crime*.

Her house, a tired-looking cabin built just after World War Two, rested near the edge of Cliffside's south end. It was only about eight hundred square feet, but for Tessa and her small family of Sunrise Guppies, it was comfortable and quaint.

She had twenty minutes before he would arrive, so she straightened up, then went into the bathroom. She brushed her teeth, teased her hair, applied a new layer of underarm deodorant and spritzed her womanhood with a lilac-scented feminine spray. Then she donned a white transparent net-and-lace negligee. She pinched her nipples so they jutted against the fabric, then sat at the edge of the couch and filed down the nail of the Chocolate Wanderer. She wanted this to be the first thing the doctor saw when he entered the house.

# 50
## *Magnets and Salt*

Sara and Maisy sat in the Theodosia Suite. They had been discussing the recent ghostly encounters ever since Luke went back to the gym.

"There are several things that might help stop the problems you're having," Maisy said.

There was a knock on the door. "Hold that thought. I'll be right back." Sara rose and let her dads in.

"Ready to go to the lake party?" Teddy asked, then saw Maisy. "Are you coming too?" He smiled at her.

"Me, oh my, no. Not unless Jon wants to escort me."

"Sit down a minute," Sara said. "Aunt Maisy was just about to tell me some things that might help stop our problems with the Blue Lady or whatever it is."

"I'm all ears," Teddy said as the men took seats.

"One possibility for stopping these problems is salting," Maisy said.

"Salting?" asked Teddy and Adam in unison.

"Well, you could use gold dust but that might get a little expensive."

The Baxter-Bellamys blinked at her.

"They're both neutral elements," Maisy explained. "Think of them as paranormal baking soda. They absorb things and neutralize them like baking soda does in your refrigerator."

"How do we do it?" asked Adam. Sara and Teddy both stared in surprise.

"Lay a thin layer of salt in small dishes and place them throughout the rooms, especially in windows and doorways. It may work, but to be honest, I've had better luck with rare earth magnets."

"Magnets?" Adam asked.

Maisy nodded. "Very strong, natural magnets. Years ago, I was asked by a very famous - and very desperate - actor if I could do anything about the spirits in his house. He and his wife had been plagued since the day they moved in. A silent movie actor owned it previously and he was known for having thrown wild satanic orgies and eventually committed suicide there. The mansion passed through a number of hands very rapidly. Charles, the actor, didn't believe any of it of course, and bought it." She finished her sherry and poured another. "He soon found out it wasn't nonsense. Name a phenomenon and this house had it - apparitions, phantom sounds from footsteps to crying, doors slamming, and cold spots." Maisy laughed. "It was a regular supernatural Disneyland.

"I wasn't sure what I could do, but I'd heard from a respectable parapsychologist to try magnets if salt didn't work. He'd had excellent results when he used them to disrupt a haunting in a private residence. He expected the fix to be temporary, but ..."

"But?" asked Adam.

"They weren't," said Maisy. "They continued to work for a long time. I'd first tried salting Charles and Leona's house, but it wasn't enough, so I switched to magnets. Voila. The activity stopped almost completely."

"But why?" asked Adam. "I don't understand how it worked."

"It disrupts the haunting, but that's all I can really tell you. Maybe it's a little like the way magnets ruin credit cards. I don't know."

Adam looked thoughtful.

"I've used them in other cases too, over the years. It doesn't always work, but when it does, it's great." She finished her sherry. "I think it might work here."

"Why?" Adam asked.

She fixed him with a stare. "Because what's going on here is tied to the land, to the lake. It's elemental. And magnets are elemental, too. As I said, I don't understand it, Adam, but I do believe science is involved."

"It's worth a try," Teddy said. "Where do we get a load of magnets?"

Maisy smiled. "That, I can answer. A scientific supply house. If there's not one in Santo Verde, there will be plenty in Los Angeles. I'll bet you could pick them up tomorrow or have them shipped overnight."

"Let's do it," Teddy said.

"It won't hurt," Sara agreed.

Adam looked at the floor, but nodded.

"And you may have a pleasant surprise," Maisy said, then looked directly at Adam. "We can't explain everything, and we don't have to. Most phenomena are not caused by spirits. Though we can't explain something, it's foolish to deny its existence." As she set her glass down, someone knocked on the door. Teddy stood and answered it.

Sara's heart beat a little faster when she heard Luke's voice. "Hi, Mr. Bellamy. Is Sara here? I didn't mean to be late."

"We're coming!" she called. Grabbing her jacket, she followed Adam out the door and smiled at Luke, handsome in dark jeans and a pale blue shirt under a short leather jacket.

He looked at her dads. "I hope you don't mind me tagging along."

"Glad to have you," Teddy said.

"You kids have fun," Aunt Maisy said. "It's time for my bath."

# 51
## *Siechert Strikes*

"Come in."

Siechert heard the voice from the other side of the door and could immediately tell Tessa had misinterpreted his mood on the phone. Which was exactly what he'd wanted.

*No, what* we *wanted.*

The Lady's voice, a silky whisper, continued urging him on even as he stepped into Tessa's tiny living room. *Yes,* it whispered, soft and sensual and he was overcome by an inexplicable alien hunger. The painful ache buzzed in every cell of his body.

Tessa sat on the couch wearing something gauzy. She had her right index finger - *the Chocolate Wanderer* - raised as she dragged the edge of a nail file over it, teasing him. Under normal circumstances he would have been instantly turned on - but tonight he was hungry for something new.

She stood, a stocky silhouette backlit by a gooseneck lamp, and approached him. "Doctor. I think the Chocolate Wanderer is getting restless." She circled his nipples with her index finger, then moved lower, teasing his belly button before heading to his backside, slipping under the band of his gray sweatpants, and inching down to wriggle in the crack of his buttocks. "And inquisitive," she said, dipping the finger up and down in his man-chasm, gliding - *up and down, up and down* - in his mossy ravine, creeping lower with each stroke.

For a moment, the hunger was forgotten as a small part of him surrendered to the pleasure. Just another quarter of an inch and the Chocolate Wanderer would make exquisite contact with his puckered mahogany knot. He grabbed her shoulders.

*She wants to hurt you again, to cut you,* said the Lady.

The new hunger flared like a revived flame.

"Oh, Doctor!" The sadistic nurse withdrew her finger from his warmest cranny. "I like it when you're aggressive. Are you going to pull my hair?" Her eyes blazed with naked need as she brought her wandering finger to her lips and ran her tongue up its length.

In his head, he heard the Lady's laughter, delightful and deadly.

"As a matter of fact ..." Siechert's voice was dry, strained. He twisted a hand into Tessa's short hair and pulled her head back.

She gasped with evident pleasure.

*She's a whore.* The Lady was getting impatient. *Treat her as such.*

With one hand on her shoulder and one in her hair, Siechert backed Cornhull into the kitchen, trapping her against the refrigerator.

"Oh, Doctor." Her eyes were swimming in raw lust as he pinned her against the surface. "Does this mean you want something to eat?" She widened her stance and smiled at him, ignorant of the ache that pumped under his skin, moving through his veins like a toxic disease, twisting his thoughts into new lunatic shapes.

"I vajazzled for you!" She lifted the hem of her baby doll nightie and pulled her panties aside to reveal a shaved beaver decorated with green rhinestones that spelled "Eat Me."

"Yes. Let's eat." He lowered himself to his knees and used his face to nudge her thighs further apart.

She giggled and opened them.

He sniffed her crotch. Through the mesh fabric of panties he scented the synthetic fragrance of an unpleasant floral deodorant, but underneath it was the spice he and the Lady longed for; the unmistakable incense of wetness. He inhaled, relishing the tang of it - like rain, like a streaming meadow brook, like ... *lakewater. Yes. Lakewater!*

He lowered her onto her back and tore her panties off, taking a few rhinestones with them.

"I think I need an exam, Doctor." She spread wider.

The dark scent of lakewater was everywhere.

The hunger reached its apex, as fine, as irrefutable, and as fatal as a razor's edge. Dr. Siechert pinned the nurse down with one arm. *Take her*, the Lady commanded. He plowed, face-first, into the hateful bitch's cunt.

She screamed, thrashed, and bled.

Siechert gnashed at her core, tore pieces of slick warm flesh away from her body with his teeth, spat them to the floor in his search to sate the new hunger.

At first, he thought the blood itself was slaking his thirst - then he realized that wasn't it. It was what the blood represented: Life.

Siechert savaged the nurse, oblivious to the ineffectual thrashing of her legs. Her hands clutched her throat as water gurgled from her mouth and nose.

The Lady was everywhere now, in him, around him. Her perfume was water, cold and dark and deep, soothing him as he watched Tessa's eyes rake the ceiling and bulge until he was certain they would burst. A purple vein, like a tine of frozen lightning, throbbed at the center of her forehead, cracking her face in half. Her skin turned purple-red, then a sickly suffocated blue, and finally, as her body went slack, that indescribable absence of color that only death could invoke.

He blinked, and stood. The house was so quiet that he wondered if even the Lady had left.

*No,* she whispered, surrounding him with her wet scent. *I am here.*

He nodded.

The refrigerator clicked.

Siechert looked down at his nurse.

She stared blindly from lidded eyes. Her mouth was slack. Water streamed from her nose. Her clawed hands began to relax.

His eyes traveled lower. There was no longer a vagina, only a ground up void between her legs, as if a firecracker had gone off in her twat. As Siechert bent closer, fascinated, he could see the wax-white edge of pelvic bone gleaming amidst the bloody muck. He thought of a white rose growing from a mound of ground beef.

He himself looked like a butcher on a busy day. The Lady whispered to him, giving him an idea he quite liked.

Crouching into the warm, slippery mess between Cornhull's splayed legs, he cocked his head one way, then the other, trying to determine the best approach.

*You know what to do.*

He knew what to do.

It was like sticking his hand into a big, warm blackberry pie. He heard wet sucking noises as he felt around. He found the posterior wall of the vagina and pressed on the fascia, but it was strong, not easily broken. Withdrawing, he stood, wiping gore on his shirt, then stepped over to the counter. He wanted a drink of water and took it directly from the faucet, rinsing his face while there. When he finished, he lifted her hot pink Cuisinart immersion blender off its charger. He smiled; he'd given it to her as a birthday gift and they'd laughed at the color that made it look like a perverse marital aid; that was why he'd chosen it.

Revving it, he brought it to the nurse's body. "All charged up, Tessa. Let's give you that exam you asked for." He giggled.

He knelt in the blood between her legs and thrust the hooded stainless steel blades of the appliance inside her. "Let's mix things up a little, shall we?" He thought of her jagged fingernail poking his anus. He was still sore. Pressing the business end of the blender into the posterior wall of her vagina, he said, "Just a little pinch. Hold still." He pushed the button and the blender came to life. It only took two one-second bursts to get through the thick fascia. "Cuisinart makes a damn fine blender, Tessa. You were right about that."

He set it aside and inserted his hand. "This won't hurt a bit." He tugged. Tessa's entrails felt like slippery tube sausages; he wound a length around his hand and pulled. They came out, wet, steaming, and reeking as they spilled into a puddle on the kitchen floor.

Human intestines were surprisingly long, but few people appreciated how durable they were. He draped the bloody rope up over her head, coiled it around her neck a few times, and chuckled at the sight. "You've been hoisted by your own innards, my dear!" He fought down the giggles, blinked away tears, and wrapped the rest of her intestines around her wrists and ankles.

Finished, he took a moment to admire his work. It was as creative as it was clever. He felt the Lady's pleasure.

He stripped off his clothes and shoes and stuffed them in a couple of Cliffside Market bags he found under the sink before padding naked to the bathroom, where he showered. Afterward, he used one of Tessa's bath towels to wipe his fingerprints away, then dried the shower and the floor.

He brought the towel to the kitchen and wiped away all his bloody footprints. Better the police find towel fibers than anything incriminating. He scrubbed the floor, trying to figure out an alibi. He was one of Tessa's few friends and he had a feeling it was no secret that they were seeing each other outside the office. He'd have to think on that.

*One thing at a time.* He shoved the towel in one of the grocery sacks then used wadded paper towels to remove the rest of the evidence on the Cuisinart, faucets, and counters. The towels went into a bag, too. With one final towel covering each hand, he took a bottle of Clorox from beneath the sink and returned to the ex-nurse.

Uncapping the bleach, he stared at her. "We must keep the clam clean, mustn't we?" He poured the pungent liquid all over the ex-vagina, recapped it and put it away, then paused to examine the scene. "Aha," he said. He took more paper towels, wet them, squeezed Palmolive Dish Soap on them, then carefully wiped her arms, neck, and abdomen. He tossed the soap bottle and towels in the bag with his shoes.

Had she scratched him? *No. Thank heaven for short nails.* There wasn't a mark on him, so there was no need to take her fingers to hide evidence. "Except, Tessa, for that very special finger." He grabbed another towel, opened a drawer by the stove and took out poultry shears and a Baggie before bending over Tessa Cornhull one last time.

He smiled at her as he pulled her index finger straight, snipped off the Chocolate Wanderer and zipped it up in the Baggie. He rinsed the shears clean, dried them, and put them away.

"I'm taking the Chocolate Wanderer with me," he told the mangled, bloody heap of meat on the floor. "I'm sure you won't miss him as much as I would."

After dressing himself in a pair of her sweat pants - thank God for chunky butt - and a too-small T-shirt, he gathered the sacks and the Wanderer. He heard his cell phone chirp. He withdrew it from his pocket and read another senseless come-on from Constance Welling. She seemed even more inebriated now than she had been earlier. This gave him an idea that would clear his name if and when the police started asking questions about Tessa.

Just before exiting, he stopped and sprinkled some fish food into the aquarium, three small pinches, just as Tessa had instructed. The fish swam to the top of the tank, eager to devour the flakes of food.

He left the house, whistling *The Happy Wanderer* as he closed the door behind him. "Goodbye, Tessa. You were a mediocre nurse. Roger, over, and out." He giggled to himself.

In the car, he texted Constance: *Where are you?* The reply didn't come through until he was almost home:

*Im ootside onn the lwan at Cliifhouse. Its the olny place I can gett any cell fone receptoin.*

Siechert felt a rising surge of hope: *Are there any people around you?*

It took a while, but her response finally came through: *Noone. Im out here all by meself. Im very lonley...I wuold enjoy sum male companyship.*

Siechert smiled and typed: *Great. Don't leave. I'll come pick you up.*

# 52
## *The End of Summer Party*

There was something in the air tonight. It wasn't just that summer was over and the first chill breezes of autumn whispered through the pines, speaking of hot chocolate, mittens and soon, the smell of burnt pumpkin. There was more. Jackson Ballou stood at the edge of the lake, remembering the feel of sand between his toes on a summer's day, and felt the hair on the back of his neck prickle up. *Something's in the air.* Something that made him uneasy.

He closed his eyes and inhaled. The air was fragrant with pine and lakewater behind the delectable scents of hot dogs, burgers, and gourmet items being sold by vendors from local restaurants. People laughed and talked and yelled as they picnicked and played volleyball or table tennis. The clink of horseshoes hitting stakes was familiar and comfortable. A guitar strummed in the background. Everything was as it should be, but anxiety gripped him.

He shivered though he wasn't cold.

"Something wrong, Jackson?" Polly slipped her arm through his.

"Someone just walked over my grave."

They watched the wind ripple tiny waves across the black water. "Do you think Norma Bailey's murderer is here tonight?" she asked.

"Could be."

"Well, we still need to eat."

He looked at her and smiled, feeling better. "What's your pleasure?"

"Fish and chips?" She nodded toward the London Frog cart sent over by a hole-in-the-wall joint that made crisp beer-battered cod and thick, perfect chips.

"Let's do it. Why don't you go grab that bench over there? I'll get the food."

"It's a deal." Polly headed for the picnic bench just as another group hurried toward it. He couldn't see who they were in the twilight, but watched, amused, as she sped up. Polly always won bench disputes. That was one of the things he liked about her. She got the bench first, then started talking to the people and they all sat down. He wondered who they were and found himself resenting their intrusion on his date - *yes, date!* - with Polly.

*Date? How'd that happen after so many years?* He grinned to himself, then headed over to London Frog.

\*\*\*

"Well, there's our lawman," Teddy said as Jackson approached with a tray of fish and chips.

"I hope you don't mind us joining you," Sara said. "Just say the word and we'll shove off."

Polly smiled as Jackson set the tray down. "I told them we wouldn't have taken such a big table if we hadn't wanted company."

"That's right," Jackson agreed. "Where's your better half, Ted?"

"Better? I prefer to think of him as my *other* half." Teddy grinned. "He and Luke are getting our food."

"Luke?"

"Our newest employee, and Sara's date. I believe once you see him, he'll need no introduction. And here they come now." Teddy waved at Adam and Luke, who each carried a tray of food. Adam nodded at Jackson as they sat down across from Teddy. Luke's smile was shy and his eyes went to Sara, who scooted over. Luke sat across from Jackson.

"I hear you've found a better job," Jackson said.

Luke nodded. "I sure have." His eyes returned to Sara.

"Hawaiian barbecue from Hula Jack's," Adam said. "Who gets the pineapple shakes?" Teddy and Luke raised their hands, and he passed them out, then gave himself and Sara bottles of Blue Springs. "Mahi mahi for me," Adam continued, "Kahlua pork for my husband, chicken teriyaki for Sara and Luke." He passed the food out and Jackson found himself wishing he'd noticed Hula Jack's cart.

"Maybe we can split a pineapple shake for dessert," Polly said.

"Hey, I'm a big spender. We can each have one." Their eyes met, and Jackson felt himself blush.

By mountain standards the night was still warm but the cool breeze became invigorating as they ate. A little ways away, by a bonfire on the beach, Troy Doheny and Derek Sand had traded their barber shears for guitars and were tuning up, their wives smiling nearby. The sounds of ping pong balls being swatted and the calls of people playing volleyball drifted over, but mostly Jackson heard a constant happy chatter from all the tables around them. The End of Summer Party was strictly for the locals - they never advertised it since a few of the traditions poked fun at the tourists. It looked like most of the town had turned out.

Troy and Derek broke into a duet, *"Surfing USA,"* and the crowd cheered. The duo was always a hit; there was something about Beach Boys songs sung beside a mountain lake that appealed.

Jackson squeezed fresh lemon onto his last bite of fish, then popped it in his mouth before turning to Polly. "You still want that shake?"

"In a little while?"

"Sure." Jackson said. "So Luke, how do you like our little town so far?"

"I haven't seen much of it yet, but I love it. I'm looking forward to seeing all of it." He paused, glanced at Sara. "I hope to make Cliffside my permanent home."

She looked back. They were obviously smitten.

"Jacky-Boy!" Lee Ballou's hand clapped hard on Jackson's shoulder and the stink of cheap whiskey came down in a cloud. Jackson jumped. His father might be a drunk, but he could be as silent as a jungle cat stalking prey.

"Dad," Jackson said. He couldn't bring himself to say more.

"Why Polly," Lee said, bending to kiss her cheek. "What are you doing here instead of frying up those eggs of yours?"

"Dale cooks those eggs you like so much, Lee. I only run the place."

"Still, I think you're a fine little cook." He clapped Jackson's shoulder again. "You need to make an honest woman out of this one, Jacky-Boy. She can cook *and* keep the books."

"Who are you with tonight, Dad? Where are your friends?"

"Oh, I'm here with Miss Kitty and Red."

"Daddy!" came Kitty's voice. "There you are!"

Kitty Ballou and her boyfriend Red Mackintosh arrived, out of breath. "We've been looking all over for you, Daddy! We were afraid you fell in the lake."

Lee burst out laughing. "Wouldn't be the first time."

"Hi, folks. Sorry about disturbing you." Red's face looked as red as his hair.

"Red's the finest produce man on the mountain," Teddy told Luke.

Red laughed. "I'm Cliffside Market's Manager of Fruits and Nuts."

"He specializes in nuts," Kitty said. "Come on, Daddy. I told you not to bother Jacky."

"Jacky-Boy needs some bothering."

"No, he doesn't."

"Kitty's right. I'm busy right now, Dad."

"Nah, let's stay a minute."

The old man tousled Jackson's hair, making him feel five years old.

"Lee," Red said. "Look here." He brought a bottle of Bud out from behind him.

Lee almost fell on Jackson as he lunged to snag it, but Red stepped back. "Let's go to our own bench first, Lee."

"You betcha." Lee paused. "Red's a man's man, Jacky-Boy. Maybe you could learn from him."

"Come on, Daddy. Let's go." Kitty nudged her father toward Red, and the drunk trailed him like a puppy dog back into the crowd. "Sorry about that, Jacky."

"Yeah, me too."

Polly laid her hand over his as he watched them disappear. "Takes all kinds."

"It does, indeed," Teddy agreed.

# 53
## *Drinking Games*

The End of Summer Party was going strong. Laurel Lutz took another shot of Wild Turkey, chased it with a swig of Sprite, and slammed the shot glass on the table. Whoops and hollers from the other actors ensued. Laurel had beaten the others yet again. When it came to drinking games, Laurel Lutz was the queen.

"I swear to Christ she has a hollow leg!" said Roman Rathbone as he slammed his shot glass down.

"And thighs," said Laurel, lifting the hem of her skirt a little. "I have wonderful, hollow thighs, just like my mother."

"Like you inherited those tits." Roman was showing signs of serious inebriation.

"Nah," said Finn Cooper, laughing. "She paid good money for those."

Laurel burst out in raucous laughter. "That's right! My momma had no tits!"

Roman swayed a little. "I guess this means your sister's are plastic, too."

Laurel narrowed her eyes. If there was one thing she couldn't tolerate, it was being compared to her sister, who thought she was a big shot because she'd done a couple of TV commercials. "There's nothing real about my sister. Not. One. Single. Fucking. Thing." She grabbed the bottle of whiskey and drank from it directly, no chaser.

The other actors watched in awe.

## 54
### *Polly's Sweater*

"The breeze is getting chilly," Polly said. "What would you say to taking a quick walk up to the cafe to get my sweater?"

"Sounds like a plan." Jackson looked at the Bellamy men. "Will you gentlemen excuse us?"

"Certainly," Teddy said. As he spoke, Paul Butters approached, dressed in all black. It was dark enough that he almost looked like a bodiless head bobbing closer, but as he neared, Jackson saw he held a bottle of wine in one hand and several glasses in the other. Only Paul would bring real glasses to a picnic on the beach.

"Care to join us, Chief? Polly?"

Jackson shook his head. "Not now, thanks. We're heading off for a bit."

"Are you sure? It's chardonnay. Inexpensive and simple, but I'm sure you'll agree it's an excellent wine."

"No, thanks," said Jackson. "But you kids enjoy yourselves."

Polly stepped closer to him and slipped her arm through his. They started toward the beach, and waved at Luke and Sara, who'd begun a walk of their own, but they didn't even notice; they were too wrapped up in each other.

"Are they holding hands?" asked Polly.

Jackson looked closer. "They sure are."

"Isn't that sweet," said Polly. "Young love." She snuggled closer.

Jackson covered her hand with his as they walked through the partygoers. "Fall's coming."

Several yards ahead of them, a shrill voice sliced the air: "Ensign! Twyla Dawn! You get back here this minute!" Two of the Matthews children came into view, followed by Taffilynn and the rest of her herd. The two breakaways bolted toward Jackson and Polly. "You stop this instant!" Taffilynn's orders were ignored.

"Oh, no," Polly said under her breath.

"Oh, crap."

When the children were no more than a few feet away, the girl tripped, fell in the sand, and squealed in enraged agony as her brother toppled over her.

Taffilynn broke into a lazy half-run that Jackson was sure was only for effect.

When she reached the pile of children, she grabbed the boy's arm, yanking him upright. He screamed.

"Ouch! Mommy!"

"Ensign hurt me!" The girl wailed as she was also yanked to her feet.

"Do you know what that is, Twyla Dawn?" Taffilynn looked furious. "That's Jesus telling you to knock it off!" She gave the girl a few unnecessary jerks, one direction then the other, as pretend wails of suffering rent the air.

People were staring and Jackson feared he might have to intervene, but Taffilynn's temper cooled. "Be reverent!" She hollered at the little girl as all her other children gaped.

"Everything okay, Taffilynn?" Jackson asked.

She suddenly looked older. "Oh," she said, waving a hand, "it's fine. Pat always wanders off at the worst times."

Jackson laughed. "Well, I hope he comes back soon. Enjoy your evening."

"You too, Chief." Taffilynn hissed something at the sniveling girl, then began herding her children toward a concession stand.

A few yards ahead, a lone figure in dark clothing sat on a smooth boulder. As they neared, Jackson saw the blond ponytail that could only belong to Merlin Skinner, the Wizard of Ink himself. His eyes were on a volleyball game in the sand.

"Nice night," Jackson said as they passed.

Merlin nodded. "Indeed." His eyes never strayed from the game.

# 55
## *Hammerhead at the Party*

His hand caressed the mirror case in his pocket as he watched the party.

The actors, drinking heavily, made fools of themselves. The fitness instructor from Cliffhouse and several others played volleyball against a group of giggling girls that included one he found particularly intriguing.

The police chief and Polly Owen were walking away, and that was good news. A young stranger held hands with Sara Bellamy not far from where her sinful fathers sat talking and drinking with Paul Butters.

That wrinkled, white-haired couple, Francis Trudy and Prudence Pender Pope, had the audacity to kiss in public, the wine they shared apparently loosening their morals. *No one should have to witness that.*

The smell of lakewater strengthened and he was certain the Lady drew near.

As he listened to the insipid singing of the aging, would-be Beach Boys, he looked from table to table, observing people carry on as if they were in the privacy of their own homes. It was foul. He wanted to do something about it.

The most raucous of all the tables belonged to the actors. He moved closer. Laurel Lutz broadcast that she needed to relieve herself. Unfortunately, her language was not so delicate. *I need to piss* were her precise words. It was crude. One of the men offered to walk her to the restrooms, but she declined. She began walking away from the others. Excitement filled him as he stepped into the shadows.

The dank fragrance of lakewater enveloped him, cool, invigorating. *It is time.*

# 56
## *Hot Chocolate*

They entered the diner by the backdoor. Polly left the lights off; there was enough light from the street lamps outside to see by. Jackson stood in the shadows while Polly grabbed her black sweater and shrugged it on. "That's better," she said. She moved closer to him. "While we're here, can I get you anything? I could make us hot chocolate?"

"With whipped cream on top?"

"Of course. Go have a seat."

Jackson sat while Polly clinked and clacked in the kitchen. He could just hear music coming from the beach area and he smiled to himself, appreciating his small-town life. Yes, he had an unsolved murder on his hands, but in the city he'd have half a dozen. *Cliffside is heaven.*

"Here you go." Polly slid onto the bench opposite him and set two mugs of rich dark cocoa between them. The whipped cream was mounded high.

Jackson drank deeply. "This is perfect."

Polly laughed. "Stay still," she ordered, and touched his nose with her finger, coming away with a dollop of cream. "It wouldn't be dignified for the Chief of Police to be seen like that." Holding his gaze, she licked the cream off her finger.

"No, it wouldn't."

They reverted to small talk while they enjoyed their cocoa; when they were done, Polly whisked the mugs away and returned a moment later. He stood. "Back to the party?"

"Yes. In a minute. I want to check the front door. It's silly, but…"

"It's not silly," he told her. She was looking toward the glass entry doors and he could smell her shampoo, clean, fresh. He touched her shoulder and she turned. Their eyes locked. He inclined his head and kissed her.

She responded, gently at first, then with a passion that matched his own.

"Well," she said at last. "Well, well."

"Well, what?" he asked, afraid he'd just ruined their long friendship.

"Well … I've been waiting a long time for that."

"And?" He knew she would say it wasn't what she'd hoped for.

"Even better than I imagined."

Relief flooded him.

"We'd better get back," she said. "You have to preside over the ritual dunking of the tourist, right?"

"Right."

"Just a sec." She walked up the aisle to check the front door, then paused, looking out. "Jackson. Come here."

He heard urgency in her voice and he was at her side in an instant.

"Look. Across the street at Zizi & Zob's."

Someone was in front of the darkened sub shop, doing something, moving their arm in broad strokes.

"Is that the graffiti artist?" Polly whispered.

"I bet it is. Unlock the door. Quietly."

She did but the hinge creaked as he pushed the door open. The person across the street looked around, then took off running, heading straight for the shadows.

"Shit." Jackson ran, chasing the man up a short street that led into a suburb of trees and cabins. He stopped running, caught his breath. The guy could be anywhere.

He returned to Zizi & Zob's and there it was, the big red Johnson. It spanned the entire shop, from one edge of the plate glass window to the other. The perp had sprayed big red clouds of sperm onto the glass door for added effect. "Shit."

He returned to the diner. "I need to use the phone."

"Go ahead." She locked up after him.

He called the station and reported the incident, determined to continue with his night off. The owners - Zizi and Zob - were a pair of dickheads, truth be told, and he wasn't in the mood to talk to them himself. *It's good to have minions.*

He hung up and turned to Polly. "Let's get back to the party."

# 57
## *Lost*

"Pardon me," he said. "Are you lost?"

Laurel Lutz had been wandering in circles for fifteen minutes after walking too far from her friends in her quest for the perfect place to pee. She turned and asked, "How did you know?"

"I was walking along the lake to get away from all the noise. I saw movement." He smiled. "At first I thought you were a deer, so I stood very still to avoid startling you. The deer, I mean."

He was a local, she knew, but she couldn't place him because she was just a wee bit too snockered. And it didn't matter. He was cute; she was lost. "Who are you?" She giggled.

"Anyone you want me to be. Who are you?"

"An actress. Anyone you want *me* to be." She felt terribly clever.

"Would you like me to walk you back to your friends?"

"Come closer. I can barely see you."

He stepped nearer, his dark clothing revealing nothing except that he was tall and slender. "Is that better?"

"It is." She paused, thinking that screwing Roman exclusively was getting pretty old. This guy might spice things up a little. "What would you say to walking a little farther from the party before we turn around? You know, for some more peace and quiet? Or whatever." She giggled.

"That's an excellent idea," he said. He extended his arm, and she took it, nearly knocking him down when she stumbled against him, but he steadied them both.

*Nice and strong.*

# 58
## *Too Soon*

Luke could smell the scent of the lake as it merged with Sara's sweet fragrance. It was light, floral, and made him want to get closer to her.

Sara snuggled against him as they walked the path a few feet from the lake's edge. "Want to sit down?"

"Sure."

She led him to a bench. They sat, and Luke looked up at the sky. Away from the lights, the stars shone brightly. Despite the moonlight, they glittered, millions of them, against the black velvet sky.

Sara moved even closer and his heart felt like it was going to beat out of his chest. "Have you ever met someone new and felt like you've known them forever?" she asked.

"Not until now." He fought the urge to kiss her. *Too soon.*

## 59
## *The Dunking Man*

"Well, there he is!" Teddy Bellamy boomed as Jackson and Polly walked onto the sandy beach. "We've been waiting for you!"

"It's time for you to do your duty, sir!" Derek Sand said as Troy handed Jackson a big fake gavel.

A spotlight shone on the swimmer's raft a couple of pool lengths out in the lake. Someone in a black scuba suit stood behind the tourist effigy, holding it up. It was made of twigs and branches bound together with vines; Cliffside's own version of the Burning Man, this was the Dunking Man.

Feeling as silly as he always did, Jackson stepped forward to the cheers of the crowd. He cleared his throat, took the bullhorn from Troy, then spoke, hoping no stray tourists had infiltrated the party. "For impeding traffic and playing radios too loud, for making drunken passes at every waitress and waiter in town, for littering, for trespassing, for taking pictures of us townsfolk because we're "colorful," for wearing Speedos when you shouldn't, and for general mayhem, I hereby arrest you for making all of Cliffside cringe. In lieu of jail time, I declare this an official dunking."

The crowd erupted in cheers and applause. Out on the raft, the 'executioner' made a big show of tossing the effigy into the lake. "It is done, Chief," he intoned in his own bullhorn.

On the shore, everyone whooped and hollered.

After lighting a series of fireworks on the raft, the executioner slipped into the dark water.

# 60
## *Fireworks*

Fireworks blossomed in the sky - gold, silver, blue - as Luke took Sara's hand and looked into her eyes. More fireworks exploded over the lake and Luke saw the silhouettes of two people, perhaps fifty feet down the path, walking out of some trees together. Sara looked up, saw them, too, but turned her attention back to Luke.

"I'm so glad you quit that job. What a horrible woman."

"You have no idea. I'm glad I quit, too." He bent to her and their lips came together in a long kiss. The fireworks he felt inside dwarfed the ones in the sky.

# 61
## *Siechert Does His Duty*

It was like fucking a corpse. Except corpses didn't drool.

Roger Siechert banged away. Constance Welling messed up on pills and booze, barely moved. Occasionally, she grunted and patted his back, before falling back into Stuporville. He wasn't enjoying himself, but that wasn't the point. *The point is to place myself - and my seed, ha ha! - somewhere at the time of Tessa's death!* And given Welling's inebriated state, he doubted he'd have much trouble convincing her they'd been together all evening.

He grunted, squeezed off round two into the tattooed bag of bones, and rolled off.

She mumbled something that might have been, "Good boy."

"Whatever." He cocked his leg and broke wind.

Constance smiled and her eyes swam toward the ceiling before closing again.

Siechert felt good. The chill inside of him was long gone; he hadn't noticed it since sometime before he left Tessa's. "Hey." He nudged Constance.

She drooled.

"Hey," he said a little louder, jabbing an elbow into her ribs.

"Whaaaat ..." She opened her eyes. They floated around, unfocused.

"May I spend the night?"

"Of course." She closed her eyes again and continued drooling.

*Perfect.* He'd picked her up outside and there'd been no witnesses. There were cameras in the hotel that would show him coming in with Constance and leaving in the morning. The only thing he had to worry about was the hour or so before they entered, when Cornhull was killed. And it wasn't as if Constance Welling had the clarity to know they hadn't been together since much earlier. *They'll be none the wiser...*

Once Constance began to snore, he reached over, grabbed her cell phone off the nightstand, and deleted all the texts between them. He then did the same with his own phone. He doubted an investigation would ever get this far, but you couldn't be too careful. He squeezed out another stink bomb and giggled.

# 62
## *Hammerhead and the Actress*

The fireworks burst in rapid succession, the kaleidoscopic frenzy overhead strobing in a way he found aesthetically pleasing. Still, the creature at his side put a damper on the beauty.

After relieving herself behind a tree, the actress rejoined him. She smelled terrible. Too much of too many things: garlic, perfume, and alcoholic sweat. He knew she wanted to have sexual relations with him; she'd said as much. The thought sickened him. The Lady, however, assured him that he must pretend to be interested.

"Right this way." Hammerhead urged her forward. "Let's find a place a bit more private."

*Yes,* said the Lady.

"Outdoor sex?" the actress asked. "That's naughty. Are you always this kinky?"

"I love nature," he said.

*Stop here,* the Lady ordered when they reached a small clearing.

"Here," he said, looking around. "This will be perfect."

The actress smiled at him. "I've never done it in the woods."

*And you never will,* he thought.

Laurel Lutz unbuttoned her blouse, exposing her too-large, too-round mammaries. "I don't wear a bra," she said. "Or panties." She lifted her skirt. She had told him no lies.

"Do you want me this way ..." she exposed her pudenda, "or from behind?" She turned, wiggling her hips so her bare buttocks swayed.

A bubble of acid rose to the top of his esophagus, leaving a bitter taste in his throat as brilliant red fireworks exploded.

"Turn toward me." He placed his hand on her shoulder and turned her around. He added slight pressure, indicating what he wanted next.

Laurel Lutz didn't hesitate. She dropped to her knees and began unzipping him.

Keeping the hand on her shoulder, guiding her, he reached into his pocket with the other and withdrew the mirror and opened it. He felt the cool rush of the Blue Lady building inside him, moving through him, making her way into his arms, his hands, his fingertips.

Laurel coughed, reached inside his boxers, withdrew his flaccid manhood, and coughed again, harder.

He pressed her shoulder, reminding her why she was here.

The coughing turned into a fit and she swayed to one side.

Holding her in place, he brought the mirror up and held it in front of her.

Her hands shot to her throat. Her eyes bulged as she looked up at him.

He grabbed her by the hair and forced her to look at herself.

Her mouth moved as if she was trying to speak, but there was no sound except a gurgle. Her face reddened and streams of water poured from her nose and mouth.

The Lady was working her magic.

The actress spasmed and it took effort to keep her in place.

The smell of lakewater was powerful.

She made a final desperate rattling sound and toppled over. She twitched; her foot kicked once, twice, and then she was still.

He snapped the compact shut and tucked his penis back into his pants.

*Well done,* said the Lady, and parted from him. He saw her, but only her back. She was a silky blue figure in flowing robes. She disappeared almost instantly.

# 63
## *2 A.M.*

At two a.m., the lake was all but deserted. On the beach, the trash bins had been emptied. The only signs of humanity were sandy footprints and the faint lingering smell of barbecued meat. Now, the only sounds came from nature: the lap of small waves kissing the shoreline, the occasional calls of night birds, a chitter of bats chasing insects.

Out on the swimmer's float, the last ashes of the burnt-out fireworks blew into the black water. The tourist effigy bumped against the raft, making a sound like fingernails scratching for purchase. In a small clearing far down the west side of the lake, Laurel Lutz's body lay dripping water and playing host to night insects.

The Blue Lady, empowered by the kill, glided along the lake's edge, surveying her domain.

Up near the beach's cement concession stand, out of the chill wind, Jackson Ballou and Polly Owen sat together on a bench in the building's shadows. They had lost track of time as they talked and talked. And talked. Jackson thought he had known everything about this woman, his best friend, but there was so much more than he'd ever dreamed of before their first kiss.

"We should probably call it a night," Polly said as the wind ruffled through her hair. "Morning is too close."

"That it is." Jackson stood up and offered her his hand.

"It's a beautiful night," she said. They surveyed the lake together.

"Indeed." He spotted something, a faint blue glow near the lake, and pointed. "Polly? Do you see that?"

She followed his finger. "What the heck is it?"

"I have no idea."

"It kind of looks like a person," she said. "But people don't glow."

All the hairs on Jackson's neck saluted. "It's probably some sort of fog."

"Or the Blue Lady," she murmured.

Jackson watched the pale blue figure glide toward them. It was still a long way off, but moved faster than a human could. And more smoothly.

"Jackson?" Polly tugged his sleeve.

"What?"

"I think we should leave. Now. We're not supposed to be here."

"Magic hour?" he asked, trying to overcome the cold fear growing in his belly.

"Might be. Come on."

As they walked toward the parking lot, a horrible sound rent the air. It had to be a night bird, but it sounded like the laugh of a banshee.

# 64
## *Of Tubs and Tantrums*

**SATURDAY**

Every time she closed her eyes, Constance saw that face - blue-gray, furious, evil. The whole thing was throwing her chakras out of balance and making her tremble with anxiety.

Then there was the humiliation she'd endured at Luke's hand. It was the reason she'd foregone the lake party last night. She was in no mood to deal with the jubilance of these inbred small-towners. Also, it had been her hope that Luke might come looking for her when he realized she wasn't there. He hadn't, of course. *And isn't that just the shits!* She'd lost him to another man. It was the ultimate blow. Her head throbbed from Friday night's excesses, but she'd taken a Percocet and that would cure her soon enough.

Last night, the handsome red-haired doctor had come, bedded her, and if her sore body was any indication, he'd done it well. *Did he take me up the ass? She wished she could remember.*

From the time he'd sat down on the bench next to her and put his arm around her until she woke alone in the morning - *why did he leave so early?* - she had enjoyed herself, had enjoyed him, but the details were lost.

She looked down at her body as she stretched out in the tub. She looked good and she knew it. Her double Ds were as flawless as ever. Her long legs were shapely. It was no wonder the doctor couldn't resist her. She'd found another man, and when Luke found out, he'd be furious. As an added bonus, that manly Nurse Cornhull would be devastated when she returned from her vacation. Constance chuckled.

As she soaked, she made plans for tonight. She'd dress to kill, go to the winetasting, and surely Dr. Siechert - *Roger* - would be there. He was a man who could handle a real woman; and this time, she'd remember every detail.

She added warm water to her bath and as it ran, the stink of the lake arose. She sat up and turned the water off, a chill slithering up her spine.

*Constance ...*

She jumped, sloshing water over the side of the tub. "Who is it? Who's there?"

The room was silent.

*Constance ... you belong to me ...*

"Eliza? Is that you?" She knew her imaginary spirit guide wouldn't answer back.

*Constance ...*

"Leave me alone," she whispered.

The tub handle turned and hot water exploded from the faucet.

Constance shrieked, bolted to her feet, slipping and sliding, barely maintaining her balance. She grappled for a towel, threw it around herself and watched as the tub filled. She didn't want to touch it.

*Constance ...*

She backed away. Then, as suddenly as it began, the water stopped.

Her own breathing echoed through the room. She stepped closer and gazed into the water. Mirror-like, and so unnaturally still that the water reflected her image. She gasped, then screamed as her reflection transformed, distorting into the blue-white face she'd seen in the closet.

*Constance ... you are mine.*

Screaming, she shot from the room.

Behind her, unseen, wet footprints followed.

*\*\*\**

Sara sat on a stool at the registration desk going through the records for complaints about the most recently renovated rooms, but had found very little. All she wanted to think about was Luke Donovan, who was currently leading a spinning class for Chad. Teddy and Adam were down the hill picking up magnets. When they returned, they would place them in 337, 339, and the other affected rooms.

She found a complaint about 330's bathroom steaming up by itself three weeks ago, and added it to the list.

*Luke.* She couldn't keep him off her mind. She knew very little about him, but as they'd joked last night, she also felt as if she'd always known him. It worried - and thrilled - her. She'd been attracted to a few guys, and had even gone exclusive with an accounting undergrad for six months back in college, but what she had thought was love began fading the first time he had decided to wax poetic about doing a general ledger. *I was so young and stupid!*

But Luke ... Luke was different.

In the morning quiet, she heard the guest elevator arrive, then what sounded like bare feet slapping the floor. A moment later, Constance Welling, wearing only a flapping white bath towel careened into the lobby.

Sara slid off the stool as Constance approached. *Thank God the lobby's empty.* Constance looked rabid and a solid stream of obscenities sputtered from her lips. Sara pressed her two-way radio and called the only other person on duty: "Jerry, come to the front desk ASAP."

"May I help you?"

"'May I help you? May I help you?'" Constance's face was a mask of fury. "What the hell do you think? You better shitting help me, and right now!"

Sara kept an innocent smile plastered on her face. "What seems to be the matter?"

"Oh, you figured out something's the matter?"

Calmly, Sara wiped spittle off her arm as Jerry Belvedere trotted toward them.

"Your shitting hotel is the problem. I can't believe you have the nerve to charge so much when the plumbing doesn't even work. I was nearly killed!"

*Oh, crap. Not again.* "I'm sorry, Ms. Welling. What room are you in?"

"I'm in 202, but I want a different room. A better room, and it had better not cost more. I want a Jacuzzi. And not on the third floor!"

Jerry Belvedere watched from a safe distance as Sara took a deep breath. "I don't think we have any Jacuzzi rooms available on the second floor, but I can move you a few doors down."

Constance glared at her.

Sara remained outwardly peaceful but wondered why the other woman didn't want anything on three. *She's been snooping!*

"Why don't you tell me what happened in 202?"

"It's haunted!"

"I can't leave the desk at the moment, Ms. Welling, but Jerry will go up and make sure it's safe so you can dress, won't you Jerry?"

"Glad to." Belvedere stepped forward as Constance whirled and saw him for the first time.

She *tsked.* "Were you *ogling* me?"

"He was not ogling you, Ms. Welling. I paged him."

Belvedere nodded. "Would you like me to bring some clothing down for you instead, Ms. Welling?"

"I do not want you going through my underwear! I'll get dressed after you check the room."

Sara handed him a keycard and he disappeared.

Welling snapped her fingers twice. "Give me a key to another room, right now, or I'm checking out."

"I can put you in 226. It's the same layout as you have now, but with a partial view of the lake."

"What's my discount?"

"There's no discount."

*Tsk.* "Not even for my pain and suffering?"

"Pain?"

"I nearly fell in the tub!"

"Are you injured?"

"I can't stop shaking." She held out her hand, which commenced shaking about half a second later.

"I'm sorry. That's the best I can do."

A local shuttle pulled up out front and disgorged half a dozen people and their luggage. *Why now?*

"Give me a key. After I dress I'll want that bellboy to come and move my things. And just so you know," she said, "these are grounds for a lawsuit, and I have a good lawyer."

"We have a lawyer too, Miss Welling."

Constance's eyes blazed. "Well, *mine* works for free, so there's no limit to how far we can press the matter!"

*You must give him great blowjobs then.* Sara smiled sweetly. It didn't surprise her a bit that Welling was one of those litigious types.

Welling glared at her, then started toward the nearest leather chair. The thought of her bare ass assaulting it made Sara cringe. "Wait!"

The woman turned. "What?"

"Stay right where you are one moment, please." She called down to the gym and asked them to bring up a robe, figuring that was faster than waiting for Housekeeping; sure enough, not thirty seconds passed before Luke Donovan appeared with a big white terrycloth robe. Constance had her back to him, unaware her former assistant had arrived.

He set the robe on the counter. "Chad asked me to bring this to you, Sara."

Sara gave a slight nod toward Constance.

He looked and Sara saw his color drain away.

It was too late. Constance spun and was up in Luke's face, her finger jabbing, wagging, and pointing as her mouth began to work. "You ungrateful little bitch! How *dare* you humiliate me like you have! After all I've done for you! You'll never be a writer now! How dare you leave me! And for a *man!*"

"What?"

"You heard me! How dare you!" Her voice echoed through the lobby and the new arrivals, just inside the doors, paused to gawk at the spectacle. Sara raced around the counter, had them set their bags in a corner, then herded them out to the veranda coffee shop for free refreshments and hurried back in.

"I have given and given and *given* to you!" Constance pounded both fists into Luke's chest.

He grappled for her flying fists.

"You dirty piece of scum!" Veins in her neck bulged and one throbbed on her temple. Her face contorted, her lips peeling back in a hideous grimace. She relaunched her attack.

Luke stepped back.

"If you keep hitting this man, I will call the police and have you arrested," Sara said.

"This is none of your business, you slut! Until you understand my humiliation, don't you judge me! He left me for a man. A *man!*"

"Please, Ms. Welling," Sara said. "Keep your voice down and listen to me."

Constance glowered at Sara, who let a smile slip onto her lips. "Luke did not leave you for a man. He left you because of the way you treated him." She paused. "And I can personally assure you ... he is *not* gay."

Constance's eyes darted between the two of them and Sara could almost see the realization dawning. At that moment, Constance collapsed onto the floor in a heap, arms flailing and legs kicking as she rolled, wailed, and screamed. "Oh God! I'm having an anxiety attack!"

Luke took several steps back.

"Call 911!" Constance rolled on the floor like a woman on fire, her towel taking its leave of her body as she floundered.

Sara's breath hitched as breasts were displayed. Then her crotch.

She gasped as the silver barbell attached to the wailing woman's privates glinted.

"I'm shaking! I can't stop shaking!"

Luke snagged the towel and tried to throw it over her, but she swatted it away and spat. A gob of saliva hit him in the face.

"You get the hell away from me, you cheating shit! Call 911!"

Sara grabbed the robe and threw it over the woman while Luke wiped his face with his sleeve.

Jerry Belvedere reappeared and Constance gave him an eyeful.

"Why isn't anyone calling 911!" Constance's voice ricocheted off the walls as Sara and Jerry tried to bundle her, but she held her arms stiff at her sides and kept up the shaking.

Luke stepped close to Sara. "You don't need to call 911. She has plenty of tranquilizers in her room."

Jerry bent down and she allowed him to help her up.

"I'll go along," Sara said, handing him a key. Constance was lawsuit-happy and Sara didn't want Jerry to end up being accused of harassment. "Luke, hold down the fort? If guests come in before I get back, just stall them. I'll only be a minute."

"Will do."

Calmer now, Constance leaned against Jerry and fake-sobbed as they took the elevator to the second floor. Sara grabbed a luggage cart and pushed it to 202. As they entered the room, she smelled lakewater. Her hackles rose.

Jerry left the trembling woman on the couch while he got her a glass of water. She threw it on the floor, sniffling between fake sobs.

"Would you like help packing your things?" Jerry asked.

Constance ignored him.

Sara suppressed a shiver when she noticed the wet footprints leading from the bathroom. The tub was full. She leaned down and pulled the stopper and water flowed smoothly down the drain. If it weren't for the lake smell, she would have assumed Welling's histrionics were manufactured. *But maybe not entirely.* Again, she wondered why Constance was afraid of the third floor. *She must have gone. Has she been up there?*

After packing up Welling's toiletries, she opened the closet, filled the suitcases, and stacked them on the luggage cart.

As Constance whimpered into Jerry's chest, Sara inspected the wet footprints. They were sodden like the others. Constance couldn't have made them.

"All done," Sara said, pushing the cart to the door. "Let's get you to your new room, Ms. Welling."

Her head still buried, Welling stood, clinging to Jerry and glaring at Sara as they headed to 226.

Once inside, Sara's radio buzzed. Luke told her the guests were waiting at the desk.

"I'll get her settled," Jerry said. He pulled Constance's hands off his shirt and left her on a chair.

"Don't be long."

Jerry gave Sara a little smile. "I'll handle her."

# 65
## *The Chocolate Wanderer*

It was Roger Siechert's turn to take the clinic's short Saturday hours and it was a good thing nobody was sick - he didn't feel so well himself. Only he and the receptionist were in the building as he sat in his office doodling in the margins of the latest Physician's Desk Reference. He drew a finger and sighed. The Chocolate Wanderer was currently sheathed in Saran Wrap and stashed in his freezer at home between a bag of frozen string beans and a leftover kielbasa and Brussels sprouts casserole.

The thought made him a little hungry for the first time this morning. He looked forward to Oktoberfest. *German beer and sausages!*

Last year, he'd taken Tessa to the celebration. Cliffside would be at it again in a couple of weeks, and he would go, but Tessa wouldn't be joining him this year.

*What to do? What to do?* That's what he'd thought in one form or another ever since he'd pulled away from her house with the Chocolate Wanderer in his pocket. *At least I still have the best part of her.* Constance Welling had all but absolved his fears. Between Tessa's vacation and Constance's muddled memories, he had an airtight alibi and plenty of time to put things right.

"Doctor?" The receptionist's voice came through the intercom.

"What is it?"

"A Constance Welling is on the phone. She says you saw her the other day and prescribed some Temazepam for her?"

*Oh shit, now she probably thinks we're a couple.* He sighed. "Put her on hold and bring me her chart."

A moment later, he had the chart and picked up the phone. "Ms. Welling?"

"Yes, Doctor. I was beginning to think we'd lost our connection, it took so long for you to come to the phone." He heard her make that irritating *tsking* noise. "I tried to text you but it wouldn't send."

"I'm working and need to keep this brief. What can I help you with?"

"I had a panic attack this morning, and the Temazepam isn't strong enough."

He was glad she understood the need to keep the call professional. "Take two."

"I did. I need Xanax. I have a workshop to do in a little while."

"I'll call a prescription for Xanax in to Main Street Pharmacy." He paused, added warmth to his voice. "I hope your workshop goes splendidly."

"Thank you. Roger, I mean, Doctor, I was wondering …" Her voice turned flirtatious.

"Yes?"

"Are you coming to the wine tasting at Cliffhouse tonight?"

"I don't know. Why?"

"Maybe we could have dinner and a drink beforehand."

*Jesus Christ.* "Okay. I'll talk to you later." He dropped the phone in its cradle and stared at it. *She might be the very definition of the word clingy, but at least she's handy.*

Tessa was clingy, too, but she knew how to make him happy. He drew another well-manicured finger in the PDR. His anus twitched a little and he began whistling *The Happy Wanderer* to himself.

# 66
## *Missing*

*It's always something.* Jackson Ballou had gotten a call from the director at the Cliffside Little Theater. An actress, one Laurel Lutz, hadn't shown up for rehearsal today. Drunk, she'd wandered away last night. Evidently, this wasn't unusual except that she hadn't shown up for rehearsal.

He parked behind Cliffhouse and walked inside. It was cool and quiet, peaceful. There were a few clutches of tourists sitting in chairs in the lobby, their voices mingling with the bubbling of the brook. He approached the desk. Louis was manning it. "I'm looking for any of the Bellamys," Jackson said.

"Teddy and Adam just got back and they and Miss Bellamy are upstairs. Third floor, I believe, taking care of something. I can call them if you like."

"I'll go up," Jackson said. He paused. "Were you at the party last night?"

"Uh, yeah. Why? I mean-"

"Did you happen to see a woman wandering around? Young, pretty, short blond hair. Nice figure. She's an actress at the theater. Laurel Lutz."

"Not that I recall."

"She was drunk."

"Doesn't ring any bells. Is something wrong?"

"She's missing." He handed the man a card. "If you hear anything, give me a call, will you?"

"I'll do that."

"Thanks." Jackson headed for the elevators. When he arrived on the third floor, it appeared empty: no *Do Not Disturb* signs on the doors, no maids, no guests. It was silent as a tomb, which seemed peculiar on a Saturday.

As he approached 337, he heard voices. He knocked. Adam Bellamy opened the door. "Jackson! Come on in!"

He stepped inside. Teddy and Sara greeted him. "You guys having a party?"

"Sort of," Sara said.

Teddy laughed. "We're doing more than that." He held up a dark disk the size of a quarter. "We're ghost busting."

"Hopefully." Sara pointed at a box on the table half full of various small disks, squares, and rectangles. "We're putting these all over this floor. We'll do the second floor next."

"Why?" Jackson asked.

"We've tucked magnets between the molding and the carpet in the halls and rooms," Adam said. "They'll hopefully stop or disrupt any anomalous activity that might occur."

"Busting the ghosts," Teddy said. He was obviously enjoying himself.

"Have you done this room yet?" Jackson asked.

"No. We're taking a break and sort of hoping something will pop up and say boo." Teddy grinned.

"Speak for yourself," Sara said. "I thought those footprints were scary enough without hearing any voices."

*Jackson ...*

Jackson looked to Sara. "Did you say that?"

"Say what?" Sara asked.

"My name."

"Seriously?" Sara asked. "You heard your name?"

"Of course I heard my name." He laughed. "Are you trying to gaslight me?"

*Jackson ...*

He jumped. They stared at him. "Don't tell me you didn't say my name, Sara."

"On my honor."

"And none of you even heard it?"

"Nope," Adam said. "You heard your name?"

"Female voice, right in my ear. I think Sara must be taking ventriloquism classes." He forced a smile, but gooseflesh rose.

"She's here," Sara said. "The Blue Lady."

"Rosa calls her Santa Muerte," Teddy explained. As if that explained anything.

"Is this the ghost your maids and the tourists were talking about?"

"Evidently," Adam said.

"But it isn't a ghost," Teddy said. "It's not a human spirit. It's stronger than that, and has the potential to do real damage, according to what I'm reading. It's called an elemental force. A water elemental to be precise."

That was too much for Jackson. "Okay, but none of you heard anything?"

Everyone shook their heads.

*Jackson ... You are mine ...*

"What the hell!"

"Again?" Sara asked, her eyes bright.

"Yes. She says I'm hers." The voice in his ear chilled him but he wasn't about to show it. Hearing voices was *not* his style. "Listen, I've got to get back to work. I just stopped by to ask if any of you know who Laurel Lutz is."

The Bellamys nodded. "She's playing Ado Annie at the Cliffside Little Theater," Adam said.

"She's known around town as Laurel Lush," Teddy added.

"What about her?"

"They haven't seen her since last night at the party. She wandered off. Did any of you see her last night, by any chance?"

The husbands shook their heads. "Not that I recall," said Teddy. "I did notice her at their table. The actors' table is always loud and she's usually the loudest."

Jackson looked at Sara. "You and Luke walked that way, right? Along the west side of the lake?"

Sara nodded. "We probably walked a mile. We went way beyond the picnic area. There was no one else on the path. Except ..."

"Except?" Jackson asked.

*Jackson ...*

With great effort, he ignored the whispering voice.

"A couple. We only saw them for an instant during the fireworks. They were too far away to even be sure it was a man and a woman. They disappeared into the trees, or that's how it looked. It was really dark. I wish we'd paid more attention."

"It's helpful. Thank you."

"Laurel Lutz has a reputation as a party girl," Adam said. "Maybe she picked someone up."

"Maybe," Jackson said. "Or maybe it's coincidence."

*Jackson ... You are mine ...*

"Is it getting damp in here?" Teddy asked.

"I think you ought to put those magnets out now," Jackson said.

"You heard it again?" Sara looked at him, hope in her eyes.

"Several times." The air felt heavy.

"Look!" Sara pointed toward the open bathroom door. Ribbons of mist curled out.

"Holy crap," Adam said. He stepped toward the bathroom.

"No, Dad," Sara whispered. "Don't."

"Last night," Jackson said, "Polly and I stayed at the lake quite late. We were the last ones there." He hesitated. "We saw something. It looked like a blue glow. It was gliding along the edge of the lake, headed for the beach. We thought maybe it was some kind of unusual fog or ball lightning or something." He glanced at Adam, then Sara.

"Something that science could explain." He stared at the mist curling out of the bathroom.

*Jackson ...*

"Do you think it was the Blue Lady?" Sara asked.

"Actually," he lied, unable to admit it, "I was thinking maybe Laurel Lutz was on her way back and wearing something phosphorescent or reflective."

*You are mine ...*

"Oh hell," Jackson said. "I've had enough of this." He walked straight to the bathroom, hand resting on his weapon. The room was so damp it was nearly raining. He couldn't see through the white mist, but with a sudden burst of cold wind, the fog disappeared, leaving only damp towels and walls behind.

He returned to the main room.

"What did you see?" asked Sara.

"Nothing. Not a damned thing."

They all looked disappointed.

"Be careful what you wish for. And put those magnets out, will you?" Jackson went to the room door and looked back. "Sara, I might ask you and Luke to take a walk with me if Laurel Lutz doesn't reappear soon. What do you say?"

"Glad to."

Jackson left, forcing himself not to run to the elevators.

# 67
## *Constance, Rebuffed*

"Well, the turnout for my writer's workshop today was a complete disaster. It's all the fault of the Crystal Cavern. They did *nothing* to promote my event. Clearly, they have no business savvy," Constance told Merlin Skinner.

"I didn't realize you were qualified to teach," he said.

She *tsked*. "Well, I *am* a published authoress. If that doesn't qualify me to teach writing, I don't know *what* does!"

"Don't move."

Constance lay on her stomach on the tattoo chair and concentrated on the needle pricking her skin. It was like a series of tiny erotic spankings on her derriere. Her lady parts were moist and hungry, and she rolled her hips a little in hopes of getting some extra attention from the blond artist.

He was gorgeous: tall and thin, with Nordic cheekbones, smooth skin, blue eyes, a straight nose and perfectly kissable lips. He was the epitome of a poet, a true aesthete, and if the needle in his long, slender-fingered hands was his paintbrush, Constance Wellings' ass was his canvas. Percy Shelley had nothing on Merlin Skinner.

A firm hand landed on her rocking hips. "Hold still, please," he said.

She giggled. "Sorry. It tickles."

He said nothing, just kept drawing. "We're almost done."

"Since I'm here, I was wondering if you could give me another tattoo today."

"It depends on what you want." His voice was flat. "I have another appointment in about ninety minutes."

"Just a tiny, little dragonfly." She craned her neck to look at him.

"Hold still, please."

"And do you want to know where I want it?"

Only the movement and buzz of his electric needle gave any indication that the man was even conscious. "Where?"

"Well," she said. "It's kind of embarrassing …"

"I don't do genital art."

Embarrassed anger surged through her. "Well then. I guess I'll have to go somewhere else."

"I guess so."

Although she wanted to despise the man for his lack of interest, she couldn't. His refusal only made him more appealing. Perhaps he was a religious man. Even that possibility turned her on. She'd love to corrupt a man like Merlin Skinner.

# 68
## *Wine Tasting*

Cliffhouse was only half full, but the winetasting was as much for the locals as the tourists, perhaps more, and business was booming.

Sara and Luke had a wonderful meal at La Chatte Rouge, hitting the bistro early to avoid the crowds. She told him about the magnets over dinner. They strolled the shoreline path, arm in arm, enjoying the cool breeze that drifted off the water. The tour boat, lit with white lights, circled the lake.

"That looks like fun," Luke said.

"It is. Would you like to do it?"

"I'd love it." Feeling cold, he snuggled deeper into his jacket and drew Sara closer. "Cliffside is great."

"I've always loved it, but it's even better with you."

Another couple approached and they stepped back to let them by.

"Dr. Siechert," Sara said. "Ms. Welling."

The doctor nodded and Constance glared, clutching Siechert's arm. Alcohol wafted off them as they brushed by.

"You hate her as much as I do," Luke said.

"How can you tell?"

"I can feel it."

"I didn't like her before she rolled around and showed me her privates," Sara said.

"I worked for her for three weeks. She wanted to show them to me, too."

"Did she?" Sara asked. "Show you?"

"Not until yesterday."

"She thought you and Chad were a couple," Sara said.

He stopped walking and laughed heartily. "Of course she did. No straight man could turn her down, after all." Noticing Constance had stopped moving and was looking back at them, he said, *"You're so Vain* was written about her, I'm sure of it."

"So is she." Sara chuckled. "It's sort of sad, really. What must it be like to be her? All she cares about is impressing other people."

"You're being much too kind," Luke said. "She also cares about controlling everyone she meets."

"I think she's been snooping around the lodge," Sara said as they took up their stroll. "She's aware something's happening on the third floor. My dads think she's trying to write a book about Cliffhouse's ghosts."

"I'm sure she's been snooping. She showed me some sort of gadget she said she could use to get inside rooms."

"Oh, crap. I wonder if there's any point in warning my dads. It would piss them off."

"I don't know," Luke said. "She claims to be a psychic, so that gives her permission to make things up. Unless you want to search her room, I'd probably say nothing."

"God, psychic. She's pathetic. Just another fraud." Sara laughed. "Maybe she's for real - I loathe her so much I don't know."

"Me, too." A cold gust of wind hit them in the face. "Did you hear anything more from Chief Ballou about that actress?"

"My dads said the police went out on the lake but found nothing. No one's seen her." She snuggled closer. "I think fall is finally here. I'm getting cold. Shall we go inside?"

\*\*\*

The wine tasting was in full swing, and Cliffhouse's lobby looked like an elegant poster, from the tall-beamed ceiling to the clutches of well-dressed guests who murmured in hushed, civilized tones. Jordan played soft jazz on the grand piano and a fire crackled in the stone fireplace on the west wall. Along the south wall, in front of the tall windows, linen-covered tables were manned by wine experts who poured samples for visitors. Blue Springs Sparkling Water bottles stood like soldiers on each table, ready to be poured into small paper cups to serve as palate cleansers. The accompanying trays of appetizers looked, well, good enough to eat.

Sara waved at Maisy Hart as she exited Omar's Tavern. The woman, dressed in a black cocktail dress with chiffon sleeves that did little to hide the sag of her age-weary arms, clutched a small handbag in her left hand and twisted a longish string of pearls in the other. She looked slightly lost as she approached.

"Sara, dear. Where might I find Jon? He's not at his usual post in the bar."

"I'm sure he'll be right back. He's probably checking stock in the wine cellar. I can page him if you like."

"Oh, no, that's all right. I'll wait."

"Why don't you try one of the wines?" Sara said.

"I will. And Sara? Would you send someone up with more towels? Somehow the ones in my bathroom got damp. It's the oddest thing."

"I'll do it right now."

"And dear?"

"Yes?"

"Would you have them drop off some more of that wonderful bubble bath? I'm running low."

"Of course."

Maisy left for the wine tables as Jordan launched into *Harlem Nocturne*. It was perfect.

"Come on," Sara said. "There are magnets in my office. Let's grab those and the towels and take care of Aunt Maisy's room."

"Don't forget the bubble bath," Luke added.

Sara smiled.

\*\*\*

"She loves this room," Sara said as they entered Maisy's suite.

"I can see why." Luke looked around at the art deco furnishings. "It looks lost in time."

"It does, but it's the bathroom she loves most. It's the second biggest one in the hotel. Come on," she said. "Let's change the towels."

They entered the bathroom, mint green tile with matching fixtures - two sinks, a toilet, bidet, and tub. The ceiling was white, as were the upper portions of the walls and a yellow band of trim edged the tile. The tub, also backed by mint tile, had an arched surround built into the wall and a lacy curtain that was halfway open. The sinks and toilets were set into similar arches and a vase of Easter lilies was set on the countertop. Their sweetness cloyed in Luke's nose and made him think of funerals. White ceiling globes lit the room. The floor was tiled in pale yellow and white throw rugs were placed in front of all the fixtures. Chrome towel racks gleamed from beneath neat, unused white towels.

The room *was* damp; Luke could see the moisture clinging to the walls. He shivered. At least there was no fog or mist, but as Sara pulled the towels from the racks, he could see their dampness. He helped her place the new ones. She felt the toilet paper, then removed and tossed it, then replaced it with a fresh roll from a small linen cabinet just outside the bathroom.

Finally, she fished a handful of bubble bath packets from her pocket and placed them on the counter. "I hope the damp doesn't ruin these."

"Ready for the magnets?" He brought a dozen out of his pocket and they placed them discreetly before moving into the bedroom and living room. They put the final two on either side of the entry door.

"I hope this works," Sara said. "What do you say we go downstairs?"

# 69
## *Constance Complains*

Jordan Cartwright stood in Omar's Tavern enjoying the dark, relative quiet as he sipped from a bottle of Blue Springs. This was his first break in two hours and he intended to enjoy it.

Those intentions fell away when he saw Constance Welling heading toward him. "You've lost me a lot of money, Mr. Man," said Cliffhouse's most dreadful guest. She leaned against the bar beside him.

"Excuse me?"

"You didn't put my flyers up." Her tone was clipped. "I ended up with far too few attendees at my writing workshop. These things cost money, you know."

Jordan said nothing. He sipped water, told himself to be calm, and gave her a weak one-shouldered shrug.

She huffed. "I drove by the library. I guess you didn't think I would, but I did. That's how I know you didn't post my flyers."

Jordan Cartwright inhaled slowly, looking for a reply that would move this conversation to a quick and quiet conclusion. "I meant no offense to you. I simply forgot." *You miserable old bag of bones.*

Constance made a disgusted clicking sound with her tongue. "You just *forgot?* How nice for you. I am an author. I don't have the luxury of simply forgetting the details of *my* job."

*An author? You wouldn't know good writing if you were sleeping with William Shakespeare.* Wishing he could punch her, he smiled instead. "I hope you'll forgive my absent mindedness. Now if you'll exc-"

"No, I am not finished." Constance placed a hand on his shoulder.

He suppressed a cringe. He felt eyes watching them.

"I have sensed your self-righteous attitude toward me since I arrived in this backward, illiterate little town, and I must say, I do not appreciate it."

*Self-righteous? You're calling* me *self-righteous?* "Madam, I'm sorry if I, and the rest of our town, have given you a bad impression." He felt the color in his cheeks deepening and his gaze shifted toward the small audience they'd acquired.

Constance Welling looked smug. The expression, much like the pink belly shirt she wore, did not flatter her. He couldn't help staring at the tattoos that peeked out from under her skin-tight stonewashed jeans. *A high-school dropout with a can of spray paint could have done a better job.*

"Pardon me," Jon Daniels said as he slipped behind the bar. "Is there anything I can do?"

Constance glared at the man. "Nothing *you* can fix. But if you want to be useful, you can bring a bottle of champagne over to *Dr.* Siechert's table." She nodded her head toward the rear of the bar.

Daniels arched a brow. "Any particular brand?"

"Whatever's good." She waved her hand in a dismissive gesture. "My date, *Dr.* Siechert, only drinks the best."

"Very well." He brought a cloth up from under the teakwood bar and began polishing. "Jordan, would you care for another water?"

"Yes, thank you." Jordan accepted the frosty blue bottle and excused himself.

As he left, he heard Constance clicking and *tsking*. "I suppose he has a tab?"

"Madam, he is our pianist," Daniels said frigidly.

Jordan, grateful for a clean getaway, didn't look back.

\*\*\*

"I never liked that piano player, lady, so bravo. You sure stirred that stick up his ass!"

The scarecrow of a man hovering over their table, staring at Constance's cleavage and their champagne, smelled of liquor and filth. She glanced at him then looked at Roger to urge him to get rid of this bum.

Roger, however, was smiling. "Well, Loyd McRoid, I haven't seen you for a while. How's the arthritis?"

"Can't complain. Not much, anyhow. You going to Oktoberfest this year?"

Constance glared at Roger, but his eyes slid right past her. "I never miss it."

"Beer. Sausages. Doesn't get any better, right, Doc?"

"Right." Siechert brought a ten out of his pocket and handed it to Loyd. "Buy yourself a drink, my friend. I'm a little busy right now."

Loyd fisted the bill. "I can see that." He ogled Constance. "Hope you get lucky tonight, Doc!"

Roger just smiled as the drunk wandered out of the bar. Constance wanted to tear the doctor a new one for letting the bum talk about her like that, but the relationship was too new. "He's a friend of yours?"

"No, a patient."

"I see. You must have to treat horrible people every day in this shitty little town."

He laughed. "Loyd's all right." He paused. "So," he said. "Am I?"

"Are you what?"

"Getting lucky tonight?"

"Maybe," she said, not wanting to appear too eager.

"I hope so." He sipped champagne, then winked at her. "You were wild last night."

"Unfortunately, I wouldn't know." She dabbed the corners of her lips with a napkin. "I'm afraid you took advantage of me, Doctor." She batted her lashes.

He smiled. "I told you not to drink with those pills."

She wanted to reach across the table and run her fingers through his wavy, auburn hair. "It was just a little."

"I look forward to refreshing your memory. What *do* you remember? I'd like to know what I need to focus on."

Her lady parts tingled. "Well, not much. I know you picked me up, then we went to my room." She admired his broad shoulders. "I hope you didn't have to carry me."

He shook his head. "You were walking fine. You started sending me provocative texts around five in the afternoon and I picked you up at about six-thirty. Remember, I brought a bottle of wine and some cheese and crackers?"

Constance shrugged. "I don't know. But I *do* remember being in my room. I just wish I remembered more of what we did while we were in it."

"I'm glad you don't remember, you dirty girl. I'm looking forward to reminding you." He winked at her. "I think Dr. Feelgood needs to make another house call, don't you?"

His eyes were bold. Mysterious, playful, just a little bit dangerous. Constance tingled. "Okay, Dr. Feelgood."

# 70
## *Something Stinks*

**SUNDAY**

"Something stinks!" Joey Haskell wrinkled his nose.

"You stink!" said his friend, Jason.

"No, really!" Joey stood still. He and Jason had been playing explorer and the woods around Blue Lady Lake was the jungle, where vicious cannibals hid buried treasure.

"Gross!" said Jason as he came abreast of Joey. "Something's dead."

"A squirrel, probably."

Jason shook his head. "Nah. I had a dead squirrel in my closet for a week and my mom didn't even know. This is bigger. Like a deer, maybe."

"You wanna see what it is?" Joey pointed. "It's over there, I think."

"Yeah."

Excited, a little grossed out, Joey led the way deeper into the woods, stopping so suddenly that Jason ran into him. "Hey, what the-"

Joey turned to Jason, his face white as milk. "It's not a deer."

The boys ran.

# 71
## *Miss Maisy*

Sara brought two mugs of coffee from her kitchen and set them on the table. Luke took his and inhaled. "Smells great. I'm so glad we ran into each other at the buffet this morning."

"Me, too." Sara sat down, pleased that Luke had off-loaded the trays they'd brought upstairs. She'd invited him up without a thought, except for the one that made her want to be alone with him.

"Have you had any trouble in this room?" Luke asked between bites of toast.

"My towels got a little damp once. I think my great-great-aunt and Omar are looking out for me."

"What do you mean?"

"Well, when it was happening, I smelled Aunt Theodosia's perfume and I heard a meow, not once but twice in the bedroom. I think they stopped the Blue Lady."

"Really?"

"You think I'm crazy, right?"

"Not after what happened to Chad, I don't! These waffles are incredible!"

They sat in silence for a few minutes, then Sara told him some stories about her colorful aunt and her Siamese cat. She told him about Cliffhouse during Prohibition, when Theodosia had been a teenager, about the serial killer - the Bodice Ripper - who had terrorized the town, and about famous guests - even a couple of presidents - who had stayed at the lodge. As they finished their breakfasts, Sara smiled. "I've been talking way too much. You must be bored to tears."

"Not at all. I want to hear more." He paused. "Maybe we could take a walk on the nature trail in a while? I'm so full I'm afraid I'll fall asleep if I don't get some exercise."

Someone knocked on the door.

Sara answered it and Miss Maisy entered the room. She seemed anxious.

"Aunt Maisy," said Sara. "Come in. Is everything okay?"

The older woman smiled. "Yes, dear," she said. "I'm here because I think it's time I told you something." She took a seat on the sofa and settled in.

Sara sat beside her.

Aunt Maisy was silent a long moment. Finally, she looked up at Sara. "I'm afraid I've lied to you, dear, and I feel terrible about it."

"Lied to me? About what?"

Aunt Maisy looked at Sara a moment before answering. "Theodosia's journals. They still exist," she said. "She asked me to keep them safe, and I have done that. She asked me not to read them, but to leave them to you in my will. I've honored these wishes, but I feel there may be information in them that would be of use to you now."

Sara was intrigued.

"Theodosia told me most are simply filled with records and receipts. Recipes, things of that nature. But she said a few deal with the news of the day and that she had also written about Cliffside's folklore; I believe that would mean the Blue Lady. She told me very little about seeing wet footprints here in the lodge, and I'm hoping that you'll find more about it within these pages. Perhaps they'll help you understand what's going on in Cliffhouse." She glanced around the room. "And in this town. I wish I could be of more help, but that's all I know. I've sent for them and once they arrive, they're yours." She looked at her hands. "I hope you aren't angry with me."

Sara leaned in and put an arm around the woman. "Of course I'm not angry, Aunt Maisy. I respect you for keeping your word to Aunt Theodosia. She would have appreciated it."

Maisy stood. "Well," she said. "They ought to arrive this afternoon. I'll let you know as soon as they're here."

# 72
## *Sunday Night Autopsy*

"It's the same as it was with Norma Bailey. Not a mark on her and her lungs are completely saturated, as if she drowned, yet she obviously died on land. My bet is it's lakewater again, too." Gene Holmes syringed greenish fluid from one of Laurel Lutz's lungs into a test tube. He labeled it and placed it next to the ones holding water from her mouth and sinuses. "This is what I was telling you about, Roger."

Dr. Siechert nodded as he bit back an irritated giggle. He had other things to think about - like the fact that Constance Welling was trying to dominate his time as much as Tessa Cornhull had. "It's peculiar, Gene. Very peculiar." He looked to the mortician. "Have you ever seen anything like this before, Casper?"

Hill shook his head. "Not until recently."

"There's no sign of lakewater on her hair or clothing?" Jackson asked.

"Well, we'll have it all tested, but no, I don't think so. Whatever killed Norma Bailey also killed Laurel Lutz."

"*Whatever* killed her," Jackson muttered.

Gene Holmes looked at the chief. "What do you mean?"

Jackson shook his head. "We've got a very clever killer here."

Siechert remembered seeing water dripping from Tessa's nose and mouth, but he also knew he killed the nurse. He thought of the Lady's voice and he thought there was probably a connection, though he'd be a hot dog in heaven before he'd say anything.

Gene Holmes began replacing Laurel Lutz's parts. They looked like sweetbreads at the butcher shop. "I don't know what to tell you, Jackson. Maybe the tests will turn something up this time."

"I hope so."

The workroom door opened and Beverly Hill walked in. "It's Sunday night, for God's sake, Casper. Why are you playing with your friends down here? You're supposed to be watching *Tomorrow's Singing Stars* with me!"

"There's been another murder, sweetie."

"I don't care if there's been a dozen murders. The doctors and policeman don't need you to supervise them. Get upstairs now. It's your turn to make popcorn!"

"Yes, Beverly, I'll be right up." Casper cringed as she stomped out, leaving the door wide open.

Her voice echoed from the stairs. "And don't forget the goddamned butter, Casper!"

Dr. Siechert burst into raucous laughter. "I bet you'd like to shove a trocar up her ass sometimes," he said. "What a cunt!"

"Roger!" Holmes said.

Casper looked like a choirboy singing Christmas carols, with his mouth open in an O, and Jackson - well, Jackson appeared to be trying not to laugh.

*One out of three isn't bad!* "Oops. Loose lips sink ships. Sorry." Siechert winked at the chief, but it was not returned.

"Roger, why don't you go on home?" Gene said.

"I- I'd better get up to Beverly." Casper's stammer was showing, but Roger felt good about that as the mortician left the room. Poor little man really needed to grow a pair.

"By the way, Roger, a little bird told me you and Constance Welling are an item." Jackson said.

"Who told you that?"

"Oh, half a dozen people. You know, that sort of thing makes for pretty hot small town gossip."

"She's ... interesting."

"And Tessa's out of town," Gene Holmes added. He covered Lutz's torso and went to the sink to wash up.

Siechert's stomach growled. *Mmm, sweetbreads.* Whenever he bagged a buck, the liver and lights were his favorite parts. "I have a need for female companionship," he said, shrugging into his jacket. "So sue me." He crossed to the doorway. "See you Monday morning, Gene?"

"Yes, but Jesus Christ, get a grip on your tongue before you alienate half our patients."

"Will do." Roger Siechert walked up the stairs whistling *The Happy Wanderer* all the way.

His anus twitched in anticipation of the evening ahead.

# 73
## *Back to Cliffhouse*

### THURSDAY

Chad and Luke moved back into Suite 310 on Tuesday and the place had been totally normal for two nights and counting. They heard no strange voices and nothing damp and scary happened in the bathroom. It was good to have normalcy return. It was also good to have a roommate, just in case. Luke had told him all about the magnets and Chad had gotten a dozen extra from Sara. He felt safe now.

# 74
## *About the Journals*

"My dad, Adam, saw Omar once," Sara told Luke as they strolled along the cliffs. Old-fashioned street lamps lit their path. "He doesn't like to admit it, though, so don't ever ask him about it. When we used to rent out the Theodosia Suite, guests sometimes reported hearing the cat and smelling White Shoulders, my aunt's perfume. Since we reopened the lodge three years ago, we've been asked at least a dozen times if we have a hotel cat - a big Siamese with crossed eyes."

"What do you say when guests ask about the cat?"

"We say yes, we have one, because it's true." She smiled. "I'm so glad Aunt Maisy sent for the journals. I've barely had time to look at them, but my dads are eating them up. One of them is about the Bodice Ripper murders in the 1920s." She gazed at the lake. "It looks so cold."

"Have they found anything about the Blue Lady yet?" He took her hand.

"No."

"I'm sure glad your dads and Miss Maisy decided to try out those magnets."

"They're amazing. There hasn't been an incident since Sunday. That's a huge relief because we're going to be filled up this weekend for the Civil War Festival. My dads have booked most of the rooms except 339 and 337. They set up motion sensor cameras in them and if nothing happens, they'll rent them, too." She laughed. "They'll take the cameras out first, though."

"I hope the magnets keep working."

"Let's cross our fingers."

# 75
## *Santa Muerte*

Rosa Morales was certain things at Cliffhouse weren't as calm as the rest of the staff believed. Maggie O'Connor hadn't bought into it, either, and had left to work at the Doc Holiday Inn, leaving Rosa and Jenna to train a couple of new maids. She missed Maggie but couldn't blame her.

The Bellamys had placed magnets throughout the third floor, where the majority of the activity was. They seemed satisfied with this, and Rosa had to admit things had quieted down. But it wasn't over. She could feel it.

She crossed herself and whispered a prayer. It was going to take more than a few magnets to scare Santa Muerte off. After ending the plea to the Lord, she reached into the top drawer of her nightstand and extracted the black-beaded rosary with the silver crucifix that had been passed down in her family for many generations. She kissed it, stroked the savior's face, crossed herself, and mumbled the Apostle's Creed.

# 76
## *Constance Clings*

Constance Welling's perfume was giving him a migraine.

Roger Siechert was tired of her. He'd taken her for a drive around the lake because he couldn't bear the thought of spending any more time in the bedroom with her. She was a great alibi, but it ended there.

Now they were headed back to his house. The seats in the Jaguar were small and set close together, but Constance didn't seem to think that was close enough - she practically sat on his lap. One of her hands rested on his thigh and he prayed to whatever gods might exist that she wouldn't let it slide any higher than it was right now.

They arrived at Bavarian Pines and he felt like telling her to hunker down so Larry the Gate Guy wouldn't see her, but figured she'd take offense. She took offense at everything.

"Evening, Doctor," Larry drawled as the gate opened. He stared at Constance's boobs, which were trussed up so high you could eat off them. "Ma'am."

Constance *tsk*ed. "'Ma'am' my sweet ass," she muttered.

Roger almost told her about his golf buddy, Phil, a plastic surgeon who could smooth out some of those crow's feet and lift her eyes as high as her boobs, but stopped himself because he already knew she'd just go off on a self-pity binge. God, she was tedious. She was making him start to miss Tessa.

*Poor old Tessa.* He'd spent most of Monday night disposing of her and cleaning up the mess she'd made. He'd rented a car and parked it in her dinky garage just in case anyone drove by. Oh, what a job. *Why did I fuck with her intestines? What the hell was I thinking?* God, what a stinking mess she'd made. He realized Constance was babbling. "What?"

"I said, penny for your thoughts?" Her hand was moving north. "You're very quiet tonight, Roger."

"Oh, sorry. Lots on my mind."

"Yes, I know."

He almost went over the curb as he rounded the corner to his street. "What? What do you know?"

She giggled. It was an unfortunate sound. "I know you have a lot on your mind."

He pulled into his driveway and parked, not garaging the Jag because there was no way he was letting this bitch spend the night. "And how do you know that?"

"I'm psychic."

He unfolded himself out of the car and then opened the door for her. She took his hand and made a show of straightening her pink mini-skirt and matching cowboy boots, then wiggled her sweater-clad dish of titties at him. When she was finally aloft, she stuck out her lower lip. "I thought we were going to line dance at Doc Holiday's tonight."

He wanted to punch her in the neck for using that childish creaky voice on him. Instead, he smiled. "Perhaps another evening. I have a long day tomorrow, so we'll have to be content with a quick nightcap."

She clung to him like stink on a beaver as he unlocked his front doors and escorted her in. "Oh, Roger, I just love this big beautiful house. Isn't it lonely rattling around in here all by yourself?"

"Nope."

She gave him a sharp look.

"But I'm glad you're here for a quick drink tonight," he lied. He'd been going to let her off at Cliffhouse, but she'd asked to come back with him. *This has to be karma for disposing of Tessa.* He stifled a giggle. And, oh, how he wanted to laugh, despite his god-awful headache. He'd wanted to ever since he'd picked her up for dinner - she had managed to get him to take her out every fucking night this week with a combination of flirting, flattery, and a vague threat of histrionics that might be visible from the moon. She was due to leave town in just a few weeks. He would stick it out until then because he had to.

"I just love this one!" Constance crossed to his Hummel collection and - *oh crap* - opened the glass doors. She was fondling "Strolling Along," a prized antique. It was a little boy with a folded umbrella and a terrier at his feet. She held it between her fingers as if it were a pubic hair plucked from a sandwich.

He stopped himself from yelling for fear he'd startle her. Instead, he moved to her side and put his hands over hers, gently extracting the figurine. He placed it back on the shelf and locked the case. "That's a very expensive family heirloom."

She looked at him. "I think it's cute that you collect all these statues of little kids. It's sweet. I have a collection of Beanie Babies. I'll show you sometime."

He didn't trust himself to speak but nodded and, as he crossed the room, he stopped in front of his gun cabinet and discreetly locked it before leading her to his impressive refrigerated cabinet of wines, just inside his kitchen. "Would you care for a glass?"

"You bet," she said. "Something red."

"I have a lovely merlot."

"Whatever."

The cretinous woman stood too close to him as he studied the bottles. The merlot was only a fifty-dollar wine, but she didn't seem to know the difference between that and Two Buck Chuck, so at the last minute he pulled a far less expensive burgundy from the bottom of the cabinet. It had been a Christmas present from Tessa, who was also ignorant in the ways of civilized drinking.

He took the wine to the counter and opened it. "Constance, the wine glasses are just there, in that cabinet. Would you fetch two?"

"You're going to make me work? Just kidding." She opened it, made some noises, then brought out goblets and one of his Bavarian beer steins. One of his expensive Bavarian steins.

"Here you go. Don't fill mine to the very top." She pushed the glasses over to him, then took the stein to the fridge.

He watched her, mystified. "Only a teenager would fill a wine glass to the brim," he said as she pushed the stein - the stein with the hounds and partridges on it - against the ice dispenser. Clinking commenced. "What are you doing?"

"Getting us some ice."

"Oh." *This is only for a little while. Only a very short while. She'll be gone soon.*

He led her into his living room and placed the bottle and the still empty glasses on a glass coffee table. With a click of the remote, his fireplace came to life. She snorted and set the stein on the table. He gestured for her to take a chair opposite the one he had chosen, but she fluttered around, first admiring the fire, then touching, touching, touching, every blessed thing on the mantelpiece. She even reached up to touch his prize Black Forest cuckoo clock, but the mechanism whirred and the cuckoo read his mind, bursting forth to chide her.

Relieved, he poured her half a goblet of burgundy and a quarter-glass of the undoubtedly dreadful vintage for himself.

"Are you trying to get me drunk, Roger?"

"What makes you say that?"

"You're drinking like a bird." She smiled and glanced at the clock. "A little cuckoo bird."

"I have to drive you home in a little while."

"You don't *have* to. My mother won't know." Her laugh ratcheted up and down.

"I'm sorry, but I have some early conference calls to make from the office, and I'm afraid if you stay, I won't do my duty."

"Silly man." She tasted the wine, wrinkled her nose, and dug her claws into the ice cubes, plopping two in. Roger watched her bring the slopping glass to her lips. Sure enough, several drops of Burgundy spilled onto his spotless white carpet. She put her glass down, this time spilling wine on the table. "I'll wipe it up." She trotted to the kitchen and returned with paper towels and a bottle of his sparkling water. Before he could stop her, she was pouring the elixir into a paper towel. "This'll do the trick." She went to work on the carpet with the wet towel. "There, good as new."

He snatched the water from the table and sipped it. It calmed him better than the dreadful wine.

Constance gulped her iced wine and looked at his glass. "Aren't you going to have yours?"

"No. You go ahead."

She poured his wine over the ice and finished it in one gulp as he nursed the sparkling water. "So," she said. "I'll get you up in plenty of time and make you breakfast. Would you like that?"

Of course, sex would be a given. She was mechanical about it and her nails were worthy of a dragon, so he couldn't even bring up his favorite foreplay. Still, it was sex, and he needed that. And perhaps he could talk her into a nice short manicure. "I suppose that's a good idea." He gulped his water, hoping to feel that wonderful coolness again, but there didn't seem to be any magic tonight. "You know how to cook breakfast, huh?" He thought of German potato pancakes and waffles and eggs over easy.

"Of course. You have corn flakes, right?"

Roger Siechert groaned.

# 77
## *Merlin Skinner*

Merlin Skinner had locked up his art studio and headed upstairs to his apartment. He got into his favorite emerald pajamas, to spend a few hours with the book he'd begun last week.

He sat nestled into the far end of his sofa. Next to him, incense swirled, filling the air with the smell of Nag Champa. Chopin nocturnes played so softly that even the fussiest baby would have given up. Chopin was a blessing after hearing so much noise all day. He hated noise. He turned a page, then paused as a sound from downstairs destroyed his bliss. It sounded a little like pennies rattling in a soda can. He went to the window.

Below, he saw the silhouette of a man moving back and forth. Merlin tiptoed to the kitchen, returning with a large butcher knife, then watched, transfixed, as the shadow of the stranger swayed one way, then the other. When he heard the fizzing sound and saw a burst of red paint, he knew he was being vandalized.

His hand tightened on the knife and his pulse rang in his ears. Waves of anger crashed over him. He'd just retouched the window a week ago. He took a slow deep breath and reminded himself to be calm, to remain centered. Still, his grip on the knife handle was almost painful and his temper buzzed like a livewire. He stepped closer and tried to see the man's face but the shadows were too dense. Based on his size, though, this was a grown man, not a rebellious pre-pubescent, and this fact unhinged Merlin's temper.

Without another thought, he raced downstairs, the slapping of his bare feet lending rhythm to the uncontrolled obscenities flying from his lips; words he hadn't used in ages suddenly became the only ones that made sense. He was at the door, unlocking it. As he thrust it open, the vandal took to the darkened street, moving more quickly than Skinner expected.

"That's right! Run!" Merlin hollered after him. The shadow-man's footfalls dissolved as he disappeared around a corner. Merlin turned to look at the window.

Half a cock, giant and red, of course, had been painted right over the *Wizard of Ink* on his window. "You son of a bitch!" he shouted again in the direction of the long gone criminal.

The echo of his words resonated off the buildings and reminded him why he'd taken up meditation and yoga. He took a deep, slow breath and envisioned the fresh air cleansing him from the inside out.

# 78
## *Reville*

**SATURDAY**

The great lawn at Cliffhouse was a battleground. The North had encamped near Walleyed Walter's cabin and the South was, ironically, camped on the north side of the lodge, near the Kelly Forest. Late into the evening sweet strains of Civil War music had echoed across the property and seeped through windows. Flutes, violins, guitars, harmonicas. Teddy loved listening. Now, he peered out their cabin window and spotted some of the South's ghostly white tents between the trees.

"Adam, let's take a stroll." His husband groaned and pulled the covers over his head. Teddy glanced at his watch - it was only six, a half-hour until dawn. Normally, Adam was the early riser, but not during the Civil War Days Festival. "Suit yourself." He quickly dressed, shrugged on a jacket, grabbed a flashlight, and walked into the chilly morning air.

Stars were fading and lamps glowed in many tents. A sleepy guard looked up from his lawn chair and saluted. Teddy saluted back and passed the Confederate camp. He neared the springhouse and a bluish light caught his eye. *Is someone in there?*

He peered in the window, saw nothing. *Must've been a reflection.* Still he unlocked the building to check. His hackles rose; the air was redolent of lakewater and that wasn't normal. He shined his flashlight around, saw nothing unusual, though the wooden well cover was, as usual, askew. Teddy pushed it back into place, noting that there was no lake smell coming from the depths of the dark well. That was a good thing. It wouldn't do to have lakewater contaminate the spring.

Uneasy, he locked up and headed for the Union encampment. Dawn was breaking as a bugle played reveille. The first campfires crackled and he heard the clanging of pots and pans as the rich aroma of coffee twined into his nose, and the scents of bacon and sausage began to seduce him.

Stomach growling, he saluted another guard in another lawn chair, then made for the tent he knew Colonel Dale Ham inhabited. He stood outside the tent. "Colonel Dale! Permission to enter."

"Permission granted."

Teddy dipped his head and stepped inside. Polly's cook had just finished dressing and he looked every bit an officer, at least after he glued his sandy goatee into place.

"What can I do for you?" Dale asked.

"Need a hand cooking your breakfast?"

Dale laughed. "Nope. The privates will do that. You're welcome to join me fireside."

"I wouldn't miss it."

"Last night we had some interesting reports," Dale said after they seated themselves on a log by the fire. A private handed them tin cups of coffee.

"How so?"

"Some of the guys swore they saw the Blue Lady walking along the cliffs."

Teddy looked up. "Really? What did she look like?"

Dale chuckled. "Blue, self-lit. Gliding. Ever hear of such a thing?"

"I have," Teddy said slowly. "We've had several reports lately, and I don't have to tell you that she goes way, way back. I don't know what the Blue Lady really is, but she does exist."

"One of the Rebs chased her and nearly went over the cliff."

Teddy was alarmed. "Dale, this is important. Get the word out to everyone in your camp that if they see her, stay away. No chasing, no yelling, no nothing. I think that Reb is probably lucky to be alive."

Dale studied him, long and hard. "I don't even see the beginning of a smile there, Ted. You're serious, aren't you?"

"Dead serious."

Dale nodded. "I'll take care of it right after breakfast. You'll talk to the Rebs?"

"As soon as we've eaten. There's nothing better than bacon and eggs cooked over a campfire."

"Can't argue that."

# 79
## *Another Big Red One*

Jackson Ballou wanted to be in a good mood; after all, he had a date with Polly this evening. But between the lack of evidence in the Bailey and Lutz murders and the fact that the damned graffiti artist, still unidentified, was going nuts painting the town red, Jackson was none too happy. Yesterday morning, Roger Siechert called the station at 8 a.m., livid about the obscene artwork sprayed across the clinic windows. The dispatcher said she'd had to hold the phone away from her ear, he was so loud. And early this morning, Polly had been hit. But it was the two deaths that really ate on him as he pulled into the crowded lot behind Cliffhouse.

He had nothing. Holmes had nothing. The county coroner had autopsied both bodies as well and had nothing. Lungs just didn't fill up with water on their own. It made no sense. Because the first body was found in a Dumpster, and the second victim had been seen disappearing into the woods with someone, Jackson knew he was dealing with homicide, despite the lack of any concrete signs of foul play. He'd just have to dig deeper.

He entered the lodge and crossed to the front desk, ignoring the enticing aromas of the breakfast buffet lining the south wall. He nodded at a few curious tourists. *Nothing to see here folks, Cliffside is Mayberry for Civil War buffs today. We only have fake deaths here ...*

"There you are!" Adam said. "I had to run without you this morning."

"I'm sorry. Somebody stole the pole from in front of the barbershop. My guys were all busy with tourist and graffiti problems, so I went on duty early. I should've called."

"Forget about it. Graffiti? Another big red one?"

"Uh huh. Polly got it this time."

"That's horrible."

"She had it half cleaned up before we could even take the report." He shook his head. "But Roger Siechert is screaming about the one on the clinic. Noble Mason removed it within two hours, but Siechert's still grousing. Something's up with him. I think he needs a vacation." He tried not to smile. "He called Casper's wife a very bad name right to his face the other day."

"Can't say I blame him. She's unbearable. Poor Casper. Can you imagine living with a person like that?"

"No, I can't." Jackson paused. "Is everything running smoothly? Anything my men should keep an eye on?"

"Not that I know of. Teddy did the recon this morning." He picked up his radio. "Ted? Come to Registration when you have a chance." He beckoned to Jackson. "Let's have some privacy."

Once inside the employee break room, they sat down at a lunch table with cups of coffee. Teddy arrived, carrying a trio of slim books, grabbed a cup, and joined them.

"Are we likely to have any unplanned skirmishes today, Ted?" Adam asked.

"I doubt it. Both sides banned the bad boys from last year." He shook his head. "I have never seen such a debacle as the one between hardcore authentics and the farbs. Who would think anyone would come to blows over appropriate Civil War underwear?" Teddy pitched his voice up a notch. "Tighty-whities didn't exist during the Civil War! Have you no respect for history?"

Jackson and Adam chuckled.

"Shoot," Teddy said. "The hardcores even give the mainstream guys shit if their traditional underwear doesn't have the correct stitching. It's underwear, for Christ's sake. It's not like anyone's going to see it."

Adam rolled his eyes.

"Takes all kinds," Jackson said. "Many hardcore authentics out there, today?"

"Not many, and not the ones who started the fight with the farbs last year. Each side has about four tents' worth and they camp a good distance from the regulars. Everybody's happier that way. I don't expect trouble, but if there is, tell your guys to look to the isolated tents for the culprits."

"Will do." Jackson rolled coffee around in his mouth and felt better.

"There were sightings last night," Teddy said.

"Sightings?" Adam asked. "Movie stars? UFOs?"

"The Blue Lady."

"Seriously?"

"That's what I was told. Both sides saw her along the cliff."

"Crazy stuff," Jackson said, thinking of his and Polly's sighting last weekend.

"Likely ball lightning," said Adam.

Teddy nodded. "That's what I suggested. I told them not to chase it."

Jackson nodded at the books. "What'cha got there?"

"These are some of Aunt Theodosia's journals."

"Good reading?"

"The best. At least these three are. There are two dozen more, but most appear to be pretty dry, though there's one from the cathouse days labeled *Quirks of Gentlemen Callers* that'll keep you up all night." Teddy grinned and tapped the books. "But these. These deal with history and lore. One whole journal is devoted to the Bodice Ripper murders in the late 20s. Did you know the Blue Lady was seen a lot during those years?"

"No, I didn't," Jackson said. "May I?"

"Of course."

He carefully opened to a random page in the first journal. Theodosia's handwriting was graceful. "'September 17, 1928,'" he read aloud. "'There has been another murder in Cliffhouse. One of our working girls, Phoebe Manners, was found in her room by the maids, horribly defiled, not unlike poor Mary McGill, who was so terribly mutilated that her murder made headlines as far north as San Francisco. I took only the briefest of glances and could stand no more. I shut and locked 207 then I had Ellsworth send for the constable.'"

Jackson's radio squawked. A truck hauling a horse trailer, fully loaded, had stalled, blocking all lanes into and out of town. Heavy inbound traffic was already backed up a mile or more. A tow was on its way, but the unit on site needed help.

"Well, I'd better go see a man about a horse," Jackson said, closing the journal.

Adam stood up. "I know my way around horses a lot better than you do, Chief. I believe a ride-along might be in order?"

"You bet."

# 80
## *Painty Painty Pervert*

Roger Siechert extracted the patient files Gene's nurse had left on the door, knocked and entered. Pat Matthews rose. "Dr. Siechert." He extended his hand. "How are you?"

Siechert gave him an obligatory handshake. "I'm fine, Pat. Have a seat." He indicated the exam table.

"Great," said Pat hopping up on the papered surface. "That's just great!"

Everything was always great with Pat Matthews, and with ten thousand children and that dishrag of a wife, Siechert suspected the man was in some kind of denial. He looked at his chart: some hypertension, occasional bouts of insomnia, an allergy to penicillin. The only meds he took were for his blood pressure. "So what can I do for you today?"

"I tried to call in my prescription," said Pat, "and they told me you wouldn't refill it again without seeing me."

Siechert took a wooden tongue depressor from a large jar by the sink. "It's been almost a year since I saw you last. You're due for a checkup."

"Yeah, I guess."

"Open up."

Matthews opened his mouth. Based on the stench that wafted from the orifice, Pat needed a dentist more than a doctor. *I could pull a few teeth while he's here; that'd give him his money's worth.* He chuckled.

"Is something wrong, Doctor?" Pat asked around the depressor.

Siechert cleared his throat and tried to iron the humor out of his voice. "Oh, nothing. I'm just remembering a joke my last patient told me." Siechert removed the depressor. "Take your shirt off and let's get a listen to that ticker."

Matthews did as he was told, revealing a torso matted with body hair.

The doctor suppressed a giggle. He pressed the stethoscope to Pat's furry back and instructed him to inhale deeply.

"Exhale. So tell me," said Dr. Siechert. "Have you ever seen *Planet of the Apes*?" As soon as the words came out, Siechert flinched a little. That hadn't been what he'd meant to ask. A ferocious fit of laughter threatened to overtake him, but he kept his cool.

"Excuse me?"

"Great movie," said Siechert. "I was thinking of seeing it again." He moved the stethoscope to a new location. "The original, of course. Breathe in. Good. Exhale."

"I, uh, I can't remember if I've seen it or not. Probably, I guess."

"Oh, you'd remember if you'd seen it, Pat." He moved the stethoscope to the man's chest and practically lost it in the forest of hair. "Breathe in. Exhale. Sounds good."

"I guess I haven't then."

"Shame. Charlton Heston was a magnificent beast." He sighed. "Breathe in one more time for me."

Finished, Siechert forced a smile away and stared at the ape-man in front of him, before writing on the chart. "Everything looks tip-top, Pat," said the doctor. "Your blood pressure is a little higher, but nothing I'm too concerned about. Are you still drinking coffee?"

The man's face reddened. "No." Matthews brought his hand to his mouth, scratching at his upper lip, as if to conceal the lie.

Siechert noticed a red crescent under the man's thumbnail that was far too bright to be blood and felt a calm, patient anger begin to move inside him. It was paint. Matthews was the vandal; he was sure of it.

"I mean, maybe a little from time to time, but I've definitely cut down."

"What?"

"Coffee," said Pat. "You asked if I was still drinking coffee."

Siechert plastered a smile on his face. "Of course," he said. "Of course I did." He stared at the man. *I could turn you in, you hairy son of a bitch. I could turn you in and maybe I just will, you sick painty bastard.* And he always drew penises. *You're nothing but a fucking painty painty pervert.* A giggle escaped.

"Is something funny?"

"Oh, no, nothing, Pat. Told myself another joke. Just go easy on the coffee." Siechert wrote Pat a prescription. "And try to get a little more exercise." *You sick hairy vandal you're going to pay pay pay for your painty painty ways!*

Suppressing a giggle, Siechert handed Pat the scrip. "Here," he said. "Fill this."

The man took it, pinching it between his finger and his graffiti thumb.

Siechert didn't let go right away. *In the old days, they would have cut your goddamned thumb off, you sick painty dickhead. Your whole hairy hand.* Siechert's laughter erupted so hard he had to force it into a mock cough.

"Thanks, Doc." Pat looked worried. Replacing his shirt, he stood and held out his hand for a parting shake.

Siechert burst into laughter. "Get your hands off me, you damned dirty ape!" Tears flowed freely, but he could see Matthews's confusion. "Kidding! Kidding! See you in a couple months!" Guffaws came out of him in short, grating bursts.

Matthews left.

Alone, Siechert lay his head on the counter and let loose with a pent-up barrage of unashamed laughter. "It's a madhouse!" he hollered. "A madhouse!"

# 81
## *The Bodice Ripper*

Tommy Collins, eight-years-old today, stood by the swings with his big sister, Carrie, and studied the mass of Union tents on the cliffs near Walleye's cabin. The first battle of the day had just wound down near the mini-golf. Now it was time to play.

"Are you thinking what I'm thinking?" Carrie poked her brother in the ribs.

"Knock it off! You can't do that! You're only a year older than me, now!"

"Nuh uh, that's not how it works." Carrie stuck her tongue out.

"Is so!"

"Is not!"

"Is so!"

"You want to go look in the tents or not, Stinky-Pants?"

"You can't call me that any more, Dad said so. I'm too old. Take it back."

She stuck her tongue out again. "You want to go look or are you chicken?"

"I'm not chicken. And I'm not a stinky pan-"

"Let's go. Now!" She yanked his arm and took off at a run, jerking him behind her.

They arrived on the cliff side of the tents a moment later and hunkered down behind some bushes near Walleye's cabin. They watched the tents for signs of life, saw no one except for a soldier a ways away. He wasn't looking. "Go look in that one!" Carrie pointed at the closest tent.

"Why me? It was your idea."

"It's your birthday! You have to go first."

"Do not!"

"Do so!"

"Do-"

"What are you kids doing out here?"

They both jumped and turned to see Walleye looming behind them. "Hi! It's my birthday!"

"Well, young man, congratulations. How old are you? Twelve?"

Tommy giggled.

"He's only eight," Carrie exclaimed. "I'll be ten in two months. He's just a baby."

"Well, little lady, with maturity comes age, but age doesn't always bring maturity."

"Huh?"

"Do you remember my name?" Tommy asked. "Or hers?"

"I'm afraid not. With age comes forgetfulness."

They told him, then he began walking toward Cliffhouse. "Come on. You can't hang around out here."

"Why not?" asked Tommy.

"Because I said so. And it's dangerous."

"How's it dangerous?" Carrie asked, skipping toward the cliffs.

"Get back here, young lady. That's what's dangerous. The Blue Lady was here last night. She could still be around."

"You're making that up." Carrie moved back from the guard rail and walked to Walleye's side. "There's no such thing as the Blue Lady. I asked my father."

"He just hasn't seen her. I've seen her a lot, late at night. She might be out in the daytime, too, but she's harder to see when it's light."

"Really?" Tommy asked. "Do you think she's here now?"

"Maybe. One of those soldier boys almost fell off the cliff last night. He was chasing after her, not paying attention to where he was, and she just sorta floated right off the cliff. He'd have gone over if not for that wall. Scared him half to death, seeing her."

"You saw her?" Carrie asked. "What'd she look like?"

"She glows blue. She can look real pretty at first, but then she changes. Her eyes are the biggest blackest holes you ever saw. They'll give you nightmares for the rest of your life."

"You saw them?" Tommy asked.

Walleye looked at them both. "I did. Saturday night, maybe one in the morning. She was walking and I went out and had a look. She fairly flew at me and those eyes …" He paused. "You don't want to see those, kids, so promise me you'll stay away from the cliffs. Don't play here."

"We won't," Tommy promised. He was sure Walleye was telling the truth. "Let's go back to the playground, okay?"

Carrie sniffed and Walleye continued leading them away from the cliff.

"You ever see the ghost of the girl on the swing?" Tommy asked.

"Hmm? Mary McGill, the one the Bodice Ripper attached to the swing with her own insides?" Walleye grinned. "No, I don't think I've ever seen her. But then I've never wandered around the playground after dark."

"Did you ever see any ghosts inside Cliffhouse?" Carrie asked.

"A few now and then. The ghosts won't hurt you, except for scaring you a little." They arrived at the playground. "It's the Blue Lady you have to be careful of." He bent down and looked at Tommy then Carrie. "Promise me. No hanging around the cliffs, and no playing outside at night."

"We promise."

## 82
## *The Battle of Cliffside Market*

"You couldn't buy skinned carrots in the 1860s, you goddamned farby!" The hardcore Reb got his face into the Yank's and tried to stare the guy down. Red MacIntosh, Cliffside Market's produce manager, eyed them; he'd seen the mayhem last year during the Pickett's Charge reenactment when one of the hardcores got into a shouting match with a farby colleague who wore Nikes instead of regulation boots.

"Yeah," said the easy-going bluecoat. "There weren't any supermarkets either, so what the heck are *you* doing in here?" He scowled at the obnoxious Confederate. "I can see your cell phone, Johnnie Reb."

"You're a fucking infantry grunt. I'm a lieutenant. You shut your farby mouth!"

Red stood six inches taller and wider than either man and he stepped forward, intimidating them with his size. "Gentlemen, I'll have to ask you to take this outside."

They looked at him, fire in their eyes. "Who the fuck are you to tell me what to do?" growled the Reb.

"Yeah. You're not even a soldier," said the blue. "You're nothing but a goddamned clerk."

"Well, at least you two can agree on something," Red said, and headed for the manager's office. The truth was, both reenactors had booze on their breath, chips on their shoulders, and were big enough to do damage. He knocked on the door.

"Come," called Kitty Ballou.

He smiled. His girlfriend was the assistant manager and the store ran far more smoothly when she was in charge than when Caesar Woodcock had the reins. With any luck, the old prick would retire soon.

"Hey, Red, what's up?"

"I think the Blue and the Gray were about to join together in a war against me."

"And they're still here?"

"Possibly. I think they may go quietly, but I'm not sure."

Kitty grabbed her keys. "Let's go see what's going on."

\*\*\*

Lee Ballou enjoyed the Civil War Festival from the comfort of Cliffside Market's deli. He was settled in a white plastic chair tucked up to a one-person table in the tiny dining area. He nibbled a slice of kosher dill then picked up his Italian sub and took a healthy bite, washing it down with a long pull on his drink, which appeared to be soda but, thanks to his long friendship with deli manager, Dewey Parsons, was actually Bud. He was on his second refill.

Today, the market's music was all Civil War, and Lee loved it. *Aura Lee* played. The store was crowded, mostly with tourists and townsfolk, but with a fair contingent of reenactors, too. He saw his daughter, Miss Kitty, walk by, all business, her eyes on patrol. She gave him a nod, but obviously had other things on her mind. He was proud of that girl, just like he was proud of Jacky. Sure, the boy had a stick up his ass, but what the hell; you couldn't have everything. He drank some more beer through his straw, belched amiably, got up and went back to the counter. "Hey Dewey," he called.

Dewey came out of the food prep area. "Yeah, Lee? What can I do you for?"

"You got any of those pickled chili peppers? The green ones?"

"Sure. How many do you want?"

"Oh, maybe six."

"Not a problem." He opened a container and used tongs to place them in a little wax paper bag. "Here you go."

"Thanks, kindly."

"You forgot to charge him for those peppers, Mr. Parsons."

The Cliffside Prune herself, Beverly Hill, now stood next to Lee at the counter.

"He don't have to pay. He bought a sandwich."

"Doesn't," she said.

"Pardon?"

"I said, he *doesn't* have to pay."

"Yeah, exactly. They come with the sandwich."

"Mrs. Hill, you can't let grammar and such shit raise your blood pressure like that," Lee counseled. "It'd be a shame to see a fine, relatively young woman such as yourself end up in one of Casper's boxes, six feet under."

"How dare you!" Beverly glared at him with her beady little eyes. "How dare you! I ought to report you to the manager for your insolence!"

He held his glee at bay. "Jesus, I'm sorry. I was only trying to pay you a compliment and give you some neighborly advice." He winked at Dewey, who was doing a bad job of keeping a straight face. He looked back at Beverly, who was near to steaming. "I can call the manager over, if you like. She's my little girl." His grin could eat a mile of shit.

"You smell of alcohol."

"Thanks, you smell pretty good yourself."

The *harrumph* told him he'd better stop poking the bear. He took his peppers and went back to his seat and watched Beverly harangue Dewey. She did a fine job, put her purchases in her shopping cart and moved to the bakery, her high heels clicking in time with the music, *When Johnnie Comes Marching Home*. That was Lee's favorite tune and the store played it just about every half hour, so he guessed it was everybody's favorite.

***

Roger Siechert loved his Saturday afternoon shopping trips to Cliffside Market. Today it was crowded because of the Civil War Festival, but he was so happy to finally be out of the office, it didn't bother him one bit. It was nice to see people smiling instead of grimacing or whining because they had a backache, a mysterious mole, blood in their stools, or painty fingernails. And by God, it was good to be away from Constance, too! She wanted to be with him every moment, but appeared to be allergic to grocery stores.

He stood at the butcher case, admiring the raw meat, the light scents of blood and flesh tickling his nose and reminding him of Tessa. He reached into his pocket and stroked the Chocolate Wanderer. It had gone bendy and wasn't holding up well in the pocket heat. He made a mental note to freeze it again when he got home, or maybe pickle it.

Running his hand along the cold ridges of the packages of fresh sausages, he wished he'd done something more interesting with Tessa's intestines. He caressed the meat, and if it hadn't been for Beverly Hill approaching with a squeaking cart of groceries, he would have lifted the package to his face and given it a deep sniff. Instead, he turned and smiled at the woman, determined to be nice. "Hello, Beverly," he boomed. "Did Gene take care of that yeast infection for you?"

Mrs. Hill came to an abrupt stop.

Several nearby shoppers rubbernecked.

Two teenage girls snickered.

That hadn't been what Roger meant to say, but lately, what he intended to say and what came out were often different things.

Beverly stalked toward him, pushing her loaded cart as if she intended to run him down. "How dare you say such a thing to me?" she hissed once she was close enough not to be overheard. "What in the name of God is wrong with you? Why are you discussing my gynecological issues with Dr. Holmes, anyway?"

A woman walked by, deliberately slow, her attempts to eavesdrop obvious. Siechert tipped an imaginary hat then shrugged at Beverly, lifted a package of sausage out of the case and smiled. "We're doctors, Mrs. Hill. We consult."

Beverly set her jaw, straightened indignantly, and spat more than spoke to the doctor. "Not anymore, you don't. You can tell Dr. Holmes I'll be replacing him." She wheeled her cart around, then paused. "As a matter of fact, you let him know he'll be lucky if I don't file a lawsuit."

Roger shrugged. "I'll be sure to pass the message on, Mrs. Hill. You just be sure not to pass that nasty infection to Casper, and we'll all be happy!"

Beverly Hill stalked away, her cart chirping down the aisle like a pissed off canary.

By now, several people had gathered nearby, whispering and watching. Briefly, he thought he might have said something wrong, then realized they were surely admiring his new cream-colored cable knit wool sweater, handmade in Ireland.

*Or did I misspeak?* He couldn't quite pin it down. *No, it's the sweater.*

He walked through the small circle of admirers, a smile on his face. "Afternoon, ladies and dolls."

\*\*\*

Mrs. Mudgett stared at the reenactors arguing outside Cliffside Market. One was a Yankee, the other a Reb, and the Reb kept shouting about the Yankee's tennis shoes. She gave them a dirty look as she spoke to her son. "Come along, Herman. Get Mother a shopping cart."

"Yes, Mother." Herman Mudgett, all 280 pounds of him, the weight in all the wrong places, pushed past the soldiers and pulled out a cart. Mrs. Mudgett, Vanessa to her few friends and Nessie to her many enemies, strode into the store as the doors opened before her. Herman followed, her dutiful servant.

There were too many people shopping this afternoon. There must have been a dozen reenactors in there - even one idiot woman in a hoop skirt who kept sweeping groceries off the lowest shelves. And tourists, oh Lord, the tourists. Why did they have to invade *her* market? It was disgusting. They dressed so badly and made so much noise and their offspring had no discipline. None whatsoever. The townsfolk weren't much better. Take Beverly Hill, who was pushing a full cart her way. The woman was nothing but a mortician's wife yet she thought she was Russian caviar on toast points.

"Hello, Beverly," she said as she passed her.

"Hello, Mrs. Mudgett," Beverly said. "How are you and your fine son doing today?"

Mrs. Mudgett didn't bother to hide her eye roll. "I'll be fine once I get out of this crowded store. If only Herman, here, was better at choosing fresh produce, I wouldn't even be here." She turned to smile at her son, behind the cart. "But he's such a good boy, we'll forgive him. He reads to me every night. He has a beautiful voice, you know."

"It must be so wonderful to have a son like yours, Mrs. Mudgett. I'm afraid Casper failed to give me a child."

Mrs. Mudgett crooked her finger at Herman and they passed the pathetic social climber without dignifying her untoward remark with a reply.

\*\*\*

*I'm going to shit on your face in your coffin when you die, Nessie Mudgett!* Beverly Hill shoved her cart forward, ramming into Taffilynn Matthews' cart near the potato chips, just south of the deli. *That breeder shouldn't be allowed to bring all those rug rats into a store where* normal *people are trying to shop!*

"Excuse me," Taffilynn said. "I'm afraid I wasn't paying attention." She pulled her cart back.

Beverly shot her a dirty look and took the right of way.

"Bitch."

It was soft, but she heard it - she *knew* she heard it - so she whirled around to glare at the baby factory. "What did you say to me?"

Taffilynn looked like shit wouldn't melt in her mouth. "Excuse me?" Small blond children circled her like seagulls around a trashcan.

"I heard you. How dare you speak to me like that, you vulgar slut?"

One of the rugrats started to cry. It grated.

"I don't know what you're talking about," Taffilynn said, patting her bulging belly full of baby as if she thought she was some sort of fertility goddess. She picked up the crybaby and placed him in the cart. "If you'll excuse me ..." She tried to get by.

"There's no excuse for the likes of you," Beverly said.

"Ladies, ladies, is something wrong? May I help you?" Kitty Ballou stepped between their carts and smiled.

"This is none of your business, you skank." Beverly looked toward the deli. "You know your reprobate father is over there getting drunk, don't you? Why don't you go bother him?"

"Mrs. Matthews," Kitty said, giving the breeder an apologetic smile she didn't deserve, "I'm sorry, but would you mind shopping in another department until Mrs. Hill is done in this one?"

Taffilynn, her face red with embarrassment, smiled back. "Of course not." She looked at Beverly Hill again. "I'm so sorry if I've somehow upset you."

"Don't you suck up to me. It won't get you anywhere."

Taffilynn, with two of the brats squalling now, turned and hurried away.

"Mrs. Hill," Kitty began. "Please don't take this the wrong way, but-"

"Oh, fuck you, pretending to be a legitimate business woman when you're nothing but the town pump."

"Excuse me." Dr. Roger Siechert spoke from behind Beverly, startling her so much she forgot what she was saying. "I think you owe Miss Ballou an apology." He winked at Kitty.

"Oh. Are you fucking the doctor, too, Kitty?"

"Mrs. Hill," Siechert began, his face a mask of Welbyesque concern.

"Yes?"

"I just want to confirm to you that my diagnosis the other day is, indeed, correct. You, madam, are a cunt."

\*\*\*

Kitty Ballou had to turn away so they wouldn't see her laughing. The look on Beverly's face was so perfect she wished poor Taffilynn could have seen it.

"Miss Kitty? Anything wrong?"

She looked up to see her dad staring at her, his expression somewhere between amused and annoyed. "Not a thing."

He looked over her head and grinned at Beverly Hill. "Dr. Siechert once diagnosed me as a dirty cocksucker, so maybe we should get together, Beverly. I'm game if you are."

Siechert started laughing.

Beverly Hill reared back and then shoved her cart into Siechert's as hard as she could. It threw the doctor backward and he landed on his butt.

"Dad," Kitty said. "Go get Red, will you?" A big flashing neon "Lawsuit" sign began flashing in her head as she went to Siechert who was struggling to his feet. "Are you okay?" She helped him up.

"Nothing wounded but my pride," he told her, looking at Beverly Hill in disgust. He bent and whispered in Kitty's ear, "She's a bitch. And she has a yeast infection. Shhhh. Don't tell."

"Uh, okay. As long as you're all right."

"I'm absolutely tip-top. I'm just going over to see Dewey about my meat order so I can make my special German brats for Oktoberfest. I do hope you'll be there."

"I wouldn't miss it," Kitty told him. "Excuse me."

"Of course." He pushed off and Kitty pulled herself up tall and squared her shoulders.

"Mrs. Hill, I'm afraid I must ask you to leave if you can't behave." She saw Red and her dad approaching. "Do you feel able to finish your shopping trip in peace or would you like to be escorted off the property?"

Red arrived, standing behind her in his emerald apron, a not-so-jolly green giant.

Beverly *humphed* and narrowed her eyes. "I will tell the *real* manager about this," she said, as she looked Red up and down before turning her cart toward the produce section.

"I hope you do," Kitty said.

Beverly *humphed* again and left.

"Doc Siechert's right," Lee Ballou announced. "That woman is a c-u-n-t." He chortled.

Red snickered and Kitty gave them both dirty looks. "This place is a regular zoo today," she said. "Keep an eye open, Red. And Dad, there'd better not be anything but soda in that cup you're holding."

He raised his free hand. "Swear to God. If you'll excuse me, I haven't finished my sandwich yet." He brandished the cup. "Need a refill on this, too. See you later, Miss Kitty. I'm proud of you."

Kitty sighed as she watched him go, then turned to Red. "I wonder why Beverly Hill's so nasty today."

"She's always nasty. When I die, I'd rather drop dead in the woods and be eaten by coyotes and bears than have her put makeup on my cold dead face."

"No kidding."

\*\*\*

Lee Ballou watched Beverly Hill disappear into the produce department as he finished his sandwich. He absently chewed on a pepper, then washed the heat away with a straw full of beer. Things were hopping at the market today, and he was enjoying the show. Put a bunch of half-drunk reenactors in with the likes of Beverly Hill and Nessie Mudgett and there were bound to be fireworks. He thought about getting a slice of cheesecake - beer and cheesecake was what they served in heaven, he was certain. He listened to Doc Siechert and Dewey discussing the merits of Schinkenwurst sausage over Krakauer. Lee didn't know what either of those was made of, but if Siechert thought they were worth eating, they probably were.

"YOU LITTLE BASTARD!"

Beverly Hill's voice triumphed over *"The Battle Hymn of the Republic."*

Lee got up and ambled toward the produce department where he saw Beverly Hill with red splattered all over her face. For a second he thought it was blood, but then he spotted a Matthews boy picking up a big fat tomato. The boy took aim and lobbed it at Beverly Hill. It exploded on her neck. "Don't you call my mommy names you mean old witch!" he cried.

"Anakin Lehi!" Just as Taffilynn got hold of the boy's arm, another child launched a tomato.

"You sons of bitches!" Beverly's voice was a shrill echo ricocheting through the store. The tomato struck her in the chest, exploding like a gunshot wound.

"Brigham!" Two more boys and one girl joined in the assault, pitching tomatoes at the mortician's wife.

"Whoa, whoa, whoa!" Red MacIntosh appeared, waving his arms.

Beverly Hill had had enough. She wiped tomato seeds from her face in a brusque motion and stalked toward the army of blond-haired children, taking the closest one by the hair. He yowled as Beverly yanked his head back and forth vigorously.

*It's the fucking Village of the Damned!* Lee chortled to himself.

Red MacIntosh was busily dropping caution cones around the whole debacle and hollering for an assistant to go get a mop.

A crowd had gathered. Several of the Matthews children assaulted Beverly Hill as she dragged their sibling around by his hair. One of them bit her leg. She howled and snagged another child by the hair.

Taffilynn stood, eyes wide, mouth covered, frozen in terrible shock.

Beverly howled again as she was pelted upside the head by a flying brussel sprout which struck hard enough that Lee could hear the impact, though it didn't slow Beverly down any. A big russet potato followed, but glanced off her giant handbag, then rolled under Mrs. Mudgett's cart where it stuck.

"Someone call the police!" Red MacIntosh, out of caution cones, yelled over the ruckus.

Beverly Hill, a Matthews child at the end of each arm, began shrieking as she swung the children in semi-circles while several of the other kids climbed on her in attempts to free their siblings.

Mrs. Mudgett bent down and unstuck the potato, turning it over as if inspecting it for damage. She seemed pleased with it and put it in her cart.

"Get off me, you little bastards!" Beverly Hill released the two boys she had by the hair and they went spinning in different directions, each coming to a hard stop against a produce bin. They both commenced screaming.

"Control your children!" Beverly shrieked at Taffilynn who remained frozen in place.

"My arm's broke!" one boy cried.

"Broken," yelled Beverly.

"Dr. Siechert to Produce," Lee Ballou called out in his rich baritone. "Dr. Siechert to Produce, stat!"

Miss Kitty, a banana peel in her hair, arrived, looking somewhat put upon. "What the heck is going on here?"

"Beverly Hill threw that boy, there, and broke his arm. I've been paging Dr. Siechert." Lee reconsidered. "I'll go find him."

"Good idea." Kitty knelt to examine the boy.

Following a hunch, Lee went back to the deli. Sure enough, there was Doc Siechert, jawing with Dewey. Now they had several strands of sausage links on the counter and were sniffing them, poking them, eyeing them, and just generally feeling the damn things up. "Could you two stop comparing sausages for a moment? Doc, I think you have a patient over there by the tomatoes."

Siechert looked up, surprised. "Sure. As long as it's not Beverly Hill. That's way too much cunt for me."

"Come on." Lee led the doctor to the boy and within moments, Siechert was splinting the kid's arm and telling Taffilynn she could meet them at the clinic. He picked the boy up, then cast a dire look at Beverly Hill. "You are in deep trouble, Missy! Are you going to tell your husband, or am I? Either way, I suspect a serious spanking is in your future."

Lee stared at him and as Siechert strode by, boy in his arms, he stared back and grinned. *What the hell?* Lee had never seen the doc quite so tweaky before.

Beverly looked almost as shell-shocked as Taffilynn, who had recovered enough now to start gathering her brood. Miss Kitty and Red appeared to still be digesting what was going on.

"It's not my fault," Beverly declared, nose in the air. "They attacked me. And mark my words, Taffilynn Matthews, you're going to pay for my ruined clothing and my dry-cleaning. Then, we'll talk about the stress this has caused me and *then* you can take it up with my lawyer."

Taffilynn didn't answer, just held her kids close and stared. Lee saw real shock in her face. "Mrs. Hill," he said sternly. "I saw everything that happened. You reached out and grabbed that boy. You grabbed the other one, too. The one whose arm you broke." He glanced around, making lots of eye contact and saw that no one was going to contradict him.

The woman huffed. "I did no such thing."

"I saw you do it, too," said Merlin Skinner, who had joined the growing crowd. Belle Tabrum, at his side, nodded.

"So did I," said Jerry Belvedere, cradling a jug of Clorox in his arms.

"Liars!" shrieked Beverly. "You're all liars!"

"Anyone else see it?" asked Lee.

"She started it," said Francis Trudy. His girlfriend, Prudence, nodded.

"It's entirely her fault the little boy is wounded," said Mrs. Mudgett. She stalked forward, stopping two feet from Beverly Hill. "You have no class. None whatsoever. You are lucky, Mrs. Hill, that it wasn't my Herman you injured. I would tear your eyes out one by one and feed them to Truffles."

"Truffles?" Lee asked.

"That's my guinea pig," Herman explained.

Jackson ran into Roger Siechert, carrying one of the Matthews boys in his arms, when he came into Cliffside Market. "Broken arm," Siechert said, rushing past.

The market was oddly quiet as he strode into a knot of people near a huge display of tomatoes. And there, in the middle of it all, were his sister and Red, Taffilynn Matthews, Beverly Hill and Mrs. Mudgett and her boy, Herman.

And Lee Ballou. *Of course.* At least he appeared to only be an onlooker this time. "What's going on?"

"We've had a tussle," Kitty said.

"I'll say," Lee piped up.

Jackson ignored him.

"This woman," said Mrs. Mudgett in her no-nonsense rumble, "broke a little boy's arm."

"She threw me, too," cried another boy as he clung to his mother.

"Are you hurt, son?" Jackson asked.

"No. But she threw me!"

"What happened here?"

"Beverly Hill hates children." Mrs. Mudgett reached up and pinched Herman's cheek fondly. "She hates them! She just grabbed those sweet little boys and started yanking them around like they were monkeys on sticks. Then she let go and …" She paused for dramatic effect. "And the poor babies just flew into the produce bins. They never had a chance."

Jackson knew Mudgett hated Hill and looked around. "Is that what happened?"

Jon Daniels, the Cliffhouse avoided his eyes, as did several others, including Derek Sand and Jordan Cartwright. Jackson turned to Taffilynn Matthews. "Do you have any idea why Mrs. Hill would attack your children?"

Taffilynn looked at him. Before she could speak, Kitty said, "Mrs. Matthews has no idea. No one does."

"Liar!" screeched Beverly Hill. "You lying skank."

"Mrs. Hill, be quiet." Jackson looked at Taffilynn. "Mrs. Matthews, want to tell me what happened?"

She looked sheepish. "I'm afraid one of my boys threw the first tomato after Mrs. Hill called me a very bad name."

"She called our mother a bitch!"

"Shh!" Taffilynn covered her child's mouth. "Be reverent."

Jackson looked from Taffilynn to Beverly. "So do you want to press charges?"

"I want to press charges!" bellowed Beverly Hill.

"That's a possibility, though I wouldn't recommend it given that you've evidently broken a child's arm and will be in a great deal of trouble if Mrs. Matthews presses charges." He looked at Taffilynn.

She stared back. "Can I think about it? I want to go to the doctor's office to be with Brigham."

"Yes. Go ahead." He watched her herd her children out the door then looked at Beverly. "You're under arrest for disturbing the peace, Mrs. Hill. More charges may be filed at a later time." He brandished his handcuffs. "I'll read you your rights in a moment. For now, turn around."

"I will not!"

"Shall I add resisting arrest to the charges?"

"Cocksucking bastard," she muttered, but she turned.

Jackson clicked the cuffs on with just a little more enthusiasm than necessary. "You shouldn't call my sister names," he said in her ear as he guided her toward the exit.

"Jackson." Lee Ballou stepped out of the crowd. "You're a hell of a good cop. I'm proud of you, son."

Jackson, surprised by the compliment, stared at his father. "Thanks, Dad."

The doors slid open and Jackson escorted Mrs. Hill in the direction of his cruiser. He heard the entire store erupt with applause as they exited.

# 83
## *Night Swim*

It had been Tommy's best birthday ever. All day long he and Carrie had watched the Civil War battles with their parents. In between, they learned how soldiers cooked, what they wore, and how their weapons worked. Even better, he got to ride the carousel half a dozen times and, in La Chatte Rouge, for lunch, the waiters and waitresses had sung *"Happy Birthday"* to him and presented him with a great big fancy chocolate cupcake that he didn't have to share with Carrie.

Later, they had fried chicken on the riverboat tour and he and his sister watched for the Blue Lady as dusk fell, but she was nowhere to be seen. After that, they went bowling, just like he wanted, then had cake and ice cream.

Now, it was almost ten at night and their parents had disappeared into their bedroom about half an hour before. Tommy heard lots of noises, some growly and scary, but mostly happy, as usual. Everything was quiet now. Their parents always fell asleep right after making noises. He wondered what games they played. Not Chutes and Ladders, he was sure.

"Hey, you wanna go swimming?" Carrie whispered as another episode of Monk started on the TV.

"Huh?"

"In the pool downstairs."

"We can't do that."

"Yes we can. It's your birthday, remember?"

That was true. It was his birthday, the day his parents let him do whatever he wanted. "Okay," he said. They quietly changed into their suits and as they let themselves out of the room, Tommy whispered, "I'll race you!" and took off, Carrie chasing after him.

Downstairs, the pool room was silent and empty and kind of spooky. The overhead lights were turned way down, but the lamps in the pool lit the water a beautiful blue and its movement cast weird shadows on the walls and ceiling. A tiny thrill of fear shot through him as he smelled the chlorine and water and listened to the echoes.

They walked to the deep end of the pool and gazed into the blue water.

"I dare you to jump in." Carrie's voice echoed.

"No," said Tommy. "What if it's cold?"

"There's only one way to find out!" She shoved her brother into the water, towel and all.

The warmth of the water was a welcome surprise. He kicked to the surface, forgetting his towel as he dog-paddled to the edge. "I'm telling Mom!" He spit water out and bobbed in place, one hand on the concrete lip of the pool.

"Will not," said Carrie, staring down at him. "Or I'll tell her you eat your boogers."

"I do not!"

"Do so!"

"*You* eat *my* boogers!" He giggled like a maniac.

Carrie cannonballed into the water then came up next to him, spitting a mouthful in his face.

"Eww!" Tommy cried. "I peed in the water! You just drank my pee!"

"You're a liar and I'm telling!"

"You're telling that you drank my pee!" Tommy's words echoed through the room.

"Shh!" said Carrie. "Did you hear that?"

Tommy went still. "Hear what?"

She shushed him again. "I heard someone whisper your name."

Suddenly scared, he really did have to pee. "Knock it off, Carrie. Mom said you're not supposed to scare me anymore."

Carrie's eyes went wide. "There it was again. Don't you hear it?"

"Stop it." Panic filled him.

"I think it's the spirit of the Bodice Ripper."

Tommy swallowed hard, remembering the terrible story Walleye had told them. *But it didn't happen in here. Nothing bad ever happened in here.* "You're being mean!"

She hesitated, then grinned. "You're a scaredy-cat!"

"Am not!" Tommy splashed water into her face.

She splashed him back.

Half a dozen splashes later, Carrie swam to the edge of the pool. "You better dive down there and get that," she said, pointing to his towel which was floating near the bottom of the pool.

"Or what?"

"Or the hotel people will tell Mom and Dad we ruined one of their towels, and then they'll know we snuck out and went swimming."

Tommy wondered if that was true. *It might be.* "You go down and get it," he said.

"Why? Are you scared?"

"No."

"You're eight now; you shouldn't be scared of stuff anymore," she said. "I wasn't. I guess you'll always be a scaredy-cat."

"I'm not scared!"

Carrie smiled. "Then go get your towel. Or maybe you're afraid the Bodice Ripper will grab you."

Despite his determination to show no fear, an icy finger moved down his spine as he thought of the story. *It didn't happen in here. He killed her on the swing.* He took a deep breath then went under the water, blocking out Carrie's words.

He kicked downward and, though his vision was blurry, he saw the towel floating just a few inches above the bottom. Once he got close, he swiped at it, tried to grab it, but his fingers moved through it - he felt a little disoriented. He was certain he was close enough, so he swiped at it once more. Again, his hands touched nothing, but the move set the towel in motion. It spun lazily, and he watched as it changed from white to a pale shade of blue.

He couldn't hold his breath much longer. He kicked again, moving several inches closer to snatch it. Again, he felt nothing, but the towel moved, swirled, and through blurred vision, he watched a form take shape.

What had appeared to be the edge of his towel now looked more like a blue-white halo of hair, and as the material shifted, it looked like there was a face in the middle.

Tommy's heart jackhammered against his ribs.

The towel-face moved closer, till it was inches away. As he watched, frozen in terror, two black holes suddenly appeared, as if the face had opened its eyes. A mouth formed and Tommy, frantic, swam backward.

The towel-face came at him and arms formed to reach for him. His lungs were ready to burst. He pushed himself off the bottom of the pool, swimming as hard and fast as he could.

He shot through the surface, took in a deep lungful of air, and thrashed and kicked, swimming hard to the edge of the pool, hopping out of the water and onto the cement. "Get out of the water!" he shouted at his sister. "Get out!"

For a moment, Carrie looked as if she were going to say something smart-alecky, then she read the terror on his face.

"Get out!" He pointed at the towel, which wasn't a towel anymore at all.

Carrie followed his finger, spotted the thing, shrieked, and shot out of the water the same way she'd entered it: like a cannon ball.

Tommy and Carrie ran to the door, but it wouldn't open.

They took turns banging on it, then the noises behind them - sucking, rushing water sounds - forced their attention to the pool.

They clutched each other, screaming as the water bubbled and boiled up not twenty feet from them. From the roiling center, something rose; something blue, white, terrible. A woman.

Carrie screamed.

Both yelled for help and yanked on the door. It wouldn't budge.

The phantom rose higher, until it appeared to be standing on the water, then it raised its arms, stretching them outward. *Tommy, you are mine. Carrie, come to me.*

The kids looked at each other and screamed again.

The Blue Lady stood an inch or two above the water and began to glide toward them, her black eyes wide and fixed on them. *Come to me.* The mouth didn't move, but they heard the words just the same.

They kept pounding the door.

The ghost stepped onto the cement and stared at them with those big, black eyes as it beckoned to them. *Come, children. Don't be afraid.*

"You leave us alone!" Tommy cried, squaring his trembling shoulders. "I'll tell my daddy on you!"

Carrie pounded on the door.

*Do not fear me, Tommy. Let me hold you in my arms. Come to me.*

"Go away! You go away, now!"

The spectral woman laughed and it was the most horrible sound Tommy had ever heard. He looked at Carrie, who was trembling, tears running down her cheeks. She was saying "No, no, no, no ..." under her breath and pulling the door handle uselessly.

The Blue Lady walked toward them.

"Go back! You just go back right now!"

She was only five feet away. *Tommy. Carrie. You are mine.*

"AM NOT!" Tommy yelled and pushed with all his might.

The door opened and both kids tumbled into the lobby.

\*\*\*

Sara Bellamy stepped back and watched in amazement as the Collins kids fell onto the carpet. She had checked the pool area and locked it herself at nine o'clock. *But these two ... How?*

The panicked kids stumbled to their feet. Both tried to race past her but she grabbed their arms.

"What's the matter? What were you doing in the pool room?"

"She's gonna get us!" blurted Carrie.

"Who? What are you talking about?"

"The Blue Lady!" the little boy cried. "She's after us. Let us go, please!"

"In a minute. How did you get in there, kids? The door was locked."

"No, it wasn't," said the girl. "We went to swim. You won't tell our parents, will you? They'll be mad."

"And it's my birthday," the boy said.

"You saw a blue woman in there?" Sara asked, trying hard to keep her voice calm and steady.

"She came out of the water and almost got us before you opened the door. We were locked in."

"That's not possible. It must have been stuck. And there's no such thing as … as a blue ghost."

"Is so," the girl insisted. "She's in there."

"Yes!"

"Okay. If you'll wait here while I look, we'll talk about whether or not I should tell your parents."

"Okay." Carrie sniffed and wiped her eyes.

"Don't go in there," Tommy said.

"I'll only be a minute. Will you hold the door open for me in case it sticks again?"

The children nodded, but looked scared spitless.

Sara felt pretty scared herself as she pushed the door open and peered inside. She saw nothing unusual. "Hang on to the door really tight, okay?"

"Okay," the kids said.

She stepped in and flipped the main switch. Shadows fled as the lights blossomed overhead. The pool was still. She started to take another step then noticed there were three sets of wet footprints, two belonging to the kids. The third set was different, larger. They came up to the door, disappeared into the puddle the kids had left, then walked in a straight line back to the pool.

Suddenly, the smell of lakewater rose, so strong that it drowned the sharp scent of chlorine. It swirled around her, chill and immediate. Her stomach flipped as she stepped back, shutting and locking the door before turning to the kids. "I won't tell your parents as long as you promise me you'll never wander around alone again - inside or outside of the hotel."

The kids' gratitude was obvious. Sara rode up the elevator and saw them to their door, using a passkey to let them sneak in. "Listen," she whispered before opening the door. "You two stay out of trouble, okay?"

"We will," Tommy said. "We're going home as soon as the Civil War is done."

# 84
## *Siechert has Insomnia*

Roger Siechert lay staring at the crescent moon that shone between the tops of the tall pines. It was two in the morning - the cuckoo clocks had just sung of the number - and he hadn't been able to get to sleep. He sat up and turned on the lamp. Maybe a glass of wine would help.

He padded to the kitchen where he poured himself half an inch of merlot, retrieved a cold bottle of sparkling water, and took both to the kitchen table. He sat.

Though his day had been delightfully Constance-free, it had been a long one, starting with the discovery that Pat Matthews was the graffiti painter. He downed the merlot in one swallow. He had yet to report this to the authorities; he was still sitting on it. Roger uncapped the Blue Springs and took a long, lovely pull. It tickled all the way down.

His morning clinic hours had run a little longer than usual, and then his shopping trip to Cliffside Market had been ruined by Beverly, Queen of the Dead, when she went off her rocker and broke the Matthews kid's arm. *At least it made me look like a knight in shining Armor All.* Smiling to himself, he polished off the Blue Springs then went to the fridge for another.

He took the bottle to his bedroom and opened the French doors leading to his balcony. Autumn whispered to him in the chilly breeze as he stepped out to study the moon, which appeared as a sickle balanced on the treetops.

The moon shed light on the bottle, making it glow blue. He saw an image of that prick Pat Matthews in his mind's eye, saw himself punching him in the face for vandalizing his clinic. He took another sip of water, then held the bottle up to the moonlight. The sparkling water moved like an ocean trapped in blue; it was beautiful. Soothing.

But Pat Matthews would not leave his thoughts and he realized he wanted to confront the man himself, maybe rough him up a little, before turning him in. *You're a painty pervert, Pat!* He giggled.

*Someone will teach him a lesson, Roger, but not you. I have someone else for you.* The Lady's voice came, calm and almost comforting.

He took another drink of water. "Who?"

Chill laughter swept around him. *Patience. I will show you.*

Roger smiled.

# 85
## *Hammerhead and the Lady*

"Where are you?" he whispered into the mirror. "Where are you?"

He felt no cool breath in his ear, heard no words, saw nothing but his own reflection. He had barely felt the Lady's presence in recent days and he knew she was visiting someone else. He could almost sense the other man's identity, but not quite.

He knew the Lady was growing stronger, and understood on a very deep level that this meant she could now enter other hosts - *lesser hosts* - more easily, and for some reason, this bothered him. *Is this what jealousy feels like?*

Uneasy, he left the Hall of Souls and walked out onto his deck.

*We have work to do together.*

"You're here!" he said as the lake smell whirled around him in cold bursts.

*I will be back soon. You must rest now.*

Calm and expectation filled him. He went back inside. Five minutes later, he was deeply asleep.

# 86
## *At the Crimson Corset*

An hour before dawn he watched Pat Matthews spray painting a monstrous penis on the exterior of the Crimson Corset, the strip joint where Booteous Maxima once hung her thong. If there was ever a place the scarlet atrocity belonged, this was it. He stood in the shadows, waiting.

As Matthews added the final details, the Lady spoke. *Go now.*

"Well, well," he said, stepping into sight. "I wouldn't have guessed you were the vandal in a million years, Pat Matthews."

Matthews gasped. "I ... uh ..."

The man held up a hand and drew closer. "Not to worry, my friend. Your secret is safe."

For a moment, Matthews looked like he might dart away, but he knew he'd been caught - red-handed as it were - and instead of running, he spoke rapidly. "It's just that, you see, I get paid when we have to come clean up. It's kind of like a commission, you know, and I uh, I have another kid on the way, and we're really hurting for money. I always make sure and do a really good job cleaning up. So really, it's not like any of the damage is permanent, you know?"

The man smiled, crossed his arms over his chest, and leaned against the side of the building.

"You won't tell anyone, will you? I mean, gosh, this is so embarrassing, it's just that-"

"No, I won't tell." He stepped closer and uncrossed his arms. "And to put your mind at ease, I will give you my word as a gentleman." He held out his hand. "Let's shake on it."

Pat Matthews stared, swallowed, looked quickly around, then took the hand. "You're a real pal," he said.

He held tight to Matthew's hand as the dark odor of water grew overwhelming.

Matthews didn't seem to notice the smell. "It's so nice to talk to someone who understands about hard times, you know?" Matthews coughed. "I wouldn't have-" he coughed harder "-done this if I didn't have to." Matthews doubled over in a fit of wracking, wet coughs that soon became gasps for air.

The man let go of his hand and watched as water drooled out of Pat Matthews' nose and mouth.

Grabbing at his throat, eyes bulging, Matthews dropped to his knees.

"Considering your crimes, this really is quite merciful." Hammerhead produced a compact mirror. "Now look into this."

Matthews reached for him. He stepped back, keeping the mirror in place.

Pat Matthews fell, face first, onto the pavement. He gurgled, water pooling around his face.

Hammerhead tucked the trapped soul into his front pocket.

Headlights moved over them as a car turned onto the street.

He returned to the shadows as the smell of the lake faded. The Lady had left him.

A dark SUV pulled up and he heard the door open, footsteps, and the low, soft whistle of a familiar tune. He considered leaving, but curiosity held him in place.

The footsteps stopped. "Well, fuck-a-doodle-doo."

He recognized Roger Siechert's voice. As he glanced around the building's edge to confirm it, he smelled the lake again. The Lady had returned, but with Siechert. *That's my competition?* He smiled in the dark.

The doctor was poking at Pat Matthews' corpse. "Looks like somebody beat me to it, old buddy."

*Beat him to it?* This was becoming very interesting.

"Yep. You're dead as grandpa's hard-on, Painty, my boy. That's no reason I can't get my two cents in, though, is it? And I don't even need an apron. Isn't that convenient?"

Hammerhead heard latex gloves snapping. Cautiously, he looked again.

The doctor bent over the body, pulled a large knife from inside his jacket, and held it above Matthews a moment before ripping into the body.

The squishy wet sounds as the doctor stuck his hands inside the dead man were revolting. The doctor brought out the endless string of guts and began draping them around the corpse's arms and legs, whistling as casually as a man trimming a Christmas tree.

When he finished, Siechert appraised his work. "There," he said. "That's how it's done." He returned to his car, still whistling.

\*\*\*

"Oh, crap," Jackson said when he arrived at the Crimson Corset. His officers had the crime scene cordoned off and it was still early enough that there weren't many looky-loos. *Thank heaven it's Sunday.*

Somehow, Gene Holmes had beaten him to the scene and was already kneeling by the body. He looked up. "Jackson, take a look at this. It's fascinating."

He moved closer, his nose wrinkling at the odor. "What's fascinating?"

Dr. Holmes pointed at Pat Matthews' dripping wet face. "I bet his lungs are full of water. But this-" He gestured at the guts and gore. "This is new. It's post-mortem."

Jackson stared at the damage and wondered how to break the news to Taffilynn.

# 87
## *Dinner with Polly*

"Thanks for coming over," Jackson said as Polly came out of the cabin and joined him on the front porch. "It's been quite a day."

"Dinner will be ready soon."

"You didn't have to cook."

She smiled. Jackson looked as tired as he sounded. "I didn't cook. I brought some of Dale's chili and cornbread. It's heating." She paused. "Tell me about your day."

"I got up at five a.m."

"And?"

"Isn't that enough?"

"I get up that early every day, Jacky. Cry me a river."

"The homicide this morning was messy. Really messy. But the worst part was telling Taffilynn."

"How did she take it?"

"Devastated. I wonder how she'll get by."

Polly patted his hand. "She'll get by, don't you worry."

"You sound pretty confident."

"I am. There are things about Taffilynn you don't know. She's a resourceful woman."

"I'm intrigued."

Polly looked at him a moment. "Well," she said. "Can we keep it between us?"

"Don't we always?"

"Taffilynn runs a phone sex business. She's been doing it for years and has managed to save a pretty good bundle. Pat never knew."

Jackson blinked at her. "You can't be serious."

"As a heart attack."

"Who told you?"

"Taffilynn. She'll be fine. She has a good job and something to fall back on, so to speak."

Jackson laughed. It was a nice sound. "I never would have guessed."

"It's always the quiet ones." Polly chuckled. "She made up the story about consulting with new mothers on the Internet so she could hand Pat a little money when necessary, but she couldn't tell him what she really does."

"He'd have flipped," Jackson said.

"True, but the real reason is that whenever Pat had an extra dime it went for tranquilizers and comic books. He couldn't hang onto a cent."

They sat in companionable silence for several minutes. Finally, Polly spoke up. "They did the autopsy on Pat today?"

"Yep."

"And?"

"This is between us."

"Of course."

"He died with his lungs full of water. The wounds were post mortem. And we still haven't got a damn clue." He seemed to think a moment. "The worst part is, there's nothing I can do. These deaths are all natural causes."

"But you don't think they are?"

He sighed. "I know they're not. I just can't figure out what's happening. Gene's as stumped as I am. We're working on it, though."

"So you think maybe he vandalized the wrong building, and someone was getting even?"

"Could be. Or he was just a convenient target." Jackson rubbed his chin. "Of course, that still doesn't tell me how people on land are drowning. There's a medical condition called dry drowning, but this isn't it. Not by a long shot. This is just ... weird. It makes no sense."

"Maybe it has to do with what we saw at the End of Summer Party."

He raised his eyebrows. "The Blue Lady?"

"Um-hmm."

"At this point, I wouldn't be surprised."

# 88
## *Roger in Elfland*

**THURSDAY**

Roger Siechert's new hobby was trailing Beverly Hill. Only a few days had passed, but he already had a handle on her: Beverly was a creature of habit. Each morning at 8 a.m., she drove her silver Escalade down into town to a little place called The Awareness Institute, tucked between La Dee Da's Bar and the Peppermint Stix Motel. This was the heart of Cliffside's blessedly small low-rent district.

The Awareness Institute turned out to be some sort of woo-woo meditation center. There were statues of Buddha in the windows and old hippie posters about karma and dogma and war. She took a meditation class every morning, then drove back home to the mortuary. In the afternoon - probably after she smeared make-up on a few corpses and gave Casper a little hell - she went out again, this time to run errands.

He had decided they'd have their little tête-à-tête after meditation this morning, so he'd risen and shone with the birdies that wanted to get the early worms. He thought about Beverly's worms, squishy and thick in her belly. Those were the worms he wanted.

If anyone had asked him what it was like, digging his hands into a steaming hot mound of intestines, he would have told them it was like coming home, though he wasn't really sure quite what that meant. He didn't think it was Freudian.

His two innard adventures so far had not only taken intestinal fortitude, but a certain degree of self-control due to the odors involved. Tessa had taken reasonable care with her diet, avoiding red meat in favor of fish and chicken; her odors were unpleasant, but nothing like Pat Matthews' stench, which could only come from greasy burgers, French fries, and Christ knew what else. The man positively reeked. *He probably ate fried cheese.* The thought disgusted Roger. *What a horrible thing to do to innocent cheese!*

*What will Beverly smell like?* Despite her meditative practices, he doubted she was a vegetarian - *my, wouldn't that be interesting?* - yet she was slender and middle-aged, which told him she probably watched her diet. She looked like the kind of person who ate grapefruits incessantly. And fiber. She would be a fan of seeded breads and celery. That would help her chronic constipation, too.

Once again, he left the Jag at home in favor of his unremarkable Ford SUV, and sat alone except for the invisible presence of the

Lady. He was parked just down the street from the Awareness Institute and as he waited for Beverly, he listened to a CD of German folk music and ate pumpernickel with thinly sliced turnips. *Superb. Beverly would probably like it.* Maybe he'd offer her some if she wasn't rude to him.

*Roger ... be ready.*

"I'm ready."

*Do you see her?*

"Yeah, yeah, I see her."

The Lady was kind of a nag.

Beverly dawdled with a couple of other women before getting into her Escalade. He set his food aside, glanced at a small bouquet of flowers he'd brought along, and started his engine, wasting gas while she primped in the mirror or fucked herself with a cross or whatever a corpse decorator did to kill time. Finally, she pulled out. So did he, but when she turned left, he went right, returning to Main Street ahead of her. He needed to get to their place of assignation before she did.

Beverly enjoyed taking a scenic route home more often than not and if she took it today, they'd be meeting soon. At the edge of town, Roger turned onto a dirt track that cut the travel time by fifteen minutes. He soon arrived at Elfland Road, a narrow asphalt byway once well-traveled but now nearly ignored because Elfland Park had been all but deserted for over three decades. Santaville, now a relic itself, had put it out of business.

Moments later, he reached the park and pulled over at the old entrance. The place still had a rusty-looking playground and plenty of cement mushroom houses, and restrooms no one in their right mind would enter.

*But I'm not at all sure I'm in my right mind.* Giggling, he glanced at his watch, saw he had at least ten minutes, and trotted to the lavatory. It was locked, so he pulled out his trusty trouser snake and started to write his name on the wall, realized that might be unwise, and finished off his piss by crossing out the letters. He had a fine and steady stream for a man his age.

He turned around, peering into the park. There were a few decapitated cement elves still standing. One held a defunct drinking fountain balanced on its arms. It looked like someone had taken a shit in it. He walked a little farther, remembering the old kiddie rides, wondering if the boat ride in a cement "river" was still there. He'd liked that one as a kid.

*Roger ...*

"Just a minute."

*It is time ...*

"Jesus H. Christ, I'm sick of being nagged, you blue bitch."

*Go to the road.*

Lakewater perfume swirled around him, making gooseflesh tiptoe over his balls.

*Go now!*

"I'm going, I'm going." He walked to the entrance, pausing only to examine the old swing set, just inside the low fence. It was tall and three swings hung from it, two of them unusable. He giggled and returned to his SUV, where he set his jack on the ground.

He waited. In less than sixty seconds, Beverly Hill's SUV came into view. He loosened his collar, ran his hand over his hair, mussing it a little, stepped out onto the road and waved her down.

He was certain she intended to pass him by, but at the last minute she pulled over and rolled her window down.

"Mrs. Hill," he said, "thank you so much for stopping. I was actually on my way to your house when I got a flat."

"My house? Why?" The woman was all ice.

"I wanted to apologize for the other day at the market and at the mortuary. I'm afraid I've been taking a new medication and it had some bad side effects."

"I should certainly hope you would apologize."

"It's the least I can do, and as a matter of fact, I was bringing you a gift. Saying 'I'm sorry' just isn't enough."

"A gift?" She looked interested.

"Yes," he said. "If you'd come with me, I'd like to give it to you."

She looked at him a long moment. "What about your truck? I don't see a flat tire."

"It's in front. My spare is flat, too. I wondered if you might call the auto club for me when you get home. After I give you your gift, of course. I can't give it to you in the car."

Beverly shut off her engine. She was trying to look annoyed, but, as he'd hoped, her curiosity won out. She stepped out of her vehicle.

Siechert led her a few steps closer to his Ford, then stopped. "Actually," he said, "sit right here a moment." He indicated the nearby swings. "I want it to be a surprise."

"Oh, for pity's sake," said Beverly. "I don't want to sit on the swing. I suppose you'll ask me to close my eyes next."

Siechert tried to look sheepish. "If you wouldn't mind."

Beverly's jaw tensed but the sparkle in her eye said she wanted her gift. "All right," she said. "But don't dally. I have a schedule to keep." She sat in the swing and looked down at the ground instead of closing her eyes, but that was good enough.

He jaunted back to his car, slipped on his rain poncho, slid his filleting knife beneath it, and grabbed the bouquet of flowers.

Maintaining the spring in his step and whistling *Happy Wanderer,* he returned and held the bouquet out. "You can look now."

She surveyed the flowers. "Well," she said, taking them from him. "I suppose I accept your apology, but I don't know why I had to get out of my car for these."

"Good," he said. "What a lovely day."

She nodded and brought the bouquet up to her nose. Siechert had a feeling this was the first time in a long while she'd been given flowers that weren't left over from a funeral.

"You're a dear friend to me." Siechert put his hand on Beverly's left shoulder, wonderful coolness filling him. It was bony, brittle. "You and Casper both." He felt the gentle buzz begin to build momentum in his hand, just beneath the skin. The Lady, riding him, moaned softly. It sounded almost sexual.

Beverly Hill coughed.

"I'd never deliberately do anything to compromise my relationship with you or your hus-"

Beverly began coughing hard.

Siechert tightened his grip on her shoulder.

The bouquet spilled to the earth as Beverly gasped for breath.

He held her in place.

She spasmed and brought her hands to her mouth. Water sprayed from between her fingers. Siechert giggled as urine ran down her legs.

He withdrew the knife, brought it up and, in a quick, expert motion, drew it across her throat. Blood and water spurted from the incision.

Beverly's head fell back, nearly severed, then she went limp as a rag doll.

Siechert released her, letting her crumple to the ground, crushing the bouquet.

The Blue Lady gave a sigh of satisfaction.

He looked down at Beverly. "How could you possibly think I would apologize to a harridan like you? You are, without doubt, the cuntiest human being I have ever had the misfortune to meet. You are the very Queen of Corpses."

Only the Lady could hear him now, and he knew she liked what he said.

# 89
## *Jackson and Gene on the Scene*

From the roadside, it appeared that a woman in red was sitting on a swing, and that's just what Jackson's officer had thought. But when he came back down Elfland Road, the figure was still there, so he stopped, only to find Beverly Hill tied to the swing with her own intestines.

Ted Lawson, young and still a little green, had never seen this kind of violence, but when he vomited, he did so a good ten feet from the scene. Jackson, arriving just before his forensics guys, was proud of him. He was also glad that his officer, rather than a civilian, had found the body. That cut down on all kinds of problems.

It was a horrendous scene. Mrs. Hill's head had been propped onto her neck and tied there with her intestines - but the strings of gut couldn't hold it well, so it lolled back, as if she were looking up at the sky. Everything was red, the blood thin and watery. Beneath her, it was obvious the perp had shoveled away some of the sand, perhaps removing more than footprints.

*What balls this guy has.* He had butchered the woman right here at the side of the road; anyone could have come along and caught him in the act. *Balls of steel.* He'd been parked right in front of Mrs. Hill's vehicle and had probably flagged her down - she most likely knew him. Why else would she stop? Beverly Hill was no Good Samaritan, you could bank on that. He thought back to Matthews' body. This ripper's boldness would help them catch him.

Darkness fell as his men finished the on-site forensics. Samples had been taken, photos shot. Gene Holmes was now hard at work.

Jackson found it interesting that the perp had been calm enough to stick around and sweep away both his footprints and tire tracks, but it was downright fascinating that he'd swept away the Escalade's tracks as well. Was that a sense of humor or something else?

He'd left no tracks. He must have pulled his vehicle up onto the asphalt and left it idling in the road while he swept. There wasn't a viable track anywhere - anything left had been taken by the breeze or destroyed by other vehicles. *I'll bet there's not a print to be found. Or a weapon.* He stood back as Gene examined the body.

"It's hard to say an exact time of death, but I think our guy probably did this after sunrise, judging by the rigor." Holmes lifted one of the hands and tried to move a finger. It gave with an awful sound. "It's stiff enough that it has to be broken out." He crunched another finger. "Yeah. After sunrise. The guy has nerve."

"No kidding."

Holmes peered into the neck with a flashlight. "We'll have to do an autopsy to be sure, but I believe her lungs are full of water. I can see it pooled in the larynx. I'd say it's time to get her up to Casper's." He paused. "How'd he take the news?"

"Poor guy almost fainted." By his reaction, Jackson knew Casper was an unlikely suspect.

"He'll be okay with us using his workroom for the autopsy?"

"Yes. Said he'd make sure it was ready but he won't be joining us."

An ambulance, followed by one of his squad cars, pulled up and parked. "Ready for us, Chief?" called his officer.

He looked at Gene, who nodded. "We're ready." He stared at the scene, thinking it looked, somehow, familiar.

# 90
## *Intestinal Fortitude*

### FRIDAY

Jackson sat with Teddy and Adam at the breakfast table in their cabin, thinking Polly was pretty damn smart. This morning, he'd told her about Beverly Hill at Elfland and how familiar the scene looked. Without missing a beat, she'd reminded him about the story of the Bodice Ripper and the girl on the swing, then suggested he ask Teddy and Adam for the details.

Adam poured coffee and Teddy tapped the journals. "Are you here for these?"

"Maybe. What can you tell me about the Bodice Ripper murders? Specifically, the one in your playground."

Teddy and Adam exchanged glances. "Does this have to do with Beverly Hill's murder?" Adam asked.

Jackson shifted uncomfortably. "It might."

"I hear they found her at Elfland," Teddy said.

Jackson nodded. That much was public - but only that much.

"On the swing?" Teddy asked.

"Can't say, sorry."

"Quid pro quo?"

"Sorry, Ted." Polly was the only one Jackson broke the rules for, and all she knew was that someone had slit Hill's throat and left the body on the swing. "I can't answer that."

"Does that mean Beverly might have been found on the swing?"

Jackson shrugged.

"Teddy, just tell him about the Bodice Ripper and stop badgering the poor man. He can't answer your questions."

Jackson smiled at Adam. "Yes, please, tell me. And don't leave out the gory details."

"Okay. Labor Day, 1928. A young woman named Mary McGill was staying at Cliffhouse. She was last seen alive in the cellar speakeasy, dancing and having a good time. She must've been dressed like a flapper, don't you think, Adam?"

"Most assuredly. Go on, Teddy."

"Several people reported seeing her leaving Cliffhouse with a tall gentleman late in the evening, and it was assumed they were going for a stroll on the grounds. The next morning, she was found tied to a swing in the playground."

"Tied?" Jackson's stomach did a little dance.

"The Bodice Ripper had slit her from stem to stern then pulled out the girl's intestines and twined them around her waist and forearms to attach her to the chains of the swing. According to this," he tapped one journal, "the Ripper had even laced the intestine through the swing's chains to make sure she didn't slip."

*Christ!* "Is this common knowledge?"

"The story of the girl on the swing is pretty well known," Teddy said, "but the part about lacing the intestines in the chains is new to me, so I doubt anyone knows about that. If the old files are still at your station, perhaps it's mentioned there."

"I'll check, but the station burned in the fifties and was rebuilt, so I'm not holding my breath." He sipped coffee. "So this information, to the best of your recollection, is new to you?"

"Utterly. Great Aunt Theodosia's journals are full of details about all sorts of things. For instance-"

"May I borrow them?"

"Of course. And we won't breathe a word of this to anyone." He slid the journals across to Jackson.

"Thank you." He paused. "Bring me up to speed on the Bodice Ripper, if you would."

"All the murders were committed the same way. His victims were slit from sternum to privates. They occurred over several years."

"How many?"

"A few. I don't recall offhand, but there were more each year. The last happened that same year on New Year's Eve."

Jackson looked through a few pages. "I'll take good care of these and get them back to you soon."

"Take your time," Adam said.

"Yes," Teddy echoed. "But there's one other thing we learned about the murders that's really interesting."

"What's that?"

"Theodosia said the doctor - he was a friend of hers - told her every one of them had drowned."

"What?" Jackson tried to stay calm. "The killer drowned them before mutilating them?"

"No. I mean, it doesn't say. It just says that their lungs were full of water. So full that water was dripping from their mouths and noses."

"What else?"

"She mentions that some of the hotel staff, guests, and townspeople who lived by the lake saw the Blue Lady walking near the time of the murders, but Theodosia assumed it was superstition. But read it for yourself, maybe I missed something."

"I will." Jackson stood up. "Thanks for the coffee and conversation. And for these." He picked up the journals.

"You look a little shell-shocked," Adam said. "Does that mean we've been helpful?"

Jackson looked from one to the other. "Extremely. But we'll leave it at that for now."

# 91
## *Constance Wraps It Up*

**SATURDAY**

"Good morning, Roger. Look what I have for you."

Roger Siechert opened his eyes to see Constance Welling hovering over him, her bony tattooed body wrapped in Saran Wrap. Fastened to her pelvis was a bright red bow, complete with curled red ribbon dangling from the center. It looked like a grotesque rose that had been disemboweled. Despite his repulsion, Little Roger twitched.

He searched his memory for last night's details. It was futile. Only one thing was certain: He had a hell of a hangover and was in no mood to humor Constance. *But what other choice is there?*

"Do you like it?" Constance turned this way and that, holding her arms out to display her shriveled batwings. Loose skin bulged over the top of the plastic wrap and a little bubble of stomach acid rose to the top of his esophagus.

"It's lovely." The lie came easily.

A hundred cuckoo clocks began calling. It was seven a.m. and he had to be at the clinic by nine.

Constance gave him her backside - twin sacks of flab hanging from her hipbones. She turned around again to show off breasts that jutted as proud and plastic as a Barbie's. *Amazing: Some women will pay thousands of dollars for huge gravity-defying tits and completely ignore every other body part.*

"Where did you find the bow?" He figured she'd been snooping, the stupid bitch.

"Does it matter? The important thing is what's under it." She drew closer.

"Seriously. Where did you get it?"

Constance sighed. "I found it in your closet in a box marked *Xmas* if you must know."

Siechert sat up. *If I must know? Is she serious?* He reminded himself that Constance was his alibi. With effort he plastered a smile on his face. "Well, I'm glad you did. It looks great."

"Does it?" She sat on the edge of the bed and pushed her plastic-wrapped tits into his arm. They were hard. "If you're a good boy, I was thinking I'd let you unwrap me."

Siechert, with no warning, and against his own will, broke into raucous laughter. He could tell by Constance's expression that this wasn't a proper response, so he toned it down. "And what do I have to do to earn that privilege?"

"You have to come with me to the Psychic Faire tonight."

"Tonight? I was, uh-"

"If you want to unwrap me," she said, crossing her arms, "you're going to have to do exactly as I say."

"Will you give me the finger?"

Constance's smile broadened into an unfortunate Cheshire grin. "I'll even let you watch me use my new emery board, you cute little pervert. And if you come with me today, I'll give you *two* fingers tonight."

*Two fingers?* He'd never even thought of that before. He glanced down at her hands, focused on her bony knuckles. *Ribbed ... for his pleasure.* "All right," he said. "I'll come this afternoon after clinic hours."

Constance bounced on the bed and clapped her hands. "Goodie!"

His head throbbed. "Now come here so I can skin you alive."

Constance looked confused and he knew he'd said the wrong thing again.

"I'm feeling aggressive," he explained.

This satisfied her. She climbed on top of him and ground her bow-covered bony groin into his lap. It hurt like hell. "Okay," she announced. "I'm ready to be unwrapped, Dr. Feelgood."

Siechert suppressed an urge to tear into her skin with his teeth. Instead, he began the chore of unwrapping the bitch in his lap.

## 92
## *Jackson and the Journals*

Jackson read all three journals twice and searched in vain for police records before asking Gene Holmes to come to his house for a private chat. The doctor had confirmed that Beverly Hill's lungs were sodden with lakewater, five liters worth. But she'd been alive when her throat was slit, unlike Pat Matthews, who'd been mutilated after death.

Gene sat at the kitchen table sipping a bottle of water. Arrowhead, not sparkling. Jackson grabbed a bottle for himself. "I don't buy the sparkling," he said. "Tastes bitter."

"I agree, but some people are nearly addicted to carbonated water. Roger buys it by the case. First Perrier, now Blue Springs."

"How's Casper doing?" Jackson hadn't stuck around for the autopsy.

"You know Casper. He's hard to read, but I think he misses her a lot. He told me he went in and cleaned her up after she'd been dusted for prints."

Jackson sighed. "I wish he hadn't done that."

"It's okay, there wasn't a clue left on her. Not that I could find."

"She's being sent to the county coroner?"

"Eh, fuck the county. I guarantee I didn't miss anything. I went over every inch of that body."

Jackson believed Gene.

"So what is it you want to talk about that can't be said elsewhere?"

"If anyone heard what I'm about to tell you, Gene, they'd think I lost my mind."

"I'm all ears."

Jackson nodded at the books on the table. "Those are some of Theodosia Bellamy's journals. This one is about the Bodice Ripper." He touched a slender volume with a brown cover, then he tapped a faded blue one. "This concerns Cliffside folklore, specifically the Blue Lady."

"What's the third one?"

"Ghost stories about Cliffhouse and the town."

"What do any of those things have to do with our murders?"

Jackson gave Holmes a basic history of the Bodice Ripper killings.

"Okay, so we have two people slashed open from sternum to pubic bone and that's similar to the Ripper's style, I'll grant you that, but ..."

"There's more. And this is where it starts sounding really funky."

"Let's have it."

"According to Theodosia, whenever the killer struck, there were Blue Lady sightings. Like clockwork. There were sightings throughout the years he struck - 1922 through 1928 - but when the killer was active, they increased dramatically."

Gene Holmes' face betrayed no expression. He studied Jackson a long time. "You're not taking that seriously, are you? Because, if you are, I think you may need a vacation."

"There's more."

"Tell me."

Jackson opened the brown journal to a bookmark, and passed it to Gene. "Read it for yourself. He tapped the page. "Right there."

Gene began reading aloud.

"'Sept. 15, 1928. I had the most frightening conversation with my dear friend, Doctor Frederick Phelps, this morning. He has been tasked with examining all the victims of the Bodice Ripper, a job I cannot imagine undertaking. He told me that the victims have more in common than being torn asunder, something he cannot explain.

"'Their lungs were full of water, though the victims were all on dry land. He says they drowned, but he cannot imagine how. He also said that at least half of them were dead before they were defiled and that he believes we are under attack by a monster that has powers a murderer like Jack the Ripper could only dream of.'"

Gene looked up from the book. "Jesus."

"Yeah. Keep going."

"'Frederick and I were indulging in glasses of sherry, and at this point, I poured more. We needed it, for I had decided to tell him about the reports of the Blue Lady walking when the Bodice Ripper was most active.

"'Frederick tried to laugh it off, and in all the years that followed, he never quite admitted he believed it, but he was one of those, along with Papa, who put an end to the monster on the first night of 1929. And to do that, he had to believe it, even though he could not bring himself to say as much.'"

"What is she talking about?"

"I don't know. Hopefully it's in another journal. I'm going over to Cliffhouse today to do some more reading."

Gene shook his head. "Every part of me thinks this is nuts. There's no backup for this material, is there?"

"No. Nothing, as far as I know. Maybe if Phelps' private journals still exist we might learn something, but that's unlikely. It's too long ago."

"Yeah." Gene reread the entry to himself then looked back to Jackson. "This is insane, you know."

"I know. But to paraphrase Sherlock, when you exhaust every explanation you can, whatever's left, no matter how bizarre, is the answer."

"So you're telling me the Blue Lady is killing people."

"Let's just say something we don't understand is at work here. Polly and I saw something that looked like a glowing blue figure walking by the lake after the End of Summer Party. And there have been numerous sightings on the cliffs at the lodge - one of the reenactors nearly broke his neck chasing after it. And something weird was going on inside Cliffhouse. Still is. Sara told me a couple of kids snuck into the pool area after hours and got chased by some sort of blue female phantom."

"Okay, I'm not clear. Are you saying this is a Bodice Ripper copycat or that this Lady in Blue was involved then and now, or what?" Gene asked.

"Yes. Possibly, yes."

"I'll think about all this." Gene stood up. "I'd better get going. I have a tee-time over in Lake Arrowhead in ninety minutes."

Jackson saw him to the door. "Hey, how's your partner?"

Gene paused. "Roger? He's okay. He's running the clinic today if you want to talk to him."

"No. Just wondered. He did a good job at the market with the kid with the broken arm. Levelheaded. I'm glad. I was a little worried about him at the Lutz autopsy."

"He's got a mouth on him and it's gotten him into trouble now and then, but I wouldn't worry about him. He's fine."

# 93
## *Madame Constanza*

The wind off the lake was cool and brisk this morning, but it was nice inside the tent. Constance Welling, aka Madame Constanza, wore a purple bandanna, gold hoop earrings, her tightest jeans, and a red vest over a purple sun-and-moon patterned blouse. She looked like a real gypsy, she thought, as she admired her reflection on the smooth surface of her crystal ball. She ran her hands over it, her mess of bangle bracelets jangling. "I see a man. He's very handsome."

The girl who sat in the folding chair across from Constance leaned in. "What color is his-"

"Shhh!" Constance opened her eyes. "Eliza is speaking."

"Who?"

"Eliza. My spirit guide. She says the man's hair is light brown. And he has blue eyes."

The girl frowned. "Light brown? I don't know any-"

"Shhh! She's still talking." Constance waited a beat. "Eliza says no, she was wrong. The man is blond."

The girl beamed. "She's talking about Billy!"

Constance didn't shush her this time. She never shushed a satisfied customer. "Yes. Billy. He's the one."

"You mean, the *one,* the one?"

Constance nodded. "Eliza says it's fated."

"Is there anything else?" The girl poked her lip with her tongue, concentrating hard. Her hand slid down and touched her belly.

"Yes," said Constance. "I see ... Eliza says ... there's a child ... or there will be a child ..."

The girl practically bounced in her seat. "*Really?*"

"Soon," said Constance. "Eliza says soon."

"With Billy?"

"Yes." Constance thought the girl was too young to be concerned with having children. Still, a dollar was a dollar, and the girl was paying. But Constance was bored. "I'm not getting anything else. I'm sorry."

The girl frowned again.

"Eliza is worn out. I am too. If you'd like to leave a donation," she pushed a mason jar toward the girl, "we suggest twenty-five dollars."

The girl reached into her pocket, pulled out a wad of bills, and placed a couple in the jar. "Thank you, Madam Contessa," she said.

"Constanza. And be sure to take a look at Constance Welling's books next door."

"Yes, I saw them."

"They're nine ninety-nine apiece, or twenty-five dollars for three."

The girl nodded absently and Constance waved her away. As soon as she was gone, she dug into the jar to see how badly the girl had ripped her off. A twenty and a one. *Cheap slut.*

Constance stood and walked outside. *Shitting wind!* She tightened her scarf to keep her hair in place. Small foamy white caps scudded on the lake. She watched a boat towing a water-skier and laughed aloud when he lost his balance and floundered in the water.

She looked at her watch and sighed. *Dr. Siechert. Dr. Roger Siechert.* Even his name was sexy. *Mrs. Constance Leigh Welling-Siechert.* That had a nice ring to it. Just a few more hours and he'd be here with her.

*If he was here now, I'd give his cock a psychic reading he'd never forget!* By the time he got there, the fair would be too crowded to have any fun. She noticed more people walking in from the parking lot, each one flashing like dollar signs.

Jim Stone's Crystal Cavern booth was right next to the tent he'd set up for her readings. He got a five-dollar commission on every fortune she told, so she needed to be sure that, in turn, he was featuring her books properly. They sat on a table, mixed with other titles. *Shit-diddler.* She moved hers front and center.

"How's business?" Stone asked as he came from the back of the booth.

"Slow."

"It's only eleven. It will pick up."

"I certainly hope so. Have you sold any of my books?"

"It's early," he replied. The Goth girl employees, Belle and Lacey, came giggling up behind Constance. Jim smiled. "There you two are!"

"Sorry, Jim," Belle said. "We didn't mean to take such a long break, but they're selling aura readings over at the Arrowhead Psychic Booth. I'm peach. It means I'm sweet but serious."

"And I'm violet?" Lacey added. "I'm very passionate?"

"And I'm passionate about work," Jim said. "So how about you two get back to it?"

The girls smiled and slipped into the booth.

Fuming, Constance spoke up. "Lacey, how much was your reading?"

"Twenty dollars?" she replied.
"How long did it last?"
"Five minutes, or ten?"
"You girls get a solid fifteen minutes with me and Eliza for only twenty-five dollars. I hope to see each of you soon."
"Don't we get an employee discount?" Belle asked in a cool voice.
"I don't employ you, but maybe your boss will discount you the five dollars he takes, so it'd cost twenty dollars. Eliza's very accurate, undoubtedly the most accurate here. I'm sure you girls are aware of that."

Lacey looked shame-faced, Belle defiant.

"I'll come over on my next break and get a reading," said Lacey.

"Belle?" asked Constance.

"No, thanks," said the little twat, and left it at that.

Rage coursed through Constance's veins. "At least one of you will get an accurate reading today." She began squaring up her books as Jerry Belvedere approached.

"Excuse me," he said. "I'm looking for the fortune teller, Madame Constantine? I'd like a reading."

"Madame Constanza," said Constance. "Follow me."

\*\*\*

Things were shit. Once she got the bellboy in the tent, she tried to seduce him; after all, he'd already seen her naked. But the little shit just got all huffy and left without even paying her. Then she had another customer, some fat bitch from Los Angeles who had B.O. and left her a fucking five-dollar bill.

And now Constance, on a cigarette break between her tent and the Crystal Cavern's booth, leaned close and eavesdropped on a conversation between the girls at Jim's.

"I think she's fake," Belle said.

"You're crazy," Lacey replied. "She's a brilliant psychic? Don't you know that by now?"

"Lacey, I've never seen her do anything psychic. She just talks about it. Haven't you noticed?"

*You little bitch. How dare you!*

"Have you noticed her crow's feet?" Belle continued.

"Yes! Why doesn't she get them taken care of?"

"I know, right? Belle said. "She's got those tits, but she's gotta do something about that skin. And her arms. Ugh. She must be even older than she looks. Like maybe sixty-five?"

"At least!" Lacey hissed. "God, how pathetic is that?"

"God, what kind of asshole smokes at a Psychic Faire? Smell it?"

"Constance does," Lacey said. "Maybe she's taking a break?"

"Fuck. I hope she didn't hear us," Belle spoke so softly that Constance had to strain to hear.

"Eh, she's so old she's probably lost some of her hearing, but you know what? I think the cigarettes are why she has such wrinkled skin?"

Constance could take it no longer. She dropped her smoke and stubbed it out. She was *barely* in her fifties and she used expensive placental creams daily. *How dare they, those little twits!* She turned to go confront them and there was Roger, smiling down at her. Instantly, she plastered on her most brilliant smile. "Roger! You made it!" She hugged him, then moved in for a kiss.

He backed off. "Lips that touch cigarettes will never touch mine. I told you that, Connie, on our first date."

She concealed her fury. "I have a bottle of mouthwash in my bag. Let's go in my tent."

"Let's not, honey-biscuit. Let the wind blow some of the stink off you first."

"You're judgmental this afternoon, Roger." She spoke from behind tight lips. "Did you have a hard time at work?"

"No, just another day."

She felt herself losing control, so she said, "Won't you excuse me a few minutes? I have a client waiting inside the tent. I'll just take care of him, then we can talk." With that, she stepped closer, making sure her stiletto heel came down on his sneaker, just above the toes. She put her weight on it and twisted.

"Christ, Constance, watch where you step!"

She looked up at him without moving. "Sorry." With one more hard push into his foot, she went to her tent. Inside, she peeked out and saw him limp to a bench, muttering under his breath. *Serves you right you skinny-dicked shit-diddler.* But what Belle and Lacey were going to suffer would be far, far worse.

# 94
## *Diagnosis: Psychic Faire*

He had to get away from Constance before the terrible blend of cheap perfume and cigarette smoke gave him a migraine. Not that a migraine could hold a candle to the pain he still felt just above his toes where her spiked heel had ground into him. She'd done it on purpose, the bitch.

Roger Siechert was not himself. He knew this and was sure others knew it as well. He should have been concerned, yet it didn't bother him. He was having far too good a time. He rose and limped to a concessions stand and searched the menu.

"Can I help you, sir?" A pimply-faced teen with buckteeth smiled at him.

"Do you have water?"

"Of course, sir."

"Blue Springs?"

"Sure. That'll be five dollars."

Siechert gave the kid a five - it was well worth it - and returned to his bench. He drank, watching the people, nodding politely at those who noticed him, hoping no one stopped to talk.

The lovely Sara Bellamy and Constance's former assistant, Luke Donovan, walked by, holding hands. That match-up must have burned Cunty Constance to the quick. Water shot from his mouth with the guffaw. *Cunty Constance to the quick! Cunty Constance can suck my dick! Ha!* He doubled over laughing.

Over by a trashcan, Loyd the Roid hung on a lady half his age, panhandling. *Loitering Loyd McRoid, forever unemployed. Ha!*

Loyd was a borderline diabetic and an alcoholic. Siechert gave him five years of reasonably good health before his body retaliated. After the Roid, Siechert saw ponytailed Merlin Skinner heading in the other direction. He was an odd one, a little too quiet, with very sensitive hearing, and his nose in the air. He looked somehow healthier tonight. Perhaps, he'd finally put on a few pounds. *Condescending Merlin Skinner was no thinner after dinner! Ha!*

Then he recognized Jordan Cartwright. Aside from a few allergies, Jordan had no health problems. Great blood pressure, a healthy set of lungs, good heart, and a very strong immune system. He never came down with colds or flu.

Cartwright smiled and headed toward him before he could fashion a poem. If it had been anyone else, Siechert would have been annoyed, but Jordan was all right. Nice, easygoing.

"Hello, Doctor," he said.

"What brings you here, Jordan? Doesn't seem like your scene." He sipped his water. "Have a seat."

"It isn't." The librarian sat. "I'm on my way to Cliffhouse. I thought I'd have a quick look around."

"You tickling the old bones today?"

Jordan gave him an odd look, then said, "Yes. I'm playing today."

Siechert nodded. "It's a hot day."

Jordan appeared surprised. "It's the first day of autumn and it feels like it to me. Would you prefer to sit in the shade?"

"Nonsense. A little heat never hurt anyone. Just ask my cat!" He guffawed, slapped his knee, genuinely amused by his wit.

Jordan Cartwright, however, didn't appear to get the joke. He smiled. "I didn't know you had a cat."

"I don't!" Siechert slapped his knee again and burst into laughter.

"I see," was all Cartwright said.

"What about you, old buddy? Are you seeing any ladies? You're a nice enough looking fellow."

Cartwright first appeared confused by the shift of subject, then he looked at his hands, and Siechert realized why. "Keep looking," he advised. "You'll find a lady who treats those fingers with the respect they deserve. Just don't pick up any fortunetellers. They'll be the death of you and they won't even predict it for you first. They're all bitches."

Cartwright blinked at the doctor. "I'd better be on my way." He stood and smoothed out his slacks.

"Don't want to keep your audience waiting?"

"Um, that's right." He rose then, but paused and turned to Roger. "Are you sure you're feeling okay, Doctor?"

Siechert waved him off. "Indeed. I'm tip-top!"

Cartwright nodded and left.

A moment of self-consciousness invaded Siechert. Clearly, he hadn't said the right things again. *Oh well. No use crying over split infinitives.* The doctor turned his attention to the passersby, recognizing Herman Mudgett - *high blood pressure, probably in part due to his cunt of a mother, poor circulation due to a diet too high in fat, and the slowest reflexes in Cliffside.*

"Herman Mudgett!" blurted Siechert as the fat man neared. "Where's the old ball and chain, you chubby son of a bitch?"

Mudgett looked mortified. "What do you mean? I'm not married."

"Your mother, Herman, your mother! I think we all know the two of you have *something* going on!" He slapped his knee and guffawed.

Herman Mudgett gave him a shocked look and continued on.

Roger knew he'd said something wrong again, but what the hell? Who didn't? He looked around at all the crazy people wearing jackets and announced, "It's as hot as a hooker's twat today!"

Several heads turned and a few people even avoided his bench as they passed, but they were all tourists. *Fuck 'em.*

Siechert finished his water and shook his head. It was getting worse. He didn't know what it was, but it was getting worse. *It's fun, though!*

# 95
## *Hammerhead at the Faire*

People were such silly, emotional creatures, given to embracing lies and superstitions. Whatever they wanted to believe, they clutched to their bosoms and defended to the death.

He watched the fortuneteller in her camel toe tight jeans, her purple shirt and pounds of junk jewelry, as she stood outside her tent talking to the doctor who was his competition for the Lady's attentions. The trollop touched him as she spoke, first on the arm, then the hand, then his shoulder. Finally, her hand lingered brazenly on his thigh.

The doctor was known to be susceptible to female flesh, but as he watched and wondered why the man would take up with this human trash, he noted the physician's defensive body language. He didn't want her touching him. *So why does he put up with it?*

The doctor saw him and waved. He waved back then walked on, passing booths and people until he had the lake path almost entirely to himself. It was a beautiful day, with a hint of autumn crispness in the air.

*I am here.*

He slowed, hearing the Lady's voice, feeling her on the cool breeze that kissed his ear. "I've missed you," he whispered.

*You are my favorite.*

"And do you belong to me?"

Female laughter cascaded in his ears. *I belong to no man, but you are my favorite. We shall play together tonight.*

# 96
## *The Lady Vanishes*

Jackson set a journal down and stood up to stretch. He and Teddy were in the Bellamy cabin and had been passing the journals back and forth for the last several hours. It had not been a waste of time, but it was odd and baffling. He'd read the journals at home, but he thought he might learn more discussing them with the Bellamys.

"What do you think?" Teddy asked.

"We're onto something," he said. "No doubt about that, but what, I can't begin to guess." Jackson sighed. "Okay, let's try to make sense of this. What have we learned from Theodosia's journals?"

"We know," Teddy said, "that the natives who first lived here moved away, claiming the land was cursed. Theodosia mentions 'water babies' - those are water spirits whose cries herald death in the old lore of the local tribes."

"That still leaves a lot of room," Jackson said.

"It does. The death cry puts me in mind of the Irish banshee, which takes the form of a female, ugly or beautiful, so I'm thinking that the water baby may be the historical basis for the Blue Lady in this case. We know the early Spanish settlement here moved on after a few seasons because of a woman in blue who came from the lake and took lives. They, like Rosa, called her Santa Muerte."

"The death saint," Jackson said.

"Yes. And while the winters would have been harsh, there was enough wood and game to get through them with relative ease, plus all the fresh water they needed. It's a little unusual that this natural lake was never a popular place to set up a civilization." He paused. "But all that suggests is that, generally, when there's a curse attached by the locals, there's something to it."

"Okay," Jackson said. "Sightings. Theodosia mentions the Spanish settlement and the sightings in the 1880s, but that's it."

Teddy rubbed his eyes. "The area was uninhabited until the silver rush in the late 1860s and the lodge was built in the 1880s. There's probably no information for the years in between."

"So, evidently the Blue Lady vanishes until the 1920s," Jackson said.

"There are sightings throughout the decade, ending with the reference to 'the monster' being stopped on the first of January, 1929," Teddy affirmed.

"Is she referring to the Blue Lady, the Bodice Ripper, or both? Both ceased activities at the same time."

"Both, when you take it in context, I think," Teddy said.

Jackson nodded. "That's what I thought, but now I hate to think it, because it means I'm accepting that some sort of water monster was - is - murdering people. That makes no sense."

"There's a connection," Teddy said, opening one of the journals. "There's absolutely a connection. Have you looked at this one yet?"

"No."

"Take a look." He opened to a bookmark and slid the volume to Jackson. "The entry dated September 29, 1928."

Jackson began reading aloud. "'The Bodice Ripper has struck twice more since the horrible Labor Day weekend massacre. To think that he killed three women in as many days, right here in Cliffhouse, saddens and horrifies me. I am angry, too. How dare this horrible creature first remove my right to stroll the grounds of my own home after dark and then cause me to look over my shoulder and avoid dark doorways inside my home? I hope he will be caught soon. Papa thinks he will.

"'The latest victim was Sallie Vance, the Blue Naiad Girl herself. She was here, posing for photos and paintings for labels for our bottled water venture. We had many guests who left after the poor girl's body was found floating in the outdoor hot spring on the north side of the lodge. I found her and wish I hadn't. I went out for a walk and there she was, face down, her body floating near the bottom of the pool, in bloody water. I looked away, but not before I saw that some of her innards had come out of her body. I dread my dreams tonight.

"'Last night, we had numerous reports of the Blue Lady. She was seen walking the cliffs, lingering near the pool where Miss Vance died, and standing by the springhouse. Two guests reported seeing her on the fourth floor. (I take these reports with caution, since those guests had come from the speakeasy and were very intoxicated.) It seems as if whenever the Blue Lady is seen, a murder is in the offing. Just as in 1886.'"

That was the end of the entry. "What about 1886?" Jackson asked.

"Go two pages forward and read the October first entry."

"Okay." Jackson turned the page. "'I knew from Grandfather that there was a killer here only a year after his father first opened Cliffhouse. The town was smaller, young, but doing well, and Cliffhouse quickly became its jewel. They had ladies of the evening, gambling, a fine bar and dancehall, a piano player from San Francisco. It was the finest hotel this side of the Rockies.

"The restaurant was famous for its venison steaks, broiled duck, and trout from the lake. They grew their own vegetables for the restaurant and brought in vast quantities of citrus from Santo Verde and apples from Moonfall. Both towns were well established, even then. People came from all over to use the hot springs and spa, and they had just opened up the natural spring and begun bottling sparkling water. Grandfather and Great-grandfather built the springhouse we have now.

"'That is, I think, our curse, that well. I am trying to talk Papa into closing it because *she* lives there, I'm sure of it.'"

Jackson paused, looking at Teddy as a shiver coursed through him.

"Strange stuff." Teddy said, reading Jackson's mind.

"For sure." Jackson continued reading. "'But I am ahead of myself. Grandfather told me that in early 1886, when the well was opened, the Blue Lady sightings began. So did the Gaslight Murders. They were not like the Ripper murders now. These girls - and a few men - were stabbed in the eye with a hunting knife. It happened at night. A total of eight people were killed in that fashion, most of them near the lake, and one in our grand lobby. We found him in the brook that passes through the room. Great-grandfather saw the Blue Lady for himself that night. She came gliding from the springhouse and, like a dim blue flame, meandered near Cliffhouse before moving down to the dock. He ran after her and swore to Grandfather that she floated above the lake and then disappeared into it, and that it gave him a fear like no other.

"'A few nights later, Grandfather and some other men from town spent the night in the springhouse. They came out in the morning, all terrified. They had put a thick iron cover over the well, trapping the Blue Lady inside. My grandfather told me this with an odd laugh, not six years ago, when I was still a child. He had convinced himself it was all coincidence, but now I think he was wrong. I only wish he were still alive so that I might ask more questions and perhaps convince Papa that if he covers the well, the killings will stop.'"

"Jesus," Jackson said. "That's really out there."

"Go to October 7th."

He did.

"'We lost two more at the Harvest Festival yesterday. The killer is certainly human, though Doctor Phelps says he has dissected all of the victims and water had filled their lungs even though all had been found on land. There was evidence to suggest they'd been in water. I said to him that perhaps the one who stabs the victims is working with the Blue Lady, that this is some sort of unholy duality. I am not religious, but I even said that perhaps a priest should be told. Papa laughed. I was embarrassed and said no more.'"

"Is there more in this journal?" Jackson flipped a few pages, but they were blank.

"Not in this one."

"This is crazy, Teddy. You know that, right?"

Teddy nodded.

# 97
## *Eliminating the Impossible*

A cool evening breeze, herald of autumn, twirled a few golden oak leaves through the Psychic Faire. Plenty of people wandered among the booths where palmists, mediums and various other scryers of pocketbooks and change purses plied their craft.

Jackson liked the feel of Polly's hand resting on his arm as they strolled. He had yet to tell her anything about what he'd learned from the journals today; he was still trying to make sense of it. Could it be that whoever knew how to kill bloodlessly had added copycatting the Bodice Ripper murders of the 1920s to his repertoire? If so, why? The contrast between the "Blue Lady" victims and the bloody mess this new Ripper left was stunning. Back in 1928, would they have even noticed or considered murder if they had found an untouched body leaking water from the mouth and nose? Likely they assumed the person was a drowning victim brought onto dry land. Even today, it was unlikely the deaths of Bailey and Lutz could be tagged as more than death by misadventure. He hoped not; in his gut he knew they'd been murdered.

*By the Blue Lady?* That's what it said in the journals, and he was horrified to find he was inclined to believe it. *Eliminate the impossible and what remains must be the truth. Or could Sherlock Holmes be wrong?*

"Why don't we get away from all the people for a while?" Polly said. "Want to walk along the lake?"

"Good idea. I want to tell you a story once we're alone."

# 98
## *Smell like a Man*

Constance was furious. The fourth and last séance of the night would begin soon and four chairs had yet to be filled at her table. *Cheap bastards can't even spring $25 for a séance?* She stood next to a lakeside tree and lit another cigarette. The smell of the lake irritated her. She took a long pull on her fresh butt.

"There you are, Madame Clitora!"

She jumped. "Jesus Christ! You scared the shit out of me!"

Roger Siechert looked amused. "Sorry."

"It's Madam Constanza. Why can no one remember that?"

"I'm just teasing you, Rabbit-Cakes."

"How did you find me?"

"I followed the smoke." He gave her a disapproving look.

She took a defiant drag. "Well, I still have four seats to fill. I'd hoped to see you at my earlier séances, but apparently, you had more important things to do."

He shrugged. "An emergency."

"Emergency?" She exhaled a lungful of smoke in his general direction.

Siechert stepped out of the smoke's path. "Broken leg."

Constance gave a small, bitter laugh. "Afraid of getting a little smoke on you, Doctor? Afraid you'll smell too much like a man?"

His eyes narrowed and Constance knew she'd struck a nerve. *Good.*

"It isn't healthy."

"Smelling like a man? I'm sure it's very dangerous."

Roger looked defensive as Constance kept smoking, daring him with her eyes to say more. Finally, his body relaxed. She knew she was in charge.

The lake stink became so strong she could barely smell the tobacco.

"Let's not fight, darling." His eyes looked oddly blank as he reached for her. She stepped back. *He can't touch me any time he wants. I'll teach him a lesson.*

"Constance, I want to kiss you," he said, his tone hollow. "Come to Daddy."

She avoided the touch. "Not now. First, you have to earn it. Take a seat at the séance table and then you can touch me all you want." She tossed her half-smoked cigarette toward the lake. "Come along,

Roger," she ordered, staying just out of reach. "This lake-stench is giving me a headache!" She glared at him. "Roger?"

Roger Siechert stared back, his gaze vacant and dark.

"Roger? Are you okay?"

"Huh? Oh, yes. What do you mean?"

"You're scaring me. Did you even hear a word I said?"

He laughed. Loud, raucous, abrasive, out of proportion. Suddenly, his laughter died and his eyes came to life. "What?"

"I have to go on in a few minutes. I need you to sit in. Are you coming?"

His smile was plastic, fixed, and devoid of emotion. *A doll's smile.* "Of course, Honey-Suckle," he said. "I wouldn't miss it for all the Christ in Kentucky."

*Christ in Kentucky?* Constance blinked at him. "Don't worry, you don't have to pay. Now go on up and take a seat."

Roger's strangeness faded away, as did the shit-sucking stench of the lake. "I'll do you proud." With that, he headed for the séance.

She checked her watch then lit another cigarette. It was always good to keep the audience waiting a few minutes.

*Constance ...*

The voice sounded like a breeze moving through dry weeds or a moth's wing grazing a window, but Constance recognized the soft, female whisper instantly. She dropped the cigarette and hurried back to the séance table, sensing icy fingers at her back.

She saw the table held a full roster now and that helped her quell her fear. She took her seat, sorry to see that Roger wasn't the only plant. Jim Stone, Lacey Mylett, and Belle Tabrum were seated, too. *Shit, less money for me.*

She looked beyond at the sitters at the table, into the audience, just in time to see *her* Luke Donovan kiss that shitting skank, Sara Bellamy. The skank returned the kiss. If they weren't already fucking, they would be soon. *Shit-fuckers, you'll pay for this!*

## 99
### *Loyd Takes a Leak*

Loyd McRoid, drunk as the proverbial polecat, weaved one way then the other as he looked for the public restroom. His vision swam but other than the need to pee, he felt great. "Hullo, have a dollar?" he said to everyone he passed. Mostly, he was met with looks of pity or disgust. "Fuckin' tourists," he'd mutter at the strangers who ignored him.

He was relieved when he spotted the little red brick building near the volleyball court. Then he saw the line outside the door. He couldn't wait that long. "Well, Christ," he muttered, seeing no immediate solutions to his problem.

*The lake.* The idea made his bladder jump for joy. *Yes. I'll piss in the lake.*

It was so dark he didn't even have to walk far for privacy. The shore was encased in near darkness and there were no people in the general vicinity. He assumed a wide stance to steady himself against the earth's unrelenting, stomach-turning motion, then unleashed the dog of war. He loved the smell of the lake.

He tried whistling to muffle the sound of the powerful stream hitting the water, but his lips were uncooperative. Several seconds passed and he chuckled to himself. "Christ A'mighty," he said. "I could put out a house fire!"

*Loyd ...*

His stream slowed. He wasn't sure which direction the voice had come from, but he'd heard it clear as day. "Yeah?"

Silence.

Loyd returned to his whiz and whistling as he emptied the rest of his bladder. Finally he shook off, tucked the dog in his pants, and zipped up.

*Loyd. Come to me ...*

This time, he knew exactly where the voice came from - the lake. He followed the sound and his jaw dropped.

A woman stood several yards out, up to her titties in the water. Despite the darkness, he could see her clearly. Not just a woman, no, but he knew she was the most beautiful woman he'd ever seen. "Hullo?" he called. "You okay, lady?"

The woman smiled and the bluish tint to her skin deepened. The hazy glow around her seemed to swell, and without opening her mouth, she spoke. *Come to me, Loyd. Come to me ...*

"But, I, uh ... It's cold."

*Come ...*

Loyd, unafraid, stepped into the water. It was icy but it didn't bother him. He needed to get to the lady.

*Come to me.* She held out her arms.

He stepped into her cold embrace.

# 100
## *Madame Conjob*

Constance glanced over at Madame Olga's table and saw a crowd several people deep watching her séance, even though it was after ten o'clock. Her own audience had dwindled to a single row of twenty-two. She glared at Skanky Sara and Luke Donovan - *my Luke!* - but they weren't paying any attention to anyone but one another. Her fathers were next to them, chatting up the police chief and his waitress. *Are there no polite people left in this world?*

Well, they were about to be very sorry they weren't paying attention because, with the girls, Jim Stone, and Roger sitting there, she could make up any shit she wanted and they'd swear to it. *It's always good to have a few plants at a medicine show!*

"I see an R and an S," she announced in Eliza's fluttery chipmunk voice. "Is there anyone here with the initials R S?"

Roger shit-diddling Siechert didn't even look up.

*What's wrong with him?* "An R and an S. Someone at the table has those initials," she squawked as loudly as she could. "An R and an S."

"Miss?" said a blue-haired old lady across the table. "Miss Calliope?"

"Madam Constanza. What?"

"Before I married Froederick March, my maiden initials were R S. Rose Spitake."

*When were you ever a maiden, you old bat?* "Yes, yes. Thank you. You are the RS I was referring to." She glanced at Roger, who appeared to be counting his fingers. *Fuck you, Roger. Fuck you and your pencil dick. You can shove your own finger up your shitty ass tonight!*

She put her Eliza-gaze on the old lady. "I see a man. He is calling you. 'Rose, Rose, my love, I can't wait for you to join me.'"

The old lady burst out laughing. "I doubt that."

"Ah, I see your marriage was an unhappy one. Froederick wants to see you in the beyond so that you can forgive him and spend eternity with him. He still loves you."

Rose looked surprised, then tittered up and down the scale. "Oh, Miss, Froederick doesn't want me to join him."

"What?"

"He's in Cincinnati at a Shriner's Convention. Once a year, he and his friends go and they like to watch the strippers." She laughed again. "He definitely doesn't want me with him!"

Constance was glad she'd put on theatrical makeup because it hid her flushing cheeks. "There's someone else on the other side, Rose. Someone else who is waiting for you and she - it's a she, I believe - loves you very much. Perhaps an aunt, or a great aunt ..."

"Good try, kiddo," the old lady said. "One of my ancestors was a Mormon and had a whole barnful of wives. I'll bet it's one of them." She beamed at Constance.

*She feels sorry for me! Nobody feels sorry for Constance Leigh Welling!* Two of her audience members walked away, heading toward Madame Olga's dog and pony show. *You'll be sorry, ass-faces. This show hasn't even begun yet!* She turned her Eliza-gaze on Lacey Mylett.

"You're going to meet a tall, fair stranger very soon, young lady."

Lacey looked surprised. "I am?"

"You are. You have a tattoo on your left buttock."

"I told you ab-"

Constance glared at her. *Stupid girl!* Instantly she turned to Jim Stone, who likely had double Lacey's IQ. *Which makes him average.* "You sir, I see a J."

"My first name begins with a J, yes."

*Thank Christ somebody has enough brains to play along.* Constance considered her next move. Giddy with relief, she cleared her throat and braced herself for the reaction she was about to cause. "I see great wealth and fortune in your future. But also sorrow. One of your children is going to be kidnapped before the year is out."

Jim's eyes narrowed. There was a flutter of voices in the audience. *This is working*!

"This child will suffer horribly at the hands of a criminal ... a criminal who stands among us this very night!" she said in the chipmunk voice.

"I don't think-" Jim Stone began.

"She will die unless you accept our help! Constance and Eliza will help you."

The audience started buzzing and a few more people arrived.

"It's her only chance. She will be killed by the very murderer who has struck down others in your community." She whipped her head around to Roger. "You," she said in Eliza's voice. "You will die soon, too."

"Ms. Welling!"

The female voice came from the audience, forceful and firm. She saw movement and then that little shit-bitch Sara Bellamy pushed through, right up to the table to stand directly behind old lady Rose.

"You are a monster. How dare you say things like that to Mr. Stone - to *anyone*? How *dare* you! You're nothing but a cold reader, and a poor one at that."

Sara was just a wisp of a girl, so Constance stood up to intimidate her. "Don't you talk to me like that. I'll tell your fathers."

"We approve," Teddy called as he, Adam, and Luke came to stand with Sara.

"And you are no longer welcome at Cliffhouse, Ms. Welling," Adam announced. "We would appreciate you leaving by noon tomorrow."

Applause rang out among the crowd. Even Old Lady Rose clapped. *The nerve! The raw fucking nerve!*

"SHIT-DIDDLERS!" Constance thrust a finger at the Bellamys as the wind pulled her scarf. It began unraveling. "Your hotel is the biggest piece of shit on the mountain! His daughter-" she pointed dramatically at Jim Stone "-his daughter is going to die in Cliffhouse and nobody but Constance Welling could have saved her! Now that you've thrown me out, she is doomed to die a horrible, blood-soaked death, ripped from top to bottom by the reincarnation of the *Bodice Ripper!* Her blood is on your hands, you shit-sucking Bellamys! All of you!" she shrieked. "You, too," she howled at Luke. "You pretty boy Benedict Arnold!"

She rounded on Sara. "You steaming pile of bitch!"

Sara moved so fast the men couldn't grab her. She was around the table in an instant, eye to eye with Constance. "Who do you think you are, to say such things? How can you even call yourself a human being?"

There were at least forty, maybe sixty people watching now. *At least Madame Olga's losing her audience!*

Jim Stone arrived behind Sara. "It's all right, folks," he said to the crowd. "I don't have any kids. She's making all this up."

The growing crowd became noisier. Constance smiled despite Stone's betrayal. *You can't buy this kind of publicity! It doesn't hurt what they say, as long as they spell my name right*!

"Madam Conjob is a fake!" declared Old Lady Rose.

"I don't care if his children are imaginary," Sara told the crowd. "Constance Welling, you are a psychopath, not a psychic!"

The crowd, perhaps a hundred strong, cheered. Hot fury shot into Constance's veins. She'd never literally seen red until now. "Take that back, you skanky man-stealing she-bitch."

Sara laughed and rolled her eyes. *The ultimate humiliation.* The crowd roared.

Constance glanced at Roger. He was still fucking around with his stupid fingers and whistling that stupid tune he loved so much.

"Ms. Welling." Jim Stone stood beside Sara now. "Please pack up. We are done here. And done with your readings and workshops at the Crystal Cavern." He turned to the audience. "You have my assurance this woman will never set foot inside the Crystal Cavern again."

Constance jumped on Jim Stone, knocked him to the ground and latched onto his neck. Instantly, She-Bitch Sara was on her back, pulling her away. She let go of his neck and rolled, taking Sara with her.

"I know self-defense, you stupid twat. I'll kill you, too!" Her hands closed on Sara's neck.

Sara socked her in the boob, but her boobs were hard and strong. "Stupid slut! Do your best," she hissed. "Do your fucking best before you die!"

"Girl fight!" someone yelled. "Girl fight!"

Sara was gasping but was still trying to hurt her. She tried a titty-twister, but it didn't work. Her hands moved lower, got under her blouse. Constance felt nails raking her belly, but that wouldn't stop her. Nothing would stop her.

Sara's hands found her fly, then ripped into the jeans. Lower, and lower still, then suddenly, Sara Bellamy had a grip on Constance's clit jewelry.

"You wouldn't dare," gasped Constance.

Sara dared.

Constance let go of her throat, shrieking in agony. Sara rolled away, got to her feet, and turned to run to her daddies. "No fucking way!" Constance screamed and gave chase, her gold stilettos flying. "No fucking way, you coward! Get back here!"

Sara escaped into Luke's arms and her fathers stood sentinel on either side of them. Constance saw she couldn't get at her, but she would still have her pound of flesh. Her vision was flashing red and she couldn't stop shaking.

"Jim Stone!" she cried, turning. "I'm going to kill you, you shit-packing horehound piece of shit!"

Jackson Ballou caught her arm as she started to run. "Nobody's killing anybody, tonight, Ms. Welling."

"Put that Bellamy bitch under arrest. She attacked me!"

Jackson just smiled. "I don't think so."

Constance fluttered her lashes at the chief, then brought her knee up quick and nut-clobbered him. With an *oof,* he let go, grabbed his crotch, and dropped to his knees.

His waitress girlfriend hauled off and punched Constance square in the face.

Pain flashed silver-white and she threw her hands over nose. "You low-class, cheap-shot, shit-whore waitress!"

"You sound like you have a cold, honey," said Polly with a sweet smile. "Maybe I can get you some chicken soup."

Constance screamed and lunged at her.

Polly took off running, Constance close behind, one hand grasping for the waitress's shirt, the other over her bloody nose.

Constance chased her onto the short pier. *The bitch is mine!*

At the end, Polly came to an abrupt stop and just stood there, staring at her, breathing hard. Constance rushed her, intending to push her into the lake, but Polly sidestepped.

The icy water shocked Constance as she plunged in headfirst. The world went silent. Nearby a milky-blue ball glowed. She flailed her arms and legs, trying to get back to the surface. The blue glow brightened, drew closer, and began to stretch out.

Two black holes - eyes - appeared. Blue tendrils floated around the face, moving with the waves - hair. A mouth spread like a slow-moving bloodstain across the terrible face, and Constance kicked herself upward with the strength of sheer terror.

A foot beneath the water's surface, she saw a hand, grabbed it and was pulled quickly upward. She broke the surface, gasping for breath, too horrified to care that it was Polly's.

"Oh, sweet shit! Oh, sweet shit!" Constance floundered in the water, kicking, screaming, and clawing her way up Polly's arm. She flopped onto the wooden surface, where half a dozen people stared.

"I saw a woman! There's a woman in the water!"

Looks of doubt came from all directions.

"I'm not lying! You need to investigate!" No one seemed interested. "Chief Ballou! Get Chief Ballou!"

The cop stood next to Polly, and Constance realized he'd been there all along. "That's enough, Ms. Welling. Time to go home. Everyone clear out. Show's over."

People mumbled and began moving, trying not to miss anything.

"Somebody get Dr. Siechert over here."

A couple of minutes passed before the doctor pushed through the crowd at the edge of the pier.

"Here I am." Siechert stared down at Constance, that strange smile on his face. "I'll take over from here." He offered her his hand.

Constance took it. On her feet, she looked back into the water. It was black as the night sky. There was nothing to see.

"Oh, dear," said Roger. "Are you on your monthly?"

"What?" Constance looked down at herself. Fresh blood ran down her leg.

"I would have imagined you were too old to still be visited by the curse of blood. And the curse was the curse of blood!" he quoted, then laughed heartily.

Anger blotted out fear. "What the hell is wrong with you! I'm not on my period. That little bitch tore my barbell out, and she's going to pay for every second of misery she's cost me! Do you hear me, Sara Bellamy, you skank?" She spun around, shrieking in all four directions, but didn't see her. "You'll pay! You'll pay!"

Siechert put his arm around her. "Now, now." He guided her away from the crowd. "Let's get you taken care of. I've never stitched a clitoris before." He laughed. "There's a first time for everything."

Constance pouted. "I'll never stop shaking!"

Roger chuckled. "With all that blood, it's a good thing there aren't any sharks in the lake."

# 101
## *Lacey Mylett*

Lacey and Belle watched the excitement from the séance area because Jim Stone had insisted they help him start packing up. "I really need to pee?" said Lacey.

"Then go." Belle looked tired and irritable, like her mind was somewhere else as she folded up the tablecloth.

"But it's such a long walk, and the line is probably forever?" Lacey collapsed one of the folding chairs.

"So go pee in the bushes."

Lacey thought about it and decided it would be easier than walking all the way to the restroom. "Come with?"

"You'll be fine," Belle said. "I'll be right here."

"Okay."

The forest was only a few yards away but as she moved toward the trees, she wished she had a flashlight. She stepped behind some bushes and dropped her pants then released her bladder. The sound of urine pudding in the dirt beneath her was powerful and somehow soothing.

*Snap.*

The crack of the twig - or whatever it was - sounded close. The crickets went silent.

"Belle? Is that you?"

Nothing.

Lacey finished peeing and was about to pull up her pants when she was struck by the intense smell of lakewater. A gloved hand clapped over her mouth from behind.

She couldn't scream. She tried twisting away but another hand landed on her shoulder, holding her in place. She was aware of heavy breathing - hers and her assailant's - and then suddenly, she could barely breathe at all.

She was gagging. Water shot from her nose and mouth, streaming from between the hands that covered her face. *No air. There's no air.* Panic.

The hands released her and she fell to her side. She gasped for oxygen but there was none; there was no room for it in her body. Her vision faded and just before it went dark, she saw the hovering silver disc in front of her. It was a mirror, and in it, she could see her own eye. It was wild and distended, its pupil massive, black, and wide, as if unable to contain the terror within it.

# 102
## *Surprising Dr. Siechert*

**SUNDAY**

Sudden hammering on his front door startled Roger Siechert. He jumped and dropped the Chocolate Wanderer. The frozen finger hit the floor and slid beneath the dining table. "Christ!" He bent and reached for it, but it spun away. The rapping at the door became furious, and he heard a woman's voice on the other side.

"Roger! I know you're in there!"

It was Constance Welling. *How did she get through the gate?*

Finally, he got his hands on the finger and hid it under a layer of ice cubes in the freezer. The banging continued.

"Coming!" He opened the door.

Constance Welling stood, looking like a pissed raccoon with her two black eyes. Despite the fact that her nose hadn't been broken, the Band-Aid she'd insisted he put over it last night was still in place.

"How did you get through the gate?"

Constance sniffed. "Larry let me in. He knows me."

Siechert's jaw flexed. *Note to self: no Christmas bonus for Larry!*

Constance brushed past him in a pink cotton T-shirt and an uncharacteristically loose pair of black sweats. "It's about time you answered," she said, her voice even more nasal due to her swollen nose. "I was beginning to think you were asleep or something." Slung over her shoulder was a big gym bag, stuffed full. She dragged a large suitcase behind her in one hand, and clutched a smaller travel bag in the other.

In the living room, she sat carefully on the couch, and hissed. "My clit hurts and I am absolutely exhausted. And look." She held out her hand. It trembled enough to have horrified Katherine Hepburn. "I haven't stopped shaking since last night!" As if to emphasize her words, she hugged herself, and affected a full-body shiver.

Siechert looked at her bags and suitcase. "Why the luggage?"

Constance appeared incredulous, a scandalized raccoon. "You didn't hear? Those shitters kicked me out of Cliffhouse! I haven't got anywhere to go and they don't even care!" She sank back into the couch and jutted her chin out. "I'm having the rest of my suitcases delivered later."

Before he could think, the words were out. "You're not staying here!"

Constance was on her feet, her face an immediate mask of raccoony outrage. "You son of a bitch!" She stomped toward him. "Where the hell do you expect me to go?"

"The Doc Holiday Inn. The Sleeping Zs. The Counting Sheep Hotel. Hell, the Peppermint Stix Motel. Take your pick!"

He expected her to sock him. It didn't happen. What happened instead was something Roger Siechert would never have predicted.

Constance dropped to the floor, hitting the carpet, rolling this way and that. "Oh, God! I'm having an anxiety attack!"

In all his years in the medical profession, Dr. Siechert had never seen an anxiety attack like this one. There was no doubt the whole thing was an act; still the sight of a grown woman collapsing into a real-life hissy fit was so stunning, so preposterous, that he stood frozen in place by sheer astonishment.

"Call 911! I'm having an anxiety attack!"

*Jesus Christ on his throne in heaven. Is she for real?* He wanted to yank her off the floor by her hair and kick her out of his house, but he remembered Tessa Cornhull. It wouldn't be long until the police realized she was missing and when they started sniffing around him, Constance was his alibi. His *only* alibi. *Well, fuck me with a grapefruit spoon!* He bent down and let his medical training take the fore. "Are you okay? Can you hear me?"

"Oh, God, I can't breathe!" she yelled as she continued breathing. "Call 911!"

"We don't need to call 911. I'm here, sunshine. I'm here. Shh-shh-shh." He moved in close, patted her shoulder and felt proud because he resisted the urge to give her a hard smack right upside the head. "You can stay here. It's all right."

The 'anxiety attack' came to a sudden end as Constance crawled into his arms, her body quaking with manufactured tremors. "My clit hurts!"

Siechert patted her ratty, over-sprayed hair. "There, there," he said. "Let's get you settled in and we'll take a look at your stitches. I'm sure you're healing just fine." He supposed the bright side to all this was that her snatch would be out of commission for a while.

"No I'm not!" she sobbed. "I'll need labiaplasty and a nose job! I don't want to live anymore! I'm just going to kill myself!"

*Not here, you aren't. I'm not cleaning up your fucking mess.* The doctor suppressed a giggle. "There, there," he said. "No one wants you to die."

"I'll bet Sara Bellamy and that stupid waitress do!"

*And pretty much everyone else who's ever met you, I'm sure.* "No," he said. "No one wants that." Siechert patted her head. "Let's get you unpacked, okay?"

She looked up at him, her eyes wet and swollen from last night's debacle. Polly Owen had done a number on the bitch's face that was equal to what Sara Bellamy had done to her snatch. Both were improvements, as far as Siechert was concerned. He'd had a little fun stitching her up. She would find it difficult to uncover her clitoris next time she wanted to masturbate. He swallowed a chuckle.

"Are you sure you want me to stay with you?" Constance asked in a little girl voice.

He smiled down at her. *Like you've left me with any other choice, you godforsaken cunt. Cunty-cunt-cunt-cunt!* "Of course, I'm sure."

Constance stood, pretending to test her equilibrium.

"Are you okay?" asked Siechert through the fakest smile he could muster.

"I suppose I will be," she said, her arrogance returning. "I ought to sue that Bellamy bitch. And that cop-diddling waitress."

"Would you like some water?"

She sat on the couch. "Yes, please." She answered as if he were a waiter taking her order. "But none of that bottled shit you like so much." She raised her chin. "I no longer wish to support the local businesses." She gave him a meaningful look. "I expect your *full* support on that."

"Tap water it is for both of us," he said. *I'll pour my Blue Springs into a cup and you'll never know the difference you manipulative dried-up cunt.* He smiled and went to fetch the water. "Do you want ice?" he called from the kitchen.

"Yes," she called back.

Siechert reached into the ice bin, found the Chocolate Wanderer and used it to flick some ice into Constance's glass. Then, just for good measure, he stabbed the now rotting frozen finger into the ice and gave the cubes a thorough stirring. He chuckled to himself and began to whistle *The Happy Wanderer*. That always made him feel better.

# 103
## *Afternoon Autopsies*

"At least Loyd McRoid's is a simple drowning," Gene Holmes said. "The lungs are full but that can happen in the water, especially if he passed out as he fell in. He may have even had a heart attack. There were no witnesses?"

"None yet," Jackson said. "Picnickers found him around noon. How long has he been dead?"

"I'd say he went in last night, during the Psychic Faire. Fairly late." Gene nodded toward the table where Lacey Mylett slept under a white sheet. "That one is a mystery. Lungs overflowing with lakewater, but no marks, no defensive wounds, and I'll bet the tests come back without any answers. As usual. Jackson, I've researched and can't find anything like it. Similar, yes, but not similar enough." He paused. "At least when they're ripped open we can call it homicide. But for Miss Mylett, Norma Bailey, and Laurel Lutz, death by misadventure is the best we can do unless we get a break."

"I think we may be dealing with something inexplicable."

"The Blue Lady again."

Jackson tried not to cringe. "I've read more. Evidently, back in 1928, Dr. Phelps and the police chief decided it was a mystery best buried since they found no rational explanations." Jackson sighed. "I know how they felt."

"Me, too." Holmes removed his gloves and apron and began washing up.

"There's one more thing. In 1887, when Cliffhouse was new, there was an active serial murderer called the Gaslight Killer. He was around for about a year. There was nothing about water in the lungs, but Theodosia Bellamy did say that Blue Lady sightings were constant during that time, just like in the twenties."

# 104
## *Cliffside by Night*

Most residents of Cliffside slept, cradled in quiet broken only by breezes sighing among trees and caressing eaves, the calls of owls, and the scuttling of night predators hunting for prey. The roads were empty, businesses locked up tight, and few lights burned at Cliffhouse.

Taffilynn Matthews sat up late in her old green easy chair, earning money to take care of her children by telling a stranger on the other end of the line how big and powerful his penis was and how much she wanted to blow him. As she spoke, the baby in her belly kicked and, content, she patted her stomach. She only missed her deceased husband a little, and only when she had to put the kids to bed or get them settled for meals. Pat had been too fond of tranquilizers and pain pills, and he set a bad example for the children. He had never known the truth about her business, and her only regret was that he had defaced other peoples' property to earn more money; but her regret was small because if he'd known what she earned, he would have stolen it to buy more pain pills. Next week, she thought as she hung up and got ready to answer the next call, she would hire a good live-in nanny to help her. She could afford that now, and more.

On the far northwest side of town, Casper Hill sobbed into his pillow, mourning Beverly and wishing he had her back. She had her faults, but she had loved him. No one else had ever loved him.

In the Theodosia Suite at Cliffhouse, Luke Donovan held Sara in his arms. In the darkness, he pressed his lips to the top of his lover's head, inhaled her scent, and squeezed her closer. He was lucky and he knew it. "I'll never let go of you," he whispered. A few seconds passed and then Sara whispered back to him. "I love you, too."

Across town, in a big brass bed, similar words passed between Jackson Ballou and Polly Owen.

Jerry Belvedere slept in his room at his mother's home a mile from Cliffhouse. On his small desk, a mug still held a smidge of the hot chocolate only Mom could make. His bellman's uniform hung, clean and pressed, in the armoire, and his underclothes lay folded on top of his dresser. Jerry dreamed of Sara Bellamy and smiled in his sleep.

Francis Trudy and Prudence Pender Pope were fast asleep after a rare but fierce bout of lovemaking, their twin beds pushed together.

Constance Welling snored as Roger Siechert dreamed of the delights of the Chocolate Wanderer.

Kitty Ballou shared her bed with Red Mackintosh, the door locked because her father had a habit of walking in unannounced. Tonight, Lee Ballou slept in his La-Z-Boy, Jack Daniels nestled in his arms and dreamed of playing catch with his son. He'd never done that and he was sorry now.

Merlin Skinner, the Wizard of Ink, sat up late in his little apartment above his shop watching *Memento* for perhaps the fortieth time.

Mrs. Vanessa Mudgett watched her son Herman dozing on the couch. "Herman!" she said as his head bobbed. He snapped awake. "Yes, Mother?" Mrs. Mudgett didn't even look up. "Did you say my name?" Herman asked. Mrs. Mudgett gave him a disappointed look. "I certainly did not, Herman. Are the voices back? Do we need to see Dr. Holmes again?" Herman shook his head. "I just thought I heard my name." Vanessa Mudgett clucked her tongue and returned to cross-stitching. From the corner of her eye, she watched her son, waiting for him to doze off so she could do it again.

Jordan Cartwright slept; a copy of Shakespeare's *A Midsummer Night's Dream* lay open beside him.

Rosa Morales was in and out of sleep, tossing and turning. She rolled onto her side, muttered another prayer, her rosary so tight it nearly cut off her circulation. When she did doze, she dreamed of monsters, living and dead. Santa Muerte was all around her, all around the town of Cliffside, and no one seemed to know it but her.

Out on Blue Lady Lake, three fishermen sat singing *Fair Spanish Ladies* in their open boat, their lines cast for catfish. They'd already killed two sixers of Michelob and caught nothing, but it wasn't about the fish, it was about having fun. It was a fine night until Ted Sparks stopped singing and pointed. "Lookie over there! What the hell is that?"

The others followed his hand. Gliding toward them was a blue figure, a woman. A beautiful woman. "I dunno," slurred Guy Turlock, "but I think it's a fair Spanish maiden. I'll take her over a shark - or a catfish - any day of the week!"

# 105
## *Reflections*

### WEDNESDAY

Sara asked Adam to man the desk while she did rounds outside. The gardens needed winterizing, the lawns one last mowing, and the springhouse required insulating strips for the window and door. Winter wouldn't stop the bottling of sparkling water, and the season would be cruel to anyone working there.

"Well, hello there, Miss Bellamy."

Sara turned toward the voice and saw Walter Gardner leaning on his rake.

"Hello, Walter," she called, walking toward him.

"I suppose you're checking to make sure we're prepared for the cold season."

"I was," she said. She looked at the large pile of debris he'd raked up. "It looks like you've got things under control."

He nodded. "Yep. We're getting there." He stared at the springhouse.

"Everything okay, Walter?"

He began raking. "Fine," he said. "I better get back to work."

Sara walked to the north side of Cliffhouse, crunching pine needles underfoot as she approached the springhouse.

As she neared, feminine laughter seemed to come from within the padlocked building. She came to an abrupt stop.

Cold bony fingertips played Sara's spine like a xylophone as the laughter continued. It was a high-pitched, lunatic sound. She took a few quiet steps closer. An autumn-colored leaf crackled underfoot and the deranged giggling from within came to a sudden halt.

Sara crouched next to the window and waited. After a few seconds of silence, she rose and looked inside. At first she saw nothing out of the ordinary. The racks of bottles, empty and full, the tables, chair, and the well, the cover skewed as usual.

And then she saw the face.

It didn't appear. It had been there all along, Sara realized, only she'd been looking right past it - through it - the same way a person sees through a transparent reflection, not noticing it at all if their attention is on solid objects beyond it.

But there it was, just on the other side of the glass, suddenly in focus; suddenly the only thing Sara could see. Shock and unreality immobilized her.

The woman's face was a milky death-blue. It was thin, beautiful, and - Sara realized as she looked into the eyes - not sane. The hair, the same color of blue, was a living thing, floating around her face.

Sara's skin tingled. She held her breath.

A flicker of pink as the tip of the woman's tongue poked out, then crawled, snake-like, along the scarlet edge of her upper lip. The jaw began working - open, closed, open, closed - creating a strange and hideous imitation of chewing.

*She's tasting me,* thought Sara.

# 106
## *Dead in the Water*

Teddy, Jackson, and Maisy Hart sat in Sara's apartment and pored over the journals. Sara had invited them to stay when she left for work. The three had been at the dining table for over an hour, reading, drinking coffee, and talking.

Maisy cleared her throat. "When Theodosia was quite old and asked me to look after her journals, she told me a little about them. This one-" she tapped a red volume with a blue ribbon bookmark "- she mentioned specifically. As I recall, she said she had thought of showing it to you, Teddy, then decided against it. It's all about the Blue Lady in the 1920s." She looked at Teddy. "Perhaps she thought you should know about her. I just read an entry. She'd seen the phantom herself and feared for her life."

"May I?" Jackson asked. Maisy passed the volume to him. "'October 20, 1928,'" he read. "'I have seen her myself, and heard her call my name. Her voice was as cold as the lake in my ear. She said I belonged to her. I was terrified because I have heard that hearing her voice means there will be a death.

"'It was seven in the morning when it happened. I was downstairs, in the speakeasy, sweeping up. She said my name twice more. I looked around but didn't see her so I took my broom and started up the stairs, intending to get Jeremy to help me clean.'" He paused. "Jeremy?"

"An employee," Maisy said.

Jackson nodded and looked back to the journal. "'When I was near the door, I smelled the lake all around me. I heard my name again and something that felt like a freezing cold hand touched my shoulder. I felt a chill deep within and turned. I saw her then, right behind me. She laughed and reached for me again. I flailed the broom and I took the last two steps and tried to open the door, but it was stuck. I cried out for help and tried again as that frigid hand touched me for the second time. I felt the cold and knew I was about to die and yanked the door with all my strength. It flew open, knocking me down, and I left the speakeasy. I will not go down there again until I know the Blue Lady is gone. She is real.'"

"Christ," Jackson said. "That's where the swimming pool is now?"

"Yes," Teddy affirmed.

Jackson began flipping pages and landed on an entry dated October 31. He read through it and looked at the others. "This one is talking about several drownings that happened during the last weekend in October. Two of them walked out into the water - there were witnesses. She says, 'A Miss Frannie Bach walked into the water in the afternoon. She was fully clothed and did not respond when her friends called to her. The lake took her, they said. The other was a gentleman who was staying here at Cliffhouse. The story is the same.'"

Jackson looked up. "She says the other drownings were fishermen on All Hallows Eve. One man was alone in a rowboat. The other boat held three men and they all drowned. She says one boat was overturned, the other was not."

Teddy spoke. "That puts me in mind of our own fishermen drowning Sunday night."

"Seems more than coincidental," Maisy said.

"All three of those men were strong swimmers. The boat was overturned, but it wasn't large - any one of them could have righted it," Jackson said. "But they drowned."

"The lake temperature is around 32 degrees this time of year," Teddy added.

Jackson nodded. "Still, men who can swim should have been able to save themselves. They were close enough to shore that they could have swum the distance if they couldn't right the boat."

"Halloween," Maisy said, "is supposed to be when the veil between this world and the next is thinnest. If there's truth to the legend, perhaps the Blue Lady was strong enough to take lives without human help. All those drownings would suggest that."

Jackson, unable to buy that idea, turned more pages, stopping on one dated November 27, 1928. He read aloud: "'There have been no killings by the Bodice Ripper in a month and we think he has left our little town. However, there have been more drowning victims found in the lake, and several other people found dead in town, one here in a hydro tub inside the spa. Dr. Phelps told Papa and me that he did check their lungs and they were, indeed, full of water. He has no explanation, though the one in the hydro tub may have been a simple accident. It's sad. Old Mrs. Worrel was a lovely lady, may she rest in peace. However, I do think Dr. Phelps is beginning to heed my warnings about the Blue Lady, though he won't say so.'"

Jackson flipped more pages. "'December 5, 1928. More bodies have been found on land, but none bear marks. Most of these, Dr. Phelps cannot dissect without permission, but he has used a siphon of sorts and found the lungs to be waterlogged.

"'I told him I think the Blue Lady is strong enough on her own that she no longer needs help from the Bodice Ripper. The good doctor made a comment about my fondness for sherry, but it was a joke. He is worried, too.'"

Jackson turned more pages, scanning entries, hoping to find something definitive. He stopped on December 24. "Listen to this: 'There have been four new murders, gruesome ones, but the murderer was caught. Unfortunately, it was not the Bodice Ripper, who was far cannier. Caleb, the slow son of grocer Avery Martin, was caught hitting Mr. Snowden, the barber, over the head with a rock. His face was beyond recognition. Dr. Phelps told us that the police chief himself arrested the boy, and that he made no protest, but seemed shocked by what he had done. He then confessed to killing three others in the same fashion that same morning by breaking into their homes while they slept. The boy kept repeating, "The lady told me to do it. The lady told me to do it." Caleb Martin is in our jail now, but Dr. Phelps believes that he will be sent down to the Lichter State Asylum for the Insane and Inebriates near San Bernardino. I believe the boy was possessed by the Blue Lady.'"

"Poor guy," Teddy said.

"Yeah. Now listen to this: 'I think that the Blue Lady needed the Bodice Ripper and the Gaslight Killer of 1887 to increase her strength after being trapped so long in the spring. I feel that she looks for hollow men, those soulless or angry men whom she can fill up to create her unholy duality. That so many were both ripped open and had water in their lungs speaks of this, and now that the Ripper has gone away, we are finding people full of water on land and in the lake. I've no doubt that she is killing on her own. As for Caleb Martin, while he is not hollow, he is very simple and was once caught doing terrible things to a squirrel, so perhaps there is violence in him. At my behest, Dr. Phelps inquired as to Caleb's habits concerning the spring water from our well and he says the boy was very fond of it. Is that how she finds those she uses? She somehow communes with them through the water? And was she losing strength so that she had to use a human being to aid her once more or did she do it for her pleasure, having found another vessel? It is a terrible thing, but perhaps it is reassurance that the Ripper has indeed left our town.'"

"That's a crazy theory," Jackson said.

Maisy nodded. "At this point, do you have any sane theories?"

"None so far." Jackson returned his gaze to the journal. There were fewer entries now, except for short notations mentioning more drownings than could be considered natural as well as more of the mysterious deaths on land. She also spoke of townsfolk reporting Blue Lady sightings, mostly by night, but several by day. *At least we haven't had any daylight sightings.*

He flipped to the final pages of the journal, to an entry dated January 1, 1929. "'Yesterday evening, Dr. Phelps, Papa, Judge Hawkins, and Police Chief Edwards and his son Tom all saw the Blue Lady as they prepared New Year's Eve fireworks to be set off by the lake. It was dusk as she appeared, a blue glowing ball, from the Kelly Forest side of the lodge and glided down over the cliffs like a fallen star. They did not recognize what they saw at that point. The glow moved toward them, just above the water, and when it was fifty feet away, they saw it morph into a woman's form. They watched from the shore, with great fascination. When she was a dozen feet from them, they saw her as a beautiful woman, but then her black eyes turned into gaping holes and her face became terrible. Each heard their own name called and then the demon shrieked and rushed forward, embracing Tom Edwards. Even as the men tried to pull the strapping young man from her evil grip, he began coughing and choking and fell to the ground, dead. Water dripped from his nose and mouth. The Blue Lady shrieked as she turned back into a blue glow and sped away across the lake, disappearing among the trees.

"'I am glad I told Dr. Phelps that I thought she was from the wellspring because he took the others into town where they procured a large sheet of marble from the general store. They took it to the springhouse and when she returned at dawn, watched as she entered through the window - glass does not deter her - and floated down into the well. They waited a few minutes and then, as one, hefted the slab up to seal it.

"Instantly, she knew and was back, pushing the marble up. Three of the men sat on it and she could still rock it, but could not lift it. Papa ran for Cliffhouse and woke Jeremy, who helped him put our largest anvil and other heavy tools in a wagon that we pulled to the springhouse. These were not enough, though they helped: two men needed to remain seated on the marble while the others went to fetch more iron and boulders, the biggest they could lift, to hold the marble in place.

"'They were at last successful and came back to Cliffhouse to wash up. I made them breakfast, and took a plate to Jeremy, who was standing guard.

"'They are now at the smith's having the thickest, heaviest iron cover possible made that can be fastened down with chains and padlocks. Tomorrow, Papa says, they will have the window bricked in, the chimney covered, and the door replaced with a thicker one that can be padlocked. I asked Papa why they didn't brick the door in and he told me that perhaps they might after they were sure the iron cover would be enough.'"

"Wow, that's quite a story," Teddy said.

"There's one more entry," Jackson said. "It's dated February 1, 1929: 'I have ceased to write in this journal, hoping that we shall have a new beginning, and I believe my hope has become reality. It has been a month since the Blue Lady was imprisoned in the wellspring and there have been no more unnatural deaths on land or in water. Perhaps she is sleeping now, for we are in the deepest part of winter and snow covers everything. If she does not reappear when the snow melts and the crocuses appear, I shall know it is over.'"

There was a click and the door flew open. Sara Bellamy, white-faced and breathing hard, rushed into the room.

"Are you okay?" Teddy asked. "What happened?"

"The Blue Lady," said Sara. "I saw her. In the springhouse!"

Jackson stared at her. "In the well?"

"No," said Sara. "She was standing on the other side of the window."

"A daylight sighting," he said. "That's not good."

## 107
### *Parasite*

He looked at the new casings hanging in the Hall of Souls, and was not as pleased as he thought he should be. Hammerhead was tired of killing so randomly, so meaninglessly, even if the Lady's methods offered him anonymity. In truth, he was an artist, and doing things this way flew in the face of his creative sensibilities. It was the fault of the Lady, of course. He killed for *her* now, not for *his* art, not for *his* power. As he stared at the newest mirrors, he sensed nothing within them. *She's taking them for herself.*

A true parasite, she needed the life force of others to survive. Her plan, he knew, was to garner enough strength to exist on her own, out of the water, without help from him or anyone else. She'd promised him the souls of the dead, but he realized now that she'd taken them for herself.

He drove his fist into the wall and screamed at the mirrors. "Reveal yourselves to me!"

There was no sign of life - or even death - within them. He was supposed to own these souls. As the taker - and the keeper - of their lives, he was supposed to rule them, and they were supposed to empower *him*, edify *him*, and immortalize *him*. He was supposed to be their God.

But it seemed he'd gone the way of all gods. *In the hearts of their own creations, all gods eventually die.* And here he was, just another dead god. Anger blurred his vision.

*No. I am not dead.* The souls he'd gathered on his own remained; he sensed them. But those he'd collected in her service were gone. Gone because *she* was taking them for herself. The realization made his next move clear: He would return to killing without her.

Hammerhead began making new plans.

# 108
## *At the Springhouse*

"You were standing here at the window when you saw her, right, Sara?" Teddy asked as he touched the springhouse sill.

"That's right." Sara hung back, staying away from the window. That was unlike his daughter.

"Have either of you ever seen anything unusual through the window? Reflections, maybe?" Jackson asked.

"No," Sara said.

"Me, neither," Teddy said. "But I think perhaps a Cub Scout saw something earlier this year. The Scouts were camping and this one little guy came up to Adam and me and told us the springhouse had a ghost inside. The boy was scared. We took a look and told him he probably saw a reflection from a window at Cliffhouse that made it look like there was a ghost." He paused. "He didn't buy it. The Scoutmaster had to call his parents. He went home that day."

"What do you think it was, Ted?"

Teddy shrugged. "I never even gave it another thought. I assumed it was his imagination. You know how kids are."

Jackson looked at the window. "This used to be bricked up, right? Like it said in the journal?"

Teddy put the key in the padlock. "Yes. We had Noble open it up and install this window when we decided to bottle the water."

Teddy opened the door. Sara had her nerve back and walked in first, shoulders squared. *That's my girl.*

\*\*\*

The floor was cement and there was a boarded up stone fireplace built into the wall. Wooden tables held bottling equipment. Two walls held racks of bottles, one filled, one empty. The well stood at the far end of the room.

"Not again," Teddy said. "This happens a lot." He gestured at the wooden cover. It was half off. "Adam thinks it moves due to gasses from the spring." Teddy looked from Sara to Jackson. "He also thinks that's why they had that massive iron cover chained over it. It was a bear to remove."

Sara glanced at the old cover leaning against the wall. "Seems like overkill."

Jackson peered down into the well. He heard water moving below. It smelled fresh and pleasant, nothing like the lake.

Teddy shoved the cover into place and they left, returning to the noontime sunlight and the cool, pine-scented air. Jackson took a deep breath. The springhouse made him feel claustrophobic.

"Guys?" Sara was clearly as happy to be outside as he was. "What did Theodosia say about the well cover?"

Teddy cleared his throat. "According to Great Aunt Theodosia, that iron cover was made to keep the Blue Lady trapped in the well."

"Do you believe that, Chief?" Sara asked.

"I don't know what I believe."

"You know," Teddy said. "It is odd that we so often find the cover out of place. We've even found it on the floor a few times. I think I'll talk to Paul and make sure his employees are putting it back on correctly." Teddy paused. "Just to be safe, why don't we use the iron hooks set into the stone and chain it down now?"

"The three of us?" Jackson asked. "I doubt we can move that cover into place by ourselves."

"The *wooden* cover, Jackson," Teddy said. "We can get some new chain and padlocks."

# 109
## *Making Sausage*

    Roger Siechert whistled *The Happy Wanderer* as he ran his boning knife over the whetstone. He wore his *I'm the Sausage King* apron, and a smile. Cooking made him jolly and a jolly Roger was an erect Roger. As he turned his gaze to the twenty pounds of pork butt and four of venison on his counter, he felt unencumbered. Sausage making was his passion.

    His bratwurst had won first prize at Oktoberfest for the last five years, and would win again this year. His secret ingredients were a couple of special spices and the venison - he'd used most of the five-pronged buck in his freezer for his award-winning smoked venison landjaeger, which he cured in the special low-humidity walk-in fridge in his garage.

    He sang as he cut the butts and venison into chunks and fed them into the grinder. The machine's growl made him think of his own hungry belly's music as pink and white meat and fat oozed like limp spaghetti noodles from circular holes in the disk.

"I love to grind my Boston butt," he sang.
"I love to grind my buck.
"I love to go a 'wandering
"With my friend old King Tut!
"Valkyrie, Valdera, Valkyrie, Valder ha-ha-ha-ha, ha-ha-ha!
"With my friend old King Tut!"

    He finished the first grinding and fed the meat through again, then gathered his allspice and nutmeg, ginger root, kosher salt, milk and eggs, and his secret ingredients, star anise and annatto. He began mixing the sausage in several large stainless steel bowls, first combining the spices, eggs, and milk, then adding the meat, mixing it all with his hands. He adored the feel of the soft meat squishing between his fingers. He added powdered milk last and mauled the future bratwurst for all it was worth. It was the best he'd felt in a century, he thought, as he began singing again.

"I love to eat my five-pronged buck," he sang.
"I love my Boston butt -
"I love to eat it day and night
"And then I love to fuck!
"Valkyrie, Valdera, Valkyrie, Valder ha-ha-ha-ha, ha-ha-ha!
"And then I love to fuck!"

    He passed the meat one more time through the grinder. At last it was time to do some serious stuffing.

His equipment was already laid out, from the reel loaded with natural hog casings to his stuffer, clips, twine, and sausage pricker. He giggled a little; he loved saying "sausage pricker."

Just as he began stuffing, the intercom buzzed. He punched it with his knuckle. "Yes, Larry?"

"Just thought you'd like to know Miss Welling is back."

He sighed, his erection wilting. "Well, we can't win them all, can we, Larry?"

"Excuse me? Should I have not let her in?"

"It's okay, she's a force of nature. You'd need an elephant gun to stop her."

"Excuse-"

Roger switched off the intercom and went back to his task.

Moments later, rather than the incessant knocking he'd expected, he heard the click of a key in his door. *What the fuck?*

Constance Welling let herself in and stepped into the kitchen, holding a shipping box. She dropped it on the counter. "I had a key made so I can surprise you! Surprise!" She threw her hands in the air. Both her eyes were blackish-purple and her lip was swollen.

For a split second, Roger wanted to throttle her for this invasion of his space, but the joys of playing in the meat were too great, the sky outside too blue, his mood too good to be tainted. Besides, she was already bruised and beat up. He shrugged and smiled at her. "A nice surprise, indeed. What's in the box?"

"It's a surprise." She fluttered her eyelashes, making herself look like a gracelessly aging Shirley Temple with bad hair, an eating disorder, and big fake tits. "It's just something I ordered online." Her expression soured. "It was delivered to Cliffhouse. Thank the shitting gods I didn't have to pick it up from that little skank, but that bellboy absolutely leered at me! I think he's a pervert."

Roger sucked a dollop of raw meat off his thumb. "Jerry Belvedere?"

Constance waved a hand of dismissal. "Whatever his name is. He's creepy."

"He has mild anemia. Beyond that I think he's perfectly normal. Good blood pressure."

"Whatever." She sighed. "Aren't you going to ask where I've been?"

"Frankly, my dear, I don't give a damn."

"What? What did you say to me?"

*She must be karma for killing Tessa.* "I was thinking we might watch *Gone with the Wind* this evening."

"Oh, so that's your way of making a joke?"

Constance, he had already learned, wouldn't know a good joke if it were humping her leg. "Yes."

"Well, maybe," she said. "While I was in town I rented *When a Man Loves a Woman*. It's my favorite movie."

He hadn't even been able to sit through that train wreck the first time. *Odious. Simply odious.* "Perhaps after *Gone with the Wind*."

"*Humph.*"

He knew she'd still try forcing that whiny movie on him, but he'd deal with that later. Stuffing the casings was a labor of love and he wasn't going to let her spoil it for him. "So what else did you do in town, Bunny-Face?"

"I had a treatment at Mountain High Colonics. It was superb. I feel wonderful!"

"You had a colonic?"

"Oh, yes. I do at least once a month. It cleans all the old stuff out of your intestines and leaves you squeaky clean. You should try it. They even have a special rate for couples."

Roger silently stuffed and counted to ten. He wouldn't tell her colonics were snake oil, that the bowel was self-cleaning. He wouldn't tell her she would never see him pay to have a complete stranger ram water up his rectum. It was absurd. He picked up his fresh bottle of Blue Springs and drank. *So very good.* Ordinarily, he would be drinking a beer as he cooked, but the water was even better. His mind wandered as he let bubbles pirouette on his palate. *If one were to indulge in a Blue Springs enema in the privacy of his own bathroom, that might be quite invigorating. Perhaps I might add a handful of Pop Rocks for more enjoyment. Mmm. Or Mentos?*

"Why are you smiling, Roger? Are you listening to me?"

He glanced at her bruised face. "What did you say?"

"I stopped at Cliffside Market to get kiwis and olives. They charge too much and don't even have the right olives."

"Kiwis and olives?" He felt a chuckle coming on. "That's a strange food combination." He twinkled at her. "Maybe you're pregnant."

She *tsked* and turned on the trembling. "I *told* you I make my face mask out of them. Don't you hear anything I say?"

He calmly took a pull on his water, getting a semi-hard-on as he pictured himself pouring a couple of bottles into an enema bag later this evening. Then he turned to her, all sweetness and light. "I'm sorry, dear heart, but I'm just a man, do forgive me." Suddenly, he couldn't remember what he was apologizing for, but Constance instantly turned off the threatened histrionics and blew him a kiss. "I can't wait to watch our movie together. Now, excuse me while I go try on my new outfit."

"New outfit?"

She *tsked* and rolled her eyes. "I already told you, Roger. That's what's in the box. My Oktoberfest costume. I looked yours over and got a green dress to match your shorts and suspenders. Remember, I told you I was going to do that?" She didn't wait for a reply. "Do you want me to model it for you now?"

Siechert didn't hear a word she'd said, just kept stuffing meat into the casings as the lyrics to *The Happy Wanderer* played through his mind on a loop. He looked up and caught her watching him. He could tell he was supposed to say something, so he improvised, something he'd gotten quite good at lately. "If you say so, sunshine."

She gave him one of those weird head-tilts like the dog in the old Victrola ads. "So you do want to see it?"

*See what? Oh fuck.* "Of course I do."

Constance clapped her hands together. "Goody! I'll go change now." She grabbed the box and disappeared upstairs.

He continued stuffing sausages and within moments, she returned.

Fury, like a bolt of lightning, shot through Roger Siechert.

She was dressed in a cheap Halloween costume suitable for women less than half her age. She wore her gold stiletto sandals and white nylons with elastic tops that ended inches below the skirt, which was so short and full that it showed her ruffled panties. At the waist, it turned into a black ribbon-laced vest that ended in curves under the breasts, corseting them up and out so that white ruffled cups covered them. The top of her cross tattoo stuck out like a turd. A big brown turd. He grinned. *Just like Constance.* He stifled a giggle.

"You like it, then?" she asked.

He couldn't even think about her clinging to him at Oktoberfest in that cheap outfit, but he kept smiling. "You look lovely. Now, why don't you go play in the other room while I finish these sausages?"

"Are you saying you want to watch me play with myself in this dress? As long as I am *very* gentle, it should be okay. My stitches aren't healed." She pulled a pouty face.

Siechert thought about the bubbly water again, and the naughty, naughty places he could put it. Without Constance he never would have thought of it. *Constance.* He needed to get her out of here so he could enjoy making the sausages and then have some fun with fizzy water later.

"Well?" Constance looked at him as if she expected him to say something. "Speaking of colonics," he said stuffing meat into a casing, "you really ought to go have another session tomorrow."

Constance cocked her head. "Huh? I didn't say anything about colonics."

"You said you went today." The meat made a wet sound as he played in it. It put butterflies in his stomach. "And it's recommended you go at least twice in succession for a really proper cleansing."

"It is?"

"Would you like me to make an appointment for you?"

"No. I'll make one myself."

"For tomorrow, I hope."

She looked at him oddly. "Is there a reason you'd like me to have it done again so soon?"

His mind raced, searching for a reason. "I was thinking we could try a new position tonight. And take it further tomorrow. A position that requires a thorough cleansing."

Constance folded her arms across her boobs. "Roger Siechert, are you asking me to have anal sex with you?"

He stuffed more meat into the pig intestine. "I'm not asking you anything, you silly bitch. I'm telling you I'm going to have my way with whichever orifice of yours I damned well please. Your clitoris must be avoided so I intend to go to work on your back door and I like a clean work space." *Shit!* That hadn't at all been what he'd meant to say. He knew he'd just fucked everything up and he was about to apologize - *wait ... what did I say? What do I need to apologize for?* - when, to his surprise, Constance smiled and sidled up to him.

"Oh, Roger," she said. "I've never seen you this aggressive before. I admit I like it." She did the twisted Shirley Temple thing again with her face and Siechert blew out a relieved breath. "So yes." She stroked his arm. "I'll have another colonic done as soon as they can fit me in."

# 110
## *Whistling Dixie*

**THURSDAY**

Roger Siechert woke up Thursday to morning light filtering through the pines. He thought he was late for work, then remembered that Holmes, as always, was doing double duty so Roger could concentrate on Oktoberfest. *There's nothing better than a good partner, except for a good lay.*

He threw his arms out, stretching, groaning with pleasure and realized Constance was gone. It was unlikely she was cooking him breakfast; he doubted she could even zap a TV dinner. He opened his eyes and saw a note on the bedside table in her childish handwriting. God, he hated people who drew hearts in place of a proper 'i' dot.

*Dear Roger, I'm off to get a multi-colonic and will be a few hours. It's full of special ingredients to enhance lovemaking. I'm doing it just for you, because of the way you plowed my back door last night. I want you to do it again tonight. No one has ever made me feel so loved."*

He crumpled the note and laughed. "Loved? That had nothing to do with love."

In fact, he'd been afraid he'd hurt her, but evidently the woman loved getting anal even more than he did - her anus was so loose that it probably had a hard time whistling *Dixie*.

Laughing, he got up and stripped the bed, then hit the shower, where he nearly parboiled himself as he scrubbed Constance's stink off his body. It was going to be a good day to make the last one or two sausages for Oktoberfest: Braunschweiger or leberwurst, at least if his special order of pork liver had arrived at Cliffside Market. If not, he would just make a string of weisswurst. *Two more blue ribbons for me*, he thought as he turned off the shower.

# 111
## *Hammerhead Rebels*

In the Hall of Souls, Hammerhead sat cross-legged below the altar. In his hands, he held the rip claw hammer he'd used for the kills he had made before meeting the Blue Lady. It was barely two pounds, with a cobalt fiberglass handle, a shining steel head and straight claws meant for pulling nails from boards, but worked just as well for invading temples when blood was no object. His hands twitched with muscle memory at the thought. He doubted his chosen name, The Hammerhead Killer, would ever be used since he was too efficient and careful to be caught.

The Blue Lady provided safety, but little satisfaction and now that he understood that she had stolen all the souls she'd promised him, he itched to use the hammer. He rose to his feet and looked in the mirror. "Are you there?" he whispered, waiting for her to appear behind his own reflection.

He waited. There was no sign of her. *Perhaps she's busy with the other one she uses.* Instead of jealousy, the thought pleased him. He removed the empty mirrors and left the room to dress for a morning hike in a little-known canyon where there would undoubtedly be a few other lone hikers. The thought of capturing a new soul without the Blue Lady's voice in his ear excited him.

# 112
## *Concerning the Wellspring*

Paul Butters was checking the kitchen to make sure La Chatte Rouge had plenty of ingredients for the day's special when Teddy Bellamy poked his head in. "Paul?"

"Right here." Paul stepped out of the refrigerated room and saw Teddy's face. "What's wrong?"

"Well, I just went to check the springhouse and the cover is broken. Have any of your employees been in there since yesterday?"

"No, but I gave one of the padlock keys to Eduardo Jones; he's in charge of bottling. I kept the other one. Just a minute." He walked out to the dining room and spotted the boy putting fresh flowers on the tables. "Have you been in the springhouse?"

"No, sir. Not since Tuesday."

"Do you have your keys?"

"Yes sir." The boy displayed his key ring. "Key to the restaurant, key to the wellspring door lock, and the key to the new padlock. They're all here. Why? Is there a problem?"

"Nothing to worry about." Paul went back to Teddy and spoke softly. "Eduardo hasn't been in there in days. I trust him."

Teddy shook his head. "It doesn't make sense. The door was locked but the wood cover was shattered and the chain and locks were in place on the well."

"Were the bottles all there?"

Teddy nodded. "It didn't look like anyone had touched anything but the cover."

Baffled, Paul shrugged. "Do you want to talk to Eduardo?"

"No, not now. I trust your judgment." He sniffed. "Something smells wonderful."

"We're making onion soup."

"I may have to come by for lunch."

# 113
## *Getting Kicks with Constance*

Constance returned from Mountain High Colonics with a smile on her face and a head just as clear as her intestines. She let herself into Roger's house and heard him in the kitchen. Even that shit-forsaken song he was whistling couldn't ruin her mood.

"I'm squeaky clean." She straddled the kitchen threshold, kicking her leg up, striking a sexy pose.

"That's wonderful, Pumpkin-Face!" Roger didn't bother looking up from sausage making.

She sighed. "Eww," she said looking at what appeared to be white sausages. "What are those?"

"They're called weisswurst. It's a white breakfast sausage."

"They look like someone scared the hell out of them."

"That's wonderful, Cinnamon-Tits."

"Are you listening to me?"

Roger kept working, whistling that damned song, and ignoring her.

Then Constance had an idea. "I'll be right back."

\*\*\*

The stupid bitch mumbled something Roger didn't hear. "That's great, Kitten-Nibbles," he called after her. His weisswursts were looking great. He was bummed he wasn't able to make leberwurst as well, but the liver hadn't arrived. It didn't matter. Regardless of what he made, he reasoned, he was bound to win first prize in every category. It was a given; almost a Cliffside tradition at this point, and Roger Siechert smiled to himself while he practiced his look of surprise when they announced the winner. His penis stiffened with joy.

Something began gnawing at the edges of his consciousness, like a fly buzzing around his head.

"A-hem!"

The noise came a second time and he realized it was Constance, returned from wherever she'd gone, and intent on bothering him. He looked up, prepared to say something flattering that would shut her the fuck up for a few more minutes, but when he saw her, his words died.

She wore that horrific green Halloween costume with which she intended to humiliate him during Oktoberfest and stood in the doorway, arms raised, head tossed back, one leg cocked outward.

She'd left the corset open to expose her breasts. Draped around them - like a garland on a Christmas tree - were his own prize-winning links of smoked blutwurst. *Of course, the blutwurst.* The pig's blood had been very difficult to obtain, so she had to defile it. *She's attracted to it because she's a pig, a little piggy cunt.*

They circled her tits, trailed down around her waist, and in one hand, she swung the last several links in a circular motion, jutting her hip. "Do you want to come and eat me, big boy?" she asked in what he assumed was an attempted Mae West impersonation.

His hands fisted. His jaw flexed. His vision dimmed. His phone began to ring. He barely heard it over the buzz of rushing blood in his ears. He let it go to voicemail.

"After you're done eating me," said Constance in that same bad accent, "I'll feed you some sausage. Or," she continued, sliding the last link slowly up her thigh, "we can kill two birds with one stone and satisfy *both* your appetites at once."

The world turned red and he watched as if in slow motion as the sausage disappeared under her skirt and her face became a mask of ecstasy so overdone it could have won an award at the porn academy.

"I have had enough!" Roger rushed Constance, and in a single move, his hands circled her throat. He squeezed her chicken neck, shook her head back and forth, a delirious sound between a giggle and a scream burbling from his lips as he watched her eyes bulge and her skin change color beneath the pound of makeup she'd caked on her face. "I hate you! I fucking hate you, you goddamned, egocentric, narcissistic, self-centered, self-absorbed, self-published piece of fucking trash!"

She hacked and gagged as her hands clawed blindly at him, missing him with each swipe.

"Die! Die! Die, you fucking piggy cunt!"

He squeezed harder, shook her till his arms ached. "Don't you *ever* mess with my meat! It's *my* sausage! *Mine!* You ruined it! You ruined it, you cunting little pig!" His words struck him funny and his screams evolved into glorious giggles. He snorted at her, oinked, and laughed as he squeezed the life out of her. "Do you like that, you little piggy bitch? Oink, oink, baby!"

She was still fighting, ineffectively clawing at him and gasping for air she wasn't going to get.

It was taking too fucking long. He pushed her against the wall and slammed her head into it. "Oink, oink!" With each *oink,* he banged her head into the hard surface. Something cracked. Whether it was the wall or Constance's skull, Siechert neither knew nor cared. He continued oinking and bashing and pummeling her head until her body went slack and his arms quaked with exhaustion.

When he let go of her neck, she fell to the floor in a grotesque heap. He looked down at her for several seconds, trying to catch his breath. His arms were wasted but his legs were still buzzing with energy. He kicked her dead face once, twice, three times. "Oink! Oink! Oink!" He moved to her ribs. "Oink! Oink! Oink!" Then her diseased, disfigured, cunt. "Oink! Oink! Oink!" He kicked and kicked, wishing only that she were still alive to feel the pain. As he oinked, an idea, not yet fully formed, floated around his head like a bee trying to source a scent. As her pelvic bone caved in, the idea clicked home. Siechert stopped kicking. He bent at the waist, resting his hands on his knees as he tried to catch his breath. A droplet of sweat ran from his forehead, down the length of his nose, and plunked on Constance's wide, blind, rolled-back eye. "It's *my* sausage!"

His phone rang. Again, he let it go to voicemail as his mind returned to the idea it was forming. It was a real beauty, and even as he struggled to catch his breath, he found himself giggling. "You'll be the belle of the ball, m'dear!" he said to the corpse. "A total hit!" As the details of his plan clarified, he realized he'd need to keep her in presentable condition. He crouched, getting a closer look at her face. She certainly wasn't much uglier dead than she had been alive, but he regretted kicking her so hard. Now her nose was broken after all. She would have been pleased, but the doctor was not. He shrugged. "Nothing we can't work around," he said.

He moved her face to the side, looked inside her open mouth and cleared out a few teeth that had been knocked loose. "Nope, nothing we can't work around. Nothing at all." He fixed her hair, then stood, grabbed her by the feet, and dragged her out to the walk-in freezer where this little piggy could keep the other little piggies company till show time.

# 114
## *Drownings*

Jackson Ballou stood on the pier by the picnic area and watched as black-suited divers dragged a second body out of the lake and handed it up to the EMTs, who laid it next to the first. Gene Holmes wasn't there yet because he was working and the clinic couldn't get ahold of Siechert. Jackson finally told Holmes to just head for the mortuary when he could since these two appeared to be simple drowning victims.

The bodies hadn't been in the water long and Jackson vaguely recognized the first victim, a white female in her thirties whom he'd seen around town. The second was Bill Wasserman, the Cliffhouse employee who manned the boathouse.

Jackson wondered if Wasserman had been on the Cliffhouse docks, all the way across the lake, when he went into the water. He knew for a fact that Bill could swim, which made the possibility of homicide more likely, though it would likely be difficult to impossible to prove.

# 115
## *Bloody Gulch*

Synchronicity. Hammerhead had driven up into Holcomb Valley behind Big Bear Lake and hidden his car near the site of a long-dead ghost town called Bloody Gulch. It didn't appear on maps printed after the 1960s and all that remained was a deep pit of a well. He'd found it years before, and it already held two of his earliest victims, no doubt nothing but bones by now.

The young man hiking nearby had been very friendly when he saw Hammerhead sitting on a felled log retying his shoe. He sat down, offered him a granola bar, and told Hammerhead about his adventures along the Pacific Crest Trail. When Hammerhead became bored, he struck, and now the hiker lay at the bottom of the well at Bloody Gulch. He'd never known what hit him.

Hammerhead had his soul tucked safely in his pocket as he took a circuitous route back to Cliffside - and the Lady in Blue was none the wiser.

# 116
## *Leberwurst*

### FRIDAY

"I'm going to make some leberwurst," Siechert sang.
"For the Oktoberfest;
"The market had no pork liver,
"But Connie's is second-best!
"Valkyrie, Valdera, Valkyrie, Valder ha-ha-ha-ha, ha-ha-ha,
"Connie's is second best!"

*Roger ...*

He paused in his grinding as the Blue Bitch's voice whispered in his ear.

*Roger ... You took a life without me.*

"And your point is?" He fed chunks of pork butt - *how appropriate* - and boiled liver into the grinder.

*You must wait for me to help you.*

"I did just fine on my own." He whistled *Happy Wanderer* between his teeth. "It was just a little piggy, hardly a human at all."

This was a relatively small batch of leberwurst since the piggy's organ had only weighed 3.4 pounds and had some bad spots he had to cut off, taking it down to just 3.1 pounds. But mixed with the five pounds of pork butt, he would be able to make three good-sized sausages; one for the judges and two for Leckerwurst, the sausage stand that showcased his delectable edibles. They would slice it up and serve it with kraut or on rye with spicy mustard. *Ah, delight!* His mouth watered.

*Roger ...*

"Can't you leave me alone for a little while?" He'd had just about enough of women, even blue ones.

The smell of lakewater overpowered the good scents of the meat, chopped onions, the minced marjoram and sage as the Lady's cold breath bathed his face. His neck hairs prickled up and his serenity faded.

*Roger, you are mine. You will obey me or I will take you as easily as I took the others.*

"Okay, I'm sorry." He spoke too loudly in the silent room. "I won't do it without you again." He giggled.

*We have much work to do together tomorrow.*

"But it's Oktoberfest!"

The dark water smell had faded after his apology, but now it redoubled and, right in front of him, in front of the grinder, a face formed, translucent blue, Medusian hair, eyes black and full of fury. *You are mine and you will obey me!*

His bladder let go and she laughed. He ran from the room, afraid and humiliated. Her laughter followed him as he took two stairs at a time to his bedroom, slamming the door behind him.

Her face materialized in front of his again as he stripped off his pants and shorts. *You will obey!*

"I will obey!" he cried, terrified.

The face faded but horrible shrieking laughter swirled around him as he exchanged his sodden trousers for dry ones.

# 117
## *Oktoberfest Eve*

"We're so glad you all could join us," Teddy Bellamy told everyone at the table in La Chatte Rouge. "With everything that's been going on, I think we're all in need of a little levity."

"It was so nice of you to invite us," Polly said. She wore a black skirt with a silky matching blouse and her mother's pearls and would have felt overdressed - Teddy and Adam wore Hawaiian shirts, Jackson and Luke were nearly as casual - if not for Maisy Hart. The elderly lady was elegant in navy silk. Still, Polly tugged at the skirt and wished she'd worn pants and flats like Sara. Jackson squeezed her hand under the table. That helped.

"There are so many people out on the lawn that I'm surprised the bistro's not too crowded," Miss Maisy said.

"That's normal for Oktoberfest Eve," Teddy explained. "Those are the vendors getting their booths ready and no doubt sampling plenty of beer. And we're way past the dinner rush." He consulted his watch. "It's almost nine."

"Do they camp out like they did for the Civil War Festival?" Luke asked.

Adam laughed. "No, but a lot of the vendors sleep in RVs. Good thing - we're booked solid."

Water glasses were filled. Menus arrived. Wine was ordered. The conversation stayed light and enjoyable but Polly sensed an undercurrent, a need they shared to speak of darker things.

Yet they didn't, not until the dinner plates had been cleared and dessert and coffee arrived and the restaurant was nearly empty. The waitress set a huge slice of coconut cake and two forks between Jackson and Polly, who tasted it and closed her eyes. "I wonder if Paul would give me his recipe if I ask nicely."

"He might." Jackson tasted it. "This is great, but I like your apple pie better."

She felt herself blush. "I still haven't told you what happened at the diner this afternoon."

"What?" Jackson asked. The rest of the table looked her way.

"I heard a scream outside the diner this afternoon and the girl who works at the Crystal Cavern - you know, the one who lost her friend the other night - she was out there. It was the strangest thing - it looked like a hard wind buffeted her. She stumbled, and her hair flew in all directions. But there was no wind."

"Why did she scream?" Jackson asked.

"She was clearly frightened of something, but I couldn't see what and she wouldn't tell me, though she was staring at the lake. I asked her inside, but she said no and crossed the street and ran up Pine." Polly shook her head. "It was really odd."

"Poor thing." Maisy shook her head. "It's so sad, all these deaths."

"Jackson," Teddy said.

"What?"

"Adam and I meant to tell you something yesterday, but your news about Bill Wasserman pushed it completely out of our minds and-"

"Excuse me for interrupting." Paul Butters arrived table-side. "Is everything to your satisfaction tonight?"

"It was perfection, as always," Teddy said.

"Excellent." He turned to leave.

"Wait a minute, Paul. This concerns you, too." Teddy looked back at Jackson. "As you know, we chained down the cover on the well after Sara's experience."

"Yes."

"Yesterday morning the cover was shattered, splintered upward, as if something came out of the well. The chain was intact, as were all the padlocks. There are four keys to the door. Paul and his employee each have one and we have the other two."

"I questioned Eduardo and am convinced he had nothing to do with this," Paul said. "He's my best worker and has been in charge of bottling for months now."

"We trust him, too," Adam told Jackson.

"He's so honest, he doesn't even drink the water," Teddy added.

Jackson said nothing.

"Are you and Polly coming to Oktoberfest?" Adam asked.

"Yep. I convinced him he has to take a little time off," Polly said, "or he'll go crazy."

"Polly gives good advice," Jackson said. "So, the springhouse. What did you do about the broken cover?"

"Well," Adam said. "We cleaned up that iron cover from the twenties and hoisted it on. Nearly threw my back out."

"It was a real bear," Paul said.

"No kidding," Teddy agreed.

"Did you chain it down?" Jackson asked.

"Lord, no," Adam said. "We're going to have a new hinged cover made."

"Eduardo will appreciate it," Paul said. "He was going to do some bottling this afternoon. I helped him push the cover back; it was almost too much." He paused, concern showing. "Hmm. He never came back. He was planning on being here in time for dinner service … I hadn't thought about it because we didn't need him. I mean, I'm sure he's fine, but it's not like him to disappear."

"Let's give him a call and see if he answers," Jackson said, rising. "Excuse us, folks, we'll be right back." With that, he and Paul headed for the manager's office.

# 118
## *Finding Eduardo*

Jackson, with Adam and Paul, stood in the springhouse, staring in disbelief at the sight in front of them.

Eduardo Jones, Paul's favorite server, lay on the floor, his limbs unnaturally bent. His bronze skin was gray, his lips blue. His swollen tongue lolled, the color of death. Water dripped into a puddle below his open mouth. *Another one,* Jackson thought.

The thick iron cover lay upside down, at least five feet from the well. He saw chips in the rocky wall - the cover had been flung.

Jackson looked at Paul. The man appeared stunned. Adam Baxter-Bellamy, looking green, was about to lose his dinner.

"Well, shit," muttered Jackson. "I'd better call Gene."

# 119
## *Adam in the Lobby*

It was the last five minutes of the midnight hour and the lights in the lobby of Cliffhouse were dim, the logs in the fireplace still glowing red within their charcoal-gray husks. The brook's burble provided the only music. Jon Daniels had closed Omar's an hour before and all the guests were in now, gone to bed to rise and shine early for Oktoberfest. Only Adam stood at Reception, checking receipts and wiping down the desk in an effort to keep his mind off the image of Eduardo sprawled dead on the springhouse floor. He had never seen a body before, even at a funeral.

Jackson had come by an hour earlier, to tell them the body was being removed and not to enter the springhouse, nor unlock the door. Adam laughed bitterly. He had no intention of going in there for a long, long time.

Something Ted had said to him once bubbled into his consciousness. *You hardcore skeptics are always the easiest to scare.* He'd been joking, but the truth was in the jest. He recalled the day they'd seen the ghost of Omar Siam watching them as they buried his mistress' ashes. He'd been terrified. *Of a cat! A friendly ghostly cat who looked as real as I do!* It was humiliating.

Indeed, he thought, seeing the phantom cat had been even worse for him than seeing Eduardo's body.

Only Teddy knew the truth about his fears. He'd never been intentionally cruel, but he did tease sometimes, making Adam defensive. Other times, he tried to get him to open up about it. He couldn't though; even as a little kid, Adam hated ghost stories and clung to science to quell his fear of the unknown.

*There's nothing scientific about that poor kid dying in our springhouse.* He shivered.

The desk phone rang and he picked it up. "Cliffhouse Lodge. This is Adam. How may I help you?"

"Come home and get in bed with me. I'm cold."

"You just want to warm your frozen feet on my back." He really wanted to ask Teddy to come get him, but that would be ridiculous. "I'll be there in a few minutes."

He turned to enter the staff lounge and wake up the napping night clerk when he caught a whiff of something dark and dank, of deep water hiding moldering roots and limbs of pines trees felled a century or more ago. The scent of rotting wood from boats and rafts sunken when Cliffhouse was new. The metallic bite of lost anchors and the dry smell of bones of men long dead. Gooseflesh prickled up his back. *How many are lost out there?*

A new sound threaded into the babble of the brook. Soft, feminine, and distant, like a woman singing from some far-off place, so quiet that he thought he imagined it at first, but it grew until it mingled with the stream's murmurs. It was the most beautiful music Adam had ever heard and it chilled him beyond measure.

Keeping his gaze low, he slowly turned to face the lobby. The smell of the lake had not diminished. The song continued, and as he brought his eyes up, his body froze and his breath hitched.

Standing near the brook, smiling at him from over her shoulder, a blue woman - *The Blue Lady!* - looked coy, playful. Her hair and dress swam around her like living things. As all these impossible facts collided, Adam thought he might lose his mind.

*Do you believe in me now?* Her lips never moved.

Adam blinked hard against the vision.

The Blue Lady turned her head away and continued her slow trek, gliding along the edge of the brook, leaving wet footprints behind her even though her feet never touched the ground. As the distance between them grew, the song faded. When she neared the stone wall, she turned to him, smiled once more, moved to a window and disappeared beyond the glass. As she did, her laughter cackled through the lobby.

"She's real," Adam whispered to himself. "She's real, she's real, oh my God, she's real."

# 120
## *Lederhosen*

### SATURDAY
### Oktoberfest

Roger Siechert stood before his full-length mirror and admired his authentic Oktoberfest garb. This year, he wore forest green lederhosen with brown leather suspenders decorated with tiny pink and white edelweiss over a white trachten shirt. His knee-high socks were white with green bands at the top, and his brand new brown suede Haferl shoes were a perfect fit. Even his Jockey boxers were a special Oktoberfest edition, embroidered with edelweiss around a stag's head that rested over his package.

He picked up his green alpine hat and sighed. He had ordered and received a beautiful new gamsbart pin for the hat. It had the traditional tuft of goat hair, along with a red feather fitted into a sterling silver holder. And it was nowhere to be seen.

He set the hat down and looked through his drawers and jewelry box one more time, trying to recall the last time he'd seen it. "Damn it, where are you?" He recalled taking it to the clinic, still in its clear plastic bag, to show Gene and Tessa. Gene had admired it, but he'd never shown it to Tessa ... other things had happened instead.

He went to his closet and checked the pockets of the trousers he wore to work. No luck.

*Oh, well.* He sighed and retrieved his old goat hair hatpin. There was nothing wrong with it, even though it wasn't as ornate as the missing one. He pinned it on his hat, placed the hat on his head, and after one more admiring twirl in front of the mirror, took his .38 out of his nightstand, decided it was too big to wear without a holster and exchanged it for his .22, which he slipped into the waistband of his Oktoberfest Jockeys. Then he went downstairs.

In the garage, he opened the door to the walk-in refrigerator and retrieved the leberwurst sausages - the other varieties had been delivered to Leckerwurst the night before, all packaged in their own special coolers, complete with dispensers for easy unrolling in the mounds of chipped ice. Leckerwurst loved his packaging ... and his sausages.

"What's not to love?" He placed the plump wursts side by side in a small cooler and poured chips of ice around them, then added fresh decorative parsley sprigs. "Perfect." He closed the container and as he opened the refrigerator door, he doffed his hat and bowed slightly to Constance's legs. "I couldn't have done it without you, poodle-puss."

He placed the cooler on the Jag's passenger seat, then paused; he'd forgotten his lucky charm, the Chocolate Wanderer. He ran in and pulled it out, now wrapped in foil. He held it up at eye level. "We don't want you to get freezer burn, do we?" He waggled the finger at himself. "No we don't."

The Chocolate Wanderer didn't reply, so Roger Siechert kissed its tip and tucked it inside his shirt for safekeeping. The chill excited him.

Satisfied, he went out, raised the top on the Jag so he wouldn't lose his hat, and headed for Oktoberfest, whistling all the way.

# 121
## *Tessa's Key*

"Oh, Polly," Jackson said, shaking his head as she refilled his coffee cup. "This is all too crazy. I think I'm going to have to call in the county boys; the body count is way out of hand."

"Which bodies are you counting?"

"What do you mean?"

She glanced around the nearly empty diner to make sure no one was listening. "Well, you have only two murders for sure, right?"

"The ones resembling the Bodice Ripper, yes, but their lungs were full, too, so I'm counting the unmarked bodies on land as well. They're connected." He shook his head. "

"What about the ones in the lake?"

"I'm ignoring them for now, even though I think there's a connection there, too." He sipped coffee. "Unless there are obvious signs of violence, they'll never be tagged as murders. Just drowning, or death by misadventure."

"What about the unmarked on land? You don't know how those happened, so maybe you don't need to count them?"

"Are you trying to cheer me up or depress me?"

"I'm just saying that if they're never going to be able to explain the manner of death, maybe you don't have to worry about calling in outside forces."

"I have to worry about the next deaths. There are bound to be more."

"Probably, but if the murderer is the Blue Lady, how well is that going to go over?"

"No one's going to buy that."

"That doesn't matter. If she is responsible then no matter what you do, neither you nor anyone else is going to solve those murders. Ever."

"And your point is?"

"You need to trap the Blue Lady, just like they did in Theodosia's time."

"You're serious, aren't you?"

"Yeah. You know why?"

"Why?"

"Because of you. Because of what I've heard you say dozens of times."

"What's that?" he asked.

"'Once you eliminate the impossible, whatever remains, no matter how improbable, must be the truth. You can't go wrong with Sherlock Holmes.'"

Polly's hand was on the counter and he covered it with his own. "I'm ignoring the Blue Lady because I can't explain it. It's too improbable."

"You can't wrap your head around it so you're not taking your own advice."

He squeezed her hand. "You make a very irritating point."

"Jackson?" Gene Holmes waved as he entered the diner and took the stool the next to him.

"Coffee?"

"Love some, Polly."

"What's up, Gene?"

"There's not a mark on Eduardo Jones. Not even bruising from the fall. He was dead before he hit the ground and filled up like the others. I have no explanation."

Polly set Gene's coffee down. "We were just talking about what Sherlock Holmes said." She looked at Jackson.

"Tell him what you told me."

She did. Gene considered. "It's far-fetched."

"Polly makes sense."

"So has the well been locked down?"

"No," Jackson said. "It hasn't been touched since last night. It's off limits."

"Besides," Polly said. "If you chained it closed, you would lock the Blue Lady out, at least if I understand things correctly."

"Good point," Jackson begrudged. He looked at Gene. "Polly thinks we should do what they did in 1929."

"What's that?"

Jackson told him and waited for the shit to hit the fan.

It didn't. Gene just nodded and said, "Couldn't hurt." He paused, took out his key ring and extracted one. "I was wondering if you'd have one of your guys stop by Tessa Cornhull's place and take a look around."

"Siechert's nurse?"

"Yes. She was supposed to be back from vacation Wednesday but no one's heard from her. She probably just decided to stay in Alaska longer - she has plenty of vacation days left - but it's unlike her not to let us know. She may be so far from civilization that she can't call in. She likes camping trips."

Jackson took the key. "Not a problem."

Gene scribbled the address on a napkin. "I appreciate it. I've got to get to the clinic."

"I'll be in touch."

"Thanks. Gene stood and put a couple of bucks on the counter. "Can you put my coffee in a paper cup, Polly? I'm running behind."

She did, and Gene was out the door a moment later. Polly looked at Jackson. "So are we still meeting at Oktoberfest around eleven?"

"We sure are."

"Maybe you'll feed me a sausage. A big fat one." She winked then leaned over and pecked his forehead. "You're blushing, Chief."

He blushed again. "How about some bacon and eggs?"

"You got it." Polly wrote the order down and passed it to the kitchen.

Jackson consulted his watch. "My guys are all tied up today, so I guess I'll stop by Tessa Cornhull's myself."

Polly made a face. "I hate that woman."

"Why?"

"One time when I was there for my annual checkup, she subbed for Dr. Holmes's nurse. I swear to you, Jackson, that woman could not take her eyes off my business."

"Seriously?"

"It was humiliating. I kept wondering if I'd sat in glitter or something. She's awful."

Jackson laughed despite himself. "That's more intriguing than it ought to be."

# 122
## *Adam and Teddy in the Morning*

Teddy brought in two cups of hot cocoa, set one down on the coffee table in front of Adam, and took a seat beside him. "It's still really hot. Don't burn yourself."

Adam nodded. He wore a white robe and a pair of slippers that Teddy had gotten out for him after having talked him into taking a long, hot bath. Adam had told Teddy about his encounter with the Blue Lady in the lobby the night before. He hadn't expected any judgment from Teddy, but he was always surprised by how compassionate - and how strong - his husband really was when the chips were down.

Teddy sipped his cocoa. "Do you want some coffee instead?"

"No," Adam said. "I don't need any help being nervous."

"I think you should tell Sara, Aunt Maisy, and Jackson what you saw, Adam. I think it will help."

In the golden morning light streaming through the cabin's windows, Teddy looked cherubic, entirely untouched by the world outside. "They won't believe me," Adam said. "I thought those damned magnets were supposed to keep things quiet."

"They'll believe you, "Teddy said. "And the magnets *are* working - we didn't have enough left to cover the lobby properly, remember?"

Adam looked at Teddy a long time. "I admire you. Do you know that?"

Teddy started to laugh and caught himself. "Why's that?"

Adam shrugged and reached for his cocoa. "When it counts, you're the strong one." He sipped the sweet drink.

"Surely you don't think you're weak?" said Teddy. "I mean, of course you're rattled. Just think of what you saw last night! That's bound to shake anyone up."

"Yeah, but you accept these things more readily. Your mind is open. It's one of your greatest strengths. You aren't cynical. You aren't jaded. I admire that. Envy it, in fact."

Teddy smiled. "You aren't jaded, Adam. You're just more skeptical than I am. And that skepticism is part of why I love you. You help me keep my feet on the ground." He placed his hand on Adam's knee and beamed. "I'd float away right now if it weren't for you."

"Thanks," he said. "But it seems I never learn. I mean, even after I saw that ... that *ghost cat,* Omar Siam, I was still skeptical. I talked myself out of it." He laughed. "I talked myself out of something I saw with my own eyes, even though you saw it, too. How much ignorance does doing something like that require?"

Teddy looked at him somberly. "You are *not* ignorant, Adam."

Adam shook his head. "But I can't talk myself out of it this time," he said. "That woman - that thing - the Blue Lady, she's real. And I'll never be able to convince myself otherwise. And that scares me almost as much as the Blue Lady herself." He laughed without humor.

"Why should that scare you?"

Adam looked at his husband. "Because," he said. "It changes me."

"And what's wrong with that?"

Adam shrugged. "I don't know. I guess I like being the way I am. You said so yourself - my skepticism is something you love about me. But that's gone now, at least about the Blue Lady."

Teddy looked at him a long time. "We all change. It's inevitable. But you and I, we change together. That's why this works." He moved his finger across Adam's hand. "I'll love you no matter what, because *you* will always be *you*. And that's what I love."

Adam sipped the cocoa, enjoying the easy silence between them. Finally he sighed. "I'll tell them what I saw."

Teddy nodded. "They're trying to piece this thing together. This will help."

Adam knew it was true and he was grateful for Teddy's support. "Ted?"

"Yes?"

"You're my hero. I mean that."

# 123
## *Leckerwurst*

Three alpenhorns announced the opening of Oktoberfest, their powerful blaring rendition of *Ein Prosit* stirring such excitement in Dr. Roger Siechert he nearly soiled his lederhosen.

He stood by Leckerwurst drinking Blue Springs, since 8 a.m. was too early for beer. The stand carried more than his sausages of course, but his were the stars. Each item on the menu board would soon display a blue ribbon and there was no bigger draw than that.

Regular attendees were already lining up for his weisswurst, the best breakfast sausage at the festival. He heard a child say, "Ew, it's white," and its father laugh and tell it to be adventurous. As Max and Karl, Leckerwurst's purveyors of fine sausage and beer, kept dispensing the milky white meat links, Roger began to think he should have made more. Then he saw Karl open the huge cooler of bratwurst - the one with the special large dispenser that fed brat after brat up through the cool ice - and he knew there'd be plenty of those.

Leckerwurst was set up near the carousel end of the Budenstrasse - the avenue of booths - and he hoped hotel management had stocked the calliope with proper German Oktoberfest music. He'd talked to the Bellamys about it last year because *In the Good Old Summer Time* and *Hold that Tiger* were very distracting and interfered with the mood. They promised to try. *If they haven't, if they play the usual kiddie crap, I'm going to tell them to turn it off and to send a German band over to play. Damn it, we need accordions here!*

"Dr. Siechert! I just love your sausage," said Nessie Mudgett before chomping down on a weisswurst. Her adult son, Herman, already obese enough to be a walking heart attack, had two of the white sausages on sticks, both dripping spicy brown mustard over his hands. One was corked in his mouth like a lollipop. The slightly retarded young man had thyroid problems that, combined with his healthy appetite and his refusal to take his medications properly, kept him as wide as he was tall, and Roger thought he wouldn't live past thirty. *But his mother should be dead by then anyway, so that's a good thing.* He smiled. "There's nothing better than a nice fat sausage, is there, Nessie?"

She bit the end of her sausage with vehemence. "What did you call me?"

"What do you mean? I didn't call you anything, Mrs. Mudgett. It's a fine day for Oktoberfest, don't you think?"

She eyed him warily, glanced at Herman, who had already finished his first sausage and was licking his hand clean, then nodded. "A lovely day." She walked over to the side of the booth. "You there," she barked at Max. "Do you have beer?"

"Of course. What would you like, madam?"

"I don't care, just give me a beer, and put it in one of those glass mugs. And fill a mug with Diet Coke for my son."

"I'm sorry, we don't have any soda here."

"What do you have, then?"

Siechert snickered to himself. *God, she's an old douchebag. I'm glad Gene has to do her pelvics!*

"We have O'Doul's, Blue Springs, coffee, tea, and fresh lemonade."

"I want lemonade, Ma!" said Herman around a mouthful of sausage.

"One lemonade, then?" asked Max.

"No, he can't have lemonade. He's got the diabetes. He'll have water."

"Do you want me to pour it in a mug?"

"Of course I do!"

Roger thought it might be fun to give Mrs. Mudgett a rip later. *She's short, fat, just a little tank on pudgy legs who drinks at breakfast time. That could prove interesting, as long as I don't accidentally pierce the bowel. The old lady shit-smell would be foul indeed.* He took a healthy swig of water and it occurred to him that the Blue Bitch might add to the fun this afternoon after all. He ordered one of his own brats on a stick, and wandered away to see if the judges were getting ready to start giving him ribbons. He smiled as the carousel started up and the calliope began playing *The Happy Wanderer*. It wasn't exactly German, but it had the feel of Bavaria. Best of all, it was a sign that today would go splendidly. He began singing along.

"I love to go a-nibbling," Siechert sang.

"On sausages and nuts;

"I love to drink a pilsner beer

"And pull upon my putz!

"Valkyrie, Valdera, Valkyrie, Valder ha-ha-ha-ha, ha-ha-ha,

"And pull upon my putz!"

People stared at him. And no wonder. Even without his new hatpin, his costume was impeccable!

# 124
## *Hindrances*

Just after Jackson left to check Tessa Cornhull's residence, Dispatch handed him a call. It was only a minor fender bender but it took time. As soon as that was taken care of, Dispatch called again about a brawl at Boozehound's. He arrived just in time to see the fight stopped by the bouncer and the barkeep, but each drunk wanted him to arrest the other. It killed an hour because he ended up hauling them to the pokey. And then another 15 minutes to get the stink of vomit out of the back seat.

He finally got back on the road thinking he might as well have worn his uniform; he was doing so much work. It was going to be one of those days.

# 125
## *First Prize*

"And the first prize in the weisswurst competition goes, once again, to our favorite local sausage maker, Dr. Roger Siechert!"

Roger stepped onto the platform in front of the judging booth and nearly snatched the blue ribbon out of the judge's hand. The man was a pitiful excuse for a judge, wearing khakis with suspenders and running shoes instead of Haferi, but at least he knew what good sausage should taste like.

Finally, he handed Roger the blue ribbon and congratulated him. Roger knew the drill. The crowd was sparse, but when he lifted the ribbon high and turned so all could see it, a respectable cheer filled the air. After a moment, he turned to the judge, said, "What's the next competition?"

"Liverwurst, in about twenty minutes."

"Leberwurst! I'll be back," he assured the man, then trotted back to Leckerwurst.

"I knew you'd win," Max said, affixing the ribbon to the menu board in the appropriate spot. "Have any other sausages been judged yet?"

"Do you see any other ribbons?"

Max laughed. "I guess we'll have them all before long."

Siechert nodded. "I'm going back. Leberwurst is up next and with my secret ingredient, I'm a shoo-in. Better get ready to start frying up patties, Max!"

# 126
## *Streakers*

Jackson was halfway to Tessa Cornhull's place when four women and two men, all young, all naked except for green garlands and running shoes, ran across the street ahead of him, heading into the woods.

*What the ... ?* He gave his siren a short burst and they turned, pointed, and laughed, then took off into the woods. He ran after them, but they were fast and unencumbered, and after just a short sprint, he stopped. *To hell with it.*

He returned to the unit, pulled out, heard a *pop* and his cruiser swerved. He pulled over and after he changed the tire, headed for Nurse Cornhull's residence, hoping nothing was wrong. He was supposed to meet Polly five minutes ago.

# 127
## *Siechert's Secret*

"It's my own personal Sausage Fest!" Roger Siechert told the crowd as he accepted first place for his bratwurst. This prize came right on top of his first place wins for his leberwurst and blutwurst - a fine smoked venison blood sausage. He turned to leave, but the poorly dressed judge stopped him.

"Not just yet," the man said, smiling. "You also get the blue ribbons for your knackwurst, gelbwurst, and teewurst." The man handed them over. "Did you enter any other varieties?"

"No, that's all," he replied, feeling like the sausage in his shorts was going to explode. Roger glanced down at his lederhosen and quickly lowered his handful of ribbons to hide the raging beast.

"Congratulations," said the judge. "I'm glad this is it - if you entered every category, no one else would win a thing!"

"True, true. Thanks again." He looked back at the spectators, most of whom held beer mugs despite the fact that it was morning. "Folks, you can sample my sausage at Leckerwurst, over by the carousel!" He giggled.

He trotted away, nodding at a few familiar faces, and calling out, "Award winning sausages at Leckerwurst! Follow me if you want an orgasm in your mouth!"

People looked, many followed. Between all those ribbons and his spectacular costume, how could they resist? His erection throbbed, standing so high it nearly reached the business end of his .22. Once, he caught a whiff of the lake and wondered if the Blue Bitch was around. He hoped not.

He delivered the ribbons to the booth, happy to see they were doing a fine business. After Max put them up, Roger stayed at the counter, front and center.

"What can I get you?" Max asked, smiling broadly.

"Another bottle of Blue Springs and a sandwich: fried leberwurst on pretzel bread with honey mustard and sauerkraut. A dill pickle on the side."

"Coming right up, Dr. Sausage King!"

"I may be the King of Sausage, but you're the Master of Sandwiches. Together, we shall rule the world!" Siechert laughed heartily, throwing his head back so far that his hat nearly fell off. "It's too early to drink booze, Max!" he called, looking around. "All the other people here are swilling beer, but even Oktoberfest is no excuse to act like goddamned drunkards! I should know; I'm a doctor! I can diagnose all you motherfuckers with my eyes closed and one hand tied behind my back!" He laughed harder, joyfully, throbbingly, and thought he sounded a lot like the Jolly Green Giant, ho ho ho!

***

"Do you hear that?" Teddy asked Adam as they approached Leckerwurst, widely known as the purveyor of the best sausages at Oktoberfest.

"The laughing?" Adam asked.

"Yes. It sounds like a male version of the laughing fat lady they used to set over funhouse doors."

"Crazy."

Teddy had talked Adam into coming to the festival earlier than originally planned because his husband needed to get out in the sunshine, among people, and forget about what he'd witnessed last night. If Teddy hadn't pushed him out the door, he'd have spent the entire day holed up in front of the TV watching Downton Abbey and dwelling on last night's events.

"It's Dr. Siechert," Adam said.

"What?"

"He's the one laughing."

"Look at the ribbons on the menu board. He's probably hysterical from all the wins."

The laughter stopped when the vendor handed Siechert a paper plate and a bottle of water. The doctor moved out of the crowd, looked up and saw them. "Why, the Baxter-Bellamys, I do declare!"

"Hello, Roger," Teddy said, silently thanking the stars that Dr. Holmes was the man checking his own lungs and prostate. "What've you got there? That looks delicious."

"Leberwurst. My own, with a top-secret ingredient that makes it to die for. To *die* for! The judges proclaimed that, of all the *leberwursts* I've ever entered - and every one of them took first place, mind you - this trumps them all."

Adam smiled. "Give us a hint, Doctor. Is your secret ingredient animal, vegetable, or mineral?"

He boomed a laugh. "Animal. It's leberwurst, man! Animal!" He paused, eyes twinkling a little more than they should. "And my secret herbs and spices! It's leberwurst, and it's Siechert's secret!"

"Fair enough."

The doctor picked a big dill from his plate and bit an inch off, chewing noisily. "You fellas should go try my leberwurst. Tell Max Dr. Sausage King sent you. He'll give you a discount."

"Thanks, we'll do that," Adam said as the jolly doctor wandered off. Then he looked at Teddy. "I hate even the thought of liverwurst."

"Me, too. I think I'd like to take our business elsewhere. It's too early for lunch, anyway. Perhaps we might sample a strudel?"

"Apricot and I'm in, Teddy."

"Sweet."

# 128
## *Inside Cornhull's Cabin*

Jackson pulled up in front of Tessa Cornhull's small neat cabin and trotted to the door. He knocked, rang the bell, and called her name. Hearing nothing, he let himself in.

The cabin was empty and clean. Too clean, he thought, his nose wrinkling from the lingering scent of bleach. But nothing looked out of place. Anxious to get to Oktoberfest, he decided to send his forensics guy back in the morning if the nurse still hadn't shown up.

As he locked the door he spotted a silver glint in the juniper bush by the porch. *Some sort of jewelry.* He went to the SUV and grabbed an evidence bag and pair of tweezers, then carefully retrieved the little item. It was a silver pin that held some fur and red feather. A hatpin, dusty but new.

He carried it back to the unit. Turning the evidence bag over, he studied the pin and it hit him: This was Oktoberfest jewelry. He'd seen these ornaments on men's hats before.

*Oktoberfest is Roger's thing.* That's what Gene Holmes had said, and Jackson knew it was true - and that the physician had been seeing Tessa Cornhull.

Jackson zipped the bag, punched the gas, and headed for Cliffhouse.

# 129
## *Sausage Fest*

As noon approached, Roger Siechert wandered the festival, pausing to watch circle dancing, and even tripped the polka with some gorgeous young ladies wearing traditional German garb, their fine, bouncing bosoms plated up in low-cut peasant blouses, their long hair done in braids or hanging naturally. They were *real* women, not like Constance or the Blue Bitch. These young ladies obviously loved sex and Oktoberfest as much as he did.

As he watched a set of particularly animated breasts jiggle and jounce, he considered the question: Which is better, sex or Oktoberfest? Sex felt great, but so did the fest. Neither happened nearly often enough, but both made his blood race, his head swim, and his heart pound. He decided they were equal. *Oktobersex!*

The owner of the breasts he'd been staring at became aware of his dazed, fixed attention, and moved out of his line of sight. "What?" he asked no one in particular. "Don't get your knickers in a bunch, you randy wenches!" He laughed merrily. "You can all nibble my sausage. You just have to wait your turn!"

Several people stared and he wondered why, then remembered how fine he looked in his new outfit. People had been gawking all day; they were jealous. He looked down at himself and didn't give a second thought to the raging mastodon pressing against his lederhosen, jutting up like a proud sword raised to signify triumph. "It's a weapon of mass seduction!" he hollered down at his swollen member.

The sudden scent of lakewater sobered, nearly nauseated him. His erection withered. *Fuck you Blue Bitch!*

*Roger. You are misbehaving.*

Siechert was incredulous. "According to whom?" he shouted. More heads turned.

*Shhhh. You are forgetting why we are here today.*

He ransacked his brain, trying to remember. Then a series of pictures flashed across his mind in a rapid slideshow: *Constance. Tessa. Beverly. Pat.*

*We are not done yet. Look around, Roger. Take your pick. The choice is yours.*

His eyes roved the crowd. He saw Merlin Skinner sitting in the shade sipping a beer. Aside from not bothering to dress for the event, Siechert saw no reason to kill him.

Beyond him, he saw Chad Armstrong sharing a large drink, lemonade from the looks of it, with a big-tittied barmaid from La Chatte Rouge. Both were in magnificent physical condition, and Siechert bet their intestines were nice and clean. That was a definite plus, but still, it wasn't inspiring.

Taffilynn Matthews, surrounded by a sea of blond-haired brats, one in a cast, was divvying out snacks. He shuddered. He didn't even want to think about troubling himself with her, although he wouldn't mind taking out a few of those cunting children. *And the one in her stomach!* But, no, that would be too messy. He thought about the Hippocratic Oath for a moment, and decided his own would be called the Hippocritic Oath. He giggled.

Then he saw her. The one he knew he was going to kill. She was walking toward him, surrounded by several other people he barely noticed. All he saw was the honey-colored hair. The full lickable lips. Those nice twistable titties and those friendly slappable thighs. *Yes. She is the one.*

*Compose yourself!* The Blue Bitch's voice broke his spell and his mind cleared.

Sara Bellamy, a handsome young man, and Police Chief Ballou and Polly of Polly's Diner were heading his way. A lightning bolt of envy shot through him when he noticed that Sara held hands with the young man. *She has a boyfriend? Outrageous!* He giggled again.

*Calm yourself, Roger. This is not the time for laughter.* A strange, inexplicable feeling of calm fell over him. His mind became even clearer as the Blue Lady's dark perfume filled his senses and her coolness entered his body.

He watched himself raise his hand and wave, and walked forward to meet them. "Jackson, Sara, how are you?"

The chief put his hand out and Siechert took it. Jackson's handshake was firm, as was his eye contact.

"Roger," Jackson said. "I assume you've won lots of ribbons today?"

"First place, every one. You have got to try my leberwurst at Leckerwurst. I've outdone myself!"

Jackson nodded and looked him up and down. "Love your lederhosen." He half-smiled.

Siechert, who was having trouble concentrating because he only had eyes for Sara Bellamy, didn't quite know how to take the comment. "I can give you the webpage. Everything I'm wearing is directly from Germany."

"It's very nice," said Polly. "Jackson, we ought to dress up next year."

"Not with my legs."

"You have great legs," Polly said.

"Not like Roger's." Jackson's eyes were on him again.

Siechert almost felt uncomfortable. Almost.

"Are your shoes from Germany?"

"Absolutely. As are my knee socks, my underwear, my lederhosen, my shirt, and my hat."

"I'm impressed," Jackson said. "I'd like to get one of those hats. Do they have them on the website?"

"Absolutely."

"Does it come with the hatpin?"

Siechert absently reached up and touched it, wishing it were the new one. "It's called a gamsbart and you buy them separately. You can choose from a number of styles." He grinned. "Same website. And if you don't like your legs, you can always wear bundhosen. They cover your knees." He looked at Sara. "You, young lady, ought to be out there in full dress, dancing polkas and showing off that fine figure of yours!"

The Blue Bitch filled his senses with dark water. *Control yourself.*

"Excuse me, Sara. That came out wrong. You and your young man are such wonderful examples of healthy young people. You should *both* be dancing."

Sara turned to her date. "What do you think, Luke? Maybe next year?"

The young man smiled at her and put his arm around her waist.

Roger seethed.

*You will have her, Roger ... Be patient ...*

\*\*\*

Jackson wasn't sure what to make of Roger Siechert. He was drinking water, but seemed drunk. He didn't smell any alcohol on the man, but given the beer-scented atmosphere, he couldn't be sure.

Later, he would check and see if the hatpin he'd found at Tessa Cornhull's was purchased by Siechert on that website. He also needed to check the doctor's whereabouts at the time of the murders. Just as a precaution.

He looked at the jovial doctor and tried to envision him committing the homicides. It didn't hang, but then Jackson had learned long ago that violence came in all kinds of packages. *Maybe a doctor could figure out how to fill the lungs with water.*

It made some sense, actually. Something definitely wasn't right with the man - it was just a matter of figuring out what it was. He would keep an eye on him; there were plenty of other people to watch, too. Merlin Skinner topped that list.

"Come on," Jackson said to Polly. "Let's go take a look around."

"Okay."

"You guys want to join us?" Polly looked at Sara and Luke.

"We're going back to Cliffhouse for a while, to check on things there," said Sara. "But how about we get together later, maybe after lunch?"

"Sounds good." Jackson and Polly went one way, Sara and Luke another. As they made their way through the masses of people, Jackson kept an eye out for the Wizard of Ink. And with each face he recognized, he involuntarily imagined them in the act of murder. He shivered despite the warmth of the sun in the thin mountain air.

***

Hammerhead stood in the shade sipping lemonade, watching the people at play. Oktoberfest was a celebration of drunkenness and excess, and the costumes were embarrassing. Inebriated men in shorts and suspenders were not attractive. Nor were the equally drunken women in costumes that flaunted their breasts. Nearly all the people who passed offended his senses.

He felt the Blue Lady once or twice during the brief time he'd been at the festival. She was near, yet far, not communicating with him. That was his preference, now that he had finally killed on his own once more. He had no desire to let her use him again and thought she probably wasn't even aware of his infidelity. She was, he sensed, more interested in joining with the other one; that was a relief.

He looked at his watch and decided it was time to leave the noisy, odiferous fair.

# 130
## *Coming to a Head*

After his irritating conversation with Jackson Ballou and inhaling the lubricating beauty of Sara Bellamy, Roger strolled back to Leckerwurst. He knew the Blue Bitch was with him so he continued to examine other attendees as potential kills. But all he could think about was Sara. He didn't know her medical history, but she was obviously healthy and active with a perfect BMI, and her body, once opened, would smell as sweet as springtime in the Rockies.

He arrived at Leckerwurst and pushed through the hungry crowd to the front of the line, ignoring the grumbles of the lesser beings. If they had realized who he was, they would have parted like the Red Sea. "Karl!" he called. "How's business?"

"No complaints!" the man replied. "Can I get you anything?"

"Why yes. Do you still have leberwurst?"

"I'm sorry, not unless you made more. The fried patties were all gone by noon."

"I'll make a double batch next year." He wondered if he could freeze Sara's liver that long. It was doubtful, but he could make his own very special batch of leberwurst to savor on his own. He smiled. "How about a brat on a stick?"

"Coming right up." Karl called the order out to Max, at the grill.

Max brought him his order and nodded toward the cooler. "Did you bring any more brats with you today? We're going to be out soon. The cooler's almost empty."

"Already? I can go get more from home now, if you like. I made a lot of bratwurst. Plenty for tomorrow."

"Great. We need them soon. More weisswurst?"

"The same amount as I brought today. I'll bring them, too."

"Let me give you the ice box." Max went back to the big rolling cooler that Roger had packed the brats in and tipped it. Roger hummed *Happy Wanderer* and helped him open the side gate on the booth, then Max wheeled the cooler out and opened it.

Roger saw the big mound of ice and a sausage protruding from the dark hole in the middle that hid the bratwurst dispenser.

"There aren't many left." Max began pulling on the string of brats. "I'll take these and hopefully they'll last until you get back." About twenty sausages pulled out before one stuck on something. Max tugged a little harder and the ice began to move.

"Shit, I should've pulled all of her teeth!" Roger exclaimed.

"What?" Max looked up, tugging harder.

"Constance is being difficult," Roger said, "As usual. Here, let me get that last one. That woman just loves a big fat sausage in her mouth, I'll give her that."

Roger bent and took hold of the bratwurst.

"I don't get what you're saying," Max said, chuckling.

"She's a bitch. You know how women are. But I will say this for Constance: she makes a fine leberwurst."

"Your girlfriend helped you this year?" Max asked.

"Oh, my yes."

"Is she here?"

"Absolutely!"

"How come she isn't with you?"

"She's a bitch. I just use her for sex and cooking. She's trying to get me to propose. Gold-digger. She wants to marry a doctor."

"So you're using each other," Max said, watching Roger tug the brat. "That's life."

"It surely is!" Roger put his foot against the cooler and yanked hard.

As the brat emerged from the mounded ice, Roger's special sausage dispenser came out with it. Max stared, mouth open. Someone behind Roger shrieked so loudly it hurt his ears. There was a sudden deafening murmur of shocked voices from all sides, and scream after scream began overlapping.

*Well, shit!* Roger let go of the sausage and the entire business rolled onto the ground. The doctor giggled. "Gotta run!"

And he did.

***

"What the heck?" Polly asked as screams filled the air, drowning out the calliope music. She scanned around, and saw a surge of movement back toward the carousel.

"Stay here, Polly," Jackson said and ran toward the screams.

"Like hell!" She ran after him.

The ruckus, she saw, was at Leckerwurst. She followed Jackson as he pushed through the crowd, then ran into him when he pulled up short, nearly knocking him into the foulest thing she had ever seen.

The severed head of a woman lay in a spill of ice, two sausage links protruding from her cavernous mouth, several more poking out from the gruesome carnage of her neck stump. Her eyes were at half-mast, showing slivers of clouded icy whiteness.

Despite the horrific face, Polly's eyes were drawn to the large, hot pink hoop earrings. "Oh, my God." Polly barely heard her own words. The roaring in her ears was so loud that she couldn't even make out what Jackson was asking the vendor, but she clearly heard the man's reply.

"Roger Siechert. He took off running toward the parking lot!"

Jackson sprinted.

\*\*\*

*Goddamn it, Cunty, why'd you have to bite my sausages?* Roger Siechert made it to the parking lot and was about to unlock his car, when the Blue Bitch descended on him full force. For a moment, he felt like he was suffocating in the stink of the lake, then it lifted. Slightly.

*You have not done as I asked. You cannot leave. Not until you kill for me. I need you to kill for me.*

"Jesus fucking Christ, I'll kill for you later, you blue bitch! I have to get out of here."

*They will find you if you leave in your car. Go into Cliffhouse and make a sacrifice to me. Then I will help you escape.*

"Bullsh-" He paused. "Really?"

*No one will ever catch you. I promise. But first you must kill for me. The one you desire is there. You may sacrifice her for me if you wish."*

"But I don't have my boning knife."

*Use your pocketknife. Go, now!*

He began trotting toward the rear of the lodge. "You'd better be telling me the truth," he muttered.

*You are mine, Roger. I will not let them hurt you.*

He entered Cliffhouse and slowed to a walk so no one would pay attention to him. He heard piano music - not German, as it should be, but American. The pianist was playing *The Entertainer*. "Two sacrifices, blue bitch, it's your lucky day," he whispered. He pulled his jackknife and flipped it open and walked toward the piano. He kept his knife sharpened and knew he would be able to sever a few fingers before slitting Jordan Cartwright's throat - then he realized that if the music stopped, he might not get to Sara. He altered his path and put on his finest smile. The lobby was virtually empty, except for Sara, all alone in front of the registration desk. She was talking to someone standing behind it. A few more steps and he realized it was just Jerry Belvedere, the slightly anemic bellhop.

He strolled closer, as carefree as an old tennis shoe. When he was ten feet away, Belvedere looked up and nodded at him, and Sara turned.

She smiled. "Dr. Siechert, what can I do for you?"

"You're as lovely as a Valkyrie, my Valdera," he told her, his smile genuine.

Her smile faltered.

Inspiration struck. "I brought you a present." He reached inside his shirt to extract the foil-wrapped finger. "Chocolate." He handed it to her.

"Um, thanks. That's very nice of you. Is it from the festival?"

"No, it's from my nurse. Go on, open it."

She peeled the foil back, stared, then dropped it, her face white. Before she could even look back up at him, he grabbed her, twisting her around by the arm, and put the blade to her neck.

"Quiet, Sara, or the blade will bite you." He glared at the bellhop. "You, come out from behind the desk and sit on the floor. Stay there or she dies."

Belvedere obeyed.

Cartwright, oblivious, continued playing *The Entertainer* as Roger turned, taking Sara with him. Now he could see the entire lobby.

\*\*\*

Jackson saw Siechert's Jaguar in the parking lot and figured the man was hiding in the lodge. He entered the back door, gun drawn, then moved closer to peer into the lobby. He heard Jordan playing and then saw, up by the registration desk, Roger Siechert holding a knife to Sara's throat. His stomach flipped. Siechert hadn't seen him, so he backed up. He decided to go to the front entrance, hoping Siechert wouldn't be looking.

He ran around the building, slowing when he got to the veranda. Jackson took the steps at the far side where he couldn't be seen from the lobby. Siechert still faced away from him.

He might have a gun, but there was no way to be sure. Jackson swallowed and moved to the sliding doors. He went through the first pair and paused in the little chamber. Siechert still wasn't looking. Jackson could hear Jordan playing the piano. That was a plus.

His backup would arrive soon, but not soon enough, not today. He was on his own. "Here goes." He stepped onto the sensor that made the inner door open. He'd never noticed the *whoosh* as it opened before, but now it sounded as loud as a sonic boom.

Siechert whirled. Sara's face was bloodless. A crimson drop appeared on her neck and she moaned.

Jordan looked up and took in the scene. Never taking his hands from the keyboard, he gave Jackson a nod and continued playing. Jackson realized he had backup of a sort.

"Chief Ballou, so nice to see you again," Siechert bellowed in a jolly tone. "Drop the gun or I'll press this blade a little tighter against Miss Bellamy. Like so."

Sara whimpered as another drop of blood ran down her neck.

Jackson lowered the gun but didn't drop it. At the back of his mind he was aware of the scent of the lake drifting through the air.

Siechert called out, "Mr. Cartwright, no matter how unobservant you are, you must know it's Oktoberfest! Do play *The Happy Wanderer*, and don't stop until I tell you to."

Jordan looked at Jackson, who nodded. The pianist began playing the tune.

"I told you to drop the gun, not lower it, Chief. Do you want me to make Miss Bellamy's neck smile?"

The watery smell grew stronger as Jackson set his piece on the floor.

"Now, ever so gently, kick it away from yourself."

He did.

Siechert started walking slowly backward, taking Sara with him. He undoubtedly intended to leave by the back door. Jackson tensed, watching, then took a step forward, then another. His gun was nearly within reach.

Siechert watched him. "I warn you, another step and Miss Bellamy will lose her head." He laughed merrily. "Mr. Cartwright, stop playing! You obviously don't know how to play *Happy Wanderer* correctly. You are a disgrace to pianos everywhere." He glanced at him, then fixed his eyes on Jackson. "Sit there quietly, Mr. Cartwright. Do nothing, or I will kill Miss Bellamy, then rip you open like a Halloween pumpkin."

Jordan complied.

"Roger," Jackson said. "Can we work this out? Tell me why you're holding Sara. What happened? What did she do?"

Siechert laughed. "Are you playing with me, Chief?"

"No. I'm not. I want to help you."

Jordan Cartwright slid from his piano bench and crept up behind Siechert.

"Your cop psychology won't work and you know why!" Siechert said.

"Why?" Jackson asked. "Why are you doing this?"

Jordan sprung, tackling Siechert from behind. Jackson scrambled for his .38 as Sara slipped from the physician's grasp. She faltered but Jordan was quick, moving her away from the doctor.

Jackson retrieved his gun. Siechert had dropped the knife. Jackson rose to take aim, and Siechert drew a small pistol and pointed it at him. He pulled the trigger.

The sound was deafening and pain exploded in Jackson's right shoulder, yanking him in a half circle. He went down on one knee and dropped his gun. Siechert ran at him.

And past him. He was heading for the doors.

Before he arrived, they opened and Polly walked in. Jackson cringed; Siechert still held the gun.

Without missing a beat, Polly drove a fierce balled fist right in the center of the doctor's face. A loud crack rent the air and Siechert hit the ground, flat on his back, his pistol skittering across the floor.

Without a second look, Polly ran to Jackson as he struggled to his feet. "Are you okay?"

"Fine," he said through gritted teeth. "Hand me my gun."

She did. He took it in his left hand and started toward Siechert, Polly at his side. Instinctively, he reached for his cuffs then remembered he didn't have them. *Of course.* He wasn't even in uniform. He turned to Polly. "My key ring's in my pocket. Go out to the cruiser and get my cuffs."

She grabbed the keys and ran for the rear door as Sara and Jordan rushed forward.

Siechert was groaning and trying to roll over.

"Do you need help?" Jordan asked Jackson.

"You saved the day once already, Jordan, I've got this. If he tries to stand up, I'll just shoot him."

The lakewater smell increased, swirling around him, making him feel a little dizzy, but as he stepped forward to make the arrest, Siechert called out, "You blue bitch! You lied to me!"

As Polly raced into the lobby, Luke and the Bellamys following, the room filled with shrieking laughter. Siechert raised his head and stared at something behind Jackson. He looked. There was nothing to see, but the insane cackling continued.

"Stay back, guys," Jackson called. "Everyone but Polly and Luke, stay back. You two, come here. Got the cuffs?"

"Sure do." Polly brandished them. "You're going to have to tell me how to work them."

"I know how," Luke said. She handed them over and he approached Siechert.

"Roger Siechert," Jackson said, "You're under arrest for murder and attempted murder. Put your hands behind your back."

Siechert gave him a bloody grin. "Blue Bitch is gonna get you. She's right behind you."

It sure smelled like it, and he had to fight off nausea. "Hands behind your back."

Siechert began singing *The Happy Wanderer* at the top of his lungs. It was garbled and gurgly behind his bloody broken nose.

Jackson stepped forward and kicked him in the ribs. "Hands behind your back. Now."

"Oh, very well." Siechert grunted and obeyed. Luke squatted and cuffed him then pulled him to his feet.

"I'm going to file suit against your girly friend for assaulting my nose," said Siechert, "and I'm reporting you for abuse!" He looked at Sara, snug between her dads. "The Blue Lady wants me to have you. She promised me I could have you. She's a real bitch, too!"

"Put him in that chair, Luke." Jackson pointed. "Then you can go to Sara."

It took Luke all of five seconds to do both. Jackson turned and kept his gun on Siechert as he began reading him his rights.

Polly held her hand out. "I'll guard him. You go put some pressure on your shoulder. "You're going to pass out from blood loss if you don't."

"But-"

"Don't we go to the shooting range once a month? I can handle this. Deputize me if you want."

"Okay. Thanks." He turned. "Is there a first aid kit around here?"

Teddy nodded and headed into the back office.

Jackson took a chair near Polly and tried to tune out the maniacal laughter still shrieking through the room. Siechert began singing counterpoint.

Teddy arrived and pressed a big gauze pad to Jackson's shoulder.

"Do you hear that?" Jackson asked him.

"Yes. I'll never listen to that song again as long as I live."

"No. Do you hear the laughter? The Blue Lady? She's here."

"I certainly smell her, but I don't hear anything."

"I hear her," Polly said without looking back.

"Such a bitch," Siechert declared. "Such a cunting bitch. She lied to me. Just like Constance. They're both cunting bitches."

"The head belongs to Constance Welling," Luke said. "I recognized her earrings."

By the time a squad car pulled up out front, the laughter had faded away, along with the odor of Blue Lady Lake. *I've got my man,* Jackson thought as his vision grayed, *but I still need to get the Lady.*

# 131
## *The Springhouse*

Jackson, Polly, Luke and the three Bellamys spent most of the night sitting in camp chairs behind the springhouse. Jackson's arm, useless in a sling, ached something fierce, but he wasn't about to dope himself up and risk dulling his senses tonight.

They whispered among themselves from time to time, but there were many long moments of silence in which Jackson was certain each of them had drifted into his or her own private world, trying to put the day's events into some sort of order.

Jackson looked at each of his companions.

Polly Owen rested her head on his good shoulder, her arm laced through his. Her hand looked bruised and swollen, but she wasn't complaining. The woman had nerves as strong as her right hook, and he loved her for that. For that and much, much more. He bent and kissed the top of her head, relishing the soft scent of her shampoo.

Next to her were Adam and Teddy Baxter-Bellamy. Adam stared into the darkness, looking far away, and Teddy intermittently made conversation and dozed off. Jackson noticed Teddy's hand rested on Adam's leg the entire night, and occasionally, Adam would place his own hand over it, taking comfort from Teddy's touch.

Sara Baxter-Bellamy shared a blanket with Luke, their heads close together, their fingers entwined. Occasionally, she shuddered, and Luke held her closer.

In the silent hours, Jackson wondered how he'd handle the inexplicable deaths. He was not content with covering them up as they had in the twenties. Like Sherlock Holmes, he intended to find the truth, no matter how long it took. He'd caught Siechert and he would catch the Blue Lady. This was why he - all of them - were here.

Sometime before dawn, when the tips of the eastern peaks were just beginning to turn pink, it happened. A new light came into view - a blue light. Jackson could barely see it from behind the stone springhouse. He sat up, wide awake, and stood to peer around the side of the building. "She's coming," he whispered.

The others joined him.

The Blue Lady glided toward the springhouse, her floating mane haloing her stoney face, making her look like an angel carved out of blue moonstone. But he knew this thing wasn't an angel. This thing was the embodiment of evil, a demon, if such things existed.

They watched, transfixed, as the Blue Lady approached the springhouse and glided through the window.

They waited a moment, then Jackson went to the window's edge. He watched as the phantom floated up above the well, then slowly sank into its depths. He heard her laughter echo off its walls, distant and chilling.

He gestured to the others. They opened the door and entered.

With his arm in a sling, Jackson wouldn't be much help with the heavy well cover, but he'd try. Polly nudged him out of the way. "You just stay back and take advantage of that flesh wound," she said with a smile. He obeyed and watched as the others centered the iron disc over the well.

After the cover was chained down and padlocked, they left the springhouse, locking the door behind them. The eastern sky glowed red with the promise of the first winter storm.

# 132
## *Hammerhead*

**OCTOBER 15**

As he stood in the Hall of Souls, he pondered his good luck. He had been unable to sense the Blue Lady for a week now. He'd strolled by the lake several times and yesterday, when he walked the grounds of Cliffhouse, he found the answer: The springhouse window had been bricked up and a solid steel door replaced the wooden one. Jackson Ballou and the Bellamys had captured her.

He'd worked hard this last week, demurely accepting thanks from everyone who had heard about the standoff at Cliffhouse. He was a hero, they said. He looked in the mirror and thought that, perhaps, they were right. He *was* a hero.

It was time to give himself his own gift for acting so bravely. He left the Hall of Souls, locking it behind him, and dressed to go hiking. He gathered his gear in his knapsack, all but his rip claw hammer, which he hung in the sheath on his belt.

Outside, it was a beautiful day, clear and bright, not a rain cloud in sight. As Jordan Cartwright let himself out his front gate, he picked a single white rose to carry with him. Such a pretty thing.

# *About the Authors*

**Tamara Thorne's** first novel was published in 1991, and since then she has written many more, including international bestsellers *Haunted, Moonfall, Eternity,* and *Bad Things.* She is hard at work on more projects. Learn more about her at tamrathorne.com

**Alistair Cross** grew up on horror novels and scary movies, and by the age of eight, began writing his own stories. First published by Damnation Books in 2012, he has since co-authored *The Ghosts of Ravencrest* with Tamara Thorne and is working on several other projects. Find out more about him at alistaircross.com

**In collaboration**, Thorne and Cross are currently writing several novels, including the serial, *The Witches of Ravencrest,* which appears about every six to eight weeks. Together, they also host the horror-themed radio show Thorne & Cross: Haunted Nights LIVE! which has featured such guests as Laurell K. Hamilton, Christopher Moore, Chelsea Quinn Yarbro, Charlaine Harris, Jay Bonansinga, Andrew Neiderman aka V.C. Andrews, and Christopher Rice. Thorne and Cross are hard at work on several upcoming collaborations, including a sequel to Tamara's novel *Candle Bay*, which will feature plenty of vampy action as the Darlings and Julian Valentyn are joined on a road trip to Eternity with Michael and Winter from Alistair's novel *The Crimson Corset*. It's going to be a harrowing ride!

# *More Books by Thorne & Cross*

## The Ghosts of Ravencrest

### Darkness Never Dies

Ravencrest Manor has always been part of the family. The ancestral home of the Mannings, Ravencrest's walls have been witness to generations of unimaginable scandal, horror, and depravity. Imported stone by stone from England to northern California over a thirty-year period in the 1800s, the manor now houses widower Eric Manning, his children, and his staff. Ravencrest stands alone, holding its memories and ghosts close to its dark heart, casting long, black shadows across its grand lawns, through the surrounding forests, and over the picturesque town of Devilswood below.

### Dare to Cross the Threshold

Ravencrest Manor is the most beautiful thing new governess, Belinda Moorland, has ever seen, but as she learns more about its tangled past of romance and terror, she realizes that beauty has a dark side. Ravencrest is built on secrets, and its inhabitants seem to be keeping plenty of their own - from the handsome English butler, Grant Phister, to the power-mad administrator, Mrs. Heller, to Eric Manning himself, who watches her with dark, fathomless eyes. But Belinda soon realizes that the living who dwell in Ravencrest have nothing on the other inhabitants - the ones who walk the darkened halls by night… the ones who enter her dreams… the ones who are watching… and waiting…

### Home is Where the Horror is

Welcome to Ravencrest, magnificent by day, terrifying by night. Welcome to Ravencrest, home of sordid secrets and ghastly scandals from the past. Welcome to Ravencrest, where there is no line between the living and the dead.

The Ghosts of Ravencrest can be purchased as a full-length novel or as serialized installments. The first installment, titled Darker Shadows, includes the first three episodes, The New Governess, Awakening, and Darker Shadows. Christmas Spirits is the novella-length 4th installment which can be read as part of the series or as a standalone.

# Mother

### A Girl's Worst Nightmare is Her Mother ...
Priscilla Martin. She's the diva of Morning Glory Circle and a driving force in the quaint California town of Snapdragon. Overseer of garage sales and neighborhood Christmas decorations, she is widely admired. But few people know the real woman behind the perfectly coiffed hair and Opium perfume.

### Family is Forever. And Ever and Ever ...
No one escapes Prissy's watchful eye. No one that is, except her son, who committed suicide many years ago, and her daughter, Claire, who left home more than a decade past and hasn't spoken to her since. But now, Priscilla's daughter and son-in-law have fallen on hard times. Expecting their first child, the couple is forced to move back ... And Prissy is there to welcome them home with open arms ... and to reclaim her broken family.

### The Past Isn't Always as Bad as You Remember. Sometimes it's Worse ...
Claire has terrible memories of her mother, but now it seems Priscilla has mended her ways. When a cache of vile family secrets is uncovered, Claire struggles to determine fact from fiction, and her husband, Jason, begins to wonder who the monster really is. Lives are in danger - and Claire and Jason must face a horrifying truth ... a truth that may destroy them ... and will forever change their definition of "Mother."

# The Crimson Corset
# by Alistair Cross

## Welcome to Crimson Cove

Sheltered by ancient redwoods, nestled in mountains overlooking the California coast, the cozy village of Crimson Cove has it all: sophisticated retreats, fine dining, a beautiful lake, and a notorious nightclub, The Crimson Corset. It seems like a perfect place to relax and get close to nature. But not everything in Crimson Cove is natural.

When Cade Colter moves to town to live with his older brother, he expects it to be peaceful to the point of boredom. But he quickly learns that after the sun sets and the fog rolls in, the little tourist town takes on a whole new kind of life - and death.

## Darkness at the Edge of Town

Renowned for its wild parties and history of debauchery, The Crimson Corset looms on the edge of town, inviting patrons to sate their most depraved desires and slake their darkest thirsts. Proprietor Gretchen VanTreese has waited centuries to annihilate the Old World vampires on the other side of town and create a new race - a race that she alone will rule. When she realizes Cade Colter has the key that will unlock her plan, she begins laying an elaborate trap that will put everyone around him in mortal danger.

## Blood Wars

The streets are running red with blood, and as violence and murder ravage the night, Cade must face the darkest forces inside himself, perhaps even abandon his own humanity, in order to protect what he loves.

# Haunted
# by Tamara Thorne

## Murders and Madness
Its violent, sordid past is what draws bestselling author David Masters to the infamous Victorian mansion called Baudey House. Its shrouded history of madness and murder is just the inspiration he needs to write his ultimate masterpiece of horror. But what waits for David and his sixteen-year-old daughter, Amber, at Baudey House, is more terrifying than any legend…

## Seduction
First comes the sultry hint of jasmine…followed by the foul stench of decay. It is the dead, seducing the living, in an age-old ritual of perverted desire and unholy blood lust. For David and Amber, an unspeakable possession has begun…

# Candle Bay
# by Tamara Thorne

## Vampire Hotel
Shrouded in fog on a hillside high above an isolated California coastal town, the Candle Bay Hotel and Spa has been restored to its former glory after decades of neglect. Thanks to its new owners, the Darlings, the opulent inn is once again filled with prosperous guests. But its seemingly all-American hosts hide a chilling, age-old family secret.

## Innocent Blood
Lured to the picturesque spot, assistant concierge Amanda Pearce is mesmerized by her surroundings—and her seductive new boss, Stephen Darling. But her employers' eccentric ways and suspicious blood splatters in the hotel fill her with trepidation. Little does Amanda know that not only are the Darlings vampires, but that a murderous vampire vendetta is about to begin—and she will be caught in the middle. For as the feud unfolds and her feelings for Stephen deepen, Amanda must face the greatest decision of her life: to die, or join the forever undead.

# Eternity
# by Tamara Thorne

## Welcome To Eternity: A Little Bit of Hell on Earth

When Zach Tully leaves Los Angeles to take over as sheriff of Eternity, a tiny mountain town in northern California, he's expecting to find peace and quiet in his own private Mayberry. But he's in for a surprise. Curmudgeonly Mayor Abbott is a ringer for long-missing writer Ambrose Bierce. There are two Elvises in town, a shirtless Jim Morrison, and a woman who has more than a passing resemblance to Amelia Earhardt. And that's only the beginning.

## Icehouse Mountain Mysteries

Eternity is the sort of charming spot tourists flock to every summer and leave every fall when the heavy snows render it an isolated ghost town. Tourists and New Agers all talk about the strange energy coming from Eternity's greatest attraction: a mountain called Icehouse, replete with legends of Bigfoot, UFOs, Ascended Masters, and more. But the locals talk about something else.

## Yours Truly, Jack the Ripper

The seemingly quiet town is plagued by strange deaths, grisly murders, and unspeakable mutilations, all the work of a serial killer the locals insist is Jack the Ripper. And they want Zach Tully to stop him.

Now, as the tourists leave and the first snow starts to fall, terror grips Eternity as an undying evil begins its hunt once again…

# Moonfall
# by Tamara Thorne

## Halloween Horrors

Moonfall, the picturesque community nestled in the mountains of Southern California, is a quaint hamlet of antique stores and craft shops run by the dedicated nuns of St. Gertrude's Home for Girls. As autumn fills the air, the townspeople prepare for the festive Halloween Haunt, Moonfall's most popular tourist attraction. Even a series of unsolved deaths over the years hasn't dimmed Moonfall's renown. Maybe because anyone who knew anything about them has disappeared.

## Evil Nuns

Now, Sara Hawthorne returns to her hometown...and enters the hallowed halls of St. Gertrude's where, twelve years before, another woman died a horrible death. In Sara's old room, distant voices echo in the dark and the tormented cries of children shatter the moon-kissed night.

## Girls' School Secrets

But that's just the beginning. For Sara Hawthorne is about to uncover St. Gertrude's hellish secret...a secret she'll carry with her to the grave...

# The Forgotten
# by Tamara Thorne

### The Past...
Will Banning survived a childhood so rough, his mind has blocked it out almost entirely—especially the horrific day his brother Michael died, a memory that flickers on the edge of his consciousness as if from a dream.

### Isn't Gone...
Now, as a successful psychologist, Will helps others dispel the fears the past can conjure. But he has no explanation for the increasingly bizarre paranoia affecting the inhabitants of Caledonia, California, many of whom claim to see terrifying visions and hear ominous voices...voices that tell them to do unspeakable things....

### It's Deadly
As madness and murderous impulses grip the coastal town, Will is compelled to confront his greatest fear and unlock the terrifying secret of his own past in a place where evil isn't just a memory...it's alive and waiting to strike...

# Bad Things
# by Tamara Thorne

## Gothic California
The Piper clan emigrated from Scotland and founded the town of Santo Verde, California. The Gothic Victorian estate built there has housed the family for generations, and has also become home to an ancient evil forever linked to the Piper name...

## He has the Sight
As a boy, Rick Piper discovered he had "the sight." It was supposed to be a family myth, but Rick could see the greenjacks—the tiny mischievous demons who taunted him throughout his childhood—and who stole the soul of his twin brother Robin one Halloween night.

## Deadly Family Secrets
Now a widower with two children of his own, Rick has returned home to build a new life. He wants to believe the greenjacks don't exist, that they were a figment of his own childish fears and the vicious torment he suffered at the hands of his brother. But he can still see and hear them, and they haven't forgotten that Rick escaped them so long ago. And this time, they don't just want Rick. This time they want his children...

# Thunder Road
# by Tamara Thorne

### Cowboys and Aliens
Evoking Stephen King's terrifying novel The Gunslinger and the epic adventure film Cowboys and Aliens, Tamara Thorne delivers a tantalizing blend of horror and Western SciFi—in a dangerous arid world from which there is no escape...

### Amusement Park Apocalypse
The California desert town of Madelyn boasts all sorts of attractions for visitors. Join the audience at the El Dorado Ranch for a Wild West show. Take a ride through the haunted mine at Madland Amusement Park. Scan the horizon for UFOs. Find religion with the Prophet's Apostles—and be prepared for the coming apocalypse.

### Unstoppable Serial Killer
Because the apocalypse has arrived in Madelyn. People are disappearing. Strange shapes and lights dart across the night sky. And a young man embraces a violent destiny—inspired by a serial killer whose reign of terror was buried years ago.

### The Four Horsemen Ride
But each of these events is merely setting the stage for the final confrontation. A horror of catastrophic proportions is slouching toward Madelyn in the form of four horsemen—and they're picking up speed...

# The Sorority
# by Tamara Thorne

They are the envy of every young woman—and the fantasy of every young man. An elite sisterhood of Greenbriar University's best and brightest, their members are the most powerful girls on campus—and the most feared...

## Eve
She's the perfect pledge. A sweet, innocent, golden-haired cheerleader, Eve has so much to gain by joining Gamma Eta Pi—almost anything she desires. But only a select few can enter the sorority's inner circle—or submit to its code of blood, sacrifice, and sexual magic. Is Eve willing to pay the price?

## Merilynn
Ever since childhood, Merilynn has had a sixth sense about things to come. She's blessed with uncanny powers of perception—and cursed with unspeakable visions of unholy terror. Things that corrupt the souls of women, and crush the hearts of men. Things that can drive a girl to murder, suicide, or worse...

## Samantha
Journalism major Sam Penrose is tough, tenacious—and too curious for her own good. She's determined to unearth the truth about the sorority. But the only way to expose this twisted sisterhood is from within...

Printed in Great Britain
by Amazon